Contents

Country of the Wen

The United Tribes of Wendat

Is a federation governed by four regions.

Each with a council of elders

1

MORA'S ARRIVAL

A fire siren blared in the distance. Mora smelled smoke. It was the coughing that roused her. She tried to lift her head. *I must've blacked out.* She winced. *Oh, my head.* The painful throbbing pulsed with the siren. A wet sensation trickled through the fur on her cheek. Reaching up, her fingers tenderly probed a gushing wound. Her mane was a sticky mess of matted hair, and her fingers came away bloody.

Mora's eyes fluttered open, her slitted pupils dilating fully to allow more light into her eyes. She could just make out a hazy, roiling cloud of smoke above her. *Something's definitely burning.* The alarm continued to blare. She rolled onto her side. *My shades?* In the frantic search for her Spectra Shades, Mora felt bits and pieces of debris strewn on the floor.

Someone above her spoke urgently; his voice was loud but unintelligible. Mora saw shoes. They moved. *Someone's feet?* Painfully, she tilted her head, peering upward, but without her shades, the figure blurred into an amorphous shape. As he leaned down close to her face, he came into partial focus. A dark native dressed in what appeared to be white pajamas under a lab coat. The native male had dark teal fur. He examined her with a worried expression. His speech was a mishmash of sounds she couldn't understand. He took her hand, encouraging her to get up, gently pulling until she stood. Her legs wobbled. Supporting her, he put his strong arm around Mora's waist and hastened toward the doorway.

"What happened?" she asked him. He replied with more gibberish. "Where's Algon?" They silently rushed through the hallway. Mora examined her symptoms clinically. *I must be in shock...* "Was there an explosion?" He didn't answer.

I hit my head; I must've damaged my frontal lobe. She went through a mental checklist: *motor control, reasoning, emotion, and language. Yes, that's all possible, but such trauma would turn my speech into a meaningless jumble. Could this be some sort of auditory hallucination?*

By this point, others in the hallway ran past them, carrying armloads of papers and boxes. Her guide threw his lab coat over her protectively and urged her to keep moving. Mora followed where he pushed and pulled. Her vision was flawed without shades, and now, under his coat, she only saw the floor. Mora realized the hallways were oddly discolored. The floor tiles were different too. *When did this change?* It was one more strange detail that accentuated the feeling of being out of place. Granted, she did tend to be focused on work, but could she *really* not have noticed these new floor tiles in a hall she walked daily to her university lab? Her emotions fluctuated between frightened and perturbed.

Mora's disorientation troubled her. The layout of the hallways wasn't right somehow. *Where is he leading me?* She heard everyone running ahead and noted the cool outdoor air in passing. *Must be the main entrance.* But her guide didn't exit the burning building. He took an abrupt turn away from those doors. Instead, he hurried down an abandoned hallway. Another set of doors made a resounding bang in the empty corridor when they closed behind them. The clang of the alarm receded. Around another corner, a pause and a beep, then they entered a quiet room.

There was no smoke here. It seemed that everyone had evacuated the building. *The fire was in the other wing. We should be safe here.* When her guide removed the coat, she saw a native who sort of looked like her lab partner, Algon. He stared at her worriedly, looming close. He was trying to communicate, his tone and gestures intense and animated, but it still sounded nonsensical.

"Algon? Why are you dressed so strangely? What happened? Can you understand me?" Mora touched the cut on her forehead, crusted with dried blood. With annoyance, she repeated her question louder. "Can you understand me at all?"

His expression was puzzled. He finally said something coherent, although his Inreji was broken and childlike. "Yes, you talk, old Pink," followed by a lot of words she didn't quite catch, which were not even vaguely like the Inreji spoken in her country.

Oh, this was maddening. "Well, that settles it." Mora sounded anxious now. "I must have brain trauma from the head injury. I'm sorry, but I can't understand anything you're trying to say."

This strange version of Algon moved her hair to the side and examined the back of her neck. He was mumbling something and seemed surprised.

"The cut is here, in the front." She pointed at her forehead, but he ignored the head wounds as if they were inconsequential.

The native kept talking, but Mora didn't understand a word. He put up her hair with a clip and swabbed the nearly furless patch below the occipital bone with alcohol. Next, he pulled a case out of a cabinet. She was close enough to examine the details of the item he chose. He squeezed it out of the package. Inside was a translucent button. A tiny gelatinous blob with tentacles hanging down from it. Algon bent her head forward and pressed the wet gooey thing against the base of her skull. Immediately, the tingling spread down her neck and penetrated into her head. Waves of sensation... sharp in contrast, moved through her. Like lightning, they pierced her brain, triggering responses in all Mora's senses: words had colors like synesthesia, and her taste buds came alive. Sensory recollections fluttered through her. Smells and flavors came and went as if cataloging memories of them. All her nerves tingled. Knowledge flooded in, like flashbacks, but of things she never knew before... new languages blazed through her mind, too quickly to focus on. A blur of visual images, complete with sounds, scents, and textures. A whole complex resource of information suddenly filled her awareness and became part of her *memory*. The confusion and shock eased, and her body relaxed. Now he took her head in his hands and gazed expectantly into her eyes as if waiting for something.

"Can you understand me now?"

"Yes, and you understand me? What did you do?"

"The standard implant is mind-mapped with the common tongue. So, we should be able to communicate now. I never learned the Pink languages, I only know a few words."

"Pink language? What does that mean?" Still disconcerted about her lack of sight, she said. "Everything seems different. Without Spectra Shades, my vision is terrible. We need to go find them."

He tilted his head like he didn't know what she was referring to. "Your vision is bad? I'll fix that, too."

What did he mean by Pink language? "Fix what? Can we go back for my Spectra Shades?"

"Please lie back on the table, Zamora."

Why is he calling me that? No one used her formal birth name. She had always gone by Mora. She did what he asked, still achingly vulnerable and confused.

"Look up," he said, and put some drops in her eyes. It made everything blur more... "Blink," he told her. He opened another cabinet and took out a little box that was similar to a Spectra lens case.

"I've never been able to wear lenses. They irritate my eyes."

He shook his head. "Do you trust me?"

Frustrated, Mora held-in further protests. "Of course, but—"

"Just let me put these in, then literally you will see."

"Oh, for goodness' sake, this is no time for jokes." But Mora lay still and let him insert the disc, which did not feel like a Spectra lens at all. He inserted the second disc; a warming sensation caused her eyes to tear. It wasn't painful, but it created a lot of lubrication. Then intense itchiness made Mora want to rub her eyes. He caught her hand to stop her.

"Let it work. Close your eyes."

Mora lay there with closed eyes, thinking about how strange all of this was, and how she still didn't know what had happened. A twisty, crawly sensation inside her eyeballs wormed its way in, followed by a creepy coldness. The itching stopped, replaced with numbness. Mora opened her eyes to a very unusual sight. Her vision was perfect now, better than with her Spectra Shades. Every detail of every object, near and far, was clear. Gazing out the window, she saw trees in the distance, and on them, leaves! Faraway things had always been soft shapes before. "What?" With an expression of wonder on her face, Mora took in this strange new world.

"Can you see better now?" he asked.

Mora turned to the stranger, who had Algon's face. The weird longish haircut, his clothing that resembled pajamas. Now that she had a clear view, she took note of the differences. His fur was too dark and the wrong color, more cobalt than teal. She noticed the paler shade was still peeking through in the tuffs of his ears. Algon had always been a little shy of the fact that his ear fans were a bit smaller than they should be for a grownup. And these were the same, yet different... Something unprecedented had happened. A dawning awareness came as her glance wandered the room. She scanned the odd squiggled writing on some sort of translucent wall panels. Not Inreji, yet she could read it. "Algon?" Mora felt the fur on her body stand on end as a monstrous terror overwhelmed her. It was all too much. She blacked out.

"Zamora!?"

She heard Algon's panicked cry and opened her eyes to his worried face. His golden eyes widened. The narrow, slitted pupils dilated with his fear.

"It's not a dream... *not a dream*." She shut her eyes again.

"Zamora, please, are you able to sit up?"

"My name is Mora." She told him as she let him lift her to a seated position.

"The portal transformed you, even your appearance, and clothing. Why did it do that?" He shook his head. "As it did with everything else we sent through, even your implant was missing. You couldn't talk, and your vision was impaired. It's like the portal removed all your upgrades." Algon's ear-fans flattened back against his head as he considered her, expressing his irritation. "If that's going to happen, this form of transportation will be useless!"

Mora had tuned-out most of what Algon was saying. A discord of ideas, questions, and theories... was pushing her toward chaos, and she was trying to hold on to reason. "Where am I?"

Algon had a puzzled expression, as if he was trying to decide what to say.

"Your name is Algon, right?"

He took a deep breath but didn't answer her question, which was not uncommon with *the Algon* she knew. He had a way of focusing so much on his own concerns that he didn't always listen to what other people said. "Let's get that cut cleaned. I think it needs stitches."

He's avoiding what he can't deal with, Mora thought.

He set to work on her head. He rubbed something with a swab around the laceration to numb the skin and washed off the caked blood. By the time he sewed up the wound, she felt no pain. Mora remained still and silent until he finished. With that task done, he said, "I'll walk you to your place after dark. Your head covering and veil were left behind, but we should be able to get you home the back way without being seen. Here, drink some water." He gave her a cup. Mora drank, not knowing what he meant by anything he just said, but it confirmed that she couldn't be in the United Colonies of Inoti anymore.

The water tasted delicious. She stared down at the empty cup.

"Want some more?"

Mora nodded and held it out. He refilled it from the sink. *Tap water?* Municipal water in her lab wasn't filtered and didn't taste this good.

"Zamora, we will figure this out, but I think you must know our project is in ruins. There is no way we can meet our deadlines now. Everything will have to be rebuilt!" Denial was his coping mechanism during times of intense stress. Dejectedly, he shook his head.

"If they deem us worthy of a new lab, after all the damage we caused. Our portal was utterly demolished! Everything we worked so hard to create, lost."

Of course, he would be more concerned about the portal project. Algon could be self-absorbed and always nothing but practical. He didn't have a creative mind. Mora recognized he didn't grasp the reality of her being out of place. Why wasn't he shocked by this? He's speaking to me as if I'm someone he's been working with. His Zamora, which means she is probably in my lab, and this is, what, an alternative world? I don't think he considered this possibility, or he's blind to the obvious.

Still talking about the accident, Algon rambled on. Mora ignored him. Her mind kept wandering through the implications. She had so many questions. "Algon, who do you think I am?"

That made him stop complaining about the lab. He inspected her now, noticing the differences. She watched him working it out. "You're not Zamora. The portal didn't change you. It *replaced...* Zamora... Who are you?" Dismay and acceptance settled over him.

Mora watched as the realization unnerved him. This wasn't the partner he knew.

"Now you're on track," she said. "And maybe you can understand that we have bigger problems than whatever happened in that lab."

"Are you even a scientist?" He asked with a hint of bitterness.

"What? Yes, of course, I am. We were developing portal technology in my lab, as I assume you are here?"

His ear-fans stood outward in an alert position, then wiggled a little. He smiled at her, obviously relieved. "Portals to travel within our city, eventually to other places, other cities, or continents. But not... other worlds!"

"Right, that was our aim as well," Mora confirmed. "But now you understand why objects we teleported were not transformed as we thought. At least that mystery is solved."

"Oh! You sent a similar object, the same thing, but a different color!"

"Right, all along we had a portal open to our separate worlds, and now *your* Zamora is in my world, and I am stuck here with no way to return."

"May I ask then, where am I?"

Algon tilted his head as if puzzled.

"My country is the UCI, which stands for United Colonies of Inoti. Our world is called Hadot. What is this country called?"

He nodded. "You are in Wendat now. We are the Wen of Hadot."

A look of bewilderment settled over Algon's face as if he were worried. "Zamora. My partner, do you think she is in your world now?"

"Yes, it could be that we traded places." Mora thought of Fenmore ... *Fen... was it only this morning when they sat in her sunny kitchen drinking Kav?* His laugh, his kiss, and her distracted goodbye as she left for the university... flashed through her mind. She now understood why he always insisted on a proper parting. And why he never failed to say he loved her. It had seemed like an unnecessary ritual that she did because it made him happy. But Fen warned her often: "You never know what might happen. Every time we part, it might be the last time we see each other." And she had laughed.

The setting sun made her stomach grumble loud enough for Algon to notice. "Let's go to the canteen. Everyone's gone, but we can get in and find some leftovers. It won't be safe for you to go out until dark, anyway."

"And why is that?"

"Because..." he said as if she should know, "you're Fog."

2

INSIGHTS

Mora glanced down at her arm with confusion. She *had* in fact transformed!

"Oh!" She jumped off the table, holding her arms out and turning them over to view all sides. She spun around, found the mirror over a sink, and ran to it. "What's happened!"

The reflection showed an image of a female with beautiful lavender fur, a white mane, and intense green eyes. Her slitted pupils had widened to full dilation, expressing her excitement. "My eyes... they've always been green, but not so bright!"

Her mane, as usual, was a little too wild and unkempt. The tufts on her ear-fans were tangled in the mess, visible only because her ears were lavender and not white. They stuck straight out from the sides of her head, a sign of acute attention, and in this case, wonder.

Her whole life, she had lived with gray fur. A common shade in her world, where mixed-race people made up a third of the population. The dull grayness of her existence was nothing special, and she'd never thought of herself as pretty.

There was still a smear of blood on one side of her face. Which she promptly washed away, and then she turned back to see amusement on the face of this strange new Algon.

He fluttered his ear-fans and smiled. "You were always this shade, but your eyes didn't have the visual range to perceive it. Our eyes see tone better than color. Things appear pastel or gray to our unaided eye, but implants enhance our vision."

As they walked back through the now abandoned hallways, Mora took notice of the walls. "When we came this way before, the halls were a muddy gray, and without this pattern detail. Now, I can see the intricate design and soft colors. This is amazing!"

Algon's grin widened, the first sign his tension was easing. Her enthusiasm about such normal things was delightful, and her joy infectious. They spent over an hour in the cafeteria eating and talking until she was feeling more grounded. Algon got up and suggested they head out. "It should be safe to walk home. The sun's set."

But as soon as they exited the building, Algon stiffened with a jolt. Mora bumped into him when his footsteps faltered. "I didn't expect such a crowd to gather outside, especially at this hour!" He hesitated, blocking their movement forward. "Fire isn't very common; the explosion has everyone curious."

There were in fact a lot of students milling around, watching the spectacle. They were mostly facing the university. But Algon directed Mora down a side path away from the crowd and tried to shield her from view.

Mora objected and kept pushing aside the coat, which he repeatedly attempted to cover her with.

"I thought the campus would be empty at this hour, at least they aren't looking this way," Algon said this quietly, as if to himself. Then in frustration he added, "Mora, please, you must not be seen!"

She wondered at this drastic change in mood, the happiness of only a moment ago was suddenly overwrought with some sort of anxiety, which seemed to make no sense, *why should she not be seen*? She thought. But then her attention was distracted with the novelty of the place.

While they navigated their way, Mora noted the differences. This morning, she had walked across her campus to the Inoti University of Technology. Where old stone build-ings with stained glass windows were nestled between covered archways and central gardens. All very traditional and old-fashioned. This was not at all like her campus. The structures were made of some sort of translucent material, which varied between an opalescent opaque that glowed from the light within to the sharp translucent panels where you could see into the laboratories and classrooms. The surrounding shrubbery and plant life were innately atypical, less manicured, more natural... every detail was oddly different from how things might be put together at home.

Mora asked. "Zamora's country of origin is Zenda, right?"

Algon nodded. "Yours is not?"

"No, my mother immigrated before I was born. There was some sort of war, she never talks about it. The Zenda seem to have a huge influence here." She pointed at all the signs which were in both the native language Salagi and the Zendali common tongue Neofinga.

"They're a wealthy country, with territories on several continents. And yes, they do a lot of business here. The Zenda Sovereign Nation has trade agreements with Wendat."

Mora raised her brow ridge at that. "They are politically dominant?"

"Depends on how you look at it, they have more territory after their expansion wars, but we have influence due to our ties with the Star People."

Star People? What could that mean? But she didn't give it more than a moment's thought. She was focused on other things.

Mora understood now that this continent wasn't colonized. The native population called it Wendat, an ancient term for *island dwellers.*

This mind-mapping of languages intrigued her. She could now read and speak them fluently, but she knew almost nothing of the cultures or history.

Across the square, groups of students were making their way toward a crowd that had gathered outside the lab that was still burning. Smoke billowed out of an exploded window. None of them paid attention to Algon and Mora. But Mora felt Algon's apprehension each time someone came near, and his sigh of relief when they would pass.

"Everything is so beautiful. The clothing, the ornaments, and the hair!" Mora exclaimed. "Inoti styles are nothing like what I see here!"

Algon gave her an anxious look, his ear-fans flattened back against his head. "Please don't draw attention to us."

Mora gave him a sideways glance, but she was too absorbed in this new world to see how panicked he actually was. The native students wore their hair long. Both sexes. She'd never seen such intricate plaited styles, beautifully embellished with shells, feathers, and beads. Seeing so many people with dark fur was especially strange. Here, most of the Wen had deep teal or green pelts. In her world, they were lighter. Maybe due to being mixed race.

Occasionally she recognized someone with a crest. The average Zendali had fur on the sides of their head, except along the crest from forehead to nape, where a brush of stiff hair grew. These Zendali students they saw in passing had indigo body fur. It reflected an iridescent rainbow of color under the lights. Otherwise, their dark pelts became one with the shadows. "All the Zenda students look pure Oji. Definitely darker than anyone I've met in my country, and I haven't seen a single Awo like me."

Algon didn't seem to be listening to her. He was distracted.

Mora was too fascinated by everything to heed his warning. "I don't see any Ocha either." Mora pointed out.

Algon looked at her strangely, then she realized he was puzzled by the terms she had used.

"I don't know the corrected term in your language for *white-furred students.*"

Algon shook his head, with a pinched brow. "The Pinks don't attend our institutions. Well, except you, I mean, Zamora. Her family gave generously to the university. When she was accepted into the undergrad program, she was only fifteen. Her family darkened her fur and mane, so the school board didn't realize she was Fog. Otherwise, it wouldn't work. They wouldn't have let her in. Now they can't force her out until the project's completed." He paused... "Or you..." His fur shivered, showing his stress. "I hope they'll allow us to continue."

Mora tried to digest what that meant, all the implications, the lack of diversity, the refusal to allow students education because of the color of their fur... "Why?" She wanted to know everything at once.

"Her science is too valuable, and no one else can do it."

Of course, he is focused on their project. Mora thought.

Mora held onto all the details he had revealed. Each point remained an enigma to unravel. "You call Ocha people Pinks? I'm not Ocha," she began with this because in her world the Oji, the darkest race, and the Awo, mixed like her, were lumped together as one. Zenda, in her world, was an impoverished country. In Inoti, anyone mixed with the Oji was marginalized. No one would have considered her Ocha, or Pink as they seem to be called here.

At home, she was a pale shade of gray. But *any amount* of Oji meant you were *Oji.* Compared to the Zendali she saw here, she realized that most Oji in her world were not pure Oji at all. They were Awo... mixed with generations of Ocha. They were *all mixed* to some degree. She had a curious thought then: *I wonder what they would look like now that I have this implant?*

While all these thoughts were running through her mind, Algon had been staring at her oddly. He finally asked, "Ocha?"

"With white fur," Mora confirmed.

"Of course, I'm aware you're Fog."

"Fog?" *There's that word again.* She thought.

Algon tilted his head side-to-side, side-to-side. *What does that mean?* She wondered... and he continued to talk...

"But that makes it more unusual. Not even Pinks are allowed to attend our university. But someone like you getting a degree is unheard of anywhere in this world. You're the only one. And there's not a single person in charge of this institution who would want to admit you're smarter than they are." He hesitated. "And when I say *you,* I mean Zamora... and you... *too,* I assume."

She smiled at his confusion. Mora was accustomed to the limitations female scientists faced in academia. Especially Oji females had to prove themselves. She expected it would be the same in any job she took after college, but she did not understand what Algon was going on about. "Explain to me what the fog has to do with me, and why *Pinks*?"

"Mora, enough for tonight. Here, this is Zamora's home." He pushed a soft leather bag into her hands. "Find the token to activate her door."

"You saved her purse?"

"I grabbed whatever was close and valuable. Here, I'll show you how it works." He poked around in Zamora's bag, brought out a disk, pressed it to the center of the door and it irised open.

3

ZAMORA'S HOME

The buildings in this neighborhood all looked like dark stone towers with glass domes. Different from the construction at the university. The house lights brightened as they entered. Mora stood in the foyer, looking at this strange place that would be her home. Algon used a device on his wrist to call someone named Asha. It didn't look quite like the communication devices from her world. It was a translucent, pliable band that fit like a bracelet on his wrist. There was a bump on the top, which glowed a little when he tapped it. He had rubbed his finger along it a few times, and then it made the connection.

Mora followed one side of the conversation. "Can you meet me at Zamora's place?... Yes, we got out... I'm fine... I'll explain when you arrive." He tapped off the device. "She's coming." With a sigh of exhaustion, Algon said, "Help is on the way."

Mora wondered how Zamora and *her* Algon were getting along on the other end of this debacle. Then it hit her. How would Zamora deal with Fen? The thought of never returning to him was like a solid rock in her heart. A wave of sadness passed over her. *My parents will be worried too!* The enormity of her loss was suddenly overwhelming.

The room seemed to tilt sideways; she reached for the counter to steady herself. Algon moved to her side protectively. "I think you're concussed. How's your head?"

This Algon was a kind sort too, his own discomforts forgotten as soon as he noticed she needed help. She didn't feel comfortable speaking about her personal losses and worries. Instead, she told him another truth.

"All of this is very... unfamiliar. I think I'll need your help to adjust." She gazed with worry at the apartment, taking in the oddness of it all. But of course, she meant the whole world outside that door as well.

"I understand. I will do what I can. Also, I called Asha. She will know your specific needs better than me."

"She's your... partner? Or do you say, mate?"

This question made Algon visibly uncomfortable. He evaded her question. Instead, he asked, "Can you walk? You'd better take a seat at the table." He nudged her toward the kitchen.

"She is a close friend of Zamora too."

Mora gave him a slight smile and a nod. "I'll make some tea while we wait."

Algon kept glancing at Mora. Which made her realize he was uncomfortable with the silence, but she was too out of sorts to say much.

"What is my counterpart like in your world?"

"He's got shorter hair, and his fur is lighter too."

The question caused Mora to reflect again on the students she'd seen on the way. Wendat natives generally had long straight hair, which was black and often braided. This Algon kept his hair shorter but not as short as the styles in her country... world... In contrast, her hair was stiffer, and stuck out in every direction in a curly mop. It didn't grow very long. That was her Zendali heritage, although most Zendali were crested, not with a full mane like she had. Hers was an unseemly mess most of the time, because she couldn't be bothered to take care of it like her mother taught her. She'd been told it wasn't very presentable, or professional... but she didn't care. Come to think of it, her mother was the only other person she'd known with a full mane.

Hearing Mora's comment about his coloring, Algon glanced at her with embarrassment, his ears flattened. Then he turned away, taking his time with the teapot as if it was a more complicated process than putting leaves in and adding hot water.

"Please don't mention that to Asha."

This brought Mora out of her reverie. When she glared at him, waiting for an explanation, he groaned. "I darken my fur. Dye shops are common here, fashionable, but no one wants to admit they aren't naturally dark. I never told Asha."

Mora kept staring like she didn't understand. He turned his back to her again, took down three cups, and changed the subject. "You didn't answer my question."

"Well, *my* lab partner dresses conservatively. The styles are different there."

Algon obviously wanted more details.

"It wouldn't make sense to you if I described what he wears."

"Try."

"Traditional tailored jumpsuit, blue lab coat."

There were no descriptive words in any of the new mind-mapped languages that described *jumpsuit* properly, but Algon accepted this and nodded. "So, you think nothing about him is interesting? Nothing worth telling me?"

"My Lab partner doesn't have a mate. He never makes time for social activities."

"You don't socialize much either, I assume? Can you tell me anything personal about him?"

Mora didn't like his tone, sensed his judgment, and felt insulted. It was true, though, about the relationship with *her* Algon. They worked long hours and kept their discussions on point, about the project, not personal things. She never asked how he spent his leisure time or if he had hobbies. She decided to ignore the barb. "Tell me about the device you used to contact your mate."

Algon reacted as if she should be familiar with such a common thing. Then, his ears perked up as recognition came over him. "Oh, of course you don't have receptors, because you don't have implants!" He turned his arm to show her. "This communication device can interface with our implants. It allows us to contact and receive calls from others who have an implant. You can only connect with someone who is on your contact list, and only if they're in range."

"You can also use the receptor screen." He pointed to something on the wall that resembled a video station, a huge device with a vertical orientation. "If you bounce the signal to the screen, you'll get a visual of the caller, and their voice will come through the speakers." He thought for a moment and realized more warning was necessary. "Zamora *never* linked it to her receptor. She just used the screen for local news and programs."

"We have a different sort of communication device; it requires two things. She showed him her wrist, a hairless spot near her palm was engraved with a circular symbol. We call this a MobiMark, Mobi for short. We wear a HelioLoop over it, which activates the mark and connects it to the VelNet. The HelioLoop is also worn as a bracelet."

"Do you have it with you?" he asked with interest.

"No, it was in my bag at the lab. It got left behind."

"I'm interested in how the technologies differ," he said.

"We use a StrataKite system."

"StrataKite?" He pronounced the strange word with a heavy accent.

"Don't you have those? Telecommunication constructs in the exosphere."

Algon didn't seem to understand. But then his eyes widened, and he said with astonishment, "In space?"

Mora nodded. "Above the planet in the upper atmosphere. We send them up with blazerockets. They're positioned high enough to maintain their geostationary orbits. They connect all our devices."

Algon's ear-fans wiggled with excitement, but before he could question her about those fascinating things, a chime rang at the door. Algon walked to the counter, picked up the entry disk, and pointed it at the door to make it open.

Asha came in, dressed in black head to toe, with a veil obscuring her face. When she removed the head covering, a beautiful Zendali with deep indigo fur was revealed. Her crest was woven into rows of braids close to her scalp. This was not common for crested people. Normally it stood stiffly along the top ridge of their heads. Back in her world, the Zendali kept their crests cut shorter, like a thick brush, but here, it was in fashion to grow them long. Mora saw some during their walk here which stood two hands tall!

It might be necessary to braid a longer crest if she wears that veil over her head all the time, Mora reflected.

Asha crossed the room to embrace Algon. "I got worried when I heard about the fire in your lab and I didn't get a call from you. I checked at the clinic if you'd been injured. Where were you?" When she glanced at Mora, her eyes widened. "You have Zamora's face." Her appraisal was immediate. Unlike Algon, she recognized something was off or different about Mora. "Who is she?"

"How do you know?" Algon asked.

Her mane is messy and loose. She smells strange, and there's something else about how she moves... it's wrong. Her body language is distinctly at odds with what is familiar. "Who is this?" She asked again. "Does Zamora have a twin we didn't know about?"

"That is why I wanted you to come here. This is Mora."

Asha waited for an explanation while staring at Mora in fascination. "And?"

"I'm a counterpart of your friend... from a multiverse variant of Hadot."

Asha raised one brow ridge in doubt.

"I'm from another world."

Asha started to laugh.

Algon stared at her with a grave expression. "Not a joke, she's telling you the truth. Our portal wasn't malfunctioning; it just wasn't what we thought."

"This needs to be kept between us, Algon," Mora warned.

"Asha, we can't talk about this unexpected outcome to *anyone* else. Can you imagine what would happen if people knew where I came from, and what is... possible?"

Somehow that made it real for her, Asha sobered. She examined Mora with curiosity. "You're a doppelgänger of my friend, but you are not Zamora. How will you survive here?"

Algon understood. Apprehension furrowed his brow. His ears flattened. They all realized the complications this situation created. But Algon seemed less interested in Asha's concerns and answered Mora's.

"Of course, Mora is right. Opportunity and greed would most certainly cause unexpected and unwanted repercussions if the multiverse were open to all. It would get out of hand..." He said this in such a quiet voice, trailing off with a worried sigh.

"We don't understand how it happened or why. I'm not sure I can rebuild Zamora's design, and I might not be able to build mine *here*, because you will have different components and materials. I need time to become familiar with what's available and how those elements can be incorporated into my portal design," Mora said.

This caused Algon to shake his head and moan with frustration. "We might not obtain a new lab, we caused so much damage."

"Everything is uncertain, don't you see? For now, I need to pretend to be your Zamora. Can you both help me do that?"

"It will take a week or more to deal with the lab. I'll take care of the negotiations with the university board. I'll tell them you're injured; it should give you time to get acclimated. Asha will help you adjust."

Asha looked at Mora with pity. "You must be fatigued. Let me show you where things are. I'm sure you need to rest. And we should find Zamora's journals."

Mora was impressed with how task-oriented Asha was. As soon as she realized something remarkable had happened, she transitioned into the altered reality without hesitation. Instead of wasting time with questions about how it happened, she just got down to business.

After they left her alone, Mora wandered the house feeling like an intruder. She was exhausted, yet she couldn't sleep. The question of returning home was doubtful. The edge of panic intruded on her normally rational mind. She liked to think of herself as brave, but this was a bigger challenge than Mora ever imagined she would face. She didn't feel brave at all. She was scared.

4

ZAMORA

Comcomly Hardihood was the dean of Muwioni University, and he was losing his patience. "Did I not demand that you expel the Fog student on principle?"

The other members of the university board looked at the dean with stubborn expressions. They had resisted and argued among themselves and didn't do anything he asked of them.

"I am an honorable elder, and where I come from, people obey my requests and respect my advice. This necessity to convince you of proper procedure has put me in a foul mood."

His exhaustive bellowing, objections, and complaints grew more insistent as the meeting dragged on until everyone's nerves were frazzled.

"If they discover her, our treaty with the Sovereign Zenda Nation will be in question. We should never have allowed someone like her to attend this institution!" His gaze bore down heavily on the other members of the board. "We will pay dearly for that infraction if we allow her to stay!"

Aiyana Bly, Zamora's professor, had realized during the course of this morning's meeting that she was perhaps the only one who knew it was Zamora's lab that had caught on fire. She didn't want to mention it because it may give them a reason to terminate the project. She waited for a pause in the dean's tirade and spoke up in her student's defense: "She became a follower of Bicara. Since the Sisters' of Justice shroud themselves completely under black garments and veil. It would be unlikely for anyone to discover what she is."

Professor Bly was a small native with moxie, and often the only one on the board willing to confront the dean. "I chose Zamora's lab partner, Algon, to monitor her progress; with the expectation he could take over if you forced her to leave the University."

Professor Bly also told Algon to vet the other members of Zamora's team to be sure none of them would disclose her abnormality or the nature of her invention. But she decided not to mention any of that. It would just complicate the discussion.

Delsin Diwali, the director of finance, spoke. "May I remind you Ekon Darego donated directly to the research headed by Zamora? If you replace her, as the dean has insisted, then we would be obliged to return his money, which they already spent a significant portion of when they bought her equipment."

"It wouldn't be possible to replace her anyway," Professor Bly told them. "There's no one else who understands her work. Algon's one of my best students, but he hasn't a clue what Zamora's doing, and, to be quite clear, neither do I."

"Was she secretive? Were her calculations hidden? Why don't you have a complete understanding?" Enapay Pool, the president of the University, asked. She was a handsome executive, dressed in an elegant suit in the Zendali style. In her prime years, she was younger than the others but formidable enough that she held her own.

Professor Bly shook her head. "There are calculations and formulas on every memory surface. Papers with her designs and doodles litter the laboratory. Algon keeps everything documented. A good part of the puzzle must be in her head. How all these pieces fit together..." She sighed in frustration, looking directly at the president with all the sincerity she could muster. "It's known only to her. She's not secretive in the least. When asked questions, Zamora does her best to explain, but this invention... it's beyond our grasp."

President Pool exchanged a look of disapproval with the dean.

"You're exaggerating, Bly." The president admonished her. "You've got all her designs and calculations. Just put more people on it."

Professor Bly knew what that meant for Zamora.

The dean was nodding in agreement.

"It won't matter how many others are looped into this project..."

Before Professor Bly could say more, President Pool interrupted with a razor edge to her tone. "You want me to believe there's no one on her team who can complete the portal technology? Not even you?"

"I'm telling you, if you want the portals, keep her in that laboratory and let her finish her work."

Director Diwali spoke then with some apprehension. "You are all aware we had a fire in the science wing last night?"

No one replied, but President Pool gave the finance director an impatient glance. That was one of the topics for discussion which she felt might not get dealt with today because of all this arguing over the Fog student.

"The fire was in Zamora's lab. It was her portal that blew up. It will need rebuilding."

Professor Bly's fur stood on end. She glared at the finance director, Diwali, with flattened ears. Her ire was hard not to notice.

He spoke softly to Bly, so only she could hear. "There was no avoiding it."

The dean's livid stare expressed his disdain. "We've got a perfect excuse to get her out then and a lot to lose if we keep her. Do you have any idea what the Zenda conservatives will do if they find out we're harboring a Fog, and she's intelligent? They'll do everything in their power to destroy her and everyone connected to her research."

It annoyed Zamora's professor having to defend an obviously false claim about the Pinks and Fog being mentally deficient. "Maybe we should challenge this charade the Zenda have postured for generations about the Pinks? She's proof they're capable of much more than the Zendali gave them credit for. Isn't it clearly a matter of education and opportunity?"

"Exactly what I've been saying. She is proof, and that makes her dangerous!"

"Sometimes I think you only hear what supports your opinion, and all the rest is ignored. She is not only intelligent, but she's astute, imaginative, and resourceful."

The director of finance interrupted their argument again: "You're missing the point! The portals would revolutionize travel. The profits from manufacturing them would support the University in perpetuity." He understood precisely the value of Zamora's work and didn't want her removed.

The Vice President, Istas Moki, had been silent thus far, when she spoke in a timid voice, the others turned in surprise that she had something to add. "Zamora's invention would also be the only technology developed in Wendat, which hadn't been given to us by the Star People."

Zamora had been an early admission at age fifteen. An exceptionally brilliant student who finished her undergrad studies quickly, entering the graduate program at eighteen, she was awarded a laboratory and team to complete her project. Only then had the University board discovered she was a Fog child. Of course, it was too late. They were invested, and they wanted ownership of her invention.

President Pool stood, startling them all. She glared at the dean. "I agree with your assessment. Ekon Darego deceived us. It rankles that he thrust such a devious situation upon us, but at the moment, we're locked in. Let her continue for now, but as soon as the Fog student completes this project, I want her gone!" She looked at Professor Bly. "I'm putting you in charge of managing her exit, whatever that means. Just get her out."

Istas Moki's dismay was obvious. The burden of this assignment should have been delegated to her, as Pool's vice president. "I don't want the task, but giving the duty to someone else shows a lack of respect." She said it without emotion, and without looking at her superiors.

"You have to admit, Istas, you are too accommodating and sympathetic of the Fog. At least Bly has shown some resolve regarding the matter," Pool said.

At this, Professor Bly's ears flattened back. She had not meant to cause any harm. Bly, too, was supportive of Zamora. She had taken action to preserve the work; in case they cast her student out. Zamora's invention was too valuable.

President Pool ignored the signs of distress among the board members, who had fallen into quiet mumbling with each other. Her voice rose with her last words. "We will not allow this to take us down. I want her out as soon as possible!"

5

OReNDA

Orenda wanted to please her parents, but she never could. Her dreaming didn't work as tradition instructed. Plagued by dreadful visions, she was a witness to impossible things. She lived with constant feelings of shame and concern for what her dreams foretold. She kept all of it secret because she couldn't fathom what the visions meant. Certainly, they were of no use to her tribe.

Troubled by her inadequacies from a young age, Orenda sought relief in her art. It tempered the fear. Drawing allowed her mind to wander. There was something comforting about releasing those visions onto paper. It bled the life from them, trapping their power between the pages, keeping them safely hidden. Her sketchbooks, which were now stuffed full of strange things, stayed hidden in an old trunk. She shared them with no one.

The tribe relentlessly pressured Orenda to study the medicinal arts. Without realizing it, they pushed her further from that destiny, not closer. They expected her to train seriously, spending quality time with her grandfather Ezno. The entire clan took it as an inevitable fact that she would be their spiritual leader when her grandfather passed. Her inadequacy made it a burden to live among them. Ezno would soon be gone from their world. This surety caused dread to curl tight within her gut.

Everyone gave her respect, special favors and even gifts to encourage her, but apprehension followed her every action. She'd convinced herself that she didn't deserve any of it. Accepting humiliated her, but to refuse was discourteous. Instead, she graciously took them for Ezno. Which then gave everyone the impression of modesty, another falsehood. No matter what she did, they interpreted it as the right behavior for an apprentice. Orenda realized that taking that role in the community should be an honor. She couldn't explain why she felt conflicted.

Ezno believed that dreams told the future and gave the medicine practitioner important messages that needed to be interpreted. In this way, the world spirit worked through the healer, directing the life force, which was all-pervasive, flowing through all beings and things. The Sacred Prime was the heart of any tribe. As a medicine practitioner, Orenda would need to give guidance and support to rid someone of sickness or create balance in other ways. But she was certain her tribe had chosen wrongly by entrusting her with this duty. Eventually, they'd realize her visions were useless and call her an imposter.

Because Orenda's family needed her to take this burden from her grandfather and give guidance to the tribe, her youth was spent learning ceremonies and following in his path. Now, with a good grasp of medicine and herbal lore, it should've given her confidence, but it wasn't enough. How could she be a spiritual leader without insight from the Sacred Prime to assist the tribe as her grandfather did? Every practitioner in their lineage had clear sight, but she did not. Orenda argued that her dreams made no sense, and they were not of this world, and not for her people.

Her family made light of her claims, saying whatever the Sacred Prime brought to her had to be meaningful. She just needed to discover through ritual and ceremony what the dreams portended. Wanting with all her heart to be the dutiful daughter, Orenda tried to adopt the path they chose for her. She took their advice and did everything expected, but to no avail. Her mysterious visions remained as frightening as ever.

Orenda sat by a bonfire with other teenagers. Her status set her apart. Lately, she'd been ignoring her lessons in herbal medicine, avoiding her grandfather as well, and trying to keep herself awake. She slept as little as possible to avoid the nightmares. Her desire to be a part of this greater family seemed impossible now. Despite her efforts to join in, something elusive separated her from them.

Sitting near the light of the fire and drawing, Orenda listened to the other kids laughing and flirting. The females talked in whispers about who held hands with whom, or who kissed, or gave love gifts to each other. The young Wen males teased them. Their dramas and desires didn't interest her. She couldn't be a part of their lives like that. She didn't have any wish to find a mate or settle down. At least not yet, and not here.

Silently, she sat in their company as they gossiped and carried on in front of her as if she weren't there. A ghost, something superfluous. Orenda had made a tough decision to renounce her obligations to the village. She would travel west and study art. Orenda hadn't found the courage to tell her family. She was terrified of facing them with the news.

Guilt kept her from leaving until now. She'd finally bought a ticket to the west coast, and the train left in the morning.

"What are you doing here?"

At the sound of her mother's voice, Orenda shut her sketchbook and turned from the fire. Her mother expressed exasperation. "Wasting your time drawing again? Why don't you take your studies seriously? Ezno won't be with us much longer, and then where will we be without a spiritual leader and medicine guardian?"

Orenda didn't bother replying. Her family had ignored her concerns. She followed her mother back to their lodge. When she entered, the others were waiting. They had set the ritual objects out for an evening blessing. She took her place in front of her mother.

Orenda lit the pungent burning herbs and blew smoke toward her mother, reciting the prayer ritual. "Daughter of knowledge, Minda, and the white moon, Muraco." She let the smoke waft toward her father. Next, she faced her grandfather; his eyes twinkled at her. "Honored seer, Ezno." She lifted the bowl of burning herbs above her head. "And, Grandmother Nokomis, daughter of the moon, who passed into your care. I, Orenda, call on the Sacred Prime, the life force in all beings and all things, infinitely divine and all-pervasive. Bless this family and our clan. Lead us faithfully. Give us purpose and strength." She set the bowl with the burning herbs on the table.

After a brief pause, where they all silently said their personal prayers, Orenda gathered her courage and cleared her throat to get everyone's attention. They opened their eyes; confusion exhibited in their body language for the abrupt intrusion during this introspective time of blessing. Orenda's ears flattened back against her head with shame for her rude invasion of their privacy. There was something she needed to say. She planned to leave in the morning. She'd put off this announcement for as long as possible.

"I have decided to go to the West Coast and study art."

Her father gazed past her without comment, as if he'd expected something like this. Her grandfather patted her on the shoulder. His sympathetic glance told her *everything would be all right*. But her mother's eyes filled with tears, and she left the room. Minda's exit left a stone in Orenda's heart.

"The train leaves tomorrow." Then, to avoid further discussion or questions, she left the family patriarchs' and went to pack her belongings.

6

BI

I t was quite unusual for the Brainery Institute to send a bellwether to confirm a candidate's test scores. Younger invigilators conducted the child's first imperial exams the previous week. Yet the results confounded them.

Bi overheard part of a conversation Bellwether Ah Lam was having with her parents.

"I believe a compassionate disposition is required."

She looked sincere, a formidable figure. It appears she took her duties to heart. "After all," Ah Lam continued, "most gifted children are outcasts, and they usually experience abuse before their talents emerge."

Bi's mother was outraged at this accusation. "I assure you, we have always been supportive of our oldest daughter, despite her abnormalities."

"Yes, of course," the bellwether said without conviction. "But this past week of testing has been exhausting and has perhaps made the candidate nervous. So much waiting, so many expectations, and few other prospects if this doesn't work out."

Bi took one look at Bellwether Ah Lam and was reassured that everything would be fine. The bellwether was of average height, with a soft, round, grandmotherly figure. Her gray fur was speckled with white around the face. A sign of her advanced age, but Ah Lam appeared agile enough. Her hazel eyes twinkled with amusement. With a genuine smile, disarming in itself, she looked respectful, and kind. The traditional costume of the invigilator was plain and unassuming. The only embellishment for Ah Lam was a black sash at her waist, pinned with an imperial signet.

She gave Bi a small bow. "Pleased to meet you, Bi."

Bi returned a deeper bow, showing her respect and appreciation, but didn't speak.

A riotous strand of gray hair escaped Ah Lam's black cornette headpiece, which sat above her ears. Bi found herself fixated on that one little imperfection. Somehow this made the bellwether less intimidating, and for the first time in days, Bi felt at ease. The other invigilators, with their crisp precision, caused her to suspect something was wrong with her test results.

All the invigilators lined up behind the bellwether, an imposing contingent of starched white cornettes. Bi sensed they were suspicious. The high deputation made quite an impression on the household too. Even though Ah Lam had requested family and servants not to intrude on the proceedings, the other children and some of the staff were occasionally hanging around the periphery of the room, unable to resist their curiosity.

Bi had lucid dreams all her life and did not know this was unusual. Her recall was precise and detailed. But she decided to keep this to herself, partly because she thought it was normal for the Gifted, and partly because the invigilators were acting strangely after the initial testing, which frightened her. She would learn in time that this level of control developed during puberty for most Gifted children, and even then, wasn't easily mastered.

By the end of the final day, Bi was confused. Her family was also concerned for her. No one had ever heard of more than one invigilator testing a candidate, or taking more than a day to arrive at a conclusion.

When Ah Lam assumed a confident posture and made her announcement: "I am secure in my assessment of this candidate." Bi and all her family sighed with relief.

"Your daughter will be expected at the Brainery Institute for training. Our new semester begins next month. Keep in mind, personal effects should be kept to a minimum. This is a list of items she should *not* have in her possession."

The bellwether handed her mother a document. Then she ushered the invigilators out and said her goodbyes to Bi.

***

Her acceptance was the only thing that mattered. Bi loved her family, but she'd always known she would leave them. She saw her path forward, which began at the institute. There would be hardships to follow, but she could be useful this way. She was ready for the challenge.

Bi wasn't at all heartsick when she arrived at the institute. But her roommates carried emotional ties to their families, even though most of them were not treated well. It was incomprehensible why they held on to their past when it was so unfavorable. Bi had spent the first few days listening to their stories. Most had been physically and verbally abused on a regular basis because their families were ashamed to have a defective child. Their difference was a burden on them.

"I didn't experience such cruelty." She told her roommates with sympathy. "My siblings' father treated me unfairly, but that was nothing really, in comparison to how you were afflicted."

"You were lucky," Far told her with some envy. She had cream-colored fur and eyes like honey. She was also sporting a bruise on the side of her face. She had admitted it was a parting declaration from her father; he'd told her that she was not welcome to return if she didn't pass.

"Maybe it was better for me because my mother was able to give birth to my siblings," Bi told her roommates. "They're ideal examples of what the Empress considers acceptable."

"You must hate them," Far said.

Bi was stunned by this. "Why would I?"

"You have a younger sister, right? She will inherit the household. Which isn't right. You are the oldest daughter!"

It was true that Bi's younger sister, Genji, would be the next matriarch of their family. But Bi had never resented her for it. Bi fluttered her ears with nervous annoyance. "I... don't really care to have that responsibility."

Far and the other roommates stared at her. An uncomfortable silence followed.

Bi pictured her sister, an exceptional beauty. Her raven-black hair fell to the floor in a smooth, luxurious fullness, although most of the time it was piled up by her servants into complicated hairstyles, with jeweled hair clips. Genji had white fur, dark almond eyes, and a pink nose. She was the ideal example of beauty in the Eastern Empire, easily fitting into the royal court.

"My sister Genji was born with a tail," Bi said, to ease the tension.

Her roommates reacted with surprise. Some of them giggled.

"That is an imperfection easily hidden, some northern ancestry? Chopped off at birth, I suspect?" asked Far.

Bi agreed and was immediately ashamed that she had revealed this family secret.

She didn't say anything about her beautiful brother Bao. She had discovered before she left home that he too had the Gift. But males were not allowed at the institute. He's not physically defective, like she was. *Maybe he can hide his Gift.* Bi thought. People have the idea that the Gift comes only to the outcast, Bi was sure that wasn't true. Bao had pure white fur, dark amber eyes, and long black hair. He was outwardly perfect.

Bi thought of him now, how she loved watching his delicate hands as he played musical instruments. Bao tried to fit within the expectations of his class. He memorized poetry, learned to knit and paint, and studied various forms of art, hoping to attract a mate of high standing. He often shared his art with Bi or recited a poem. Her heart twisted for him, knowing he would be facing difficulties if anyone learned the truth.

"No," Bi told Far, "I'm not bitter about my siblings' opportunities, or their beauty and talent. I love and admire them. I have adventure in my future; their lives will be boring in comparison." Her smile was genuine, yet Far looked at her with doubt.

***

Over the years at the institute, Bi made a regular habit of eavesdropping on conversations related to her. She would send her spirit body into meetings where they talked about her progress and their plans for her. Bi realized the administration never seemed to sense her presence when she used astral projection to spy. They were completely oblivious. This was also how she had come to know that her test scores exceeded those of any other gifted child for generations.

Bi was determined to test the limits of her gift. She began by extending her reach to her family across town, keeping a remote view of their lives. Eventually, emboldened by this success, she did something unforgivable... she dared to spy on the royals. She just wanted to understand why the Empress thought so little of people like her. But Bi never learned why the caste system was allowed to persist. Conversations among the elite never mentioned the outcast.

What Bi learned by eavesdropping on the Empress Li Niyama was her fear of the Shadowland. All the royals were obsessed with the Zenda Nation. The Empress believed the Zendali would attack again. She wanted to be ready.

Bi had to ask herself... *Am I able to do what the others can't? Was that why my instructors never suspected when my spirit was right there in the room watching them? Surely the Empress would shut down the school if she knew what was possible!*

She could enter anyone's private space and observe them. She didn't want to divulge her abilities to the other students. She reasoned, if they were able to do what she did, they would be talking about it. Not everyone was as private as she was. Most of them talked about their experiences and challenges a lot.

The average student only learned to control their lucid dreaming. They could project themselves into a mental construct, which was used for creative purposes called a Focal Space. These took many forms, but most often mimicked a room in a house, a work-room, or a laboratory. More creative students might create something unusual, adding embellishments and unique details. The students were required to visit each other in these spaces. For training purposes, this practice of holding the vision and sharing it with others prepared the spies and their invigilators for future missions. A spy and her invigilator would meet in the focal space to communicate, make their reports, and in turn get instructions. This alone was at the heart of the institute's training. Bi could do much more. She could move within a waking dream. She could send her spirit anywhere. Now that her training had ended, the institute was preparing her for a mission. She was called to a meeting and was expected to just observe and listen. A military representative was speaking with the school's administration.

"She's not dark enough to infiltrate the Shadowland. But the Zendali do business with the Wen. The Empress wants her sent there." General Zhuhui told the institute council. She was a large female with a mottled grayish-yellow pelt. Zhuhui had once attended the institute herself, but failed. She had then enlisted in the armed forces, and unexpectedly rose to the Imperial Guard.

"The Wen have green pelts, I do not. How am I expected to blend in with the natives there?" Bi asked.

The general turned her attention to Bi with a scowl.

"Yellowish, greenish, is there really that much difference? Just cover your fur with garments and keep your head down. Don't draw attention to yourself."

"The last report on the country was before the Shadow Wars, and before we closed our borders. Our information is outdated." This was the Bellwether Ah Lam, who was opposed to the mission.

"We understand you have misgivings, Ah Lam, but the Empress has been waiting for such an opportunity and she will not listen to reason. She is insisting that we send Bi to learn what the Shadowfolk are planning. You are in the business of training spies. We have more important information to gather than knowing what the Northern Tribes are doing. Have you forgotten your place?"

"It is a dangerous mission for one so young. You have chosen to send her there without knowing what their current culture is like, and without knowing how the shadowland might have corrupted the Wen? It feels hasty, to say the least!"

"The student's own fever dreams foretold she would travel to Wendat. Should we not trust that she knows her destiny?"

"I have always questioned the veracity of the fever dreams. Are they predicting what should come to be, or are the students seeing what we chose for them? Your argument does not convince me." The bellwether argued.

Bi viewed most adults with wary skepticism, especially those who made decisions that affected her life. At least the bellwether had always championed her. All the others seemed to exist in a constant contradictory mode. On the one hand, they put a great deal of effort into training the gifted at the Brainery Institute. Yet they rarely trusted the information that the students' lucid dreams provided. They doubted and debated every detail. This made Bi angry, but she was trained not to show her emotions.

The worst doubters were the military generals, followed by the royals. Bi was no great fan of the Empress, who mandated laws that were frivolous and unnecessary, and which put herself and others like her in a sort of untouchable caste with very few rights.

"This is to be an information-gathering mission. The Empress has wanted to send someone there for a very long time. Bi is the first candidate who saw herself interacting with the shadow people, and it placed her in Wendat. So that is where she will go, and I will hear no further arguments," the general said.

Bi had repeating nightmares that foretold dangerous encounters. However, the nature of her visions didn't seem to matter to her superiors.

From what she had witnessed during her years of spying on her teachers and other adults, the attention surrounding Bi was unusual, and now this mission would be either a tremendous success giving the Empress all she hoped for... or the biggest loss imaginable, and a personal tragedy for Bi. The expectations were incredibly high. Unreasonably so, considering how little they knew.

7

FEVER DREAMS

*T*he air was salty and smelled like fish. The boat had looked so much bigger before. Now Bi regretted not having a larger vessel. With the mist over the water, there was no direction to aim the little boat. All around, it looked the same. She couldn't see the shore. Her one flimsy sail came untied and was flapping like an angry bird. Bi stood suddenly, reaching out to catch the tether, nearly tipping the boat over. Grabbing the end of the rope, she pulled it down to the boom and fastened it securely. Her fingers were so cold there was no feeling in them.

The waves had picked up. Nausea was constant. These discomforts impeded her ability to focus when full attention was needed to maneuver through the turbulent waters. To be incapacitated in these conditions could be fatal. Bi's extremities were raw with the incessant spray of cold water and wind. The storm was coming on quickly. Ominous black clouds rolled above. Icy fear crawled under her skin. Then the first big raindrops fell on Bi's face, slapping hard against her already damp fur. The full force of the storm unleashed a torrent and drenched her thoroughly.

Lightning struck the water, and the luminous column electrified the air. When the thunder boomed right overhead, Bi cried out, her heart pounding. The waves poured over the edge. She tried to bail the water with a small bucket, but the boat was thrusting back and forth violently. Both hands were needed just to keep herself aboard. Bi held tight, gripping the mast and the hull as the boat was flung with a fierce intent to dislodge one small female from a ridiculously tiny vessel. She was going to capsize! All would be lost!

Suddenly, Bi caught sight of a light, a flash that pierced the gloom. More lightning? Then she heard a bell clanging, harsh and demanding. A fishing boat! The vessel appeared out of *the fog, hung with lights that swung in the wind. It lit up the night like a beacon of hope. Bi yelled, "I'm here!" She kept shouting and shouting, her voice lost in the wind...*

Bi sat up, gasping. "What!"

"Another fever dream?" Far asked. Her calming voice brought Bi back to the present.

Too out of breath to speak, she nodded and fell back on the mattress, her shirt damp and clinging to her.

All the recruits in Bi's class at the Brainery Institute neared the age of puberty. As their day of acceptance approached, fever dreams haunted them, growing stronger, more frequent, and so real.

Fur matted with sweat, and long tangled hair had become a constant discomfort lately. Bi got off the cot where she slept in the shared dormitory room. Still shaken from the vision of near-drowning, she went to the sink to freshen up. In the mirror above it, she frowned at her sallow complexion, the yellow-grey pelt, and her straw yellow hair twisted all around her fan-shaped ears. She started pulling it away, working through the knots. "Sometimes I'm tempted to cut it short." Bi looked sallow in the dim light of the room. Her eyes were green. Not amber or brown... and too round. Her fur was too dark, and her hair was too light. In every way, she was ugly by her country's standards. The low caste was determined by the color of your fur, rather than birthright. The only thing that saved her from mediocrity was her Gift.

Far hugged her from behind. "I hope you don't. It's pretty." She ran her fingers through a few strands. "Let it be. I like your green eyes too."

In their language, Shinutta, *bi* was not a name, but a specific color of green. The shade of spring leaves, it described the color of her eyes. This was the first thing her father had said when he saw her, and the name stuck. He liked her eyes too, even if her birth meant he wouldn't father any other children. Unfortunately, her coloring was unsightly to most citizens.

Bi sighed. "But the Empress does not."

Far gave her a knowing smile and went back to folding her clothes.

Bi didn't want to mention it, but soon she would be able to hide her eye color. Once on a mission, she would be provided with colored lenses that fit over her irises, making them brown. These lenses, created for spies at the Brainery Institute, were extremely expensive to produce.

Not every spy was so lucky. The others envied those who got them. Being able to fit in with local beauty standards mattered to many of the displaced population. Some people with gray fur saved their hard-earned wages for full-body bleaching treatments. But this extreme and toxic solution, in Bi's opinion, was a stupid idea.

She shared a room with five other recruits. Far, her dearest friend and reticent lover, was beautiful by Bi's estimation. Her sunny appearance, however, contrasted with her serious nature. Far held an aloof and practical mask to cover her insecurities. But with Bi, she was passionate and demanding of attention. "We will always be connected, no matter how distant," Far said. "We're corded."

Bi assumed she meant they could share lucid dreaming. Rather than commenting on that, she tenderly ran her claws through Far's fur.

"It's a tether that lovers share." Far explained, "I read about it in the archives. Intimacy creates a strong energetic connection. Which means we will always be united even after graduation."

Bi had never heard of tethers or cording and had become a little annoyed with how clingy Far had become. She nodded but paid little attention to what her friend was hinting at.

The housing arrangements within the institute intentionally grouped students with a mix of personalities, chosen carefully to elevate everyone's training. Once inducted into the Brainery Institute, the propaganda began instilling pride and purpose into the students, producing spies born to protect the Empire from a war that the Eastern Empress Li Niyama believed inevitable. Bi did not agree with this assessment and resented the misinformation, yet she dared not speak openly about it.

An absence of respect for her superiors would express Bi's general mindset. A capricious attitude for someone in her position. The scarcity of options defined the lower castes in their society. It wouldn't be advantageous for a spy to be less than loyal to the Empress.

8

A Journey West

After Orenda finally confessed her plans to her family, much of her anxiety dissipated, and she was able to sleep without troublesome dreams. During the morning meal with her family, she told them she had applied to the university months ago and got a full scholarship. Her father shook his head and said art wasn't a noble profession, just a hobby. Her grandfather had left in the night without saying goodbye. Which was beyond hurtful, considering she had spent more time with him over the years than anyone. Though Orenda did not consider herself a good apprentice, she loved him and felt guilty for disappointing him. Her mother wouldn't speak to her at all, ignoring her attempts to talk.

Orenda believed with all her heart she had to go. She had packed all her books and art materials, clothing and a few ceremonial items and herbs (just in case). Her father, Muraco, ordered a ground vehicle and took her to the train. When they said goodbye, Muraco handed his daughter a package. "From your mother." Orenda took this as acceptance and forgiveness, and it made her cry.

"Please tell grandfather I'm sorry."

"Ezno said you need to go. He understands. He told me to give you this." He handed her a folded note. When she cocked her head in a questioning gesture, he said, "Your great aunt, his sister Coso, that's her contact information. She's invited you to stay. She'll also make introductions for you in the city. Best if you're with family when you arrive. City life differs from the village."

"The scholarship provides a dormitory, but I'm grateful to have a place to stay until they open, much better than the student hostel!"

"I'd feel better knowing you're with family." Her dad looked worried.

This family connection was unexpected and lifted her spirits a little. Her guilt about abandoning her grandfather was the hardest part about leaving. Knowing she had Ezno's support meant everything. She had taken a big, impulsive leap without considering all the details. A do-it-now or never situation had driven her to this point of departure. Then, this morning, she started to worry. Having family in Muwioni was reassuring. It didn't feel so much like she was stepping off a cliff.

Muraco embraced his daughter, holding her tight. When a whistle signaled boarding time, he helped to carry her things onto the train, grumbling about the heavy trunk and asking who would help her get it off in Muwioni.

"I'll find a way, Dad. Everything will work out."

"Your dreaming has told you?"

She looked down. "No, not exactly. I only know that I have to go, not why."

Muraco accepted this. It was the way of seers. Once all her belongings were on the train, he hugged her one last time, then left without looking back.

The hovertrain was not fast. The trip would take several days to cross the whole of Wendat from one coast to the next. Orenda had expected to feel excited about the adventure, but she was like a butterfly in a cocoon, wrapped in apprehension and doubts. She didn't have a sleeping compartment, but she had taken over a section in the back corner of one train car, where two bench seats faced each other. Her trunk and cases surrounded her. Orenda spent her time staring out the window or drawing in her journal. The package from Minda contained home-cooked treats. She was going to miss her mother's cooking. The train was never crowded. Along the way, people got on and off, but on average, only a handful of other passengers came into her section. The light traffic allowed her to keep that corner to herself.

Whenever she slept, she dreamt of two females. Although she had never met them, they were not strangers to her. The sketchbooks were filled with images of their faces and the exotic places they were from.

As Orenda sat daydreaming and sketching, she nodded off again, thinking about the two mysterious females. Suddenly she jerked upright, dropping her journal. The heavy book clattered to the floor, making a loud thwack, startling the others seated near her. Everyone turned to see what the fuss was about. They observed with concern a frightened young native with teal fur and blue hair, her hand pressed against her heart to calm her rapid breathing.

Orenda realized she was traveling to meet them. She would soon have to face whatever secrets they carried. This is what her grandfather understood, and possibly discerned from his own visions. Inevitably, Orenda would seek them out. Even though she had told no one about her dreams, Ezno understood. She had no doubt in her mind that she was connected in some inexplicable way to these strange foreigners. Her life and theirs were intertwined. She was not running away from her burdens as she had thought. She could not escape her destiny.

9

MUWIONI

When Algon and Asha arrived in the morning, Mora had finally fallen asleep on the couch with one of Zamora's journals in her lap. She realized the chiming sound had to be the door. Still only half awake, she pointed the disk in the approximate direction of the entryway to let them in. They gave her a bewildered look.

"I couldn't sleep," was all she said.

Algon announced he would make tea and breakfast while Asha helped Mora get ready. Though she was exhausted, her anticipation of seeing this new world gave her strength.

Asha first braided Mora's mane very close to her scalp, using an underhand-upward motion to make continuous, raised rows along her scalp. Asha told her she did the same with her crest, so it would fit under the headdress. It was tight and a little painful, but Mora didn't complain.

"Zamora shaved the sides of her head for a time to hide the fact that she had a mane. But after joining the Sisters, she didn't have to."

"Why would she shave the sides of her head? Is that another fashion here?"

Asha paused. Her fingers stopped moving for a moment; as if she were considering what to say. "Most Zendali have a crest of hair from their forehead to the nape of their neck, like me. Not a full mane like yours."

Mora nodded. "Where I'm from, most people are mixed race. So, I've rarely seen anyone with a crest, not until I came here."

"Interesting. Well, Zamora didn't want anyone to know her heritage."

"Oh," Mora said, but she still had no idea what Asha was talking about.

Then Asha instructed Mora in how to dress like a member of the Sisters of Justice, a follower of the Goddess Bicara.

"These garments are all black! They'll be stifling in the heat!" Mora exclaimed.

A slightly peeved expression crossed Asha's face, but then she smiled. "They really are more comfortable than they look. In any case, you don't have a choice."

The undergarment was a form-fitting black bodysuit. Over this went robe-like apparel, which was topped with a sort of turban headpiece and black veil. The whole outfit looked confining, but Mora didn't want to be ill-mannered. She went along with all of Asha's instructions.

"This is a perfect way to disguise your pallid pelt. It's either this or the dye shops."

Mora wondered if Asha was insulting her. She didn't like the sound of *pallid*. She'd only just decided she was pretty with this lavender fur. Now she had to hide it! "Did Zamora dye her hair?"

"When she first got here, she was dark indigo. Both hair and fur. She hated the upkeep, and she hated pretending to be something she wasn't."

Algon called from the kitchen that breakfast was ready.

"Let's go eat," Asha said.

Mora had so many questions. The weight of her ignorance was heavier than the Sisters' robes.

***

"Mora doesn't know why some Zendali have a mane!" Asha announced with some mirth as they joined Algon in the kitchen.He looked at Mora in surprise. "You are not aware you have royal blood?"Mora stared at them both like they had to be joking, waiting for the punchline.

"Only the Royal Zendali are born with a mane. All others have a crest," Algon told her.

If a child is born to a royal without a mane, they cannot rule." Asha confirmed.

They seemed dead-serious. Mora looked at them with an incredulous expression, still amused. "The Zenda Nation in my world doesn't have royalty... So, you're saying I'm a princess here?" She laughed.

"Ah..." Algon gave Asha a worried look. "No, Mora, you are Fog here. Your royal blood means nothing to them."

"Your blood is mixed with the Pinks. Which is considered an abomination in Zenda, even more so because of your royal heritage. It might have no significance in your world, but your mother was related to the royals. That's why you have such a full head of wild hair," Asha explained.

Algon looked impatient. "We'd better have breakfast, then get going." He had cut fruit with yogurt in bowls. Unleavened bread with butter and preserves was also on the table. The scent of spicy herbal tea smelled wonderful, which astonished Mora. She had never liked tea, and least of all the herbal blends. She took a sip, relishing the flavor. It tasted as delightful as it had smelled. "Oh, I like that! It surprised me because I'm a Kav drinker. I've never liked tea before." Mora savored everything Algon had prepared with obvious delight. When she exclaimed how exceptionally wonderful everything was, Asha mentioned her cuisine preferences would change.

"You're going to crave healthier foods now because of the implant."

Algon and Asha had their implants since they were young. They didn't recall what it was like without them. But they related a few humorous stories about students from Zenda having new experiences with food when they got theirs.

Watching Algon cleaning up the dishes, Mora said, "I've got no clue how to operate anything in this kitchen. All these knobs and buttons are just dreadful. Nothing is like what I'm used to."

"We'll show you later. I think we should spend the early part of the day out. Might get too hot to wander around in the afternoon."

Both had put on the headpieces and covered their faces with the black veil. Mora was astonished that her vision was unobstructed by the fabric. The outer surface of the veil had a sheen prohibiting a clear view of her face. She could see out. But others could not see in.

"The city center isn't far away. Let's walk through the park," Algon suggested.

In daylight, Mora realized the entire neighborhood was bigger than she'd thought. Asha explained that some Zendali used their homes here seasonally. Many were currently unoccupied.

At the end of the street, they saw larger homes. "This is where I live with my father and brother," Asha told her. "The Zendali contractor who built this community used a typical structure style that's common in the Zenda Capital, Ekene."

Mora took note that Asha's family home was much bigger, with three towers. Her father was obviously affluent.

"Top two floors in the back tower are mine," Asha said.

They took a shortcut through a park dense with deciduous trees. The flower beds were filled with native plants and herbs. The bushes were flowering, too. Asha named the plants as they walked by. Benches lined the path, where a few people sat chatting and mothers watched their children play. Everyone in the park was Zendali. "This resembles my world, but greener, I suppose. There's a drought after the heat of the summer there." Asha and Algon exchanged knowing glances. On the other side of the park was a wall and a huge gate standing open. "This is where the foreign sector ends," Asha told her.

"It is also where anything that might be familiar ends," Algon's ear-fans wiggled in anticipation of her reaction.

The first thing Mora saw was fascinating enough to make her pause. Across from the gate, a tall building made of Energy Crystal towered over them, with greenery on every level. Mora peered through the walls into a forest of plants. "They made the buildings of the same material as your dome. " Asha explained.

Mora tilted her head up to take in the full view. It was unique, appearing both delicate in detail, and solid... as if a garden was frozen in ice.

"The crystal gathers nourishment from the sun?" She asked.

"Yes," Algon affirmed. "It generates and stores energy to power the building. And it's unbreakable, of course. The city encourages patio gardens for residential housing, but this one is specially designed for food production. Vegetable gardens are on every level, and they grow fruit trees in a central atrium."

"It's much taller than we build in our city. We have earthquakes. Isn't height a problem here?" Asked Mora.

"The construction accommodates tremors." Algon reassured her. "The buildings move fluidly with the quakes. Unless the land opens below them, of course. This construction is completely safe at any height."

When they turned the corner on the street, a panoramic view of the city opened below them. A wide road led down an incline to the city market. Mora stopped in place, astonished and speechless. The city was extraordinary, a mixture of natural wonders and futuristically surreal structures unlike anything known in her world. The early morning sun sparkled off the crystalline walls, making all the structures seem like they were made of diamonds. But the most notable oddities were the floating structures, made of some soft glowing material, fluffy, oblong things Mora couldn't quite find the right words to describe. "What *are* they?" she asked.

"We call them Floaters. A gift from the Star People. They're alive but not conscious, laboratory-grown."

Still transfixed, she asked in a barely audible voice. "What do they do?"

"Think of them as an enormous data core, or libraries, giant storage centers of knowledge," Algon explained. "We mostly use them for immersive learning and entertainment. They interface with our implants."

"You go inside them?"

Algon nodded. "They're hollow, but the living material on the inside adapts to your presence and accommodates your form."

Mora looked at him in awe. "What is it like?"

"Floaters have a symbiotic relationship with our implants. When we get inside, the walls surround our bodies, and tendrils reach out to connect with our implants. They have stored information in their cells: entertainments, travel adventures, or mind-maps that we can access."

"But what are they made of?"

"I'm unable to tell you, mainly because I am not involved in floater science, but if I knew, I shouldn't say."

"Can you tell me why they float?"

"They produce gas, which gets trapped between the outside layer of skin and the inside body of morphing flesh. This gas makes them rise."

"Let's go then! How do we get inside?"

"I'm sorry, Mora," Algon looked uncomfortable. "They are off-limits for anyone but native born Wen. This is an agreement enforced by the Star People. But to answer your question, there's a lift that gives us access."

"But the Zendali are allowed the implants?"

"Not just allowed, but required if they come to Wendat," Asha told her.

Mora had not taken her eyes off the scene before her. She was completely mesmerized by this marvel of a city.

"I can't experience them either." Asha sighed. "I grew up here, and I've always been curious. I tried to get in once when I was little, and the orifice wouldn't open for me." She smiled now, accepting the frustration with enviable grace.

Mora was so eager to see everything that her disappointment regarding Floaters was only a minor blow. There was so much here to experience! As an outsider, she didn't expect to have access to everything. After all, she was but a visitor here.

"Shall we proceed?" Algon asked her with amusement.

Mora beamed with expectation. "Absolutely! Lead on." Her first glimpse of Muwioni was honestly overwhelming. What followed would be indescribable to anyone in her world.

10

The Spy

"You will be traveling by air to an eastern port in the Empire's territory." Bellwether Ah Lam told Bi.

"I've never been on an aircraft."

"Does it frighten you?" Ah Lam asked.

Bi nodded, "Yes, but it is also... thrilling?"

"Then, the military submarine will take you across the ocean. Traveling southeast," Ah Lam used a pointer to indicate the route on a map that hung on her office wall. "They will get you close to the continent of Wendat, leaving you in the open sea, here." She tapped the map. This looked very close to the western coast.

Bi imagined herself in the little sailboat. In that vast ocean, and was somewhat comforted by the idea she would be near the shore.

"The generals have been debating for days, as no ships have made this crossing into the territory of Wendat for generations. The weakest point of the plan is in making sure there are no witnesses. If a native of that country saw the submarine emerge, your mission would be exposed."

"Yes, I was part of that discussion. I suggested they surface under the cover of night." Bi said, then with a certain amount of caution she shared one of her biggest concerns... "I've never been in a boat on the water."

Ah Lam gave her an incredulous glare. Which was unlike her. Bi shrunk back as if she had stepped out of line.

"I don't mean to complain. It just has me a little worried," Bi admitted.

"As you should be! I was informed that you had been given rigorous training! I only *assumed*... they would have you in the water."

"It was mostly theoretical training in a classroom. I understand the workings of a sail."

"That is absurd!"

"It is a lot of faith to put in a dream," Bi said. "I just hope to keep the little craft afloat until I'm rescued."

The plan was simple yet seemed improbable. She would be expected to survive a storm in a tiny boat, hoping the Wen would discover her in time. Her dreams foretold a rescue. Even with zero practical sailing experience, Bi was expected to trust that she would not be lost at sea. She was troubled by other doubts as well. Bi honestly wasn't sure where this adventure would lead, but she was quite certain it would not be what they expected. In some of her visions, she wore a strange costume. Maybe she'd take the advice of the military general, Zhuhui, and wear a disguise.

If things were not so uncertain, and the variables so confounding, her dreams might make more sense. Bi mostly saw the first scenes of the journey to come. The boat people, then some danger in the forest. These were the visions that repeated. She occasionally caught glimpses of the shadow people, but nothing was clear beyond the forest episode. Perhaps the outcome of the encounter was undetermined. Bi had not had even one glimpse of the city. Maybe she wouldn't survive long enough to get to her destination. This worried her more than she was willing to admit.

The Brainery Institute's recordings of Salagi, which was the Wen's prime language, were created long ago. Neofinga was also quite common, because so many Zendali traveled there. Bi had spent time studying these. But she had no one to confirm whether her diction was correct. Now that she was finally scheduled for departure, she hoped her languages were proficient enough and her pronunciation wouldn't give her away as a foreigner. All language forms are a sort of living thing, just as theirs had changed from Shin to Shinutta once the Empire overtook the North-Western tribes.

***

Excitement outweighed Bi's trepidation, but she didn't want to show how eager she was to leave, especially to her friend Far. She had conflicting emotions regarding Far. Bi was sometimes irked by her comments and judgments of their roommates. Far was also possessive and selfish. She saw faults in others, but never in herself. Yet at the same time, Bi deeply cared about her.

It was likely that Far would fail her final exams. There were few outside options in the service industry that would be anything but drudgery. Bi wanted to secure something for her friend before she left. She had some influence at the institute and was able to get a small accommodation, which allowed Far to be her invigilator. In this case, it meant someone who kept watch over a lucid dreamer operative while they were away on a mission.

Invigilators also tested new candidates, but that was a job for mature members of the institute who became instructors or part of the administration. Some of her friends may end up staying on, and training for that position.

Bi would report to Far about her progress through lucid dreaming while she was traveling. Then Far would make her reports to her superiors, and they, in turn, would report to the royals. This was how it should have been. A recruit on mission needs to know they can count on their one connection to the Empire.

11

DISPARITY OF DISTANCE

F ar disliked being cheated. She imagined a more exciting life for herself. Like the opportunities they gave to Bi... exploring the world, leaving the county, and meeting new people! She wanted that.

With Bi gone, Far had started speaking openly to the other roommates about her dissatisfaction. For the most part, they ignored her grumbling. They were accustomed to her contrary nature and claims that she was treated unfairly. But when it had to do with Bi, they showed bewilderment. Lai, Niu, Sying and Yin were still waiting for placement. They were all nervous to learn where they would be assigned, and they knew if it were not for Bi, Far would be out already. They gave Far embarrassed sideways looks. Her roommates told her she was fortunate to be an invigilator, and she should be proud to have that honor. But none of them informed Far how much Bi had fought for her.

Yin, who was the bossiest of the roommates, finally spoke up. "Bi loved you, Far, why are you speaking ill of her?"

"Bi has the mistaken impression that I'm *happy* to be assigned as her invigilator!" Far scoffed. "Who does she think she is? It's like being a servant to the royals."

"That is the job of an invigilator, Far, if you didn't want the assignment, why did you agree to it?" Sying asked.

"I thought she would share her adventures with me. But her communication is all business, no interesting details. It's like we were never close. I've no wish to be subservient to Bi, or anyone else!"

"Why even come to the institute then? We are all servants of the Empress, isn't that evident? We do her bidding one way or another; there is no point being bitter about it," Lai said.

"I assumed by entering the Institute my status would be raised." Far admitted.

"There is little glory in being a spy," Niu said. "I've heard most of the work we do in the northwestern provinces is harmful. We expose the petty crimes of the commoners. Do you realize how many foolish laws they are expected to adhere to? The Empress decrees something is illegal. And we are expected to expose anyone who disobeys! Yet, most of those activities are just ways they make ends meet. Once we report them, they end up being heavily taxed."

Far didn't seem concerned. She didn't comment on the hardships of the northern tribes.

"Did you hear anything I said? Do you care about anything but yourself?" Niu asked.

"I told you, Far is entirely self-absorbed lately. Just look at her. When was the last time she bathed or combed her hair?" Lai said.

Far ignored the criticism. "So, I've ended up just *watching*, while Queen Bi gets all the adventure!"

"She is also at *risk* and faces unknown dangers." Sying told her with an edge of worry.

"Unfortunately, our superiors have made it clear I have no choice in the matter. I have to do what I'm told."

As the weeks progressed, Far expected Bi to share her personal thoughts and feelings about her adventures in Wendat. But each time they connected in the Focal Space, Bi was all business. She didn't say she missed Far or ask anything personal about how life was back at the institute.

Most of the students weren't aloof like Bi. They shared all their feelings and fears and talked about their experiences. But the further away from her country Bi traveled, the less she seemed to be willing to share with Far.

Filled with indignation, Far's thoughts became increasingly negative and brooding.

"Bi never said she loved me. She's always been a little too detached." Far told Sying. *Privately scheming to get the best position for herself and leave me behind!* She thought to herself.

"Bi's position as a field agent doesn't allow for the sort of relationship you expect, Far. I'm sure she must be overwhelmed with all she is trying to accomplish."

"She isn't supposed to make independent assessments! She's required to report her findings and observations to me... then get instructions from the institute. I am the conduit for that process!" Far complained.

Sying cringed at the bitterness. "I imagine she reports what she believes is most important. Why do you doubt her?"

Far couldn't explain because her reason wasn't professional, or in the least rational. She
felt emotionally cut off. Nor could she admit that her jealousy made her doubt that Bi was
being completely honest.

"It isn't right that she doesn't tell me everything. I'm her invigilator!"

"Your duty as an invigilator is to be *available for contact* when the field agent reports.
It's a simple job, really, to receive the agent's report, and then keep our superiors informed
of the progress during the mission. I don't understand why you are making this so
personal," Sying said.

"You are not an invigilator, Sying, how dare you tell me how to do my job!"

***

Something about absence and longing, some strong affinity...drove her. Desire and attachment motivated her. Far reached with her yearning, extending outward in search of
Bi. Suddenly, her spirit body detached and flew across the distance, uncontrolled, tum-
bling through time and space. To her astonishment, her desperation led to a connection!
Far had exceeded even her own expectations.

Then Far was there with Bi in Wendat! Her spirit floated above the room. She observed
everything Bi was doing, but when she tried to communicate... as they might do in the
focal space, Bi didn't hear her. She didn't seem aware Far was with her.

Then suddenly, as fast as it had happened, she snapped back into her body. Startled by
this, she jumped off her bed.

"What's going on?" Niu asked. "A fever dream frighten you?"

Far couldn't speak. She stood in the dormitory breathing heavily, wide-eyed, staring at
her roommates.

"Far, what's gotten into you?" Lai asked.

But it was Yin who came over to Far and sat her down, running her fingers through
Far's pelt the way she had seen Bi do. Gradually Far calmed. But she didn't speak of what
happened.

It never occurred to Far that this *special ability* was not *her* gift. This newly discovered
ability to astral project was merely a flawed echo of her friend and lover's capability. This
was happening because of her intimate link to Bi.

Until this happened, no one had come close to experiencing what Bi could do, and Bi had never told Far what she was capable of. If Far had tried to connect with anyone else, she would have discovered she couldn't make it happen with them. The link existed only with Bi. Far was too excited for such rational experiments. She just *assumed* that she'd had some sort of breakthrough.

Her lack of talent was well established. She wasn't able to visit the other student's Focal Spaces. This had not changed, but she had long ago stopped trying. To pass as an invigilator, the student was required to manifest her dream body in their field agent's Focal Space.

Yet, Bi chose not to inform her superiors that Far wasn't able to do this. Bi had always accommodated Far by coming to her Focal Space. As time permitted, Far experimented with her new abilities, flinging her spirit body outward to where Bi was, watching undetected what was happening.

Bi would never suspect I could penetrate her carefully protected privacy! Far mused...

She knew it was wrong, but still, she felt justified because Bi was not being completely honest with her, and she wanted to know what was actually going on.

Far knew all the other students pitied her, even Bi. They thought she was less talented than they were. The lowest of the low. She heard them whisper sometimes about her lack of talent and how they didn't expect her to pass. *Now, if they only knew my secret talent, they would think differently! They would be impressed, envious even.* The more she thought about it, the more impressed with herself she became. It was nothing less than a miracle what she was capable of! Pride in her ability swelled inside Far. It was an unbearable secret to bear. She desperately wanted to brag about it.

Observing Bi's life in Wendat was an irresistible compulsion. Far hardly rested or ate. Her body hygiene suffered. The others observed Far and whispered among themselves. Far ignored them.

When out of body, achieving visual perfection was impossible. There were obstacles. Most of the time it was like peering through a smoky window or seeing something at the bottom of a pond, in murky water. Images shifted and faded. It took concentration, and it was exhausting. The whole experience was shaky and easily disrupted. But she persisted, she lingered, she tried to make sense of things. What she observed, she didn't like.

Soon Far's jealousy twisted her opinion of Bi, and she started to imagine Bi was a defector. Fear of being associated with that crime caused her to make irrational choices. Far decided her only option was to distance herself by cutting direct communication at the focal Space. She didn't tell her superiors that she was doing this. After all, what could she tell them? How could she explain what she was able to do?

Her obsessive monitoring of Bi continued. Taking the place of what she should do as an invigilator. This left Bi isolated and unable to get help when she needed advice.

Far's observations were seriously hindered by her lack of control. It was much harder than visiting someone's Focal Space because other people were involved. Any sudden energetic disruption or unexpected movement broke Far's concentration and threw her out. Conversations were unclear, jumbled, and slurred. She couldn't maintain the necessary focus to see and hear things properly in these real-life environments. So, she filled in what she didn't understand with her own version of reality.

12

STUDENT OF ART

On the fourth day of Orenda's train ride to the west coast, she suddenly woke from a dream, picked up her journal, and began to write and sketch. *I have dreams about places that don't exist and people I have never met. The landscape of those dreams was confusing. I know they're not real, but the experience is as true as my waking reality. I see places, mountains or features I recognize, but the buildings and environments around them are different, alien, and wrong. The ancient forests are gone; the lakes and rivers are brown with waste. Fences and walls divide the country, and endless roads block animal migration. I sometimes wake from these nightmares crying, heartbroken by the loss of our natural wonders, then I'm relieved to know I was just dreaming. But is this just a nightmare? What if this is our future? The strange structures are not in harmony with nature. The vehicles wait end-to-end on the long roads, emitting toxic fumes. Inside them are ghostly white-furred people, pallid and strange. This dream world is truly frightening. I pray for these nightmares to end.*

By the time Orenda finished the sketch, the train was passing through the outskirts of Muwioni. She moved closer to the window, taking in the wonders of the city as it passed by. Her dark mood soon evaporated as anticipation of this new adventure lifted her spirits. This city was a jewel, sparkling in the sun. Light reflecting off the windows and domes gave it a magical quality.

They passed wondrous things as they entered the city, towering mesh-like structures that captured water from the air. These were common on the West Coast, where summers were dry. She noticed the factory where Energy Crystal was produced, which was why in the heart of Muwioni most of the city buildings were made of this translucent material.

With all the plants on balconies and rooftop gardens, it was a bright and gleaming emerald city, truly awe-inspiring!

As the train got closer to the station, Orenda pondered on how unprepared she was for city life. She had grown up in a remote place. Her father's parting words mentioned that her tribal ways were far removed from city norms. She had lived in a large East-Coast settlement, but it was old-fashioned compared to Muwioni. Her community was built within the forest by a lake; the structures were mostly wooden longhouses. The center of the village was occupied by communal buildings, where governing took place. Being the largest village in those parts, it gave her the false impression she wasn't back-country raised. Her community was substantial, more so with the adjacent farmlands, but there was nothing sophisticated or modern about it.

The only other place Orenda had traveled to was the northeastern city of Seneca, where she and her grandfather attended a gathering of medicine people. Seneca had been dark and heavy, crowded with perilous characters. There had been a menacing aspect to that city, which made her timid and cautious. The only safety in the area was near the medicine circle, which gathered for the World Renewal Ceremonies. These yearly events prevented catastrophes like crop failure, earthquakes, and floods.

There was a reason Muwioni was called the Crystal City. It had an extraordinary luminous quality. Everything appeared bright, as if nothing untoward could happen. Still, it was staggering to imagine she would ever find her way around this maze of buildings.

Orenda's great-aunt, Coso Winnemucca, was waiting at the station. She was easy to find in the crowd because she looked so much like her grandfather Ezno. Orenda was amazed that she had come in person. She was an important member of the city government, a council elder. A personal greeting wasn't expected!

Two young males took charge of Orenda's baggage and trunk, moving them to a cart. Coso introduced them as Kinache and Yuma.

Orenda wondered how her aunt knew them. Only when Kinache mentioned that Holata Tyee, the famous local medicine guardian, was expecting to see her the following day did Orenda realize the connection. Her aunt took it for granted that she was here to study medicine. Orenda realized this was a natural assumption, considering her aunt knew she'd been Ezno's only apprentice. There had been preparations and expectations preceding her arrival. Coso would not take the news of art school well.

13

The Castaway

As in her visions, the shore couldn't be seen, and a thick mist rose off the water, obscuring visibility. The claustrophobic haze gave Bi a strange and lonely sensation of hopelessness, as if she were lost, never to be found. She shouldn't doubt they would arrive in time. As it was one of her repetitive dreams, she had seen the rescue over and over again. Still, it didn't stop her from worrying. Enveloped and hidden from view, the panic now threatened to imbalance her sensible nature.

If only there had been time to sail closer to shore; it looked suspicious being so far from land in such a tiny boat. No matter how often Bi had this dream, it never told her the whole truth of the situation. All it did was prepare her for a leap of faith.

It got darker. The vapory gloom dissipated, and the rain started. The storm raged right above her, tossing the tiny vessel about like a toy. The vast sky and sea made it seem unlikely that she would be found. She was minuscule and insignificant in that infinite expanse of angry water, helpless to save herself. Bi feared she would not be seen.

It is so often truer than not when hope is lost... what you desire finally comes to you. So, it was for Bi. The moment she resigned herself to facing her death, the fishing boat appeared, penetrating the misty gloom. A string of lights swayed wildly in the wind. The bell clanged with an urgent promise of rescue. She shouted over the raging storm, not knowing if they would hear. Desperation made her cry out until her voice was hoarse. As the boat got closer, she saw people on deck pointing. They saw her!

Bi's boat was flooding by the time the family on the fishing vessel pulled her on board. Moments after they retrieved her scanty gear and supplies, it was swallowed by the sea.

The Wen native who had helped her on deck was as drenched as she was. "You're fortunate we came this way. It isn't our normal route. The storm pushed us in this direction."

"I'm grateful you did," was all Bi could say. They talked very fast. She only got the general meaning of what was said.

This seemed to be a family business. The crew were obviously related. The father was an older, more weathered version of his sons, with dark teal fur and a muscular frame, while the daughter had the softer look of their mother, with dusky greenish fur. Bi held her pack tightly to her chest, as if it could protect her from all the strangeness. Father and sons piled her other things on deck and secured them with a net and rope. They led Bi below deck into a warm cabin and gave her a soft blanket to dry herself and some garments.

"I'm sure everything in that pack of yours is wet. Take these and change," the elder female said.

As Bi shyly thanked them, they left her alone to change. The little stove warmed the room, making the space quite cozy. She pulled off the sodden garments and put her little slip-on boots close to the heat. Bi was pulling on the sweater when she heard a light knock on the door.

Mother and daughter peeked in. "You must be hungry," the daughter said. "Mom heated some leftovers for you. Please," she motioned to the chair, "have a seat by the stove and get warmed up."

The mother handed her a plate with grilled fish, root vegetables, and wild rice. Herbs gave it a savory aroma.

Motion sickness had prevented Bi from eating on her boat, even though she had brought provisions with her. The incessant rocking of the waves made her woozy. When it got more turbulent, she was heaving over the side. For the last couple of days, she couldn't keep anything down. Having stepped onto a much bigger vessel, with people around, she felt better almost at once, and she was hungry!

The family seemed accustomed to the motion of the boat, untroubled by the storm. They behaved as if it were normal. Their fishing vessel was quite large and felt safe despite the rocking. They sat silently in the chairs beside Bi, the mother with her knitting, the daughter mending a shirt. Bi felt their curiosity, but they were too polite to ask questions. They let her eat in peace. Grateful for their silence, Bi relaxed and enjoyed the meal.

The whole scene was a little strange... so homey and calm after the intensity she went through. Yet Bi had to admit: living the dream was far worse than her nightmares. Getting it over with was a relief. And knowing she was on the right track was helpful. She felt her rescue was verification. It spoke to the accuracy of her visions.

Now she knew without a doubt she could trust the dreams.

During the storm, she had lost faith. It was just a bit too close for comfort. Lost in her thoughts, Bi hadn't paid attention to how fast she'd eaten everything until she heard the mother asking, "Was it enough?"

"Yes, thank you."

The daughter jumped up, took her plate, and left the room. An uncomfortable silence filled the emptiness again. The mother, trying not to be intrusive, kept moving her knitting sticks back and forth. The daughter returned and handed Bi an herbal tea. Just holding the steaming cup was comforting, and the sweet aroma of the flowers had a calming effect.

Sipping the tea, Bi mentally reviewed her previous visions of this event. Her foresight didn't contain details of these pleasant moments. She was only shown what she needed to survive. The best and the worst of the experience were obscured, flattened, muted... as if the life was removed from it. The reality was different... much harder, and deeper, and richer. Those raw emotions were missing in the dreams... the terror of the storm holding her life in its grasp, with only a slim chance of a passing boat... Bi understood now, as frightening as the fever dreams were, she was only a witness in them. She would never have been able to fully understand that until she lived through the real thing. It had truly shaken her.

The young native broke Bi's ruminations by introducing herself. "I'm Aponi and my mother is Dyani. My father and brothers are still dealing with the nets and securing the boat. You'll meet them later."

Bi felt a moment of trepidation; she needed to introduce herself and use a name familiar to them. The only native name she found on record, similar to her own, was normally given to a male, but she chose to use it, anyway. "I'm Bimisi," she told them.

Aponi looked at her with surprise. "An unusual name for a female!"

"My mother named me after her brother, who died right before my birth."

They nodded in acceptance. This sounded true enough, and bringing up a personal tragedy had the effect she hoped... stopping further questions on the subject.

"I'm from a coastal tribe further north. I was traveling to visit friends, but got caught in the storm and carried too far from land. When I lost sight of the shore, I didn't know which way to sail." That was partly true. Hopefully, they would believe her.

Dyani and her daughter exchanged a knowing look and nodded. "Well, you're safe with us now. We'll make sure you arrive without further trauma. I'm sorry we couldn't save your boat, but we managed to get most of your supplies."

Bi thanked them, knowing she would no longer need the boat. Getting to Wendat was her objective.

"You've all been so kind. Thank you for saving me from the storm." After everything they had done for her, any words of appreciation sounded insufficient and lacked the depth of her real feeling. And Bi did sense a debt of gratitude to these strangers, which fate had delivered her to.

They gave her a blanket and a soft pallet.

"This was taken from our dinner table bench. Sorry, it's a little small," said the daughter.

"Actually, that's perfect. I'm not very big."

"Our sleeping cabins are down the hall to the right. The latrine is the first door on the left."

They let her rest without further questions. Bi expected to tell the story she'd prepared, and was nervous about being able to properly answer detailed inquiries, especially not knowing what region or tribe they were from. But thankfully, they didn't ask.

She would worry about that tomorrow. As soon as Bi snuggled down on the pallet near the stove, she fell into a deep sleep.

Bi was awakened by a new and strangely vivid dream. She lay in the dark trying to figure out where she was. The rocking of the boat reminded her. Bi felt she urgently needed to find the latrine. She snuck down the hall and lingered outside the parent's room because they were talking with a tone of disagreement. Suddenly, the father exclaimed, "Bimisi?"

Bi waited a while longer, hoping to catch something more, but heard only muffled whispers. Finally, she got chilled, so she used the toilet and went back to her nest on the floor, falling back to sleep without any concerns.

In the morning, a gentle rocking of the boat made it difficult to leave the comfort of her bed. The sound made by the wake of the waves kept lulling her back to sleep. The movement of the ship was now peaceful and soothing. A breeze whistled through the rigging, and the halyards slapped the mast. Bi lay on the pallet listening to the gooseneck squeaking on a taut main sheet, the dinghy slapping against the lapping waves, the anchor rollers creaking, and the blocks squawking. She couldn't have known what made these sounds, but she listened and examined every noise. The cry of hungry gulls, then laughter and a playful ruckus from above, changed the tone of the morning. Time to get up.

Bi was folding her blanket when Aponi peeked around the door. "Oh good, you're awake. Here, I made biscuits and eggs, and we have some apples too." She handed the plate over and turned to leave.

"Wait, is there anything I can do to help?" Bi asked.

The daughter shook her head. "We will come to keep you company in a bit; I'm just cleaning up right now. My brothers want to meet you if you don't mind. They're setting the crab cages now. We decided to hang out close to the coast for the day, then we will head further south."

Bi sat by the stove and enjoyed her meal, trying not to eat too fast. With her breakfast finished, her calm morning was over. The thought of meeting the others made her heart thump loudly. Her pulse was rushing and roaring in her ears. The door opened, and the whole family entered, making the room crowded and the air thick with the scent of their bodies. Ellute, the father, was polite but worried and reticent. His skeptical expression said more than enough about his concerns. The youngest of the two, who was introduced as Chitto, behaved with open friendliness. The older one, Askook, hung back and didn't speak until all the introductions and pleasantries were exchanged. Then he began to ask Bi specific questions about her home and tribe. It was clear he didn't believe her.

"Let's not bother her with all these unimportant details," Ellute interceded. "Let her rest. She experienced a traumatic event."

Ellute stared pointedly at his son Askook as if in warning. He glared back at his father, defiant. Ellute spoke with a kinder tone, hoping to elicit compassion, but his elder son's expression didn't change. If anything, it made him angrier.

"She lost everything," his father told him. "The least we can do is give her some time to recover."

The youth was visibly offended when his interrogation of the stranger was thwarted. He stomped away, glaring back at Bi and his father.

"Don't mind him," Aponi consoled her. "He's often troubled about things that are not his business, and he gets... disruptive."

The look of frustration on Aponi's face gave Bi the feeling she meant to say something more critical of her brother.

Then, she turned to her younger brother with a smile. "Chitto is the nice one." Aponi pinched his ear affectionately.

Chitto smiled shyly at Bi.

A short time later, Bi heard a heated argument on the deck above, loud enough to draw her attention. The raised voices were too muffled to distinguish what the fuss was about. She suspected, however, it was about her. What else could it be? Aponi excused herself and went up to settle the dispute. Bi followed at a distance and hid behind the door to the upper deck.

"Why are you talking about a reward?" Aponi asked Askook.

"Because we may as well be law-abiding citizens and collect what is our due, instead of harboring a fugitive."

"You don't know that she is."

"Don't tell me you think she is really from a coastal tribe. Look at her yellowish fur, her light hair and those green eyes! Can you explain how any of that is possible?"

Bi's priceless Specta-Shade lenses were lost in the storm. She realized how it compromised her mission. Her green eyes had always been a problem.

"She doesn't have Zendali features," Aponi said. "She has no crest! But even if you're right, and one of her parents is from Zenda, then we would be causing the tribe and the council grief. Why would we want to bring trouble down on anyone?"

"From Zenda? With that fur? I'd say more likely she's some sort of Native-Pink mix!" Askook's tone was full of ire.

"You are just causing problems with that kind of accusation!" Aponi was losing hope that she could make her brother see reason.

"Am I? Why?" Askook taunted. "Because whoever they are, they broke the treaty with our allies! What do you think you can do to help her? The nearest reservation is inland and not easily reached on foot. Besides, she's not our responsibility!"

"You just want the reward!" This was Chitto, the accusation flung at his brother with disgust.

"No, worse!" said Aponi. "He wants to impress his Zendali friends. Turning her in would give him credibility. It's acceptance he's after!"

"I'm already *in*, you idiot, and you know nothing! They're patriots!" Askook's voice lowered an octave. "It's important. I'll get a better job. I don't want to be fishing for the rest of my life."

"Patriots?" Aponi shouted at him. "What, you think I'm a child? You think I'm not aware of their history? There are facts about their past you aren't willing to accept. They are not clean. They have genocides to account for, don't you realize? Or do you just not care?"

"Genocide? Please, don't be so dramatic!" Askook practically spit the words out. "And those are exaggerations! Why would you listen to such nonsense? We need this alliance. We can't afford to challenge them about ancient history. Whatever happened in the past has nothing to do with us."

"Of course, you would take that position!" said Aponi. "You have no compassion for the refugees! We give sanctuary to the Pinks, and you're perfectly aware they are not animals! Your friends hunt and kill them still. It is not only in the past! We don't need that kind of help!"

"We are not going to solve anything with such talk. Let it go," Dyani's voice interceded. She looked imploringly into the eyes of her oldest son. With a challenging glare, he walked away.

To get the last word in, the youngest shouted after his brother. "We're independent! We don't need the Zendali at all!"

His mother patted him on the shoulder. "We care little about politics, son, and this is not our business."

From her hiding place, Bi watched Aponi smile at her younger brother.

Their father came into view, telling the them to tend to the crab pots and prepare to leave. "Boat won't sail itself," he told them, and they dispersed.

Bi didn't understand everything they had said. She grasped that they were talking about her, and that Askook didn't believe her. But most of the exchange was spoken too fast for comprehension.

"He's gotten involved with a radical nationalist group out of Zenda. I'm telling you; he is not going to let this go." Aponi was worried.

"We have treaties that we cannot break," reminded Dyani. "We have to be mindful, no matter how we feel about the Fog."

"And that is what those Zendali gangs do. They hunt them. They kill the Fog if they wander off the reservation! I've been told they harass and molest the Pinks too. We should warn Bimisi."

"That's hearsay," Ellute objected. "There has been no proof of murder and no convictions."

"Well, I don't think she's Fog," Aponi exclaimed with some frustration.

Both her parents stared at her.

"Do you recognize any Zendali traits in her features? I'm just pointing that out... because I don't."

"Doesn't mean she isn't mixed with Pinks," Ellute cautioned, and they all thought about what that implied.

Bi crept back down to the room where she'd slept and closed the door. She understood they thought she was in danger. She didn't understand what they meant by Pinks or Fog.

***

Later in the day, Bi was on the quarterdeck, leaning against the railing, watching the coast and enjoying the sun. Askook stormed by Bi giving her a hostile glare. Then Chitto came up to chat, idly toying with a piece of rope. "What kind of name is Bimisi?" he asked her in a friendly tone.

Bi wasn't sure how to answer. "It means slippery. Not a very attractive reference, but it was my uncle's name. He was a fisher too." She thought the lie might work.

But Chitto had sensed her indecision. "Sorry, I don't mean to be rude, but didn't your tribe give you a spirit name?" Seeing her puzzled expression, it was clear she didn't understand what he meant.

"It is so unlikely the elders would choose not to give you a spirit name, considering your parents named you improperly."

Bi could feel the flush rise to her face. With the heat of her embarrassment, her ears flattened back. She tried to hide her frustration with a simple admission. "My name is strange, and I'm different." She turned her face to look out at the waves.

"Don't worry," Chitto told her with compassion, as if he understood. But he had no idea how out of her element she was. Bi was lucky that these people were her first encounter. She was learning from watching their reactions every time she made a mistake. Chitto didn't try to question her anymore. He casually moved away and went back to his chores.

The next day they were trolling near the coast, and Bi asked to be taken to shore. "Better for all of us if I leave you now. I don't want to cause you any trouble."

Aponi nodded. "I'll tell my dad to stop the boat so we can take you ashore."

Bi went to gather her things. Her backpack and clothing were all dry now. They had also moved her provisions downstairs. She stuffed her pack with as much dried meat and fruit as she could fit, and filled her canteen with fresh water. She would leave what she wasn't able to carry with the family. When her back was to the door, someone came quietly in behind her. She caught movement from the corner of her eye and jumped. "You startled me!"

"Sorry." It was Chitto again. He was shy, but inquisitive. "I admit I'm too curious. I'm sorry. But you're so mysterious... and... I just want you to be safe. I wish we could do more to help you."

Bi wasn't sure how to respond. It seemed like Chitto genuinely wanted to protect her, but she should not let him think she needed help. "Not your problem." Her tone was a little too sharp. Noting his hurt expression, Bi shook her head with resignation and said in a softer tone, "I'll be fine, thank you."

He pulled out a map, laying it flat on the small table. "Look, we are here. The city is on the other side of this woodland." His finger moved across the map inland. "You shouldn't go in that direction. It's really too dangerous for you. But if you follow the coast further until the beaches are shallow and the cliffs are high, you come to this place, where the mountains part, dipping down to a river valley. You can't miss it. If you follow the river inland, you'll come to the Nisnap reservation farms. You would be safe with them. They'll give you sanctuary. If you stay with us a couple more days, we can bring you closer."

Bi examined the map. But not to find sanctuary. She had to go to the city. "Thank you, Chitto. I will keep it in mind, but I do have to go to the city. I'll take my chances."

"Here, take these." He handed her a cloth with something hard inside. She unwrapped it to find goggles.

"What are they for? I mean, why do you have them?"

"We sometimes dive for shellfish; the goggles make it easier to see in the saltwater. I also use them on the boat because of the salty wind."

"Won't you miss them?"

"I have an extra pair."

"This is sweet of you." Bi tried them on. The room became dark and rose-colored. "Oh! They're amazing!" She took the goggles off and handed them back to Chitto. "I can't take these. They're too valuable."

With a worried expression, Chitto wrapped the goggles back into the scarf and pushed them into Bi's hands. "You'll need them. Keep the scarf too."

"Why are you protecting me? Who do you think I am?"

He stared at Bi like he wasn't sure what to say or how to answer without offending her.

"It doesn't matter," he said finally, looking down.

"You gave her the scarf?" Aponi asked as she entered.

Chitto nodded.

"You wrap it like this," Aponi said. "Let me show you." She took the scarf and wrapped it around her own head and across her face.

"You can wear the goggles on top," Chitto suggested. With the scarf and goggles, her whole face would be hidden. "You'll look exotic, but no one will bother you." He smiled encouragingly.

The sister unwrapped her head and folded the scarf, giving it back to Bi. "I wish we could do more."

This was unforeseen. Bi was more than astonished by such kindness from strangers. It was all far more than she'd expected. She turned away and stuffed the items into the pockets of her bag, a little overwhelmed with emotion.

The older brother, Askook, knocked loudly and said, "Time to go."

"He doesn't like me." Bi wasn't sure why she'd said that. What did it matter? Today she would be out of their lives.

"He's a radical." Chitto's hackles were raised and his ear-fans flattened back. He was obviously angered by his brother's behavior.

Bi was going to ask what he meant, but Aponi shushed him. "We shouldn't talk about it, and Bimisi doesn't need to share our worries."

Bi picked up her pack, and they made their way to the upper deck.

It was a calm, sunny day. A small dinghy was lowered off the side. Everyone gathered around to say their goodbyes, and Dyani handed her a small package of grilled fish. "For your supper," she said.

Bi had no room in her bag, so she tied the package to the straps. "Thank you for everything."

Dyani gave her a sad smile in return. "Of course."

It was Chitto who rowed her to shore. He was silent all the way. He pulled the dinghy onto the sand and gave her his hand to help her out, lifting her pack from the boat to the dry sand. She thought he might leave her without a word, but he finally said, "This is a mistake. They will find you."

"Who?" Bi asked. "Who will find me? Why are you so worried?"

"You're brave." He shook his head. "I'll give you that."

Without another word, he pushed the dingy back into the water. Got in and started rowing back to his family. She could still see them on deck. The mother and daughter waved, and Bi waved back. The father pulled on ropes to adjust the sails and got ready to leave. Askook glared at the shore in her direction. His expression gave her chills. The fur on her arms stood on end. Bi rubbed them vigorously as if it could dispel the menacing portent of his leering gaze.

14

The Ziv

Algon managed to acquire a new lab for their research, and Mora spent the week with him at Muwi University, where they began to rebuild their portal apparatus. She also worked on calculations through the night at home to make necessary adjustments.

The idea of breaking everything down into molecules, to beam a person or a thing somewhere, and then reassembling those particles in another place, was a mystery she'd wanted to solve since she was little. It had become an obsession after watching a popular series on the family video station (or receptor screen, as they called them in Muwioni). Now she'd accomplished a lifelong dream. She'd taken an idea from some fantasy writer and made it a reality!

Well, at least it had gotten her here in one piece. Feeling unmoored and somewhat sullen, she found herself wondering how to take the next step. How would she realize the big dream... to make this invention transport the living, what had caused it to blow up, and how would she get herself home? The hours had been long, and she needed a break. Algon agreed to accompany her to the city.

They were walking through the public market when Mora suddenly grabbed Algon's arm. He turned back, wondering what was wrong. Her grip on his biceps was tight. She was distressed. Following her gaze, Algon saw she was watching a procession of Star People crossing the public square as they made their way to the embassy building, adjacent to the Council chambers.

They were a good head taller than most native men, so you couldn't miss them. Similar in form, with two sexes. They all had slender bodies, with fine, diaphanous fur. It was so white it was blinding in the daylight. Their fine hair was long and nearly translucent. They had quite large eyes, which appeared completely black. The Ziv turned toward Mora, staring across the crowd, right at her! An overwhelming sense of fear was triggered when they focused on her. It was like an animal response to danger, and she wanted to run.

"Their eyes," she spoke softly.

"Oh, yes, that does look eerie. The Ziv and Elo, both have an inner eyelid. You've never seen them?"

"Inner lid?"

"A nictitating membrane, which shields the daylight glare. They have sensitive eyes. It looks opaque to us, but the lid is a natural shade against brightness." Algon told her this in a calm voice, as if it were the most normal thing to have aliens in the market. Thinking about it from a clinical view was helpful. "On a gut level, they terrify me."

"Their shaded eyes do have an ominous appearance, but when the inner lid is open, the Ziv have light-colored irises with a round pupil," Algon explained. "You really have never seen them?"

The Ziv were still honed in on Mora as if they recognized her.

"Don't stare," Algon admonished Mora. "They don't like it."

"But they're aliens!"

He looked at her curiously and asked, "You don't have a relationship with the Star People in your world?"

She couldn't tear her eyes away from them until they climbed the stairs and entered the building.

"I can't believe it! Aliens walking around the city marketplace like it's the most ordinary thing!" She turned her attention back to Algon, who looked quizzically at her, and realized she hadn't answered him. "Well, no, not that I'm aware of."

Algon's expression was perplexed. How strange that you don't, he said. But if you did, I assume your world would be more like ours. "There are three races who have had a relationship with Hadot. They helped us build many civilizations on this world. How could you not know of them? Who did you think we were talking about when we said the Star People gave us technology?"

"I don't know, some foreign company? Three alien races?"

Algon shook his head, and his ear-fans wiggled like he thought it was funny. "The Durga, Ziv, and the Elo," he told her.

"In my world, people reported sightings of extrasolar spacecraft. Most of them are saucer-shaped flyers that maneuver differently than our airships. But the government told us aliens weren't real. People who witness sightings or claim they were abducted by aliens were treated like needy fools who wanted media attention, or simply crazy idiots."

"You also believed they didn't exist? In all the vast universes, you thought we were alone? Mora, you have a scientific mind, surely you can't think we are the only life in all the worlds that exist! That would be short-sighted. Don't you think?"

"It is the predominant belief in my world that we are unique and alone."

Algon was incredulous at the thought, and Mora stared at him, understanding that it *was* unlikely. Yet she had accepted it. "If anyone of importance encounters them, and they speak publicly about it, or if they admit they believe in the existence of aliens, they may as well forget about having a successful career. They'd be ridiculed. There'd be some sort of publicity or misinformation campaign, which would ruin their credibility. For some unknown reason, our government has hidden any official relationship they have with aliens. It's been a controversial subject for a long time"

"Maybe the Star People in your world have a private relationship with the leaders, one the public is unaware of?"

"Maybe." In light of what she'd witnessed, Mora realized that was possible.

"They're more afraid of us than we are of them."

Mora considered this with doubt. "Why do you believe that?"

"They're cautious when interacting with us. I suppose, in contrast to their advancements, we're primitives with hostility issues." Algon was making a joke. But there was truth in it. He laughed, expecting her to be amused too.

"You call them Star People, but who are they really? Where are they from and why are they here?"

"They have never told us what sector of space their sun is located. We won't know that sort of information until we've evolved into a space-faring society. Then we can join the Interstellar World Alliance, of which they are all members."

"But obviously they could give you that knowledge?"

Algon was shaking his head. "They won't, in fact, they have made it clear they are here to prohibit such advancements until we are no longer engaged in war-like behavior."

"This does make me curious if they've interacted with all the other multiverses. It almost feels like *we* are *their* experiment." When Algon stared at her uncomprehendingly, she continued. "Don't you wonder what we are to them? Why get involved with us?"

Algon looked at her with a creased brow. "You have thoughts that often confounded me."

"What did you say these aliens call themselves?"

"Those are called the Ziv. You're lucky to have seen them. They don't come here often."

"And why Wendat? The aliens only interact with the Wen here, nowhere else on Hadot?"

"They tried to develop relationships with other countries, but as soon as they chose war over cooperation, they pulled away. Star People only give their advancements to nations that are non-aggressive."

"We must be like children to them." Mora pondered.

Algon agreed. "If you can call aggression childish, then yes. The Star People ended their support of Zenda and the Eastern Empire because of their wars."

"The biggest question for me is why the aliens didn't protect the Pinks and stop the invasions into their lands," Mora said.

Algon nodded. "They were offered support with conditions. The inhabitants of those lands didn't agree with the restrictions imposed. They chose to fight, and they lost. Also, they would not take the implants."

"But Wendat did."

He chuckled a little. "Yes, we did, and we prospered. If you want more details, Asha is the one you should talk to about past events. She knows our history better than I do."

"Now you're more advanced than Zenda in some ways?"

"True, the Star People worked quickly to accelerate our society. They also forbid us to share their technologies with other countries. We are allowed to implant visitors from abroad, but we are not allowed to share how the implants are made or give them a detached sample."

"Is it likely the Zendali could replicate them, even if they got their hands on a sample?"

"No, I strongly doubt it. A growth substance is necessary to breed them."

"Once they're merged with our physiology, they can't be taken out, right?"

Algon was vigorously shaking his head. "No, removing them is very dangerous. It would disrupt essential functions. The person would immediately perish."

"Why do you think the aliens are afraid of the Zenda getting a sample if it can't be reverse-engineered?"

"I would not venture to say what they think. It might be to make a point about privilege and respect."

"You mentioned they're breeding them in a growth vat. Are the implants alive?"

"Yes, and so are the floaters. In part, the trains are too. But they're not conscious beings. Or at least we don't think they are," Algon laughed.

Mora raised a brow ridge as if to indicate concern.

Algon confirmed. "All manufacturing of alien constructs are carefully monitored. The Zenda can't copy them. They are not mechanical technologies. They would need the vats and other substances to grow them."

Mora thought about it. "Do you think the aliens can monitor or control us through the implants?"

Algon looked at her funny. "Monitor or control? For what reason?" He shook his head as if such an idea were ludicrous. "You're a suspicious person, Mora."

"So, you don't think they might be programming our minds in some way through the implants, or when you're in those floaters?"

This line of questioning obviously upset Algon. His ear-fans flattened back. "Isn't it enough that we have *chosen*, of our own free will, to obey their wishes?"

Mora didn't respond. She paid no attention to Algon's agitation. She was thinking about how the Ziv had looked knowingly at her. "Algon, they were looking right at me as if they knew I didn't belong here."

Algon sighed. "I think you're getting paranoid, Mora."

15

Nightmares

The narrow dirt path through the forest was rarely traveled by villagers. This riotous mess of underbrush left little opportunity to deviate from the unwieldy trail. The bushes bent against Bi's body as she pushed forward, snapping behind her as she passed. A dark woodland that was full of shadowy thickets and tangled brush. Tree sap, musty soil, and toadstools scented the hot air. The overall feeling was oppressive. Ahead, she glimpsed a sliver of light and the promise of an exit. Her eyes were mostly focused on her feet, watching for roots, so she wouldn't trip. She looked up again and saw a tall figure blocking the exit, just a silhouette against the brightness of the sky, a hulking form, menacing and solid, waiting for her. There seemed to be nowhere to turn, just a straight path that led her to this ominous stranger. Bi slowed her pace with indecision. So firmly intent on what was ahead, that she didn't notice what came from behind, there had not been a sound, whoever followed was quiet as a whisper, just before the impact she felt them, smelled them too, but it was too late, she fell under their weight. She struggled to take a breath, but his heavy body crushed her tender flesh into the roots and stones. She tried to push him aside, kicking and jerking to get free, but her effort was futile. He grabbed at her pants, ripping her clothing away.

Suddenly, gasping for breath, she woke from the nightmare. With her heart still racing, Bi took a few practiced calming breaths in an effort to still the terror. Soaked with perspiration, she shivered from the breeze coming off the ocean, a damp cold that seeped into her bones. Her beach fire was now a pile of coals... The previous day, Bi had walked along the coast until the sun started to set. Tired of trudging through the sand, she made a small campfire on the beach with driftwood. Grateful for the food Dyani had given her, she unwrapped the fish and nibbled while she watched the sunset. The evenings remained warm here. The sand held the heat from the sunny day. The fire was a comfort, an indulgence. Her little camp was remote enough that she didn't think anyone would see her. Just behind the beach, piles of driftwood lay against a cliff. Far above, she could see the edge of a dense forest.

After her light meal, she lay back on the warm sand, resting against her pack. The bright first moon, Ifa, rose, a crescent low on the horizon. Stars filled the sky, seemingly as plentiful as sand on the beach. The vastness of all those distant suns made her feel small and alone. She *was* so very alone. She had to admit the boat people's children gave her reason for concern. They knew something she didn't. They'd tried to explain, or warn her perhaps, but she didn't understand.

Despite her worries, she had fallen asleep watching the flames of the fire. She did not reach lucid awareness, or contact her invigilator as she expected, but fell into a repeating nightmare instead. A fog had rolled inland, chilling the air. The chill of the damp air woke her. Now the tide was coming in, wave after wave. A soothing sound. It filled her with a sense of relief. She picked up her belongings and moved back closer to the driftwood to make herself comfortable, and wait for the dawn. She didn't think she would get to sleep again, but before sunrise, she got sleepy watching the second moonrise, Ife the Lover, huge and red above the sea. Finally, drifting off, she slept deeply. It was the warm sun on her face that woke her next. Parched, she reached for her water skin and found it nearly empty. She needed to find a creek or spring sometime soon.

She mulled over the dream about two dark men chasing her in the forest, which woke her in the middle of the night. It was a repeating night terror... A path, the two men, a cliff, and a cave were the vivid details. The other elements varied, always showing a different outcome. It must portend a dangerous event. The aftermath was undetermined. Chitto's last words came to mind: "This is a mistake. They will find you."

She kicked sand over the fire pit to cover the ashes, picked up her pack, and walked along the beach. She didn't go inland yet. Bi wanted to avoid the village that she'd seen on the map. When the sun made her progress unbearable, she dropped her pack, took off her garments, and went for a swim in the ocean. The water was a little cold, but welcome. Afterward, she sat on the beach to eat dried fruit, washing it down with the last of her water. *That's it,* she thought. *Now, I really must find a path into the forest.*

She needed to find water before she camped and hoped there would be a creek or river inland. She continued walking along the shore, and kept her eye on the bank, looking for egress through the thicket. The shore was strewn with palm-sized rocks, which slowed her progress. Eventually, she came to a pile of enormous boulders, which had tumbled into the sea. It blocked her way along the beach. The waves crashed across the rocks with force, making them slippery and dangerous to cross. She followed the barrier all the way from the shore to the cliff and climbed the boulders to the top. On the other side, she found runoff from the cliff above, a small waterfall descending into a cove. With relief, she drank as much as she could and filled her water skin.

Thankfully, there was also a path up the cliff into the forest.

16

BETRAYAL

The family took their fishing boat further out to sea in calm waters to fill their nets, planning to return to the harbor in the morning with their catch. The storm had put them behind schedule.

A light breeze was enough to use the sails instead of the power cells. They had chosen a perfect location, filling their storage compartment full to the brim with the prized Chum fish that were tender and delicious. They would bring a hefty price. With their hulls packed with the day's catch, they put down anchor for the night.

Askook had been brooding since they'd taken Bimisi to shore. He wanted the reward for her capture, but he also wanted to impress his friend Tao, who was the son of the Zenda Ambassador Ziyad.

By evening, they were headed back, and Askook spotted a fire on the beach. Using a spyglass, he discovered it was the fugitive who called herself Bimisi. She was camping out in the open on the shore. *She's completely oblivious*, he thought. Askook decided to contact the Order of Amon Kuroo when they reached the harbor in the morning. He said nothing to his family. They didn't understand his concerns.

He hardly slept in anticipation of her capture. As soon as the boat pulled into the port and was close enough to the pier, he jumped down. After mooring it to the pier, he yelled to his brother Chitto that he'd be back, leaving them to deal with the load.

His receptor would be out of range of the city, one of the annoying things about living on a boat. They were often too far away to connect with their friends. He reached the harbormaster's hut and requested to use their Link-Line. This was a capsule-like booth. Askook stood inside and slid the door closed. He removed the translucent armband from his wrist, which contained his receptor device. Inserting it into a slot, he waited until it glowed. The Link Line would enhance his signal and allow him to reach someone at a greater distance. All the outposts and villages had them. He signaled his contact at the Order of Amon Kuroo. An elite member who was his age, named Tao. But it didn't connect. When he couldn't speak to Tao, in desperation he contacted Chayton, whose father Mato was a council member. Like Askook, he was eager to join the resistance movement. They opposed the government-sanctioned reservations.

"I spotted a Fog fugitive; she was on the shore last night but will be heading inland to the forest path between Miwok village and the Reyfin harbor."

Chayton was excited. "I'm not far from Miwok Village now. If you're at the harbor station, we can travel from both ends and trap her in the middle. The brushwood is extremely dense along that trail. There's no getting off that path! She won't escape us!"

Askook didn't tell Chayton he had met her, or that she'd been on his family's boat. It would sully his reputation, and it might cause trouble, which he didn't want to deal with. Eager for the hunt, he agreed with what Chayton suggested. They were both hopeful that this capture would gain credibility with the Order. Askook didn't even bother to return to his family's boat. They would want him to unload, and that would cause a delay. Also, he knew without a doubt his father would forbid him to go.

With this in mind, he ran off to find the coastal path that Bimisi would have taken when she left the beach. It was little more than an animal trek. Which was annoying, because it hindered his progress. Impatient to get his hands on her, he pushed through the thicket, Adrenalin fueling his excitement and the anticipation of his reward.

He felt no guilt as he ran toward the forest. His family would finish unloading the catch. His father, Ellute, was happier than Askook had seen him in a long time. The additional deliberation about the sum due for the crabs would distract them, and his absence would go unnoticed until it was too late to stop him.

17

The Ancient Forest

M ora and Algon had another grueling week in the lab, assembling the portal apparatus. The university had imposed a timeline for delivering the project. It left little opportunity for anything else. At this point, they were not trying to construct a portal for the living. There just wasn't time for such a big plan. Mora trimmed it down to make a particle transport device to move non-living goods instead, the same principle but simpler and faster to complete in the timeline imposed.

They were both exhausted, and Algon suggested a day trip to the forest. He had booked a train to the coast, northwest of Muwioni, and from there they would drive to the rainforest, where the old giant trees lived. They had hoped Asha could take the day off for the hike, but she had exams coming up and didn't feel it was wise.

When they went to the station, Mora expected something like what they had in her world, metal constructs that ran on rails. She had seen the local trains moving in the distance and realized they had a different, sleeker look, but she didn't expect this! There were no rails because the train floated above ground! Algon told her they used the magnetic pulse of Hadot's lay-lines to draw energy. In part, they had some of the same living material in them as the floaters, which helped them rise. They also had a translucent energy crystal material, which formed an oblong bubble dome over each carriage. The energy crystal added power to other functions, which interacted in some mysterious way with the organic matter of the structure. The lower part of each carriage was made of ferrebast. It's a fibrous plant grown in our region. When processed, it's very strong.

Every time Mora encountered another alien technology, it made her introspective. She started to think about the aliens and all other multiverse versions of Hadot. She wondered if her version was the only one that didn't openly interact with them, and why they chose

Hadot to experiment on? Or were there other worlds with different species under their watch as well? And finally, why were the many versions of this world important enough to send an alien delegation to oversee us?

Algon had been talking about how the trains were made, and how they function, but Mora missed most of what he said because she was lost in her own thoughts. He was trying his best to impart some practical knowledge. Mora *was* interested but also amused. She had never seen this side of Algon.

"Now the train floats close to the ground in resting mode. It will rise up higher once it gets moving forward or back along the lay-lines, depending on how the conductor interfaces to guide it. The hover elevation above the ground level depends on the strength of each lay-line. The energy they emit from the ground varies in places. If the lay-line is strong, the train will rise to approximately twenty kin. Do you use kin as a measurement?" He asked. "I'm one kin tall," he added.

I nodded, and he continued.

"Imagine twenty Wen stacked end-to-end! That's how high. If it's a weak connection, it will fall to perhaps ten kin. But in most cases, the train will be above any animal herds, hunters, or nomadic wandering tribes who might cross the landscape."

Mora nodded and smiled and tried not to show her amusement. Something about his serious "teacher mode" was very sweet, and comical. *That really isn't fair*, she thought, but quite honestly, her Algon wasn't like this. He never took the lead. She couldn't picture him as a teacher, for example. It was enjoyable to see this version of Algon so self-possessed. She nodded to show she was listening. And then really tried to do just that.

"As mentioned, they make each car dome of energy crystal, and the lower half of the train car is ferrebast."

Mora asked, "I don't see anything that looks like the fluffy floater, but you mentioned there is organic material beneath this frame?"

Algon nodded and continued talking. "Yes, you can't see it, but it's there. It helps the train float. Also covering the lower vents are these supple tendrils." He pointed to the dangling filaments along the bottom and length of the train. "We call them the Whistle Whips."

They looked like rubbery whiskers, as thick as a finger, extending from the foot of the train about an arm's length out and down.

"When the train moves forward, they flutter and whistle. The closer to the ground, the louder the whistle."

The train looks like a many-legged bug, Mora thought.

"In places where the train drops closer to the ground, the whistle of the tendrils sends a warning far ahead of its arrival. Even if someone doesn't move out of the way, the magnetic pulse will only push them to the ground. After the train passes, they can rise unharmed."

Although probably frightened, she thought.

They finally boarded. Mora followed Algon through the train compartments. The seating arrangements were much the same as in trains where she came from, with bench seats facing each other, and tables extending from the sidewall. However, the dome provided a much greater view of the surroundings and the sky above. Storage space was below the seats for luggage, if you had any. "How does the conductor know where the Lay-Lines are on the open landscape?"

"There's a display on the forward-facing window. The glowing marks show clearly where the lines run. The conductor needs only to steer toward a line, and a magnetic pull will guide the train and hold it snugly in place. However, the train can't pass over all lines, because sometimes obstacles prohibit the crossing. Mountains can be too high to access the lay line energy through them. Bodies of water can be too wide or too deep, and water weakens the connection. There are also ancient villages in the way of some routes. They were established long before the Star People gave us this technology."

"Why not move them?" Mora asked.

"Move them?" Algon replied. As if that were unthinkable. "No, we don't touch these sites. They're sacred to the Wen whose families have lived there for generations." His ears fluttered with emotion. "Do you want me to answer your question or not?"

"Please continue," I said.

"The train design uses a second transparent map over the lay-line display, which shows the topography of the land, including the older settlements, and clearly marks the lines that can be safely traveled."

The train took two hours to reach its destination. Mora was mesmerized by the view; she didn't move from the window or engage in conversation. When they arrived, they walked to another building adjacent to the train station. It was a depot for vehicles. Algon went inside to request one for the day trip. The rental cost was minimal, a small fee for citizens. Slightly more, and with a contract for nonnatives. This was another interesting experience. Their version of the automobile was quite different. Algon returned and led her to the lot where the vehicle was parked.

"People don't own their own vehicles here?"

Algon looked at her like he couldn't imagine why anyone would. "Any citizen can check them out when they need one. They're available in various places around the city and villages. What would I do with one of my own? The maintenance alone would be a disadvantage. Also, where would I put it?"

Amused at his objection to something common in her world, she had a teasing tone. "Those are all good points. I have a parking bay for mine." When he gawked at her, she said, "That's a room for the vehicle."

"You have a separate room just for a vehicle that only you use?"

Mora had enjoyed vexing him a little, but he was right. "When you put it that way, it sounds selfish. Fenmore, my partner, uses it sometimes. But yes, most people in my city have a private transport vehicle. Hopefully, this will change with the portals we're building."

Algon tilted his head from side to side in acknowledgment of the portal's advantage.

Mora noticed he was still indignant. But had chosen not to say more about her private transport.

"These vehicles are for brief excursions or for moving things around the city."

Roads were not extensive in Wendat. They could drive wherever paved roads existed, which meant short-distance trips. For long-distance travel across the country, people took trains or floaters.

Mora could see four varieties of vehicles. All four had this in common: the wheels were like fat bicycle tires, not filled with air, but solid. The base or lower half of the vehicle was composed of ferrebast. The entire top was a transparent dome or oblong bubble, made of energy crystal to generate electricity. In this way, the designs were like the train. The dome opened on each side, level with the seat for entry. It hinged open when a small indent in the base was pressed. When the dome side was open, it reminded Mora of the wings of a bug. They made the seats of a rubbery woven mesh. This rubbery substance was another alien tech. It was grown, not manufactured. When she sat down, the seat conformed to her body. When she leaned back, cables of the rubbery material snaked over each shoulder, crossing in front of her to attach themselves to the outer edges of her seat. They were comfortably snug and adjusted to her girth, without being too tight.

Algon waited until Mora got situated. "If we stop suddenly and jerk forward, the belts will hold you firmly in place. If we impact something, the headrests will move out to cradle your head."

Mora observed the other differences from what she was used to. She didn't see a rearview mirror. Instead, they had a display panel on the dashboard that showed what was behind them. Mora found this display distracting and disorienting. No steering wheel either. Instead, handlebars sat in a resting position on the driver's side. They were flat, with the handles facing the driver, and pushed forward into a slot in the dash. Algon got seated without hindrance, then pulled the bars toward himself. To start the vehicle, he pressed a button on the floorboard located on the far left. Then he pushed the steering handles up. "If it goes up like this, it moves forward. The further up, the faster it goes." When he pulled downward, the vehicle slowed, then at a certain point, it moved backward. "It can't move backward as fast as it goes forward." The bars also tilted side to side for turns. To stop the vehicle, he used the same button on the floorboard. "When the power's cut, the car will stop suddenly. If you ever drive, remember, it's important to reduce the speed before cutting power."

Algon drove Mora out of town. The two-lane road was almost empty. Only an occasional vehicle passed them from the other direction. Since the traffic was light, she removed her head covering and veil. She still found them claustrophobic. Algon pushed a button on the dash. The clear bubble roof darkened all around except directly in front. Seeing Mora's interest... "for sun glare." He gave her a knowing look. It wasn't an exceptionally sunny day.

The landscape mesmerized Mora. "There's so much unused land! Just endless fields, rolling hills covered in wildflowers, mountains!" In the distance were copious forest clusters. It was like going back in time to witness a pristine primeval wilderness.

They turned off the main road and entered the forest park. A long road led them into the deeper forest. In this area, the undergrowth was cleared. Eventually, they came to an open space where they parked. Mora saw no other cars. "Is it normally so deserted?"

"Campers and hikers come on their days off work. Families usually picnic on weekends. I try to come when it's quiet."

"I'll walk without a head covering then. Do you think it's safe?" There was no disagreement from her companion, which Mora took to mean he agreed. She stuffed it in her bag in case she needed it.

When they got out, and she looked up, the trees were so tall the tops disappeared into the misty clouds. "I never imagined it could be like this! They're enormous. The entire forest looks primordial!"

Algon pointed to a path. "This is my favorite route; it will take us to the creek. You lead the way."

They were about halfway down, walking in companionable silence when they heard a whooshing noise, which was immediately followed by a bloom of blood on the side of Algon's forehead. An arrow had grazed him and then thwacked into a nearby tree, right behind where Mora had just stood.

"That was meant for you!" Algon was bleeding profusely. The cut was deep. "I guess we will find out if you were paying attention during my driving lessons. Now run!"

18

The Ring

Bi had begun having dreams about two men attacking her in a forest even before she entered the Brainery Institute. At the time, she had no way of knowing the event would happen in a different country. The repeated warning made her cautious about going into the woods near her family home alone. But she didn't want to give up her peaceful nature walks. Bi had given the situation a lot of thought and decided she needed to carry a weapon.

She had no knowledge of fighting techniques, and no defensive training. She imagined a knife could be easily carried, but also might get taken from her during an altercation and used against her.

Still... in the absence of anything else... She found a hunting knife with its scabbard in a storage closet and started carrying the blade everywhere. She had been tucking it in her belt under a layer of clothing for years. The weight of the weapon felt promising.

It wasn't until her sister acquired an antique ring with a poison well that Bi found her perfect weapon. It required no special training. The ring was one of many gifts her sister, Genji, received from an admirer. She was being courted by several young men from wealthy families. Most of their gifts were of little interest. Her sister was not easily impressed.

Bi recognized the antique when the young suitor gifted it. The next day, she went to her sister's room and found it tossed aside in a bowl with other trinkets.

Bi pocketed the poison ring. Most likely, her sister wouldn't care.

The ring had a lid with a garnet stone on top. The gold bezel and mounting were carved with vines and leaves. The stone was carved in relief like a flower. Under the stone lid was a hollow spike. Below this needle was a well that could be filled with poison. Bi had a passion for history, especially the ancient world. She had read about these rings and had seen drawings of them. She suspected her sister's admirer knew nothing of the hidden compartment. To the unaware, the gem looked like nothing more than an ornate antique treasure. Most likely, he hoped to impress with the cost of the item, which Bi guessed was considerable.

She had begun to look for plants from which she might extract a noxious substance. Something potent in small doses, but not deadly. She eventually found poisoned berries and soaked them in alcohol for weeks, resulting in a distillation of the toxic fruit. Bi had no way of knowing how strong this tincture was but decided it would at least make someone sick.

Knives were one of the forbidden items on the list Bellwether Ah Lahm had given her mother. Bi had reluctantly left it behind when she left for school. Jewelry was not prohibited, only discouraged. Bi had kept the ring in her room at school. Hidden away with the ear-bobs her father had made for her.

Now on the shore of Wendat, Bi dug those treasures out of her pack. She lovingly fingered the finely crafted parting gift from her father. Delicate winged bugs wrought in gold for her ears. Bi was fond of the little pollinators. They symbolized ethical virtue and purity. A silent message that her father accepted her as she was, and loved her unconditionally.

Then she filled the well in the ring from the little vial of poison, feeling a little more secure knowing the ring was ready for use. *Such an ingenious design*, she thought. If the point was pressed against a body, the needle would compress, squeezing the liquid out. This wouldn't necessarily stop whatever harm they intended. *It might take too long to work*. But it gave her courage. Before climbing up the cliff to the forest path, she put it on. Bi had a strong sense of foreboding. *Be brave. You can do this.*

19

Avoiding the Obvious

Mora was shaken after their misadventure in the forest. She had managed the vehicle with a little direction from Algon. On the train ride back to the city, Algon had found a first-aid kit. Mora bandaged the cut to staunch the bleeding, but it needed stitches. She was back in her robes and head covering, and the gloves that covered the pale fur on her hands.

"That is the best I can do while wearing these gloves," Mora said in a distracted sort of way.

"Mora, you're avoiding the fact that you were seen! Isn't it obvious you're in danger?"

He was in a foul mood. Which was understandable.

"Sure, and let me point out... that's nothing new! This world is hostile for people like me, but in order to get back to *my* rightful place, I need to focus on my work."

After getting the blood cleaned up, he insisted that they otherwise act *normal*. Mora had scoffed at that. "Normal? There is nothing normal about this Algon!"

He gave her a withering look and flattened his ear-fans.

"Do you know who that was in the forest? Did you see them?" Mora demanded.

Algon shook his head. They had the train car to themselves, but he refused to talk about the event. "We should not have been so careless."

Meaning *she* was careless, by going without the head covering. Mora mulled that over for a while and then decided it wasn't helpful to waste her energy on something that *almost happened*. She would either survive this world or she wouldn't.

You're right, she acknowledged.

After that, they talked through some points of concern about the project. Algon was still upset and didn't contribute much to the conversation. She talked *at him*, and he occasionally asked questions to clarify what she meant. It was a process. Mora was able to compartmentalize. As soon as her mind was focused on her work, the fact that she had nearly been killed was no longer in her thoughts.

When they came near Muwioni, both she and Algon's receptors got a message from Professor Bly saying the Dean had called a meeting the next day to discuss her team's progress.

"Algon, have you noticed the Dean's contempt toward me? I believe he's influenced the other board members against our project."

She noticed Algon cringe, and then he was silent for a moment. "Maybe they have issues with our lack of progress?"

This sounded like a reason, sure... but not the underlying problem. Mora squinted at him. *No, that's not all of it,* she thought. She had directed her team to stop trying to transport living things and focus on a downsized production model.

"You directed the team to stop experimenting with live subjects. It's not what they signed up for. They're disappointed." Algon suggested.

Mora pursed her lips. "I've noticed the team has lost enthusiasm about the project since we downsized to fit the timeline the board imposed. Do you think the Dean is upset about my decision, too?"

"It's not what they expected, Mora. I told you they wouldn't be happy."

To say she was frustrated with the pressure they were imposing would be putting it lightly. "Anyone who isn't part of the scientific community just won't understand what it takes to create something like this!" Mora complained.

"They don't need to understand our challenges. Zamora and I made promises. It is now our job to deliver. That's all they care about."

"Well, I told Professor Bly... in no uncertain terms, that we can give the university something fast and downsized, or the board would have to give us more time to do a larger project!"

"You know, Zamora would *never* have done something like that. How did Bly take your ultimatum?"

Mora smiled. She couldn't help feeling satisfied with the fact that she could push back when Zamora wouldn't dream of it. "I definitely sensed the undercurrents of discontent."

Algon actually laughed and then winced because his head must have hurt.

"I think there is a lot more going on," Mora said on a more serious note. "Something else that I don't understand is influencing the school's decisions. Professor Bly is being deceptive. She's not telling us the whole story."

Algon shrugged, lifting his shoulders and rotating his arms with palms up as if to say he had no idea. "We can't let those feelings interfere with our emotions now. Keep a clear head." Algon advised.

They took transportation with a driver from the train station.

When they dropped Algon at the hospital, Mora asked him: "Should I tell Asha to pick you up?"

"No, I'll be fine. See you in the morning."

20

PORTAL TECHNOLOGY

Mora made a pot of Kav and stared at the calculations on the wall panels. As she sipped her brew, she glared at the equations. At first, with a mindset of irritation, solving this problem had vexed her for so long that she felt blocked.

Mora had been stalling for a few days because she was stuck. There was something she couldn't clearly grasp. Something didn't fit. Now they had to face the university council, and she needed to have something positive to say.

She still had to figure out why her portal was accessing different worlds, well, different versions of her world. She had to know how to prevent trans-world travel. It was an awkward term she made up referring to different multiverse. She did not want to give this Hadot-line access to her Hadot-line.

She turned on the receptor screen and keyed in the nature channel, scrolling through the list to find a wooded scene. *This will have to suffice. I won't be going back to the forest anytime soon.* She let her mind wander, recalling the fresh smells in the woodland park and the supple texture of soft dirt as she walked the path. Slowly, the tension released, and her shoulders dropped.

Then, she began to review the ideas she had been mulling over on the train. As easy as sliding puzzle pieces around on a table. The design reconfigured in her mind. She stood, wiped sections from the panel, and began filling in the blanks. Before she realized it, the evening had slipped into night, and she was a little woozy.

Right, I didn't eat lunch and skipped dinner too. When at home in Inoti, she had a stack of frozen meals she could pop into the microwave. But things didn't work the same way here. No fast food. She no longer had a taste for unhealthy food either, since she got the implant. Now she craved things she'd never liked before.

Mora opened the kitchen cold-box and took out leftover food Asha had brought a few days before, took a whiff, and decided it was still edible. Gazing at her panels covered in design elements and calculations, she ate the leftovers cold. Not bad. She was more grounded now, with a little food in her stomach.

Then the missing piece stood out. She set the bowl on the counter and spent the next hour fixing her equations. When she went to bed, she slept hard and deep, but only for three hours. She didn't hear the alarm she had set and woke to Algon signaling her door.

***

They held the meeting at the university in Dean Comcomly Hardihood's conference room. Mora walked to the meeting with Algon and Professor Bly. When they entered, President Pool was sitting at the head of the table. Mora knew who she was from photographs she'd seen. Vice President Moki announced to the group: the *Fog female* has arrived. The president watched Mora as she crossed the room. She didn't speak to her but indicated with a gesture to take the empty chair. Mora took the seat next to the Director of Finance, Diwali. No one spoke to her. *Maybe it's the veil. No face to relate to*, she thought.

The meeting was called to order by President Pool. She explained to the others that Mora was attending this meeting to give them a report on how her portal project was developing. Mora looked across the table and noted the dean was scowling at her. She wasn't easily intimidated. Ignoring him, she stood to address the school board, which seemed like the right thing to do, but they all looked at her oddly.

"We've progressed with the portal project. I finally made the necessary leap, which puts us much closer to completion." This was news to Algon, as she had not had time to tell him. He looked at her curiously, perhaps wondering if she was bluffing. The others had no response at all and just stared at her. "It won't be much longer," she concluded.

They were looking at Algon now for some reason.

"What I mean is," Mora added, "we most likely will have a working prototype soon, if we are able to acquire all the parts we need." Diwali nodded, which she took to mean he would get the parts on the list Algon had given him. Some more confirmation would've been nice. "I'm confident we can meet the deadline you gave us with a downsized construction plan."

When she finished her report, the room was silent. She remained standing for a moment longer, uncomfortable with the lack of communication until the dean cleared his throat, gestured in her direction. "You wait outside. We need to speak with Algon alone."

She held up her folder. "Don't you want to see my presentation? I've outlined—"

"Please wait outside," President Pool repeated in a perfectly pleasant voice.

Mora had expected a different response, maybe some congratulations for her breakthrough, or a pat on the back, but instead she was simply dismissed! She snatched up her papers, drawings, and diagrams for the portal design, grateful they couldn't view her indignation under her veil. She had worked until late in the evening to prepare a visual presentation for this meeting. But no one had shown any interest in looking at it. Reluctantly, she left the room and waited in the hallway for Algon.

"What did they say?" She asked when he came out a short time later.

"Some official nonsense, nothing to worry about. They agreed to purchase the last items on our list. Some are not easily obtained." These were high-cost components, and the dean had been blocking the order. They had been waiting to argue their need for them at this meeting today.

Mora saw a hint of subterfuge. Another warning that she didn't fully understand what was going on. But she focused on the positive side. They needed approval from Diwali and Comcomly. Now they had it. That's what mattered.

"Well, at least we got around the dean. Now that they're willing to cooperate, we should make headway. I don't know how they imagined we could finish the project if we didn't have everything we asked for."

Algon didn't reply. He acted distant and distracted.

"Algon?"

"What? Oh right, yes, that is good."

21

THE AMBUSH

Bi had climbed the rocky cliff next to the small waterfall. She entered the forest where a trickle of water meandered through a rocky, moss-covered artery toward the cliff edge. She followed it upstream until it veered off. This is where she found the path. It was more like an animal track, narrow and overgrown. She froze. An ominous tension was building as she surveyed the dense foliage. It was gloomy and oppressively hot, making her feel claustrophobic. But it was her nightmare memories that caused her panic to rise. She tried taking a few slow deep breaths to calm her fear, but it wasn't working.

Bi looked up with apprehension. Her heart was pounding so hard she imagined it might climb right up her throat like a frightened animal. She felt dizzy with adrenaline coursing through her body. He was there in the distance! A looming silhouette against the light... blocking her path. She nearly cried out.

Although she heard nothing behind her, she knew someone was coming. A stalker, a hunter. She opened the cap on her ring. Just in time, she pivoted and slapped the needle into his arm. The motion threw him off balance, and he fell backward into the thicket. Without hesitation, she ran, knowing the two men would trap her in the middle. Her pack was a heavy thud bumping against her body with each stride, slowing her down. No escape seemed possible. The bile rose, burning her throat. This was more dreadful than the dreams. She was certain they would kill her.

Then she noticed another path that broke off into the thicket. She recalled this from a dream, a tree with the peeling red bark, and behind the bush with thorny leaves, she abruptly dove in that direction and ran full speed, trusting the memory of her visions. A clearing came next, and across it... was a rock wall. As she broke through the forest thicket, she marked the sound of someone thrashing forcefully through the underbrush in pursuit. She pushed herself to move faster. She reached the rock face, quickly scanning it for a crack. It was hidden behind the outcrop that jutted slightly away from the massive wall of stone. She slipped her pack off as she was running and threw it through the crack, then squeezed into the narrow passage. Inside was a ledge. It took a moment for her eyes to adjust. Dropping from the rim, she squatted against the inside wall of rock, trying to calm her heaving breath. She gasped as the native who was chasing her emerged from the brush and halted on the loose stones in the clearing. Bi was biting her own hand to stop herself from making noise as she cowered inside the cave. She could hear him pacing around the cliff, trying to find where she'd gone. There was no soil, only rock, no tracks. It must look as if she'd vanished. After a time, the second one joined him. She listened intently to their conversation, and one voice sounded familiar.

They were talking only a few feet from her on the other side of the rock wall. The entrance to the cave was not obvious. A vertical outcropping blocked the cave entrance. Even if you peered around that edge, it looked like an indent, nothing more. Bi was small enough to squeeze inside that space. An adult male would likely not fit. The drop into the cavern couldn't be seen until you were inside, at the end of that passageway. Her attackers obviously did not know this territory well. Perhaps the local natives didn't speak of this subterranean shelter? She realized she had been holding her breath and released it with a sigh. She focused on relaxing and kept her attention on their voices.

"Are you sure she's Fog?"

"She must be. You saw how pale her fur is, but such a strange color, not light enough to be a Pink."

"She doesn't have Zendali features, but you're right. Her fur is too light to be a member of a west coast tribe unless they're mixing with the Pinks."

Bi realized one of these men was Askook, and that gave her chills. Did he act alone, or did the boat people report her? *No, they wouldn't. He is the radical,* they'd said.

There had been no time to consider her options. She had been forced to trust her vision. In such situations, uncertainty would get you killed. This was her second leap of faith. She had an overwhelming sense of relief and gratitude for her training.

In this strange land, she was alone. She was unsure of her future, but she had a new sense of well-being and trust that she would be guided toward her destiny.

Bi was curious how they'd found her, and if the poison had any effect. The encounter had happened too fast. Everything happened in a frantic blur. She didn't even see her attacker's face.

"If she is Fog, what is she doing off the reservation? They are all told that as long as they stay put on that land, we can't touch them. I've never seen one leave the sanctuary, but a couple of our Sovereign Nation brothers bragged about killing one."

Askook's voice was low now, and a little slurred. "I tracked her here... the trail just... ended."

"Clever bitch."

Something fell. "Hey, what happened to you?"

"I'm... not well... I feel awful... strange."

"What kind of strange?"

There was no answer.

"Hey, can you walk? I have a vehicle, but it's not exactly close."

"Dizzy, my stomach..."

Bi heard a retching sound.

When they left, something was being dragged.

So, the poison is working! She couldn't help feeling justified. She had just one question on her mind. What is the Fog?

22

FOREIGN INFLUENCE

Orenda didn't have the opportunity to talk about art school with her great-aunt. Evening events kept them busy, including a tour of the city, shopping for new clothes, and dinner out at a Zendali restaurant.

Her aunt Coso frowned at her back-country clothing and said it would stand out in the city. Then she bought Orenda a whole new wardrobe. Zendali styles largely influenced the fashions in Wendat. She found a few locally made garments from a modern native designer; these she treasured most. She had never had such lovely things to wear, or so much choice!

Orenda tried bringing up the subject of school, but every time she got interrupted. The next morning, when she woke up and went in search of breakfast, she found a table set in the garden for one. Her aunt had already gone to work.

Yuma showed up at Coso's compound in the early afternoon. Orenda had been busy all morning setting up the room given to her, putting her belongings away. When Yuma interrupted her, she was organizing her art supplies.

"So, you're a painter too?" He casually toyed with the implements and brushes, showing his curiosity.

"Yes, I want to study art."

Yuma gave her an incredulous look, but his ears wiggled like he found the whole idea delightful. "That will be a surprise to Holata Tyee! I'm not sure she will like that."

"I'm not sure it matters what she thinks." She gave him a sideways look as she finished shelving some of her supplies."

Now Yuma flattened his ears. "Be careful how you challenge her. She doesn't take kindly to anyone who disobeys her."

Orenda thought about how to respond, and how much to tell him, then decided to let it go. She also didn't find a good excuse not to go with him to meet Holata Tyee. "I'm sure you're right. Well then, should we get going?" It would be impolite to refuse the medicine guardian's invitation to meet... Orenda felt a little ashamed that she didn't really care if she did. Seemed like her aunt had arranged everything ahead of time for her to study with this highly acclaimed healer, and she really should be more appreciative.

Mostly she chose to accompany Yuma because he was sweet. She wanted to learn more about him. There'd been an immediate feeling of kinship. "Did you grow up in this city?"

"No, but my father is the Quaqu Chief. He travels here from the Vilma Provence in the south a few times a year. He made the arrangements for me to apprentice."

Yuma was slim with a wiry build. Orenda took note that they were of the same height, his long black hair was loose and parted in the middle, and the only adornment he wore was a ring in his septum. His fur was darker than hers, more teal than green, and he had black tufts on his ears. Orenda found that adorable. His garments were well worn, of natural fabrics, but clean. She thought this an oddity. A wealthy young native. Son of a chief. Who is studying with such a famous medicine guardian, dressed in a simple way? She recalled the other one, Kinache, who wore expensive boots and clothing, and a lot of jewelry. He presented his wealth in a flashy way, which seemed a little foolish in contrast to Yuma's understated appearance. His modesty made her curious.

"Is Kinache an apprentice as well?"

Yuma rolled his eyes up thoughtfully. "Well, not officially."

"Care to explain?"

"Holata Tyee does not feel her son has the makings of a medicine practitioner. So, he decided to dabble in ceremonial magic without her knowledge. He has a teacher." He whispered this conspiratorially. "She's from a Zendali Sartomal Cult, a spellcaster named Mulogo. They use dark magic, with potions and blood rituals. I have only seen her once, but... well, I wouldn't want to mess with her."

Yuma's openness on this subject surprised her. What Kinache was doing was not exactly a crime, but meddling with dark arts would be frowned upon. "I see, and are you Holata Tyee's only apprentice?"

"Oh, no, you'll meet Tokala Luta today. She is second apprentice. But if you join us, I assume you will be first, as you have had years more training from your grandfather."

Orenda's ears flattened, and she grimaced. "About that, I actually came here to study art at Muwi University. I don't intend to be a medicine guardian." Yuma stared at her unbelievingly, so she continued to explain. "My dreaming is... different. I'm of no use to my tribe as a seer."

He had a worried expression. "I was honest with you about Holata Tyee's son because I thought you would be one of us, and you should be warned."

"I understand. You can trust me. I'll keep your secret."

They walked across town together. Orenda was distracted by the avatars people were wearing. These three-dimensional animal totems were projected onto faces. Sometimes expensive variants were larger and covered people's whole bodies. The cheap ones tended to flicker and glitch. Nevertheless, they were all fascinating. She had first seen them years ago when she visited the eastern city of Seneca, but they were just newly imported from the Sovereign Zenda Nation, and too costly for most Wen. Not as many people wore them then. Now they were very popular among the youth.

"What are those things people wear on chains like an ornament, but often have in their mouths?"

"Binkies. They interact with your flavor receptors, another Zendali import. They come in a lot of different flavors."

"Have you tried them?"

"Me? No." He laughed. "I'm not interested. The council members are constantly harassed by the Dean of Muwioni University, Comcomly Hardihood. He's banned them on campus and tried to get the government to ban the import of Binkies altogether, but they're especially popular with children."

"You say that like you're old already!" She laughed. "I've seen adults using them too."

He gave her a teasingly serious glance. "They don't cause any harm, and that means the council couldn't legally block them."

"Looks to me like the Zenda Nation has a huge influence on fashion here, too. I've hardly seen locals wearing traditional garments." She fluttered her ear-fans. "The first thing my aunt told me when I arrived was that I couldn't walk around in the clothes I brought from home."

"You seem fashionable to me." This was with a teasing glance that turned into a laugh when he saw it embarrassed her. "Crowds of visitors come to the city for the festivals. You'll see plenty of traditional garments then. Sometimes people come from way up north. Their beadwork is amazing!"

Orenda was so comfortable with Yuma. She felt like they could be friends. She liked his easy-going nature.

Suddenly, their peaceful stroll through the city was interrupted by a distraught young native who came running up to them out of breath. "Yuma, I'm so glad I found you. We have to hurry. Something terrible happened!"

23

THE MEDICINE GUARDIAN

They all ran through the city to Holata Tyee's compound, arriving to find a young native on the floor of her antechamber. He was moaning. His eyes would occasionally try to open when they said his name. When they shook him, he flinched but would not rouse or respond to questions. The youth was delirious, and mumbling something incomprehensible.

The medicine guardian remarked loudly, "It's about time!" and Yuma cringed. She immediately commanded him and the other native youth to bring the sick one inside.

Orenda followed them to the treatment room as they placed the suffering native on a narrow bench-like bed in the middle of the room. This was low to the ground and padded.

Holata Tyee addressed the other native male. "Chayton, what did he eat?"

"Nothing. Well, as far as I know. He was fine until he threw up and collapsed. I had to carry and drag him most of the way to the vehicle. He could barely walk. He went completely unconscious on the drive here."

"He's been poisoned, but with what plant or animal, bug, or reptile? To properly treat him, I need to know what happened!"

Orenda spoke up without thinking. "We can start with charcoal, mix the powder in liquid and get him to drink it."

Everyone turned to look at her as if her speaking startled them. The two apprentices looked at each other as if they expected some admonishment from their teacher.

But the guardian only turned to Yuma and said, "Get the Bezoars."

Orenda was a bit horrified. This was a remedy originally brought from the Zenda Territories. Now, some native healers harvested them from the digestive tract of wild game. They looked like a stone, and were made of undigested food, plant fibers, and hair.

In Orenda's opinion, bezoars had no actual effect on ridding the body of poison. They were a hoax! People who trusted this sort of thing were just gullible.

Yuma brought a box full of blackish round stones. The guardian scraped some of the Bezoar into a cup and added water to the shavings. "This should bring down his fever."

Holata Tyee gruffly told Yuma to sit the unconscious native up. Then she commanded him to drink. His lips parted. She poured the liquid into his mouth. He rolled his eyes trying to open them.

The medicine guardian instructed her other apprentice to prepare the pearls. Tokala Luta used a pestle and mortar to grind a few small, irregular pearls. Assuming a poultice was expected, she made a paste of these and handed the bowl to her mentor.

Holata Tyee peered into the bowl, then up at her apprentice. "How do you expect me to use that?" Tokala Luta winced at the rebuke and quickly added more water and handed it back.

Orenda watched the procedures without further interference. She found the remedies crude and unsound. Her grandfather taught her a different way of dealing with poison.

Holata Tyee yelled at her son. "Did you reach Tao?"

"Yes, he's on his way."

The guardian started to undress the unconscious native, asking Yuma to help her. She removed the pants first, looking at the ankles for a snake bite, but no marks were evident. When she took off his shirt, an obvious inflamed welt was exposed. "The poison entered here."

Holata Tyee scowled at Chayton. "It would be helpful if you knew what kind of poison caused this."

From everyone's reaction, Orenda concluded that this guardian, who claimed to be a medical practitioner, intimidated them. She was hostile and demanding, and as far as Orenda was concerned, she was not knowledgeable enough to warrant such notoriety.

Orenda would have put a plaster on the injury to pull out any poison still under the skin. She would have filled him with activated charcoal water until he vomited again. Then encourage him to eat more charcoal to neutralize the toxins in his system. Then she would have made a remedy with mandrake root, which would be an antidote for a wide variety of poisons, at least a far better choice than bezoars and ground pearls. Those were crude treatments with no actual effect.

At that moment, a young Zendali came in. He had an impressive crest of head hair and dark indigo fur.

"Tao, there you are!" Holata Tyee addressed him with some deference, which Orenda found a little odd. He was a youth, no older than the others.

"I knocked, but no one heard me." He regarded the male Holata Tyee was treating. "What happened to Askook? He tried to contact me, but I was hunting."

Chayton responded, "He spotted a Fog female, and we tried to capture her in the forest."

"Tried?" asked Tao.

"She got away. I'm not sure how. She must have been hiding. But I couldn't stay to search the area. When he got sick and collapsed, I brought him here."

"What's wrong with him?" Tao directed this question to Holata Tyee.

"He's poisoned," the guardian said flatly, as if this should be obvious. "You'd better bring her here and find out what she injected him with."

"Injected?" Chayton and Tao said simultaneously.

"There was no opportunity for her to do that," Chayton said. "She pushed him, that's all. He fell backward off the path into the thicket, and she ran. We couldn't find her."

"What sort of bushes?" The medicine guardian demanded.

Holata Tyee must be thinking they might have had poisonous thorns. Orenda thought.

Chayton shrugged. "I'm not sure. He got right up and ran after her, though. I wasn't far behind. She didn't touch him again."

"Nevertheless, she did somehow insert the poison into him. You can see the injection site here."

"Who is this?" Tao said, looking at Orenda.

Yuma replied, "This is Orenda, apprentice to Ezno. She arrived recently from the East Coast."

Tao glanced at Holata. "A new apprentice?"

The guardian raised her chin, looking down on Orenda. "It hasn't been decided."

"Actually, I have decided," Orenda said. "I will not be your apprentice."

Everyone in the room looked astonished, including Holata Tyee, who had an exalted opinion of herself.

Now, Tao regarded Orenda with narrowed eyes.

Her reaction to his glare was immediate and visceral. Orenda was frightened of this Zendali youth. Everything about him spoke of malice. She carefully controlled her body language, not wanting to show her trepidation.

"Don't concern yourself with her Tao. She'll be back begging. She's nothing but a backcountry hayseed."

Orenda backed out of the door. As soon as she was out of sight, she ran from the compound.

24

INFATUATION

When Mora arrived the next morning at the university, she was looking in her bag for the security disk she needed to enter a door for the wing where the new lab was located. She didn't notice the native scientist quietly approach until he was right next to her. Startled, she spun around to face him, which made him jump in surprise. He seemed nervous, which made Mora keenly aware of every detail. He wore his hair a bit short, which was unusual here. His lips were full, his face wide and soft. His big eyes were dark amber. They widened with confusion.

He reached out and lightly touched her arm. "Are you angry with me? You walked by like you don't know me. I miss you, Zamora. Won't you consider my proposal?"

"I... I need to get to the lab. Can we discuss this later?"

He seemed to deflate even further, giving her a sad sort of shrug and nod. She pushed quickly through the door and didn't look back.

Mora had noticed that she had an admirer. She'd taken note that he sometimes showed up uninvited. He wasn't part of her team. Yet he had access to her department. He usually came during informal talks about the mechanics of the apparatus while they were in the building phase. He just stood at the back of the room, observing. But it was more than the project. He followed her off-campus as well. She would see him staring at her from a distance. He sometimes attempted to signal her, but she didn't understand the intent behind the gestures until today when he hinted at intimacy with Zamora.

Now she was curious to know what his relationship with Zamora was.

"Algon, do you mind if I ask you about that young scientist who sometimes comes to observe our team?"

"Well, that could only be Ohpa."

Mora raised her brow ridge in a sign of curiosity. And waited for him to continue.

"Zamora had a team of ten assistants. I was put in charge of vetting them all to be sure they had no species-phobic tendencies, and the university made them sign strict non-disclosure forms with a penalty attachment. If they were to reveal Zamora's identity or the fact that she is"—he paused and looked befuddled, "that you both are... different."

"This is because she couldn't work in the lab with the head coverings?"

"Right."

"And by *different* you mean we are Fog and smart?"

He smiled and nodded. "I devised a questionnaire which every prospective assistant had to take, so I could identify anyone who might be loyal to those who have certain predilections or prejudices. Out of those who passed my test, Zamora conducted interviews from behind the veil to find those who could implement what she needed, and in this way, we built the team. Once they were assigned to her, the Dean brought in paperwork they had to sign. Only after all of this did she take off her veil."

"Was Ohpa a problem?"

"Oh no, I just thought you needed to have the backstory, so you'd understand how we found the people you, well, Zamora could work with."

"I don't understand. What was the issue with Ohpa? Why did he leave the team?"

"Ohpa proposed a formal mating with Zamora."

"To marry her? Isn't that illegal?"

"Yes, well, maybe? It is generally considered forbidden, but technically it is only illegal to have children with the Pinks, according to our formal agreement with Zenda. There is no mention in our agreement about the Fog, however, as they are not supposed to exist."

Mora pursed her lips. "I can see how that might complicate things." She laughed, but Algon didn't.

"No, Mora, it isn't funny. Our country gives them sanctuary, anyway. Both sides are pretending the Fog who live here are fictitious. We claim there are none, and the Sovereign Nation prefers to posture they don't exist because they should not. At the same time, they are informed we protect a few on the reservations. So unofficially, it is a point of contention, which is only tolerated because no one wants to upset the peace."

"Doesn't Ohpa understand that exposing Zamora would be detrimental to her work? I mean, I'm sure she doesn't want to hide on a reservation."

"He doesn't want to expose her. He wants to hide with her. The sanctuary document, which the refugees agreed to when they moved to the reservations, says nothing against

Wen partnering with the Pinks. I guess it wasn't something anyone considered might happen. Our treaty with Zenda officially prohibits a Pink from getting a visa. The Council gets around that by offering refugee status instead."

"So, if a Pink and a native had children, they wouldn't actually be breaking any treaties or Council laws?"

"*Officially* no, there is no such stipulation in writing. But the Zendali would definitely object. Treaty negotiations would be open for investigation, and the issue of the reservations would come up."

"Ohpa didn't want to have children?"

"Ohpa is in love with Zamora. He was willing to forgo having a family, and would even go so far as to live on a reservation with her if such a measure was ever necessary. His family lives in the Southeast, near Seneca. They are not around to influence his decisions. He is also persistent. Zamora finally gave in and made the mistake of taking him as a lover."

Now, it all made more sense. "What happened after? I mean, why did he leave her team?"

"Kai happened."

Mora looked surprised. "Who is Kai, and why didn't you tell me any of this before?"

"Zamora doesn't talk to me about personal things. I didn't think you would welcome my interference in personal matters."

"She didn't tell you, but you are fully informed... Oh, she talks to Asha?"

Algon looked apologetic. "What happens in the lab is my business, and Asha wanted me to understand the personal dynamics."

"Tell me about Kai."

"Kai was one of the candidates I vetted for our group. He passed all the assessment tests I gave in regard to social perception, but his science wasn't exceptional. Zamora chose only the brightest for her team. But during the interview, she liked his attitude and the ease of his personality, his confidence. So, she contacted him to meet her privately."

"She trusted him enough to reveal her identity?"

"It was a risk. Without the signed non-disclosure document, in my opinion letting him know her secret was a mistake, but Zamora was sometimes lonely."

"I think I need to hear more about Kai and why he has not been following me around like Ohpa."

"Kai's father is from Zenda."

Mora's ears flattened, and she looked at Algon with alarm.

"Which I didn't realize when he was vetted for our project. His father married a native and fully integrated into our culture. His bride was the daughter of a tribal chief. Kai's father took a new name and cut all ties to his previous life in Zenda. He has no connection to his homeland now. They raised Kai in native traditions. Kai also favors his mother's family genetics. He doesn't have a crest or any obvious Zenda features other than the darkness of his pelt."

"Kai is a mixed child, same as Zamora, but not considered Fog?"

"Well, no. It's not the same. He is not mixed with Pinks. When explorers from the Sovereign Zenda Nation first encountered the people here on Wendat, the natives they met were also very dark, which made them *acceptable*. There were other considerations, but instead of trying to invade our country, they made trade agreements and treaties with us. Zenda and the four councils of Wendat have lived as peaceful allies since."

"None of their claims make sense to me. Pinks are not a subspecies. We are all just different races. It's completely ridiculous to claim otherwise! There is no such thing as pureblood! In my world, we are mostly a mixed society. But we are aware of the differences in the genomes."

"There are twenty-three detected areas of the genome showing dissimilarities between Zendali and the fair races. Some have to do with brain structure and function. This science is used to devalue the Pinks, and is the Sovereign Nation's proof that Pinks are not able to process higher learning," Algon said.

"If they're not given an education, of course, they will be less capable and less intelligent. They just don't have access to the same opportunities." Mora objected.

Algon nodded agreement. "We know the truth of this, but the general population in Zenda does not. They believe what their government tells them."

"If Zamora's achievements were to be made public, it would be detrimental to the entire façade the Zenda Nation has built. These false claims about the Pinks would be exposed!"

Algon reacted to Mora's excitement with caution. "Mora, what you are saying is dangerous. You have no idea how much influence they have here. They would never let that happen."

"Was Zamora still involved with Kai when—"

"Zamora's affairs were private." He said this in a blunt tone, making it clear he didn't want to talk about it further. Seeing Mora stiffen, he softened his voice and continued. "Unknown to everyone but Asha. You'll have to ask her if you want to know the details.

I only heard that they kept their relationship secret from Kai's parents. Regarding Ohpa, his fond attention became distracting for Zamora, and she asked me to transfer him out. Then Asha told me why."

25

CONNECTIONS

I t was a few days after Orenda ran out of Holata Tyee's treatment room when her second apprentice, Tokala Luta, called to say she was sorry. She was the medicine guardian's second apprentice.

"Why are you sorry?"

"It was a highly charged day. A lot of drama..."

"Did Holata Tyee ask you to contact me on her behalf?"

"No! It was just unfortunate. Not the best situation for you to meet my mentor. I think you got the wrong impression of her."

"Did I?" Orenda paused, not wanting to sound so rude. "I'm sorry for running out like that but to be completely honest with you, it seemed like the perfect situation to get an accurate read on Holata Tyee, it is only under the worst of circumstances that you discover the true nature of a person."

There was silence on the receptor, and Orenda realized she had been too honest. It was a mistake she often made, and every time she had regrets about it. *Why can't I just keep things pleasant like my mother always cautioned?*

But the apprentice did not sound offended when she finally spoke. "I am actually calling to see if we can meet. I have a friend attending Muwi University. She is a third-year history major, and I think that she might be able to ease your transition there. It's always good to have someone who can show you around campus."

"Sure, I'd be happy to meet your friend, thank you."

"By the way, my friends call me Tokala." *She wants to be friends. Well, let's see how that goes.* Orenda was still unsure why Tokala was reaching out.

***

A couple of days later, Tokala arrived with the Zendali named Asha, who was dressed in black robes and veil. Orenda stood at the door in awe; the sight gave her chills. She thought for a moment this was one of the females she had seen in her dreams.

Asha was wearing the traditional garb of the Sisters' of Justice. But when she took off her head covering, Orenda realized with disappointment that this robed devotee wasn't either of the females from her dreaming visions. Asha had dark indigo fur, and her black crest was tightly bound to her head in a few plaited rows. She had an imposing presence, a highborn beauty anyone would envy, and Orenda thought *what a shame to hide it under a veil.*

Orenda led her guests to the courtyard garden, where a table was set with herbal tea, some small wildflower muffins, and a platter of fruit.

As they were getting seated, Asha asked: "Tokala tells me you're here to study art?"

"That's right. I was given a scholarship."

"She's also an experienced apprentice. Her grandfather is a medicine guardian of some notoriety, although, unlike Holata Tyee, he's reclusive," Tokala repeated this bit of news to open the conversation about Orenda's background.

Orenda wondered if the medicine guardian had sent her apprentice to entice her back.

Asha asked with amazement, "You gave up your medicine title, and spiritual practices?"

Orenda didn't quite know how to explain, or what to say. "I can't give up what is intrinsically part of me, but I felt guided to come here and study art. For now, art is my path."

"Holata Tyee has been in a horrible mood. There are hopeful apprentices from all over Wendat who send her gifts begging for a chance to study under her, and you turned her down!" Tokala said this with a matter-of-fact attitude and didn't seem upset about it. She had an ironic smile on her face. Asha chuckled too.

"I'm sorry if I cause you any trouble," Orenda told Tokala.

"No, not at all, but Holata Tyee still expects you to come begging her for another chance." She wiggled her ears with something akin to amusement.

"I definitely won't be doing that."

Looking a little more serious now, Tokala told Orenda. "I think if you met Holata Tyee under different circumstances, you would have a better opinion of her. She was under stress that day, and she gets a little overbearing at times, but I think she regrets you've not returned."

Tokala looked so sincere, Orenda chose not to speak ill of her mentor. She smiled instead, and for once didn't speak her mind. After a pause, when her guests were staring at her, Orenda realized she should say *something* in response. Focusing the refusal on herself, she told them: "On the contrary, the day I met your mentor, the perfect circumstances took place to inform my decision. I'm sure I didn't make a mistake. It's time for me to explore other things."

At that moment, Coso walked into the garden. She greeted her niece's guests graciously. "Did I hear correctly that you turned down the opportunity to study with Holata Tyee?"

Orenda cringed a little but answered hastily. "Yes, that's what I was saying, Auntie. If it is all right with you, I'd like to discuss my decision in private with you later."

Her aunt paused in the doorway with an indecisive expression, as if she were thinking about how to respond. Orenda didn't really know her aunt well, but she made an assumption that Coso's apprehension was because she was upset and wanted to settle things now. Or insist that Orenda return to the medicine guardian and apologize.

But suddenly Coso smiled. "Of course, have a nice visit." Then she left the room.

That was odd, and Orenda could tell her guests were uncomfortable. Before they made their excuses to depart, she wanted to ask about other members of Asha's religion. She didn't want to wait for a later opportunity when she might talk to Asha alone.

"I realize this might sound peculiar, but I keep dreaming about two females. I believe they wear the same garb as you do. I need to meet them."

Tokala Luta excused herself to find the restroom.

When Asha looked conflicted and didn't answer, Orenda decided to trust that this meeting was not a coincidence. She brought out a large sketchbook. "I have never shown these to anyone. Please take a look before Tokala returns."

Hesitantly, Asha took the book and began to flip through it. Page after page was filled with sketches of Mora and another young female she didn't know. On some pages, there were two Sisters' dressed in black with veils. She closed the book and gave it back to Orenda. Asha closed her eyes and took a few deep breaths. "One of them... is an acquaintance. I will ask if I can introduce you. But she is very private. I can't promise she will agree. Also, please don't show this book to anyone! You must know... it's dangerous."

"I understand why. Please assure her I will keep her secret."

"You are a seer?"

"I see things that I don't understand, and people I don't know."

Asha considered this with a sober expression, trying to decide if she could trust her.

When Tokala Luta returned to the garden, Asha stood, and they said their goodbyes.

Now Orenda had to face the disappointment of her aunt.

26

The Cave

B i was beginning to understand why Chitto was concerned about her. She did not expect the Wen to be so much darker. The Eastern Empire histories had indicated the natives here were descended from her people, but that was long ago.

By nightfall, Bi was too exhausted even to eat. The stress of the attack had taken its toll. She curled up in a safe, dark corner of the cave. Fragrant leaves were strewn on the ground. Sleep came quickly. The last thing she heard was an owl calling and an answer from farther away. Two owls, or maybe two men, still waiting? She wondered...

Bi stood on a patio terrace overlooking a city. The sky was black in the west where rain was falling, and strokes of lightning flashed in the distance, momentarily lighting the landscape below. With the approaching storm came a rich scent of ozone. The sun was close to the mountain ridge. Tiku was on the horizon, a huge red orb. "The corpse bleeds," she heard someone say, a reference to the dead planet descending.

Through the dark clouds, the setting sun painted the edges of the storm with a purple glow. Despite these wonders, her attention was focused on a bright spot of light directly across from where she stood, hovering over the mountains. Not first moon, Ifa, it was lower on the horizon. This anomaly was too small to be either of Hadot's moons.

She wondered if the light was a sky vessel flying toward her instead of to the north, where they would be approaching the airbase. But in her city, no traffic flew in that direction. The little light wavered back and forth, up and around. That shouldn't be possible. She glanced below, where an unknown city sprawled. The golden rays of sunset reflecting on crystal domes. This was not a place she knew. Oh! I'm dreaming... she coached herself to be a witness.

The city was glowing. Every structure was translucent, reflecting purple and orange light. Could this be my first view of Muwioni? She was standing on a terrace, transfixed on that shining speck in the sky, wondering what it might be. The orb grew brighter, rays extending finger-like toward her. Abruptly, the light shot forward, crossing the distance in a flash. She was hit by the impact, and the force took possession of her. Body and mind suspended, observed, not alone. The other presence wrapped tightly around her as if the orb were a body, with arms squeezing tight.

Bi woke gasping, and drenched in perspiration, her heart racing. "What was that?"

Late morning light filtered through the vines from an opening in the cavern above her. Rays of sunlight sparkled on dust particles in the air. Roots and tendrils of delicate vines reached toward the shallow pool of rainwater, which reflected the sky above. She'd not slept so deeply in a long while.

The evening before, when she was quietly waiting for the men to leave, she tried to make out what was marked on the cave walls. But through the gloomy expanse, the drawings were barely visible. She rose to her feet now, brushed off the dirt and leaves, and took a closer look at the flat cavern surfaces. They were completely covered with images. Some petroglyphs were of the Wen, and the animals they hunted. Some markings looked like moon cycles and the planets around Hadot's sun. Connecting these were swirls, stars, and arrows. She recognized symbols for the elements water and fire. A story was being told here.

Most interesting of all were drawings of beings that looked alien: some were small with big heads and giant dark eyes, painted in white. Another group was taller than the Wen. They also had white bodies, but with long white head hair. Some of them sat in flying ships with lines that radiated out of them. These must be the Ziv and the Elo! She had heard stories about them. Over time, aliens became nothing more than a fantasy in her country. Mythical creatures, monsters, and phantom characters in the books children read. Often cautionary tales to make them behave.

During her time spying on the royals, she learned that the aliens were real. She had been astonished to discover how much they contributed to the country's infrastructure and advancements. The Elo and Ziv had an alliance with the old patriarchal government. This was before the northern expansion and the Zenda Shadow Wars. For some unknown reason, the Empress chose to censor them from their nation's history.

Bi stood in awe of these stories left here by Wen long ago. She carried a small book in her backpack, made with plant-fiber paper. She began to copy as much of the petroglyphic story as she could. Bi wasn't an artist, but these line drawings were fairly simple. While drawing, she nibbled on the last of her dried fruit. She was running out of supplies. Her small pack didn't hold much. When she had filled several pages to document the story from the main chamber, she stood and stretched. *Time to explore what else is here.*

The cave was a series of chambers. Daylight filtered into the cave from holes in the upper dome, and all of these shafts were deep and far smaller than the one in the first chamber.

In a little chamber in the back, a trickle of fresh cold water ran down the wall and filled a basin in the sandstone. The basin was too perfectly shaped to be natural. Someone had carved it out to catch the runoff.

Beyond this was an entrance into a dark little chamber. She almost didn't explore this tiny hole in the wall, but a dripping echo made her pause. Bi crawled through the opening to find a smaller cave, which glowed with a pale phosphorescence. Steam filled the air. It rose from a pool. As her eyes adjusted, the walls of the chamber came into focus. She crawled further and put her fingers in the water; it was a hot spring!

Well, her dreams might not have warned her of some challenges, but her faith was renewed. The visions had led her here. She was optimistic that everything she would need was here in the cave or the surrounding area. She just had to trust.

Before exploring outside, she stripped down and went for a soak, washing the saltwater and dirt from her hair, and for the first time since she embarked on this journey, she felt truly safe. It couldn't hurt to stay here for a while. She needed time to think, dream, and revise her plans.

After she had bathed, her damp fur smelled like sulfur, but she didn't mind. The mineral soak had been restorative. She dressed in her spare garments and washed the ones she had been wearing for days. Laying them on stones in the outer chamber to dry.

Refreshed and relaxed, her next challenge was to explore outside. She didn't think her attackers would return, considering one of them was sick. After the men left yesterday, she had no dreams to indicate there might be further danger here. The angle of the light shining from above told her mid-day had come. She stood in the rays of the sun and inspected her fur. It wasn't as dark as the men who attacked her, and their hair had been black. She was several shades lighter. Her yellowish fur and pale hair were not going to pass in the city. These Wen are darker than expected, almost like shadow men. The boat people were quite dark as well. As Chitto had suggested, she needed to find some way to cover her pelt and hair before going to the city.

Her stomach growled like an angry beast. Before addressing other problems, her hunger came first. She'd been nibbling on dried provisions, which weren't very satisfying. Time to check the surrounding area.

The cave access was boxed-in, a tall, narrow slice between the stones. On the inside, there were no handholds to climb up. But she found that the ledge sloped downward to the corner of the cave. At that end, the ledge cut into the rock face like a ramp. She walked from the corner along the ledge to the exit. Squeezing through the stones, she stopped to listen before stepping out. High above, on top of the cliff, she saw trees and plants growing. In front of the cave was a rocky floor. Some shards of stone were strewn loosely around. To the left was a forest. Bushes, grass, and flowers grew at the edge of the thicket. On the other side was wet ground leading to a little muddy stream. Her toes sank into the clay. She quickly backtracked, covering her footprints.

The bushes near the forest were full of berries. Bi ate as she picked and collected more on a big leaf. She lifted a decaying log and found some fat white larvae. She popped one in her mouth to suck on and collected the rest on another leaf. Next, she found acorns that she could roast and grind to mix with water into a porridge, with nettles, and wild garlic. Together, that would make a good meal. She gave silent gratitude to the nature guide who taught her about foraging, fishing, and trapping in the wilds.

On her way back to the cave, she found wild indigo. This gave her an idea. She was familiar with its use, to make fabric dye. Bi had visited a processing plant her mother invested in. She had a vague memory of how to extract the color from the plant. She picked a sizable clump of the leaves to make a paste. Hoping she might darken her fur with the mixture. On closer inspection of the area, she found the raw materials for making primitive paints. White chalk was abundant, a whole vein of it on the narrow side of the cliff. Now she realized why this cave was used for the ancient tribe's story keeping. Everything was accessible to make the cave art. Red Ocher was in the clay-like soil too. *I can mix some of that into my dye.*

Her first priority was to prepare the food she'd scavenged. Bi sighed with relief, satisfied food was available. At least enough to sustain her for a few days. After that, she should be ready to leave for the city.

27

TreacherY

Chayton's father, Mato, was a council member in Muwioni. He was also a friend of Coso Winnemucca's. Generally, these two council members were in agreement on matters of government. They had been acquainted for years and grew closer during the tragedy of his wife's passing. Outside of their work relationship, they were close friends.

Chayton had fallen into bad company, spending too much time with Holata Tyee's son Kinache, and Ambassador Ziyad's son, Tao. The evening before, Mato had gotten a report that his son Chayton had brought someone in urgent need to the Medicine guardian. His friend survived but was still in recovery. A poison damaged his liver. Mato knew little to nothing about the incident. No official report had been made. He naturally assumed a snake had bitten the youth. Oddly, when he asked Chayton to explain how this happened, he was cagey and wouldn't talk. He'd grown accustomed to his son's evasive behavior, and expressed only mild concern when his attempt to discuss the event with Chayton was ignored.

Mato was at Coso Winnemucca's compound when Holata Tyee's apprentices came to visit Orenda. The young people were having an animated discussion in the hallway, and he noticed Orenda peek into the garden where he sat with her aunt. After a moment, the three of them came in and stood before them. Orenda was in front, while the other two hung back with worried expressions.

"There is something we need to tell you," Orenda said. "Well, it's *my* opinion you should be informed. Please don't reveal that you got the information from them." She motioned to the two young apprentices. "It's really important, do you agree?"

The two adults looked at each other, and they both nodded. Mato had a difficult time not chuckling at this cold, sober request. The drama invoked seemed a bit too much.

It was hard to take them seriously. What could possibly be so upsetting to these three youngsters?

But Coso was at full attention. "Of course, we will respect your wishes, won't we, Mato?"

"It concerns your son," Orenda told him, then she looked at the two apprentices, and Mato sat up straighter, now more alert.

"Yuma has seen his mentor's son Kinache practicing the dark arts on a number of occasions. He's studying under a Zendali Sorceress from the Saromal sect."

Mato flattened his ears and was about to speak.

"This is relevant because he's been giving some of these charms to Chayton."

"We don't know how he is using them, but it has something to do with a female he wanted," Yuma told them.

Tokala Luta came forward now. "Today I overheard Kinache and Chayton talking to Tao about how the fisher's son was injured. The medicine guardian wishes to keep this information from the council. But we feel the young female's life is in danger."

"What female?" The two adults asked at once.

"We don't know," Tokala said, "but they think she's Fog, and they tried to capture her in the forest. Somehow, she prevented her capture by attacking Askook with a poison barb. Now they're planning to retaliate. They want to hunt her."

Mato stood. "I am going to put a stop to this immediately!" He was deeply troubled by his son's machinations. An instinctive parental distress overcame him as he realized that something untoward was at play.

"Wait, we haven't told you everything," Orenda said.

Yuma spoke up now. "We think that the Order of Amon Kuroo is behind this and that your son and the others have pledged fealty to that organization. They are helping them in some way."

"Not my son!" Mato's conviction was fueled with pride and concern.

Coso stood to stop him from leaving. She reached out and held his arm. "Mato, I think we should be cautious, and not make any rash decisions. I realize with your son involved in this, it isn't comfortable to wait for what develops, but that is exactly what we need to do."

Mato's panic subsided, but he was obviously under strain. "It was my understanding that the Amon Kuroo was a dark blight on the past."

Coso nodded. "Why do you believe they're active now, especially here?" She asked Yuma.

"I don't have proof, just signs that would be meaningless to you." He looked at Orenda. "Which is why I hesitated to tell you."

"We will do our best to prevent any harm," Coso assured her niece and young visitors.

Orenda glanced back at her friends as if hoping they would reveal more of what they suspected, but they didn't seem willing.

***

When everyone had left, Orenda found her aunt sitting alone deep in thought. "Excuse me, Auntie, may we talk?"

Her aunt patted the seat next to her. "Are you worried?"

"I wanted to talk to you about my decision not to study with Holata Tyee. You were upset the other night and dismissed me. I was waiting for the opportunity to explain."

Coso shook her head. "I wasn't upset."

"But I thought you expected me to study with her?"

Coso smiled at her niece. "You can tell me now. What troubles you?"

"I went to the medicine guardian, thinking the visit would be an introduction, but instead a crisis was in play because a young Wen was poisoned."

Coso's ears stood rigidly alert now, as if surprised to hear her niece had witnessed something so dreadful.

"Watching her deal with him gave me a chance to observe her medical practice, and she made bad choices. If he didn't have an implant, I believe he would have died."

"Those are serious allegations," Coso said, "and also a little pretentious to think you know more than a famous healer."

"I realize that, which is why I stopped myself from speaking up. But I could tell you in detail what she did and what I would have done differently, and why. Your brother taught me how to make and properly use herbal remedies. As well as the treatment of all manner of injuries and poisons. I am young but not a novice. I am well versed in the treatment of toxins, even when the source is unknown, but Holata Tyee is not."

Coso knew Orenda had been her brother's only apprentice and had been at his knee since she was a toddler. "All right, I believe you. If I told you that I was relieved when you turned her down, would you be surprised?"

"What? Yes, I would! I thought you *expected* me to study with her!"

"No, I thought that's what *you* wanted, so I arranged the introduction. She is the one who expected that you would study under her. She would have pressured me to back her proposals endlessly as if she took you for her apprentice only as a favor to me, not because you're the best candidate. I did not look forward to being indebted to her."

"You seemed unhappy with me and told me to go to bed."

"I was not unhappy. I was exhausted! I had been worried about the situation ever since I got the word you were coming. When you chose not to study with her, then... well, case closed, and I could relax. Honestly, I did not realize how much the prospect of your being in her hands worried me."

"I'm so relieved you're not angry." Orenda sighed and took her aunt's hand affectionately.

Then Coso admitted: "I've had suspicions about her for quite some time. I didn't want to talk about my distrust. I was just glad the matter was behind us. But it seems I am not free of her influence yet. If your report is correct, she may be involved in something more nefarious than I thought. We have no choice but to monitor the movements of her son and his friends to find who is aiding them and who exactly is involved."

28

FLOATER

O renda clung to the railing as the platform rose up to meet the landing area beside the floater. A native male was loitering there and watched her with a minacious sneer. She paused, unsure what to do. He laughed and waved her forward. She touched a round, smooth spot on the side of the floater; it began to glow around her palm, and then an orifice opened. Before she could take a step forward, that young Wen pushed against her back, knocking her into the floater. She stumbled, and he jumped over her. Laughing again, he went to the back to take his place along the wall. She assumed he was just foolhardy or clumsy.

Still reeling from the rudeness of his forced entry, Orenda squinted in the direction he had gone, but in the gloomy interior, she couldn't see him. With a sigh, she decided to let it go, assuming this was to be expected in the city.

The inside of the floater was a little creepy. It was spongy and soft to the touch. She'd been told to lean against a wall. When she did, the pliable surface reached around and cradled her body, and nearly swallowed her! Orenda's heart raced with panic until filaments from the floater reached out and interacted with her implant. Then calming energy filled her.

A series of bubbles floated toward her. Each one contained a scene: landscapes, cities, and grand elaborate rooms. She moved close to see the details inside. Without intending to, she touched her forehead to the bubble, and suddenly she was inside it, falling or flying toward the landscape. *This is like a dream; there are no actual bubbles in the floater.* It was astonishing. Everything felt completely real, not just a visual experience, but also smells and sounds, textures too.

Around her, the sky and trees passed as she floated down to an expanse of gardens where everything was in bloom. Her feet landed toes first. She stood in a very realistic environment, smelling the sweet scent of the nearby flowers and cut grass. As Orenda walked through the garden, exploring and interacting with others who were also there, birds flew by, and little creatures rustled in the bushes. She was impressed with how realistic the experience was.

Then she noticed some native males leaning on the pillars of a gazebo. The one who had knocked into her on her entry was with them. She realized that all of these young Wen had been shadowing her recently. *How would they have known what virtual place I would choose to visit?* Her mood plummeted, sinking into dread... from wonder and awe to trepidation. They didn't smile at her; they watched like hungry predators. *What do they want with me?* She wondered.

She quickly signaled to disengage, pulled herself out of the floater wall, and looked around at the others in the room to find the Wen who had harassed her... *they must be here.* Could they access the same place from a different floater? It was no use. She found it impossible to distinguish anyone's identity. The figures were submerged and impossible to recognize. The sight of all the others enveloped in the floater gave her a chill. She quickly exited, feeling she had been targeted and abused.

I was so excited to do this, and they ruined it for me!

29

The Observer

What's a spy if not an observer? In order for Bi to obtain secrets, she needed to walk freely in Wendat, to encounter the Shadow People visiting from Zenda. If that meant coloring her fur, she had to try. The process took her a few days, but she managed to make a dye from a mixture of indigo and ocher. She applied this to her pelt and hair, taking care to apply the thickest amount where her fur would be visible. This would not fool anyone on close inspection; the color was uneven and motley. The dye would also wash off, eventually. She'd need a better solution. The goggles would hide her eyes, yet Bi was in doubt about wearing them in the city. *Wouldn't they draw more attention?* She wondered. The whole get-up was undoubtedly odd.

She left the cave reluctantly after having rested for nearly a full moon cycle. She'd never been so comfortable. She set traps for small game and collected herbs and roots to supplement her diet. Bi enjoyed having a place of her own a little too much. Having time to herself where no one dictated what she should do was a luxury she'd never experienced. Oddly, she wasn't at all lonely. The selfish desire to abandon her mission and live in the wild burned inside her as she enjoyed these days alone. Who among her people would ever find her? She sighed, knowing how useless it was to yearn for such things.

After a recent contact with her invigilator, Bi had to admit no further preparations for the journey were necessary. No more excuses for her procrastination came to mind. She needed to move on. Far encouraged her not to delay the inevitable.

Bi was still a few days' journey from the city on foot because she wanted to travel at night and sleep during the day. She passed Rayfin Harbor the first night and found the trail on the other side where the path toward Muwioni continued. She slept above ground in the trees. Afraid, if she camped in the forest, she would be seen.

Bi started to cross a major road when a hauler stopped and offered to take her to the city. She threw her pack in the back among the crates of vegetables and crawled in. The driver in the cab didn't say anything more before driving on. *Was giving rides to strangers normal here?* Bi began to worry that she'd been too willing. What if he wasn't a friendly farmer? What if he's with those who tried to capture her? During the entire ride into the city, she tormented herself with the worst-case scenarios.

When they arrived at a market, she jumped out, ready to run. The farmer got out and handed her a piece of fruit. Warily, she took it and thanked him. He smiled and carried on with his duties, unloading the hauler.

Bi hardly had time to feel relieved before a new unease settled in. She was searching the market for a gem dealer to trade a few stones for local currency. Her government provided a pouch of gemstones which should be highly valued here. She hoped they would be enough to pay her expenses until she found work.

The venders were interested in her gems, but she was told there was no local coin available. They offered to credit her implant for the value transfer. Evidently, currency exchange never developed here. Bi wasn't sure what they meant by *implant,* but obviously, she didn't have one. She would also not be able to work without being implanted unless she found a place that would pay her with room and board.

Language proved to be a greater challenge than expected. Everyone spoke incredibly fast. People were also amused by her accent.

While she cut through a narrow back street, going along a little too hastily, and not paying close attention to her surroundings, she turned a corner and collided with someone dressed in black. They fell, hitting the ground hard. It seemed to have knocked the breath out of her. When the stranger's head covering and veil came off, Bi saw it was not a typical native female. She had pale fur and green eyes, like herself!

Scrambling to stand, the stranger's eyes frantically searched all around and down the street. She grabbed the head-covering and quickly replaced it.

Bi reached down to help her, apologizing. "I'm sorry."

The stranger pulled away and said nothing. She looked poised to run away. Warily, she pinned the veil in place, hiding her face again.

Bi lifted her goggles to show her eyes, saying, "Look, I'm like you."

The stranger brushed dust off her garments, still seemingly poised to escape.

Bi knew she looked strange in the outfit she wore, the goggles resting on her forehead now.

"Who are you?" The stranger asked.

"I'm Bimisi, a traveler, hoping to find a room to rent and work. Maybe you could suggest where I might inquire?" Bi realized she was speaking in formal Salagi, everyone in the market seemed to use a sort of slang or a more common version of the language.

"With those eyes, you need to be careful." The stranger told her. After a pause, she added, "You can call me Mora."

"I am so happy we ran into each other. What are the chances?" Without a doubt, this was no mistake. She was in exactly the right place at that moment to meet Mora.

"The Journeyer Hotel posted a notice that they were looking for kitchen staff. I was there recently to make arrangements for a party."

"I was told about that place, but I don't have any way to pay for a room."

"I met the manager at that time. She might hire you. Follow me. I'll talk to her now."

The Journeyer was more of a rooming house for long-stay visitors. Tourists came on occasion, but most of the guests came to Muwioni on business from the Zenda continent or territories. Their notice for *help-wanted* was still posted.

"I should have asked if you have any experience with kitchen work," Mora said.

Bi nodded that she did. "I better let you know before we talk to them that I don't have an implant."

"Travelers aren't allowed into Wendat without an implant. How did you enter?"

This was news to Bi, but she needed to trust someone. "I'm a refugee of sorts. But please don't tell them. Maybe I can work for room and board?"

"That's all you want? I can help you get an implant without anyone being alerted to your situation."

"You would do that?"

They had arrived at the hotel. Mora waved her arm for Bi to follow her inside.

"Let me speak with someone and find out if they still need a worker." Mora went into the hotel to look for the proprietor and found her talking to the manager.

"Are you still looking for kitchen help?" Mora asked them.

The manager looked up, perplexed. "Why do you ask?"

"Mistress Kel, I was here recently about the university award party. Do you remember me?" Asked Mora.

"Yes. To answer your question, we are still understaffed. With that big party, it will be a problem. But no one has applied."

"I know an immigrant who's looking for work. If you'd be interested?"

"You mean a Pink?"

Mora nodded hesitantly.

The manager didn't seem happy about it. Some Pinks worked in the city. There was no ordinance against it, but she hesitated. "I suppose for kitchen work... all right, yes, I'll take her on a temporary basis."

Mora signaled to Bimisi, who had been listening to their conversation from a distance. Bi was still wrapped up in a scarf and goggles. None of her fur was showing.

Mora introduced her to the manager. "This is Mistress Kel. She's agreed to hire you."

She was a heavyset female with a dark green pelt, scruffy dark hair, and a curt attitude. The manager looked from Mora in her black robes back to Bi in her crazy outfit. Then Bi raised her goggles and her scarf unraveled, showing her green eyes and mottled dye job.

"She is not a Pink, and that bad dye job won't fool anyone." She looked at Mora with consternation. "What is she? Have you brought me a Fog, because that..."

"Fog? No, certainly not. Bimisi just wanted to fit in, didn't you?" Mora asked encouragingly.

Bi nodded, then shrugged.

"You better keep your head down, don't mingle with the guests, stay in the kitchen."

Mistress Kel turned. In a harsh whisper to Mora, she said, "What did you get me into?"

Bi did know something about prep work. She had spent a lot of time when she was little in the kitchen at her family home. She enjoyed talking to the cooks, and they often let her help. Before they knew she was gifted, they might have thought Bi would follow in their line of work.

When Mora asked about room and board in exchange for Bi's labor, the owner was a little surprised, but she happily agreed. It was cheap labor for her, and this put her in a better mood.

"We have a room Bimisi can use. But I doubt she'll like it. This used to be a storage room for linens, and it's small. Lately, we've used it as a break-room for the staff who work a double shift and need a rest in-between. If Bimisi takes the job, no one will need to do double shifts. Which means a lot less complaining, and my job will be easier." Mistress Kel led them to the little room, which truly was no bigger than a closet. This was located behind the hotel lobby and adjacent to the laundry. It had no windows.

"When the washing machines are in service, they are loud and disturbing." The manager was up-front about the disadvantages. "My other employees complained when they tried to nap here."

The room was sparsely furnished. A small cot in the corner had bedding stacked on top of it, a lamp with a bent shade sat on a little table, and a plain wooden chair was against the wall. The bare stone floor had no rug.

Bi readily accepted, despite the obvious disadvantages. "Thank you!"

Both the manager and Mora looked stunned.

"Are you sure about this?" Mora asked.

"It's perfect," Bi told them.

The manager took them to an adjacent room with a toilet, shower, and even a cabinet that dried fur with warm air! Bi had never seen one before and tried not to look awe-struck.

They walked back to the room with a cot, and Bi dropped her pack on the floor, thanked the manager again, and beamed a big smile at Mora.

"Report for work when the second-morning chime rings. If you're up by first chime, it will give you time to prepare yourself." Then she turned, and as she walked away, she warned. "Do not let the guests see you."

When Mora was alone with Bi, she took off her veil.

"You seem to be completely unconcerned about the conditions. I have to say, everything considered, you seem a bit too pleased. This arrangement isn't a beneficial exchange."

Bi smiled again. "This is perfect. Don't worry."

"What was I thinking? This is crazy! The place is full of Zendali!"

Bi was completely calm and shrugged. "I will avoid them."

"I'm pleased they have work for you, but... I was wrong to bring you here. It might not be safe. I tend to compartmentalize everything. I wasn't considering the risks, only the work."

"I'll be careful. I understand why you're worried."

"I'll be here in a week to attend a party. Tell me if you want to have the implant when I see you next, and if you do, I'll make the arraignments. Then maybe we can find a safer place for you."

"It was such good fortune that I ran into you today." Bi laughed at the fact that she had *literally* run into her. "Thank you for bringing me here.

"Bi, this was a really stupid idea."

"No, this will be fine, no worries."

"I hope you're right," Mora said as she turned to leave.

30

Unexpected Encounters

Mora noticed Asha staring across the plaza. She cursed softly and turned to warn Mora, but it was too late. He intercepted them, as if he could see right through their Sisters' of Justice garb. He moved in close to Mora, pressing his nose against her veil. "Zamora, I haven't seen you on campus lately." His tone and attitude were familiar and flirtatious.

"Kai, we don't have time for this." Asha obviously said this to inform Mora of his identity.

Kai ignored Asha and waited for a response from Zamora.

"Even under that robe, I would know you from all others."

"I doubt that, Kai. I expect you were following us from her house."

He tilted his head toward Asha and smiled.

Kai ignored Asha, and waited for a response from the sister he thought was Zamora.

Mora smelled the sandalwood soap rising off his warm fur. A suffocating panic reaction caused her to take a step back from the native stranger, and she awkwardly fell against Asha. This was not the reaction he expected. Kai's ear-fans flattened back and he said, "Have you been avoiding me for any specific reason? Did I upset you?"

When Mora didn't answer, his tone became incensed. "I'm not a fool, Zamora! Do you think you can just *dismiss* me? Are my affections so meaningless?"

Probably to diffuse his aggravation, Asha grabbed Mora's arm and said, "We apologize, but we're needed urgently elsewhere." She pulled Mora away.

Mora had not said a word. She felt completely blindsided by this admirer, who certainly had a much greater emotional connection with Zamora than Algon had told her about. He knew her intimately, and he had expectations! These secret affairs were a liability for Mora.

She whispered to Asha as they moved away from Kai. "Sorry, I just froze. That was intense! I think you saved me from a difficult exchange back there."

"I've seen him with you, I mean... with Zamora. She talked to me sometimes about their tumultuous relationship."

Mora turned to her with concern. "Was he abusive?"

"No, not physically." Asha sighed, "He treats her like a convenient distraction. Flirting, having sexual rendezvous. Then, ignoring her for a while. Then the drama starts all over again. He tells her he's sorry, that he misses her, and he needs her, and she puts up with the whole mess like she couldn't expect any better."

Mora was bewildered by this story. "Asha, why didn't you tell me about him before? All of these details about Zamora's life are like landmines for me." Asha looked confused. Mora had used an Inreji term, with no translation for landmine in Neofinga or Salagi. "Obstacles, I mean. If I don't have all the particulars of her life, it's hard for me to impersonate her."

"Haven't you read about Kai in Zamora's journals?"

"Oddly, I have found no reference to her affairs, with Kai or Ohpa. Maybe she was careful not to mention them in case she's discovered and the journals might implicate her friends? Come to think of it, she doesn't mention anyone by name. She mostly writes about her internal struggles, her work, and her life as a child in Zenda. But she does not even say who her family is. In her place, there are no family photos either. I think she was aware of the possibility she would be exposed, and she made a real effort to minimize the damage in case that happened."

"Well then, I should warn you, the one you really need to avoid is Chayton. He's a friend of my brother, and he had a possessive sort of obsession with Zamora. She told me he almost raped her once."

"A *friend* of your brother knew she was Fog?!"

Asha winced. "Maybe, but he *wants* her. If he does know, he's kept her secret."

"But after he attacked her, she managed to avoid any further contact?"

Asha did that side-to-side tilt of the head, which seemed to mean uncertainty. "No, oddly enough, she started meeting with him on occasion. I'm not sure what happened between them. She wouldn't tell me."

Mora's fur rippled with her stress. "That's disturbing to hear. Are you sure he knows what she is?"

"No, I only assumed maybe he never saw her uncovered. His attack might not have gotten that far. She didn't tell me details."

"So, he could have been following me too, all this time, and if I don't know what he looks like, how can I avoid him?"

Asha stared at Mora. Her expression was sober. "You're right. I'm sorry. I should have told you. What are you going to do about Kai now? He apparently wants to carry on his relationship with you, thinking you're Zamora."

Then something happened that took Mora's attention. As upset as she had been only a moment before, what she saw then *thoroughly* distracted her, and she didn't answer.

"Mora?"

Across the public square was a group of aliens near the pavilion. For a visitor from Inoti, where such a thing would never take place, she was absolutely riveted at the sight of them casually walking through the city in public view.

"Mora, are you intentionally trying to avoid this conversation?"

"What? No, I just don't care about him. I don't even know Kai."

Clearly displeased with the attitude, Asha's ear-fans flattened.

Mora wondered why Asha was so concerned about the guy if he was rude and possessive. "I'm not getting caught up in *any* of Zamora's relationship dramas. I have more respect for myself than that."

Asha finally noticed that Mora was looking at the Star People with an expression of awe.

"Oh, those are the Darga," Asha said. "They must be here for a meeting with the council."

"They're bald and furless!" Mora cringed. The Darga had smooth brown skin and huge heads. This naked look gave her a creepy feeling. It was so unnatural.

Asha was saying something about them. She heard her say they were binary beings, intersex. But Mora didn't hear most of what was said. There was a hollow feeling inside. Her head resonated with a buzzing noise that drowned out what Asha was saying.

The Durga moved gracefully through the crowd, and just like the Ziv had done a few days before, they recognized Mora. Or at least that is what it felt like. Before climbing the steps leading to the ornate double doors of the council building, they all paused, communicating for a moment with each other, then they turned, looking through the people milling about, and focused their gaze on her. Could it just be her imagination? Mora's attention on them was broken when Asha spoke again.

"Algon told me that in your world you don't have contact with the Star People. Is that really true?"

Mora nodded but kept her eyes glued to the Durga.

"The other day I saw the Ziv. They also stood taller than us, but they were beautiful with soft white fur and long gossamer hair." Mora spoke in a soft, distracted tone.

"I've seen them on occasion. That's the advantage of living in a capital city: you can see the Star People when they meet with the council." Asha told her.

"They wore form-fitting bodysuits. Most unusual were their ears, a curl of flesh, flat to their heads." She nodded at the aliens, like the Darga." Her gaze still looked into the distance, watching these different aliens as they entered the Council building. "The Ziv made a much different impression on the crowd," Mora continued. "The Zendali especially were disturbed by the sight of them. Today the visitors from Zenda seemed apprehensive about the Durga, but no more than that."

Asha looked at Mora with clear dismay. "Isn't it obvious why?" When Mora didn't seem to understand or nod in agreement, Asha explained. "Because the Ziv look too much like our Pinks, except they're not downtrodden servants. They're powerful extrasolar beings! The Zenda Nationalists are especially vocal about their aversion to them."

Mora ignored the reference to Pinks as if she hadn't even heard. When she spoke, she sounded uneasy. "I can't explain how I feel... to see with my own eyes that aliens actually exist."

31

AWARD RECEPTION

Their hard work paid off. Mora, Algon, and their team completed the less ambitious design by the required deadline. These portals would break down the molecules of any nonliving substance, transport them to distant portals set up across the country, then reconfigure the object at the target destination. All the tests now proved to transport objects successfully, and render them properly.

Mora was also certain no cross-world transmissions would occur with this equipment. This had been her greatest concern. Her final breakthrough, which involved closing pathways into other worlds, made it possible to wind up this project. She still didn't have a clue how to differentiate between the multiverse. She assumed there must be many. But for now, all she cared about was the completion of her responsibilities to the university.

The day had come to celebrate her achievements, and oddly, a strange sort of loss possessed her. It was often like that when a project ended, but this was more so. This wasn't just some undergrad collaboration, it was her *baby*, the dream that had been her obsession for years, and the beating heart of her waking hours. Well, it wasn't the full realization of her passion project, but one step closer. She felt gratified and a little depressed all at once.

Mulling over these thoughts caused a sort of dislocation. She stood in the ballroom of the Journeyer Hotel, where guests were milling about waiting for the ceremony, some clustered at the tables having drinks and talking. Mora watched them distractedly, lost in her ruminations and future plans.

Her eyes landed on one of the invitations on a table nearby. "A remarkable scientific achievement. A technology to change the world." The project had been advertised to investors as the only significant invention to rival the alien bioscience. The anticipation and greed in the room were palpable. She felt the buzz of expectation, and her own excitement made her edgy.

Mora watched as the guests worked the room, looking for favors and contacts. Seful and Yaful Amun—the "science twins" from Zenda—were present. Both pretentious and eccentric, they had an undercurrent of something dubious about them. Algon had told her they were Golden born. Yaful dressed in a bright, flashy outfit that seemed out of character for a scientist. His brother was more understated in his attire and his behavior. Yet Mora didn't have respect for him either. His big smile and overly careful demeanor were spurious. She still didn't understand what their scientific research entailed. Everyone she asked gave her vague answers.

Curious as she might be about them, she did not want to approach or interact with the Zendali, and the majority of these guests were from Zenda. Businessmen or corporate representatives for the most part. She saw Asha's father Ziyad and her brother Tao chatting with some of them in whispered tones.

Someone in this room was the potential buyer, but she didn't know yet who had won the contract. Algon mentioned there was a fierce bidding war taking place with the University Board for the rights to manufacture. A whole delegation of businessmen from the Sovereign Zenda Nation and Territories arrived for this evening's festivities. They all hoped to influence the board members and gain favor. Expanding the portal transportation overseas would be monumental. Mora had not realized until this moment, as she looked around the room, that this was not about celebrating a scientific breakthrough. It was more about politics and money interests.

The university hadn't requested Mora's attendance at this ceremonial gathering. She never got an invitation, but she knew that Asha had. Mora just assumed she was expected, considering the fact that it was her design, her invention... and she had even helped to plan the event! Now that she was present, not a single member of the university had greeted her.

A little niggling doubt was lodged in her chest. Algon had been the one to ask her for help in choosing the location for the event and making the arrangements, not anyone on the board. The first signs of apprehension came when Algon and Asha picked her up, and they warned her to keep a low profile at the event.

How can I keep a low profile if this event celebrates my invention?

But she only nodded, assuming Asha worried about exposing her to all the Zendali nationalists who would be in attendance. As usual, Mora wore the garb of the Sisters' of

Justice with black veil and matching formfitting gloves. The gloves were so supple that she could easily use her hands as if they were bare.

Asha was busy talking to her father's guests. Ziyad was the Zendali Ambassador, and Mora knew he had personally hosted a couple of the investors who placed bids for production rights of the Portal Technology. *Algon must have risen in stature with the completion of this project and what it promised.* Mora thought as she noticed how Ziyad introduced Algon to the business executives.

Algon noticed Mora standing at the back of the room and joined her. She'd seen Bimisi working in the kitchens and pondered how she'd done such a botched dye-job on her fur. It obviously wasn't a professional job. The dye was wearing off in places. Looking more mottled and uneven. She looked at Algon, scrutinizing his perfect color job and remembering *her* Algon, who had much lighter fur.

"I can see you staring at me," he said.

"Through the veil?"

"Don't worry, I can't see the details, just your eyes and the vague shape of your features."

"Sorry." She paused but kept staring. "I'm wondering how the dye is applied so evenly."

"Why do you bring it up now?" he said, clearly annoyed. "We've already discussed this. I assume you're referring to my counterpart, who doesn't dye his fur?"

"How do you do it?"

Whispering loudly, he leaned into her. "You think I'm vain or caving to social pressure?"

Mora frowned at his defensive tone, confused about his attitude. She just wanted the information and wasn't judging him. "I'm not criticizing your choices."

He wrinkled his brow and said, "Well, not exactly." Now he looked somewhat vexed. "My family doesn't have close ties to Zenda." He smiled. "That is an understatement. I am being polite. They are also not supportive of my desire to work for a Zendali Corporation. As you see, they are not in attendance. And then there's Asha's father." He paused, clearly not wanting to say more about how they opposed Asha's relationship with a native youth. "I have to consider my position in the scientific community, the investors, the possible job offers."

"I'm not asking *why* you do it, but *how*."

He answered with a sigh. "There are businesses which specialize in fur and hair dying. I'm sure you've seen them in the city, but maybe didn't realize what they were? They have names like Indigo Glow, Dark Beauty, Jet, Obsidian Gem. They are all imports from Zenda with competing prices and variations in the way the color is applied and how long it lasts. The Zendali use them too because plenty of citizens of the Zenda Nation and Territories are lighter than what would be considered acceptable. The darkest fur is their standard of beauty. It's also the wisest choice if you plan to compete in the business world, where investors are Zendali. Appearance matters to them."

"It's all right, really," she said. "I'm sorry for making you uncomfortable. You have every right to partake in any cosmetic changes you wish, and what you choose is none of my business."

"You know, Zamora and I had a similar discussion. She didn't know I took the treatments; she never saw my natural color. But Zamora's family, who got her settled here, told her to continue dying her hair and pelt. If she'd been willing, it would've been much easier for her. She wouldn't have had to hide under those garments every day or limit who could be involved in her project. Her stubborn nature made life difficult for everyone who knew her."

"Oh." Mora nodded approvingly. "She wouldn't hide who she was then." This was a statement, not a question, because Mora understood. She also would not want to do those procedures to fit in. Regardless of the limited social life that choice imposed, she'd rather remain as she was.

"You and Zamora never considered or cared about what comes next, but that is all I think about! You're creative and original, and your physical limitations won't prevent you from finding work. Some insightful employers might look past your religious eccentricities because they value what you contribute. What happened at the university proves my point, doesn't it? You were allowed to stay because of this project."

"Algon, what are you getting at? What's upset you?"

"I am not that clever. No one will make such exceptions for me. I can barely assist you. Most of the time, I don't have a clue how you come up with your solutions." He shook his head in regret. "Before I met Zamora, I thought I was something special, top of my class and all that. But no, she made me realize I wasn't close to her brilliance. I need to curry favor in other ways."

After this emotional confession, Mora quietly considered him, then she reached out and put her hand on his wrist. "First of all, I don't know you as well as my Algon, but if you are anything like him, you are every bit my equal. You have a different way of seeing things, and it helps me put the pieces together. I need your insights, and if Zamora has not told you this, she needed you as well. We are a team."

Algon gave her a bewildered look. "Zamora never showed appreciation. I'm a little astonished by your praise, Mora. Thank you."

Dean Comcomly Hardihood spoke from the elevated stage. "May we have your attention?"

Everyone in the room turned toward a long table on a raised dais where the bigwigs sat. Department heads, and perhaps the winning investors, were looking at the Dean, who had stood up to get everyone's attention. The set-up reminded Mora of a wedding party.

"Before the celebration begins, we have some awards to present." Dean Hardihood looked smug, obviously enjoying the attention and being in control.

Mora unconsciously stood taller and straightened her garment and veil in expectation of walking in front of the crowd. Algon was joined by Asha, who suggested they all sit.

Their table was nearby, but Algon said, "When this is over."

The dean's gravelly voice rambled on about the virtues of each person on her team as he presented awards to them, praise that was overstated, in Mora's opinion, since they had not designed anything. But that was politics.

Then Algon's name was called. He walked to the front and onto the raised stage area where everyone in the room could see him. "And now for the genius behind the creation," Dean Hardihood said. "I present this award of achievement ..."

Mora looked around, confused. She felt a wave of sadness as Asha turned toward her. *She must have known!* Mora stood rigid and furious, waiting to see if they would call her next. But it was over. She would receive no acknowledgment, no award for her invention. Betrayal from the university was no surprise, but she didn't expect this double-cross from Algon! *How could he not insist they include me? Why didn't he at least warn me?* Asha reached out to her, but she roughly pulled away and stormed toward the kitchen, headed for the back exit.

Just as Mora was about to make her way through the archway, Bimisi brought out a tray. Mora saw a Zendali male seated with a delegation of important-looking foreigners. He was dressed in elegant attire and wore a huge gold pendant. Bimisi placed the tray on his table and stared at the delegate. His eyes grew wide at the sight of her green eyes and bad dye job. Mora rushed to the table as his look of surprise turned to anger.

He stood and shouted at Bimisi. "What are you?"

Fortunately, the room at this point was noisy with everyone talking, and no one else was alerted.

Mora quickly interceded and took Bimisi's arm. "You're needed in the kitchen." She moved swiftly away with Bimisi in tow, avoiding the stares of the other guests. "You'd better evade further notice by the delegation," she whispered. "Word of this will spread, and it might cause you some real trouble. Why did you look at him? Why were you even out there?"

"I didn't mean to. It was the jewelry. It's not made in Zenda."

Mora's anger at Algon was still burning. She barely paid attention to what Bimisi was saying. She felt her emotions were pushing against a dam that was ready to burst. She had to get out and go home, where she could grieve. She started to walk across the kitchen to the door.

"Wait!" Bimisi said. She ran closer and spoke softly. "I thought it over. I'd like your help. I need the implant."

Mora nodded. "I'll come here tomorrow. Can you be ready after the noon meal?" She realized she should get Bimisi into the lab before she no longer had access.

"I'll be ready, thank you."

When Mora stepped out into the alley behind the kitchens, she was confronted by a native with such malice on his face that she understood immediately he was a danger. She backed up toward to door and then froze. Her mind was so overwhelmed with animosity and regret that she didn't respond immediately to the threat. Her hesitation was a mistake.

He quickly closed the gap between them and pushed Mora against the wall, leaning in close to see through her veil. "What? You think these robes will protect you?"

First Kai and now this? *How do they know it's me?* She thought.

"Be careful who you protect, Zamora. I know what you are. You should be grateful I *want* you, despite your defects."

Seems like my ungrateful attitude is a shared belief. This must be Chayton.

"Know this," he said, "you can't save that mutt in there." He pulled at her veil, but she'd pinned it tightly. "Your clever ruse is easy to uncover, now that you don't have the University protecting you."

Mora shoved him, but he was too heavy. He laughed at her attempt, then leaned into her harder with a menacing smile. Mora's self-defense training finally surfaced. She was not going to be handled so roughly without a fight. She jammed her knee into the orifice where his reproductive organ was sheltered. This area of the male Hadot body was tender and sensitive. All her frustration and pent-up anger went into that jab.

His look of surprise was reward enough. As he pulled away, she swept his feet and shoved his shoulder, causing him to slam against the bins, then fall to the ground. Without further hesitation, she ran down the alley. Before crossing the intersection, she glanced back. Chayton was curled on his side in pain. Satisfied he wouldn't chase her, she continued home. All the way, thoughts of deception, betrayal, and threats were reeling through her mind.

I 've got to leave this world. I need to build a new machine!

32

The Implant

After fuming over the injustice of her situation, Mora realized she would most likely be locked out of the university immediately. Also, a recent attempt to break into the Bio Labs created a rumor that the university planned to code the doors with genetic markers to prevent Zendali from entering. This was the wing where she was planning to obtain an implant for her wayward traveler.

Mora decided she'd better do what she could for Bimisi before they denied her access. When she first suggested getting an implant for her refugee friend, she'd thought to ask Algon for his help. That was no longer an option. Mora wasn't sure she'd find the room where he'd taken her on the day of her arrival. What if she couldn't figure out how to implant it correctly?

When she arrived, everything happened in a disjointed jumble. *Can I even trust my memories from that day?* She left right away to pick up Bimisi at her lodgings. Going to the university at night, when no one was around, was best. It should give her time to figure it out. At the very least, she might take the implant for Bimisi and ask someone else to help.

She made it to the hotel without incident. Only a few tourists wandered the streets. Approaching the building at night, she admired how beautiful the crystalline structures were. This one was mostly opaque and glowed from within. Shadows of moving figures could be seen through the walls. She avoided the kitchen staff entrance in the alley and went for the main lobby instead.

The waiting room floor was transparent at night, showing a garden below. Mora recalled that the floor was opaque during the daytime. Now, at this hour the garden was closed and empty of tourists, *no one wandering around to look up your skirts*, she thought.

She told the front desk she wanted Bimisi's room, and they let her go back through the kitchen.

She walked through the scullery; it was dark after hours. When she turned the corner, someone grabbed her, pulling her into an alcove. At first, she struggled, thinking it was Chayton again. But he whispered, "Shush, it's me." In one quick movement, Kai flipped her veil up and started kissing her.

She moved her head aside and swallowed the bile that had risen with her fear. "You scared me. Why are you here?"

"I followed you. And came in through the kitchen." His expression sobered. "This wasn't a pleasant surprise, was it? Please forgive me, Zamora, I just miss you."

"I had an altercation earlier today with Chayton. He threatened me."

This made him angry. "I'll deal with it. I won't let him hurt you again."

"That is not your responsibility. I don't have time for whatever this is right now. Stop following me!" Mora pulled away, put her veil in place, then walked down the hall, leaving him standing there bewildered by her rejection. Again, she wondered, *how do they know who I am when I'm robed? Kai must be watching Zamora's house!*

The room by the laundry was around the corner. Mora pressed the door signal and heard it buzz on the other side. They didn't exactly have doors here like she was used to. They were ovals that irised open. Bimisi answered the signal, looking like she'd been asleep.

"Sorry, did I wake you?"

Disoriented and befuddled, Bi stood in the doorway, clearly trying to grasp the situation. "Morning prep in the kitchen starts early. I've had to go to bed right after the evening meal to keep up."

"Bimisi, I had expected to have the help of my lab partner to get your implant, but he's betrayed me, and I think I might be locked out of the university very soon. We need to go tonight and try to find it."

Bimisi reacted with surprise, her ear-fans flattening against her head. "Is that why you left before the party even got started?"

"Yes, it is. Can we leave now?" Just the mention of the incident brought the pain to the surface again.

"Hey, you can call me Bi. All my friends do."

Mora nodded distractedly. "Urgency and tribulation don't get along well, and I'm exhausted. We should go." Without another word, Mora headed for the lobby.

Bi hurried to catch up, but once outside the hotel, she took the lead. Pointing toward a rack of pedal bikes, she asked: "Do you know how to ride, Mora? These would get us to the University faster."

Mora looked askance at them. She knew how to ride a bike in her world, but these were different. "I'm sure I can figure it out."

They took a path along the canal; it was lit by soft glow strips along the side. The surrounding area was obscured in the shady gloom of night. Moonlight glow shifted through the tall trees, throwing patterns on the path. Branches rustled in the wind, reflecting Mora's agitated mood. She felt as if someone were lurking in the dark. She rode harder and faster, rushing through the quivering shadows. A sense of urgency kept her alert.

They parked the bikes with others at the university. Mora pressed her key disk to the door and was relieved that it allowed them entry. She first went back to the room where the original lab had been. It was still blocked off and had not been restored. She turned back, retracing the steps she had blindly taken that first night with Algon. Turning to enter the other wing, through some double doors, and then she used her key disk on the first door on her right. Nothing happened. It would not open.

Deflated and concerned she might not be able to access the room, she tried the next door down. To her relief, it pinged open. She nudged Bi into the lab. Not wanting to alert any security guards, if they had them, she turned on a small light over the workstation and began to search the bins along the wall where she thought Algon had taken the implant. Then she found a cold storage canister with small packets. On close inspection, she thought they must be what she was after. No label on the package to confirm, but the instructions spelled out the process that Algon used on her.

She found the alcohol, swabbed Bi's neck in the place just below the back of the skull where the fur was rubbed bare. Mora extracted the little jellyfish-looking thing. And pushed it against Bi's neck. It was fascinating to watch the implant insert itself. The little tendrils moved into her flesh and submerged. Only a reddish bump was visible now.

"How do you feel?"

"It feels like worms in my brain... The sensation is moving down my neck and spine. It tingles a little."

"It was the same for me, then it seems to be working."

"Hey, I'm understanding your speech more clearly now!"

"You sound better when you speak, too. You'll have access to the most common local languages and the Zenda prime as well. I added more to my implant here at the university. Because I have Zenda blood, I don't have access to the Floaters that allow citizens of Wendat to download more languages and mind-maps. But you told me you're not Fog like me? So, you might be able to use them, you should try."

"I'll try." Bi said this with a hint of doubt.

Mora was observing her. She still wondered where Bi had come from. She'd decided maybe one of her parents had mixed with the Pink, which she assumed was not permissible according to the United Tribes of Wendat's treaty with The Sovereign Zenda Nation. "We should go. Do you want to stay the night at my place? I'm not far from here."

Bi was shaking her head, which made Mora realize the head signals—nodding and shaking—were a common body language in their worlds.

"I still have early morning work in the kitchen. I should return tonight." At that moment, Bi noticed her fur, and as Mora had done not long before, she completely lost her composure. "Oh, what is this? I'm a mess of different colors! Oh no! Why didn't you tell me?"

"I assumed you knew the dye you applied was uneven," Mora said. "I asked about local businesses that specialize in dyeing fur, in case you want to use them."

Bi didn't seem to be listening to the suggestion.

"You are beautiful!" Bi blurted out with obvious amazement.

Mora smirked at the compliment. "I'm not used to hearing such things."

"This is going to take some getting used to! I didn't expect it would affect my senses." Bi told her. "Thank you for this. I know it was a risk. I hope you won't be in trouble for helping me."

"I won't be if no one finds out, so please keep it between us. I'm still worried that you are in jeopardy at that hotel. Now that you have the implant, we can find you another job, and better accommodations."

"Don't worry about me. I'm happy where I am, and I better get going."

They exited the building. Bi took one of the bikes and headed toward the city center. Mora watched until she was out of sight. *Why are you so willing to live and work in that place when you're obviously in danger?*

When Mora entered Zamora's place, the wall com signaled. Multiple messages flashed expectantly for her attention. Scanning them, she saw that most were from Asha, and two were from Algon. It listed three messages from the University: Professor Bly, Vice

President Istas Moki, and Dean Hardihood. Also, one from security. She supposed it was too much to hope that they wanted to apologize for not crediting her for their amazing Portal Invention. Mora didn't know whether to laugh or cry.

She didn't have the energy to deal with this tonight.

33

Conjecture & Misfortune

Seful was a Golden-born Zendali, he was also a twin. Which was rare. Both he and his brother were scientists. Both were in Wendat to gain insight into the alien technology. Neither of them had made any headway. Seful had been in Wendat long enough to be distressed at his lack of advancement. He'd been trying to acquire a sample of the alien implant with the hope of reverse engineering it. The long-term plan was to create an implant that would shut down certain brain functions. Which would help control the Pink workforce. Thus eliminating any disobedience. He'd been conducting experiments for over a year. Because all efforts to obtain a detached sample had failed, he'd been removing them from Pinks. Young members of the Order of Amon Kuroo had recruited native youth to get the Pinks he needed for experimentation.

The implants died when removed. So did the host. It was a lot of trouble for nothing. The entire process was annoying. Pinks born and raised on the Wendat reservations still had their claws. He had taken pleasure in pulling them out. The little heathens had to be muzzled as well. They were not the docile subjects he had used in his experiments in Zenda.

The Order had Zendali students at the university, and at Seful's request, they had tried to break into the science wing where the implants were grown and stored. Unfortunately, it was not successful, and now measures were being taken to block the Zendali genetic signatures from entry to that entire area.

He was just cleaning up his work area after completing his recent extraction. A naked Pink female lay on his laboratory table, her sightless eyes retained a haunted look of desperation. Fluids from the neck wound filled the drainage trough. He was just about to call for someone to dispose of the body when his receptor buzzed. Distractedly, he whipped the blood from his hands on his lab coat and pressed the button to accept the call.

"I just followed someone who broke into the science wing where the implants are kept."

This was one of the Wen recruited by the Amon Kuroo, who had tried and failed to get him a sample of the implant from the university laboratory. He was well-placed. With a job in building security. Excitement and agitation surged through Seful as he tried to find out the details. "Did you follow them? Can you get the sample?"

"There were two of them, one who was dressed as a follower of Bicara, and the other took off on a bike toward the city."

Furious at the inadequacy of this answer and the ineptitude in general, he nearly lost his composure. "Did you see where either of them went?"

I followed the Sister of Justice toward the Zendali compound. I assume it was Tao's sibling."

"You assume?"

"I'm sorry, sir, I thought you could follow up."

Seful ended the call without further comment, furiously shoving the table, causing the Pink to roll off and land in a heap on the floor.

He shouted toward the door. "Get in here and clean this up!"

34

JUSTIFICATIONS

M ora woke late. Depressed and unmoored, she wanted to stay in bed and do nothing. Now the project was finished, and she had essentially completed her graduate work. There was nothing she *had* to do. No place she needed to rush off to. She finally went downstairs and was in the process of making herself a huge breakfast when the door announced a visitor. She took a peek at the security screen. Asha stood by her door. She hadn't yet reviewed the messages from the day before. Picking up the disc, she signaled the door to let Asha in.

Mora didn't greet her guest. At the same time, she heard her mother's voice in her head saying she was being inhospitable. Perhaps, but she didn't invite Asha to come. She kept her back to her visitor while she made a cup of Kav, which Asha didn't drink. Of course, Asha was going to side with Algon and Mora didn't know where that left their friendship.

"Algon was an idiot"

Mora's ear-fans perked to attention at this unexpected statement. She turned and gave Asha an inquisitive look, still feeling reserved, holding in her anger. She could think of nothing polite to say. Turning back to her Kav, she added some real cream, stirred, and took her breakfast plate and Kav to the table. "You know where the tea and cups are."

Asha nodded and went through the motions of making herself tea. Staying silent, as if gathering her courage or thinking about how to approach the problem. She joined Mora at the table, watching her eat and sipping her tea.

"He's not species-phobic. He just doesn't get involved in politics, which is our one point of contention."

"What do you mean by species-phobic?"

"I believe you used the term racist? But for the Zenda, the Pinks are more like livestock. The official position of the Purebloods, categorize the Pinks as a different species." Seeing Mora's look of consternation, Asha held up her hand to stop her complaint. "I agree it's bad science. You do understand the university is not giving you credit only because they found out Zamora's Fog? Once they discovered what she was, they could not abandon the project because too much money was already invested, not to mention the profits they expected to gain from the finished product."

"It is *my* invention. It could not have been created without me. They called Algon a genius! They gave me no credit whatsoever! And... he *accepted* the award!"

"I know, and the situation isn't fair. But regardless, there are a few things you need to accept." She held up her hand, her little finger raised. "First, Zamora understood this would be the outcome, and she went forward anyway." Ticking off each item on her fingers: "two, Algon warned her to continue dyeing her pelt and mane so the university wouldn't find out what she was. She didn't want to and didn't care. Because she believed they needed her so badly, they would not be able to retaliate. She was carelessly reckless and proud. Three, Wendat has treaties with Zenda, which are already stretched by the formation of reservations to protect the refugees, both Pinks and Fog. By challenging the university and tricking them into accepting Zamora as a student, her family not only put her in danger but also everyone who knew what she was. The university was just biding its time until the project was completed. When they no longer needed her or *your* expertise... of course, they quickly disassociated themselves to protect the school. How could you expect they wouldn't?" Asha paused to let all of that sink in, looking at Mora with sober concern.

Mora had stopped eating. She glared at Asha, but her tension was letting go. Her friend's message was sinking in. Maybe she had no right to be offended because even though she took the project to completion, none of this was hers.

"Unfortunately, you have to face the repercussions of your counterparts' choices. Zamora was self-centered and focused on only one thing: her work. Four," Asha continued to tick off points by raising another finger. "Algon admired her, but she was not inclusive. She did not support him the way you have. He told me what you said to him last night, how you appreciate your lab partner, his counterpart, and that you were a team, how you feel the same about him. That was not Zamora's attitude. She was condescending and treated everyone on her team dreadfully, including Algon. Like they were beneath her level of intelligence. I doubt she realized how it came across. She wasn't intentionally unkind, but her capacity for social interaction was limited by her inexperience and isolation. She had no grace or consideration when it came to other people's feelings. Five, despite all of her flaws, we protected her secrets, and we genuinely cared about her. We are your friends too, Mora. Algon did not appreciate being put in such a compromising situation by the university, but he didn't think he was in a position to object."

Mora sat in silence. All the fight had gone out of her, she was bewildered by the realization that she really had no grounds for her indignation. This was not her world or her project. It was Zamora's. She had been relating to the incident as if it were *her* loss, but it actually had nothing to do with her, and Zamora had set herself up for this. As disappointing as it felt, Mora realized she had to disengage from the ownership of the university portal project. She'd spent years developing her own portal, where deep attachments developed because she thought of it as her one great life achievement. But maybe she had more to give, other things to create.

"You're right. This is not my fight, and it is not my project or my world. But I'm stuck here with the consequences of what Zamora set up. I don't see a way forward. What comes next? All I have is defeat and loss. How do I navigate a life I don't own? There's still so much I don't understand about living here."

"Well, I can help you. So can Algon."

Mora smiled a little. "I shouldn't be, but I am still angry with Algon."

"Just give it some time."

Mora nodded. "I didn't ask you if you had breakfast. Can I cook you some eggs?"

"You're not a good cook, Mora."

Mora smirked. "I never had to cook for myself. Fenmore loved cooking."

"You've never talked much about him. What was he like?" Seeing Mora's sad face, she realized her inquiry wasn't exactly welcome. "Oh, I'm sorry. You must miss him?"

"Yes." She didn't elaborate. Her eyes stared at her hands, which were folded in her lap. She was holding back her tears, but her chin trembled. Finally, she said, "For a while when I first got here, I had access to the research facilities, so I tried to find him, to see if he was living in this world."

Asha looked surprised. "And did you find him?!"

Mora nodded. "I did. He and his family are residents of the ZendaPharm Corporation."

"A resident? Not a doctor or scientist?" Her pupils expanded from a slit, to full dilation. Signaling her full attention. "You mean he's a Pink?"

"Yes, he is. Our word for the light furred is Ocha."

Asha's ear-fans had perked up with interest. "But *how* did you find him?"

"I was astonished their database wasn't secure. There was nothing stopping me from accessing those records." Mora admitted.

"It's public information because Zendali employers or other research facilities may need access. Of course, Pinks are not taught to use it, even if they could get access. At this point, the Zenda nation as a whole is overly confident about the lies and secrets that have become normalized in that society. Even the Pinks take it as their lot, with few complaints." Asha explained.

"My partner has an old-fashioned name, Fenmore, Fen for short. I didn't expect him to have the same identity here, but I had to start somewhere."

Asha stared at her in awe. "Did he?" She cocked her head to the side, an inquisitive gesture. "They generally don't allow heritage designations."

"So, I've heard, but oddly, Fenmore *was* recorded, with a notation following it that said Ikoo. Someone in the facility gave him a pet name."

"Pinks are forbidden to use the names of their ancestors," Asha confirmed. "This was one way to erase their cultural ties."

Mora nodded. "But his parents had nevertheless used the family namesake in private. The residents don't seem to realize they have no privacy. Everything is recorded and documented. Still, I wouldn't have been certain this was my lover's counterpart if it weren't for the attached photo on his identification document. Ikoo was smiling in that picture. It felt wrong that he was so happy when, essentially, he was a test animal!"

Mora's eyes were filled with tears that she'd tried to hold back.

"Then I researched what their life was like and reviewed the contracts they signed to live in the facility. Even if I could visit Zenda, I would not be able to see him. I finally realized he'd be nothing like my love. Fen's counterpart here was raised in isolation and without education."

"Knowing what you do... about *my* country, I'm surprised you would look for him."

"I don't have anyone here who loves me like he does... he *adores* me. I didn't even appreciate his attention or know how lucky I was until I lost him. I sometimes wonder if Zamora," she stared into Asha's eyes, communicating her worries more clearly than any words could, "is with him."

Asha understood the implication and decided to change the topic. "Look, I have an idea. I've been working with a friend; we help with the reservations. Would you like to join us? We planned a trip out to the closest one tomorrow."

"What kind of work are you doing, and how are you allowed on a reservation? I thought they were off-limits to the Zenda."

"Normally they are, yes, and I did have to get special permission because I'm Zendali. Tokala Luta, who is the second apprentice of the powerful and famous Holata Tyee, vouched for me. I am Zenda by birth, *but* I grew up here in Muwioni. Even though I cannot be a citizen of this country, I am more Wen than Zendali. Tokala is my best friend. They assigned her to assist the people on the reservations with medical needs. She claims I'm there to assist her, which gets me in, but I have a different intent, and she approves."

Mora raised her eye ridge, waiting for Asha to continue...

"I come from a country which is guilty of countless injustices. This led me to my dual majors of history and anthropology. I suppose I was trying to understand why my people behaved as they did, but there isn't any excuse. This leaves me with my self-appointed purpose of making restitution. That's the Wen way. I grew up here and share their values. I came to realize there were too many lies about the fair races. I want to change that. They lost their culture and history. Zenda purposely rewrote our histories to make Pinks look like they had no higher learning skills, no cultural advancements, no civilizations! Zenda children think we discovered the Pink territories and found barbaric heathens there. Furthermore, they were taught a false purpose. Our history says the Zenda took these wild creatures to give them a better life with structure and protection. Which justifies their enslavement. Our science justifies the same false narrative. Then I met Zamora, and I realized how ridiculous it all was. The Pinks are not any less capable. They just don't have a chance to get an education!"

Asha had raised her voice during her passionate disclosure. She drew a deep, calming breath and continued. "I have been trying to pull together information for the immigrants, anything I can find about their countries before they became Zenda territories, before the expansion wars. It is of course forbidden, and my father would skin me alive if he found out."

"That is amazing, Asha! Did Zamora know about this?"

"No, not really. I wanted to tell her, but she was always so focused on her own work. Sometimes I mentioned my history studies, and my interest in ancient cultures, and she heard I had some involvement with the reservations. I mean, I tried multiple times to open that conversation... but since she never seemed to care about what I was doing, I didn't end up telling her much."

"Yes, I want to go. I am very interested, and I can contribute. If you will let me, I would like to help you build, what do you call it, a database? Or is it a mind-map?"

"It is a mind-map because the information can be transferred to the implants, and becomes a memory. It is not the same as a database where information is stored outside of yourself. There are still old archival depositories of information at the universities here, but they're rarely accessed because the implants are easier. In Zenda, all they have is the old system: digital data and old archived ledgers, books, and such. Few people are implanted there. The Zenda calls it a Digital Information Archive. That's what you used at the university when you looked for the people from your world, right?"

Mora nodded. "Yes, it was easy to access, and similar to what we have in my world."

"I am really happy you're interested and willing to help!"

"Thank you, Asha. This will take my mind off my other problems. I have to stop being focused on my disappointment and worries. I need a project... and this is perfect." She reached out and touched Asha's hand. "Also, thank you for setting me straight about Zamora. I had made some incorrect assumptions."

Asha's eyes filled with tears. She shook her head a little. "No, Mora, you could not have known. This is a difficult situation you walked into. I'm just happy you understand now. We will come by to get you tomorrow morning."

Asha got up and headed for the door... then suddenly turned around. "Oh, I keep meaning to introduce you to someone I met through Tokala. She's a seer and an artist. I'm not sure how exactly, but she's connected to you."

Mora had a puzzled expression. Introductions outside their circle were unexpected. "I assume if you want us to meet, you trust her?"

Asha had a pensive expression. "I don't even know her. But yes, for some inexplicable reason, I do."

"Asha, is Tokala Luta informed about Zamora? That she's Fog?"

"Yes, they've met, and she will keep that secret, as we have."

"Has she heard about *me*? Or will she think I'm Zamora?"

"I have not told her about you. I wouldn't know how to explain, and anyway, it is not my story to tell."

35

RUMINATIONS

Mora missed her Fenmore. The emptiness was a constant ache. Trying not to think about the fact she might never see him again just made her ruminate more about all the special little things he did when they were together. And she realized how much she'd taken for granted. He was always supportive, easy-going, and somehow knew her mood. Fen genuinely cared about her. Even though he had his own things going on, he tried to make their relationship a priority. He was a scientist with a specialization in vaccine research for infectious diseases. His work was impressive, but most of the time, he had pretty routine hours. She couldn't help contrasting her lover, the scientist, with Ikoo the subject of scientific research. In both cases, they worked for pharmaceutical companies.

Lately, without her project to occupy her mind, whenever she was alone, she was thinking of Fen, wondering if he realized she was gone, or if he thought Zamora was her. Remembering how he was never too busy for her, how he would look at her when she talked, never distracted with his Mobi or the Video Station, he was actually present, body and mind. He heard every word and paid attention to every expression. No matter what she was venting about, he would really listen to her. She didn't realize at the time how remarkable that was.

When she made her cup of Kav in the mornings here, alone in the house, she thought of him, and how he used to bring her a Kav or hot tea and say all the right things. He had a way of asking questions, which made her take a different perspective about whatever troubled her. He was her compass, and he kept her on track.

Fen had never had a friend like her, who could cite the documents word-for-word, pulling the information from memory to back up her statements. Mora laughed a little now, remembering the expression he had whenever she challenged him with the reference material. She loved being able to confound him. It was a sort of good-natured dare and defiance. Mora smiled at the memory, yet she had never felt this degree of heart-rending sadness. She sighed, knowing how unhealthy it was to mull over what was lost, yet she could not imagine losing the intimacy of that relationship forever. She had to find her way back to him.

After discovering what Fen called her "magic powers," he often used her to make a point during friendly debates when they were in the company of his colleagues and buddies, asking her for the specific information he needed to justify his argument. She missed everything: the attention, the comfort, the sex, even the arguments. Most of all, she missed the simple fact that he *knew* her and treated her with pure... was it devotion? There isn't an accurate word for it... ardor, esteem, affection. They were well-matched and had hardly ever argued or fought, and when they disagreed, they'd talked it through.

It was clear that Zamora's situation with men was complicated. Mora thought about the run-in with Kai, who grabbed her in the dark alcoves of the scullery when she went to find Bi. He leaned into her, purring with lust. His kiss was passionate, obviously expecting the sexual relationship he'd had with her counterpart to continue. He wouldn't be easily dissuaded.

More disturbing were the lewd comments and threats of Chayton, who still seemed to be stalking her. He was vulgar, and his attitude was sexually charged. His insinuation that they had unfinished business would have to do with what Asha had told her about the attempted rape of Zamora. He exhibited deviant behavior, which was out of the ordinary for this country.

Then, in contrast, there was Ohpa, who had stopped hounding her but would occasionally send her hopeful messages asking to meet with her. His proposal was honest and considerate, and she sensed that he deeply cared.

Zamora definitely had an active and varied sexual life, despite being Fog. But none of these men were in the least bit attractive to Mora.

36

LOCKED OUT

When Mora finally got around to listening to her messages, she wasn't surprised to find that Dean Hardihood had requested a meeting and asked her to bring her entry disks with her. The message was cold, blunt, and to the point.

Mora prepared for the meeting with Zamora in mind. She remembered Algon had told her that Zamora had been promised a degree, but she found no record of an undergraduate diploma, and now she had finished the course work for her graduate studies and project, which in her world would have given her a doctoral degree.

When Mora entered the conference room, she was surprised to see other professors and members of the science department, not just Professor Bly, who had overseen their project. Dean Hardihood, Director Delsin, President Pool, and her vice President Istas Moki, were all seated at the table with Algon. The room was crowded. She took the only empty chair. Dressed in her black garb with veil. They could not view her face, and she imagined this unnerved them to some degree. They could not get a read on her mood.

Dean Hardihood's voice was like a bark, sudden and sharp. "Your project is complete. We expect you to return all related property regarding the portal technology and your access disks for the department." His disdain was clear. He didn't want to waste any time with her as if he were just dumping out the trash. He'd gathered everyone in the department who could back him up on this maneuver. It was almost comical how he wanted to make a show of strength, but his body language told her he was far from self-assured.

"You are referring to *my* invention," Mora said, "which you chose not to credit me for, and you have stolen?"

The dean looked perturbed. But it was President Pool who answered. "The invention is university property, not yours. Did you honestly think we would give credit to a pretender such as yourself and take on the risk that would cause?"

"Fascinating word choice, *pretender*, considering you are all pretending you had the knowledge and ability to create the portals. I would say you're guilty of that, not me."

"You pretended to be a Pureblood Zenda," Hardihood said. "We would not have accepted you if we'd known what you are. We would never choose to break our treaty with the Sovereign Nation."

"My benefactor paid you generously for taking the risk." She could not admit that Ekon Darego was Zamora's grandfather. That would put her family at risk. It was bad enough he had called her his ward.

"They paid us generously without telling us we were taking a risk," said Pool. "We are doing them a favor by not reporting them."

"You are protecting the university, not them," Mora said. "So don't deceive yourselves into thinking you're generous. Speaking of which, you promised me a degree from this university, before and after you were aware that I am Fog."

They visibly cringed at the word, clearly not wanting to be associated with the unfavorable designation. Which made her wonder if Dean Hardihood had told the other professors whom he'd pulled into this meeting *why* they were treating her with such harsh disregard.

Hardihood looked to the department heads for support. "We cannot give the Fog a degree from this institution. It would set a precedent. It would challenge the treaty. We can't take the liability of that kind of exposure."

"Then you admit you lied to get what you wanted? You promised the degree to manipulate me, so I would complete my work."

Professor Bly said, "Zamora, you must understand what a difficult position you have put us in?"

Then the vice president, Moki, turned to Bly. "No, she's right. We knew when we met with her last that we had no intention of rewarding her. She has every right to be upset."

Everyone at the table looked at her, a little bewildered. Evidently, she was notorious for disputing the board's decisions, because President Pool said, "Not now, Istas."

All the board members and department heads stared at Mora. Obviously at a loss for words.

They didn't expect a Fog to argue these points. Mora thought to herself. She was coming to understand that Pinks were compliant creatures in this world. And the Fog were content to be hidden and safe. In either case, they would never be confrontational.

Then Algon stood. He looked calm, but Mora noticed his frustration as his claws tapped nervously on the table.

"First," he said, "I want to point out that the invention *was* the property of the university until ownership was given to the company which will produce the portals. You have relinquished your rights. If you do not give Zamora what she was promised, I will make sure no further profits come to the university, other than the award bonus you have already received for *gifting* it. Any profit sharing is discretionary at this point, as there have been no formal documents signed with the university."

He had everyone's attention. Some were obviously not aware of these conditions and looked at each other with curious or angry expressions.

"It was greedy of you to make that deal," he said. "Choosing a percentage of profits instead of a one-time payout. But that means you will receive nothing more unless you honor your promise to Zamora. I'm sure you can understand this means you have a great deal more to lose by not honoring your word to her. You've told everyone I am the creator, and I assure you, they will listen to my advice. Since this discussion is about honoring verbal agreements, you will honor yours with Zamora. Award her the diplomas as promised. She has more than earned them, or no one will honor their verbal agreements with you. Furthermore, it's unlikely anyone will discover she is Fog, unless *you* tell them." He looked directly at the dean. "She has no reason to reveal her identity, which would put herself in danger."

Mora was trying not to laugh under her veil. The whole department was staring at Algon in astonishment. She supposed they didn't know he had it in him. He's normally unobtrusive. They all thought they were using him, but maybe it was the other way around? While she was still unhappy with the whole situation, she wasn't angry with him at the moment.

Mora stood, dropped the entry disks on the conference table, and walked out. She had nothing more to say to them.

***

The next day when Algon showed up with Asha and Tokala, he had Mora's diplomas in hand.

"I'm not going with you," he said. "I just came to give you these. Can we talk sometime soon?"

Mora nodded. "Thank you for what you did for Zamora."

He looked surprised. "For Zamora?"

"I can't let myself believe I'll be here indefinitely."

Then he looked down, but nodded his understanding. He knew there wasn't much here for her to build a life on, and she was too brilliant to be content with less. "I really am sorry."

"I know," she said.

37

The Long Game

In Wendat, a dangerous joint effort had begun with Ziyad at the lead. He had been tasked as the Provost and Judge to deal with a problem in Wendat. His son Tao and daughter Asha had come to this country when they were too young to be fully indoctrinated into the ways of his ancestors. He had been personally responsible for guiding Tao. Ziyad was proud of his son's progress. But Asha had come under the influence of a cult called the Sisters' of Justice, and it felt as if she were lost to him. He had ignored it up to a point, expecting her to get tired of hiding under those dark robes and veil. But she hadn't, and now he was getting some disturbing reports about her which he could not ignore.

"The Order of Amon Kuroo is an ancient tradition into which you have all become young stewards. Until recently, we were a secret society known only to royalty and certain members of the upper class in Zenda." Ziyad was speaking to Tao and a group of young Zenda students who were here in Wendat with their parents. These families received entry visas under a ruse of business contracts but were actually part of the Order and under Ziyad's direction.

"How or when it emerged isn't recorded, but yes, we are credited with prompting the expansion wars." This was in answer to a question... one of many this evening. Ziyad's patience was wearing thin. Tao at least knew the history of the Order. *I should put my son in charge of these meetings*, he thought. But to do so, he needed to officially assign Tao the role of Master Traveler, and that required a ceremony. Making time for the rites and customs had not been at the top of his priorities, but he needed to reconsider that. If Tao were to take a leadership role, he could take over the tutelage of these youths.

"If the goal was the eradication of all Hadot species who were not pureblood, and their extermination was sanctioned by kings during that era, why were the Pinks spared at all?"

Ziyad didn't know the young Zendali's name, but he glanced at Tao with disgust, and Tao got the point and shrugged. The answer was obvious, and Ziyad was tired of ignorant children, and even *more* appalled by those who were not astute enough to understand what the Zenda Nation had built. He ignored the question and moved on; he wanted to get this meeting over.

"We are now generations past the expansion, with new objectives and challenges to face. We were sent here because the Wendat Government Council has disrespected our relationship with the Pinks, and you all know what that means. But something unexpected has occurred in Zenda. So, let me just get to the point of this meeting."

Now he finally had the rapt attention of the youth in the room. A few of the older members sat in the back, having drinks and watching with little interest, as they had already heard the news.

"Prince Nakhadot Hotep Kemel is coming of age. I have received a report that he is not being cooperative. His mother has been acting dowager queen after the death of King Nebtawi, and she has always done as she is told. But it seems that the prince has the same disposition as his father, despite all efforts to control his education."

Tao asked with concern. "Are we being recalled?"

At least his son understood the gravity of the situation. The Order of Amon Kuroo had been in control of Zenda for too long to give it up now. Despite who was on the throne, the Order was the true governing force of the country. They acted as advisors to the royals, but when advice wasn't taken, other pressures were brought to bear until they had the oversight required to rule.

"Nakhadot's ideas are dangerously disruptive and broad in scope. It is suspected that once crowned as king, he will advocate giving choice and rights to the Pinks, which will undermine the very fabric of our society."

Needless to say, the members of the Order would never let such a leader be crowned. The Amon Kuroo represented the traditional views of the Originalists, the religion of Wandrona, and the preservation and purity of their race.

"Nakhadot will never gain enough support to derail our long-held position." One of the elder Zendali spoke from the back.

"Likely not." Ziyad agreed. "But he will be an annoyance that must be dealt with."

He had not answered Tao's question. He addressed his son's concern next. "More and more Pinks have been escaping from the territories and making their way to Wendat. And, as you know, the government here has chosen to give them sanctuary. To outwardly oppose the native council might end our treaty. Which would mean we would no longer be welcome and would not have access."

The elders had come forward now, drinks in hand. They nodded and mumbled a few solemn comments, which Ziyad didn't quite hear.

"Our long-term plans concerning the situation in Wendat are too far advanced to terminate. We will proceed with our efforts here, but some families must return home."

Now the elders looked at each other wondering whose lives would be uprooted to deal with things back in Zenda.

"Before that happens, we have a ceremony to conduct. My son will take the role of Master Traveler. Thereafter, Tao will have complete charge of directing the local efforts with our young stewards."

38

OMENS OF CHANGE

The endeavor to adjust the Hadot native's behavior with implants had not been a complete failure. The Interstellar Alliance found they worked as expected for *most* people. Implant technology was an invention of the Ziv. They had been used in other sectors with different alien species with far better results. The Ziv had spent a considerable effort to acquire the Durga delegation's approval. Now, the fact that some implants were splintered was a concern. They had not been entirely successful. Unfortunately, certain Hadot individuals resisted the blunting of aggression. They called this splintering because the implant was not defective in general, but one *splinter* of its operation didn't serve as it should, to inhibit a bias for hostility.

The Durga, Ziv, and Elo debated among themselves about the inhabitants of Hadot, and those individuals with tendencies toward violence.

"It is part of the animal brain." The Ziv delegate, Prea, said.

"Self-preservation mechanisms work in tandem with aggressive behavior. The impulse to defend themselves can only be blunted so far." The Durga Superior Doyen, Mulu, argued.

Prea, the Ziven delegate, spoke with a discouraged posture: "It is an awkward admission that the implant technology is still imperfect. It's a work in progress. Having to make such a report to the Ziven Principal Senior was something I had hoped to avoid."

Mulu had long been belaboring his position, but the Ziv had not agreed. "The Zendali aggression can't be expunged with the appliance we've used on other species. We need to alter the implants to account for the differences in their genetics."

"Perhaps we can adjust future implants," Prea relented. "But what of those currently in use who can splinter? We must modify in another way."

The other point of contention was about how severely to correct the behavior of the people who had become a disruptive force in Wendat.

"True," Mulu told Prea, "the Zendali fanatics encourage some Wen youths to resist and splinter. Yet, it's against the Alliance Creed to interfere."

"The Zendali are conducting malevolent maneuvers in Wendat! We have only just begun to make progress there!"

The other Ziv delegates reacted with alarm, noting Prea's frustration. She was not usually impassioned and rarely spoke with such indignation.

The Durga kept their composure. "Removing the Zendali who have legal visas under Wendat law is not possible, nor can we tell the Council what we have learned."

"But we can insist on modifying the implants to prevent further harm."

Mulu had to comply. He had no better recommendation. Prea would force corrective measures on the council despite his warning.

39

Recalcitrance

When the Extrasolar delegation arrived in Muwioni to meet with the council, a different sort of debate took place. Coso Winnemucca reminded the Star People that the United Tribes of Wendat didn't have a system of punishment in keeping with their proposal.

The alien alliance insisted on the modifiers regardless of their recalcitrance, because they hinted that they knew things the council did not, which they also refused to divulge.

Council elder Mato was the father of one youth in question. He was speaking with sincerity and hoped to sway the direction of this meeting. "Giving support and encouragement for the right behavior is our way. Only in extreme cases do we banish a citizen if they refuse help and continue to cause harm."

The Alien delegation, however, would not change their minds. It was the first time in Wendat history that the demands of the Star People had caused disharmony and indecision among the council members.

By the time Council Elder Coso escorted the alien delegation from the council chambers, half the afternoon had passed. The Durga, Ziv, and Elo walked by the native youth who had been waiting in boredom outside the chambers. The three of them were stunned to see Star People exit.

Coso motioned, inviting them to follow her into the chambers. Chayton, Kinache, and Askook had something in common. They were able to splinter. When they were seated, Chayton's father spoke.

"The youth of Wendat have been raised with philanthropic principles. You were taught to be generous and helpful, to safeguard the weak and guard against abuse. This is why we shelter and protect the Pinks." In truth, Mato had no proof these youths had been involved in anti-Pink activities. All reports were inconclusive, nothing more than conjecture. But the Star People had singled them out and made it impossible to refuse this *correction measure*, as they had called it.

In front of the three chairs, a long table had been placed. White rings, large enough to be bracelets, were set before each of them. At a signal from Mato, manacles snapped closed over the three young Wen, their arms and ankles suddenly immobile. Shocked by this unexpected restraint, they all struggled.

Mato, feeling it was his duty, came forward to deliver the judgment. "The devices before you are new accessories, which will work in tandem with your implants. We will use them on any individual who can splinter."

Chayton pleaded with his father. "What do you think we did? Are we experimental animals now?"

Askook spoke in a whisper to Kinache. "The Order assured us the council had no evidence of our crimes!"

"Shut your mouth. They'll hear you."

Coso came forward when she saw Mato hesitate. "Maybe now you can appreciate how Pinks feel about being test subjects? But you needn't worry. The modifier is completely safe."

Kinache said, "My mother has the full power of—"

Coso interrupted him before he finished his objection. "Your mother has been notified that you are here and informed of your punishment. She did not attempt to stop these proceedings."

Only Askook sat silently, brooding and scowling.

She continued with her explanation. "The devices which you see on the table before you were designed to yoke with your implants. As mentioned, they're called modifiers, but it might be more appropriate to call them empathy amplifiers. If you're involved in causing harm to anyone, you will feel their pain. It will be unavoidable, and you will suffer whatever they experience. This includes the harm that you might do to animals. So, I would say your hunting days are over. They will be installed on your dominant arm so that you'll be reminded not to cause injury. If you do, the agony you experience will be significant."

"You can't make us wear them!" Kinache spit these words out with so much hostility he was shaking. Followed by a string of curses about Pinks.

"Oh, but we can, they will be implanted today, and it is irreversible. If you try to remove them, the modifier will kill you." With this declaration, all three of them fell silent. They suddenly realized the severity of their situation.

Coso nodded to the other council members, each taking a device from the table. These thin white circles fell open when lifted. The bands were threaded under the manacles and placed around their right arms. The ends met on the inside of their wrists. When the band was released, the ring seemed to melt through their fur and merged with their flesh.

All three young Wen cried out. These were not the gentle tingling sensations of the implants. The modifiers stung. The pain climbed up their arms, leaving a trace of white webbing in the wake of the modifier's flow. Both the flesh and the fur bleached to white as the sensation continued to travel all the way up, across their shoulders, and around their neck, finally connecting with the implants at the base of their skulls. The band was partly submerged, and the circle became a welt around their wrist. The white webbing was visible on their arms, like a bolt of lightning. "This will become known as the Sign of the Splintered. You won't be able to cover it with dyes; it will emerge through anything applied to your skin or fur."

Mato nodded to the other council members, who stepped back from the chairs. Then he released the shackles. "That will be all. You're free to go."

The three native youths were dazed and unsteady when they stood. They headed for the exit, rubbing their arms.

"It still burns," Askook said quietly to the others.

Mato was near the door. As his son, Chayton, approached, he said, "The sensation will ease. The device won't cause you any further discomfort, so long as you avoid doing harm."

Chayton's body language expressed his ill temper; he walked past his father without looking at him and said nothing.

40

INVERTED WORLDS

On the way to the Reservation, Tokala Luta was quiet, driving the transport and keeping her attention on the road while Mora and Asha had a conversation about the history of Zenda and world politics in general. They had their head coverings removed for this portion of the drive, as it was early morning, and there was almost no other traffic. The dome was also in a tinted setting, making it more difficult for anyone on the outside to see in.

When Mora met Tokala, she immediately felt a kinship. The young medicine guardian had a no-nonsense attitude, her body language made her look tough, and her facial features were austere, but in conversation, she was open and kind. So, Mora took a leap of faith and decided to tell her she wasn't Zamora.

"I think if we are going to work together you should know, I'm not Zamora. I'm not from this world."

Tokala obviously felt uncomfortable. Her earfans quivered then flattened. She turned to Asha. "What is she talking about?"

"It sounds ridiculous, I know. I'm not sure how to explain," Mora said. "There was an accident in my lab, I switched places with my counterpart in this world."

Tokala pulled the transport over. She didn't even look at Mora, but instead asked Asha. "What's really going on, is she serious?"

Asha gave Mora a look of regret. "You'll have to prove it to her in some way."

"How exactly would I do that?" Mora asked.

Tokala turned around and glared at Mora. "I don't know you; how can I trust such a fantastic story?" Then she asked Asha, "what does she hope to gain from this ruse? How will it affect my work and what we're doing at the reservation? I have half a mind to turn around right now."

"I have reason to believe her. Algon was there when it happened. He called me that night. I have been helping her acclimate to our world since she got here."

Tokala was quiet, staring at Asha. She seemed to be processing, deciding what to do. She turned back to Mora. "I do trust my friend, and she believes your story for some inexplicable reason. You better not be trying to trick us in some way because I can't afford to mess things up at the reservation."

Without saying another word, Tokala pulled back onto the road. Then Asha carried on talking about the history of their Hadot.

Mora tried to keep her focus, because she did what to learn about this world, but what Tokala had said still stung. She wasn't used to being mistrusted. But of course, it would be hard for anyone to believe! *What was I expecting?* It wasn't until Asha asked a direct question that Mora snapped out of feeling sorry for herself. "I'm sorry, what?"

"What were Pinks on your world like?" Asha asked, and Tokala gave her a sharp look of incredulity. Obviously, Asha was trying to find a way to convince her friend that Mora was sincere.

"We call them *Ocha*, the fair race. But most people there are like me, *Awo*, mixed, and appeared gray in color. The Zendali are called *Oji*, but they are not usually as dark as you, Asha. I'm realizing everyone on my world is mixed race to some degree. I've been wondering what they all would look like with my enhanced vision. I love the lavender color of my pelt. But before Algon gave me the implant, my fur, just looked grey."

"Your people are various shades of gray, then? Is that how they look without implants?" Asha asked.

Mora nodded agreement. "But they all must have color variations that I couldn't see before. For example, I met someone here who says she isn't Fog. She has golden fur under a bad dye job."

Tokala's ear-fans flattened with alarm.

"Are you referring to the female who was working in the kitchen during the party at the hotel?" Asha asked, looking worried.

"Yes, that's Bi."

"How did you meet her?" asked Tokala.

"Bi literally ran into me on a side street. Knocked me flat, and my head covering came off. Fortunately, no one else was around. She saw my green eyes and then removed her eye coverings to show me she had green eyes, too."

"How did she end up working at the Journeyer Hotel?" asked Asha.

Mora wiggled her ears.

Asha widened her eyes in surprise. "*You* got her a job at a hotel full of Zendali businessmen?"

"She must be the one who was being hunted. She isn't safe at the Journeyer Hotel!" Tokala said.

"Hunted?" Mora realized they were right. She made a poor choice, but Bi was so happy about the position. "Well, Bi was somehow very pleased to have the job. She's even working in exchange for room and board."

"She's living at the hotel too?" asked Asha with apprehension. "And without payment? Did she really believe she had no other options? Where is she from?"

Now Mora looked bewildered. "At the time, it seemed like I was helping her, arranging the job and place to stay. I admit I didn't consider her coloring and any possible repercussions from the Zendali who lodge there."

Asha shook her head. "How could you not, Mora?! You're so intelligent, yet sometimes you miss the obvious. You get so wrapped up in your own worries you don't think about others or the danger you put them in."

Mora paused for a moment, wondering if it was true. Was she really so inconsiderate of others, or was that Asha's experience of Zamora? She sat in silence for a time. It was clear that Asha was upset. They drove in silence for a while. Mora could feel the tension and unspoken blame. The issue seemed to be closed for now. Mora found she had plenty of self-critical thoughts and disappointment for her poor choices already. She didn't need their rebuke.

Finally, Asha seemed to calm down. Her curiosity being stronger than her indignation.

"In your version of Hadot, the Pinks are called Ocha? And it is commonplace to be Fog?"

"We call mixed-race people Awo, and yes, the majority of people are like me."

"If the Zendali are not world dominate? Then which country is?"

Mora thought about how to answer, wondering what Tokala would think of what she had to say in regard to colonialism in her world. "The Ocha colonized this continent.

We call it the U.C.I., the United Colonies of Inoti. They are also the dominant cultural influence worldwide."

Asha squinted her eyes, reflecting on that. "In my opinion, as a broad term for the species, Ocha is better than calling them Pinks. Our fair races are no longer from any particular place or nation."

"Was it the same in your world after being invaded? Were cultures lost?" Tokala asked.

Mora nodded. "Yes, but in our case, the Oji and the native population of Inoti are the ones who lost identity and status."

"The natives?" Tokala asked. "You mean the First People, the Wen?"

Mora felt ashamed to admit it. She nodded, but Tokala was driving and probably didn't see it. "There are few Aboriginal nations left. But numerous tribes were completely destroyed."

This was sobering. Tokala and Asha waited for more details, but Mora didn't want to talk about the shameful past of her people.

"In my country," Asha said, "the average citizen believes anything our government or scientists claim without question. Yet, I know for a fact that those different genetic markers don't make much difference."

"I'm not a biologist or geneticist, but it seems clear to me we are all much the same," Mora said in agreement. "Oddly, our ancestors said comparable nonsense about the dark races," Mora told them. "It's antithetical to what you have here."

"The problem with centuries of indoctrination is that people stick to what's familiar. If we could spread the truth to the public now, few would agree with the facts or believe in the information's veracity. The Pinks are not a separate species; they're a different race. And the mindset of a whole nation needs to be changed!"

Mora was nodding her agreement. "Unfortunately, the perceptions endure. Even if your Prince Nakhadot is able to change the laws to make conditions better for the Pinks, the view that they're less capable and therefore unworthy of equal treatment will persist. It has in my world, at least."

"A species, by definition, is not arbitrary. They represent reproductively cohesive evolutionary units. Races are part of a continuum which is arbitrarily and subjectively defined. The fact that the Zendali have bred with the Pink population is proof they are compatible. Our histories purposely leave these details out, as an act of dissimilation. To prove Pinks are fundamentally different from us. It allows the government to maintain control over them. Because if the Pinks aren't capable of doing anything more than menial tasks, it keeps them in servitude."

"Are you saying that Pinks are actually enslaved in your country?"

Asha looked at her with a mixture of sadness and embarrassment. "Everything about my country is going to be upsetting."

Mora laughed, which was clearly unexpected. "Sorry, it is just terribly familiar." Then, with a more sober tone, she told some truths about her country. "In my world, the Ocha colonized much of the world. This land was not an empty place; it was inhabited by diverse cultures and great civilizations, which they destroyed. They did unspeakable things to the natives, and most of their culture and languages are unknown to us now. A great legacy was lost. More than I realized until I came here."

"Well, I'm glad you can take the conditions here with some levity, but the truth is rather grave, and you're in a precarious position. The Zenda here do not mix with Pinks. It's forbidden, illegal."

"Yes, I clearly understood that fact. And yet Zamora did exist, and she prospered here. Did she join the Sisters' of Justice to hide who she was?"

Asha was shaking her head. "No, she was a believer. But of course, it was helpful not to be seen."

"I found a small book on Zamora's shelves about the Goddess Bicara and the origins of the Sisters' of Justice. I found it interesting... However, I'm not at all religious."

"Which puts you more at risk. You should be aware; the university may force you onto a reservation to keep their Zendali investors from finding out what you are."

"What are you suggesting I do? Isn't Zamora's home safe?"

"Zamora's family is wealthy. They bought that place for her. But Zenda contractors designed and built the foreigner's sector. It is a residential community for them alone. Isn't it obvious that being surrounded by the Zendali is dangerous?"

Mora shook her head. "Then why did her family build her home in this community?"

"It is the only land allotted to the Zendali. They could not build elsewhere. But of course, they expected her to keep coloring her pelt."

"On the other hand," Mora said, "sometimes hiding in plain sight is the best way to cheat those who want to ruin you. They would never suspect a Fog to be right under their noses. Or that I'm friends with the daughter of the Zendali Ambassador!"

Asha responded with a somewhat rueful snort. "This was a conversation I had often with Zamora. I told her it wasn't safe for her to live in that house. We argued when she gave up dying her fur and hair. But she grew tired of it and wanted to be natural. She lived among the Zenda as if nothing was different about her. And they never suspected because she was covered with the veil."

"I just realized Zamora's arguments are not unlike what Bi told me. I suggested she needed to move out of the city after what happened at the hotel on our celebration day. But she insists she isn't Fog."

Asha smiled at this. "What is she then?"

"I have no idea. Pink and native, maybe?"

Asha said, "Then maybe we have a new follower of Bicara."

Mora gave Asha a sly smile. "Doesn't your religion frown on impostors among them?"

"First of all, Zamora was not an imposter. Also, few of us live here, but in Zenda her disciples are many. Bicara has a large movement there. This garb isn't required; there are unveiled followers too. Some of us wear these robes for the isolation they provide, to avoid the complex relationships people outside of our faith impose. But it's also protective. Pinks follow Bicara too."

Mora's ear-fans perked up and straight out. "I didn't realize that. But for me, the garment will never be anything more than a convenient disguise."

Asha shrugged. "Honestly, I don't think any of the Sisters' would be upset if they knew. Our wish is to protect those who are in need."

Mora laughed again and said, "As long as I'm not offending anyone."

"Why do you laugh?" asked Tokala.

"Because it seems like my very existence here is offensive."

"Religion is full of conflict," Tokala said. "You don't need a book of rules to tell you what correct behavior is. People know in their hearts when they're doing something wrong."

Mora was nodding in agreement. She asked Asha, "What does your family think of you following Bicara's teachings?"

"They think all of this is an eccentric phase I'll grow out of. They don't like that I'm involved and don't understand my choices. It causes a lot of hostility from my father and teasing from my brother. My mother isn't with us, so what I do here doesn't matter to her. But if I were with her in Zenda, then she would probably forbid it, and force me to be the charming daughter she could take to her events and show off. She treated me as if I were one of her accessories when I was little. A pretty little bauble. Smile, sit, sing, perform."

"I'm sorry, Asha. That doesn't sound like a pleasant childhood."

"Well, I was very young. I hardly remember her. And I didn't grow up to be pretty. I look like my father, handsome at best. A stern face is what I see in the mirror."

"You are beautiful, Asha, stunningly so!" Mora told her.

Asha flattened her ear-fans and wrinkled her brow. "Anyway, if my parents knew my political leanings now, they would be much more upset."

"What are your political sentiments, Asha? I don't know much about your world politics."

This question made Asha pause. It was too much to cover with a simple answer, and some things she didn't wish to divulge. "You need to study our history. I don't mean to be evasive, and maybe that's a topic for further discussion. But right now, what I can tell you... I believe Pinks should have the right of autonomy, the right to choose, not the kind of choice my government postures now, one kind of servitude or another... but real options to be independent. At this point, those who support these new ideas are causing friction because our people don't want to change. They're comfortable with how things are, or they can't imagine giving up the advantages they have. But Prince Nakhadot is leading the reformation efforts. He's saying all the right things. He's brilliant!"

"So, he is a reformist? Passionate visionaries like that tend to get killed."

Asha shook her head sadly. "The messages of martyrs can be more poignant and effective after they are gone. But I hope that won't come to pass."

Mora observed how passionate Asha was about her country and felt a little ashamed. She had never been involved in any cause. "I admire your commitment. I am no more political than I am religious."

In fact, Mora had never taken a stand for anything meaningful. When she'd first arrived in Muwioni, she believed the two worlds had nothing in common. But now, looking at the underlying behavior of those who had influence, she realized the people of Hadot had all the same flaws, which led to all the same struggles in both worlds. They just manifested differently depending on who was in power. One race was just as likely to be the oppressor as the other. It was as if their worlds were inverted.

41

THE PERIL OF TRUTH

P ost-graduation, Algon was set up nicely, overseeing the production of what had been named Portal Pods. They had a ferrebast base where the components were located. Above this was an energy crystal cube with a simple hatch opening at one end. It was about the size of an office desk and could only transport non-living items.

One group of investors from the Sovereign Nation had offered the highest bid to own the technology and distribute the portals overseas. The University was taking a cut, and Algon was making a respectable income from the manufacturing and sales. He would also be overseeing the distribution.

Algon negotiated a sizable percentage of the future profits for himself. Unless he wanted to, he wouldn't need to work the rest of his life. The royalties alone would give him an opportunity to do whatever he pleased. But of course, he planned to give Mora or Zamora a share of those profits. He hadn't braved that conversation yet because Mora was so angry, she would hardly look at him.

His main ambition was to establish himself, so he could offer to make Asha his mate officially, because until now he had not felt stable. It was undeniable her family disapproved of him, which he had assumed was due to his modest upbringing. But lately, he started to suspect it was a race issue.

Although after the award ceremony Algon had been praised for his achievements, by Ziyad and his Zendali associates. Maybe now Ziyad would consider him an acceptable mate for Asha. He had proven that he could provide for her properly.

Algon was heading for a factory inspection when Asha's brother Tao cornered him before he entered the building, roughly pulling him aside. "I saw you with that half-breed. Who is she?"

"What are you talking about?"

"Don't pretend to be innocent. I was in the forest that day. You were with a Fog female. I followed you."

"You shot me!"

"You got in the way."

Algon kept a straight face and shook off Tao's grip on his shirt, staring him square in his eyes. "I don't know what you imagine you witnessed, but it is of no concern of yours."

Tao slammed Algon against the wall. "Don't think I won't report you. My family has no love for you as it is. Breaking treaties will bring harm your way. This cushy job you got for yourself will be over too."

Algon said the first lie that came to mind. "She's a traveler. She paid me to take her to the forest. I don't have any idea what she was looking for."

"You must have her name, where she's from? Where's she staying?"

"No, I don't. I'm sure the name she gave me was false. She met me at the train station, and I had no idea she was FOG until she removed her head covering in the vehicle. By then, we were already on our way to the location that she asked to be taken to." *Let them waste their time looking through the forest for some mysterious, non-existent clues.* Algon thought.

"Did you discover what she was looking for?"

"I might have if you hadn't started shooting at us!"

"She must have said something after you fled the forest."

"I asked questions, but she didn't give away any information which might be useful."

"How would you know what might be useful? Why was she dressed like a follower of my sister's goddess cult? Are they mixed up in that together? It seems too much of a coincidence. She was wearing the garb of a follower. Is Asha friends with her? Maybe that's how you met her, through my sister?"

Algon struggled not to react to the truth Tao was presenting. "I didn't tell Asha. She's been focused on her exams. She doesn't need to hear about strange travelers."

"Then how did this traveler find you?" Tao studied Algon suspiciously. "What a convenient excuse. You're not a talented liar, Algon. You can expect to be questioned further by people who are less tolerant than me."

"You mean by the Order of Amon Kuroo?"

Tao was so surprised at this accusation he released Algon and stepped back. That was all the confirmation Algon needed.

"I have suspected for some time you were part of that vicious order. Your father, too. No Tao, you will not touch me. If your secret little club does anything to bring harm to me, or if I were to disappear, you will discover I have more protection than you might imagine, and it will cost you."

Algon stood taller, straightened his tunic, and walked into the building, leaving Tao in stunned silence.

When inside, he went to his office first and contacted Asha. They had a Link-Line at the factory, which amplified his receptor signal, allowing him to contact her when she was out of the city. He gave her a recap of the confrontation with her brother. "You need to warn Mora, and the other Fog female too, the Order is actively looking for them. He also confirmed that he was the one who shot at us that day in the forest. You *do* understand your family is somehow mixed up with the Order and whatever they are planning?"

"I'm sorry, but the idea that Tao would shoot at Mora because she's Fog is too much. Honestly, in the depth of my core, I just can't reconcile my *brother* with such a violent act as attempted murder."

"You've told me about his temper. You don't think he is capable of cold, calculated bloodshed?"

Now, Asha was silent... *thinking, annoyed, angry?* Algon wondered.

"Asha, are you listening to me?"

"You've insinuated that before, but there is no evidence they are."

Algon was silent on his end, not knowing how to make her believe him. Asha assured him she would take care of Mora and give her his warning. When they disconnected, he kept mulling over everything in his mind. He and Asha had never really discussed the Order. He had questioned her on several occasions about things he knew Tao had done, and he'd dropped hints about what he imagined might be going on, but he had not told her his suspicions regarding the Order of Amon Kuroo for fear of upsetting her. The response she gave him indicated she had the same misgivings, but she just didn't want to believe it was true. Turning a blind eye to this was a terrible risk.

42

Reservations

Welina was the closest town to the Nisnap Reservation Farms. Anyone planning a visit to the reservation had to stop and fill out forms at the Welina registration office, and wait for confirmation to proceed. The procedure took about an hour even though everyone at the office knew Tokala very well.

Tokala showed their documents to the Sanctuary officer. They would be returned with his stamp of approval before they were allowed to drive further to the reservation. The office was stuffy and hot. When Asha's receptor buzzed, she walked outside to take the call. Mora followed to wait on the veranda in the shade. There was a bit of a breeze, which made it a lot more comfortable than it was inside.

Mora noticed the garb she and Asha wore was getting some attention from the town's people. They walked by the office glaring and brought others to show them, all openly staring and pointing. In the city, it didn't much matter if you dressed differently. There were a lot of tourists and strange fashions there. But in this small town, they had maybe never seen the Sisters' of Justice. She and Asha definitely looked peculiar.

Mora didn't mind being stared at. The only thing about having to wear this outfit all the time was that it was claustrophobic and too hot in this weather! She didn't understand why Asha would choose it when she didn't have to. This made her realize she had not asked Asha why she chose to be a follower of Bicara and what about the Sisters' of Justice appealed to her. If she was going to pretend to be a part of the sect, she should research more, learn about their history, and what motivates them.

Asha ended her call and appeared distressed.

"What is it? What happened?"

"Algon was assaulted at the factory by my brother."

"What factory?"

Asha paused in confusion at first, and then her tone was concerned. "He didn't tell you?"

"Tell me what?"

"Algon was employed to oversee production of the portals. A company from Zenda won the bidding contest. They are manufacturing them in Muwioni. Algon will also be involved with the distribution."

Mora had been feeling less upset with her previous lab partner after he defended her at the university, not that she had gotten over her indignation about the university giving him credit, but she understood he had no choice in the matter. Asha had helped her get past the hurt, but now, he was *profiting* from her invention and didn't even have the decency to tell her.

Asha moved in closer so they could see through each other's veils. "Mora, I can actually feel the fury rising in you, and I can read your body language, even under all those robes."

"I try to keep reminding myself that it was never mine. But I'm still bitter about it."

"He was going to tell you; he just didn't have the opportunity yet. Please give him a chance."

"I wanted to be free of Zamora's family money, free to build another portal device. At this point, I have no funds of my own and no way back."

Asha replied with more confidence than she felt. "We'll find a way. Have faith. Our destiny isn't random."

At that moment, Tokala came out of the office. "We're all set." When she observed the tension, she said, "Let's go. You can tell me what this is about on our way." When everyone was in the car, Tokala said, "Out with it. Which one of you is going to tell me what's going on?"

"My brother threatened Algon because he saw him with a Fog female. That was you, Mora, that day you took a hike in the forest, and Algon claims it was Tao who shot the arrow."

Mora sat up straighter. "He what?"

"Tao happened to be on a hunting trip in the forest when you and Algon showed up. He recognized Algon with a Fog female. He followed the two of you but never got a good look at your face. But he knew Algon, so he's guilty by association."

"What do you mean he *threatened* Algon?" Tokala asked. "What does he plan to do with this information?"

"Tao said he would make sure Algon didn't keep his job. He wanted to know who she was, but Algon told him the female was a traveler, and he didn't have her name. He misdirected, but he doesn't think it will hold up. Algon knows about Bi's encounter on the day of the celebration and told me we should get her to safety."

They sat in silence for a moment. "Should I head back to the city, then?"

Mora answered: "I think we should do what we came here to do. Afterward, we can go talk to Bi. She's working now, anyway. As long as she's around the hotel staff, she should be safe."

When they pulled onto the road again, an emergency vehicle driving a bit too fast in the other direction passed them. The road was narrow and dusty; it skidded and nearly side-swiped their vehicle. Tokala looked back at it. "That was a rescue transport."

The rest of the way, Mora sat in silence, thinking about what she should do. Tokala talked to Asha about reservation affairs, and Mora barely paid attention. She was too consumed with her own outrage and fear. The back road to the reservation was unpaved and, after the recent storms, was full of potholes. Tokala was a cautious driver. They bumped along at a rather slow pace, giving Mora too much time to worry.

43

STIGMA

With the university closed for the summer break, more students were in the public marketplace. They crowded the streets with activity. The summer craft festival would be held in a couple of weeks, and already visitors were arriving from other towns and cities for the event.

On this day, Orenda's goal was to collect art supplies. Her aunt had gifted her an easel, and she wanted to start painting. She'd found a few supplies in the market: hand-crafted brushes, also pigments, and binders she would have to mix herself. But she had an address for an import shop across town that sold tubes of oil paint from the Zenda Territories. They were expensive, but she wanted to try them.

She was heading in that direction when she viewed Holata Tyee's son Kinache through the crowd. Oddly, his fur was much darker than the last time she'd seen him. He was standing with that Zendali, Tao. His deep indigo fur and crest were iridescent in the sun. Most people don't realize that only a natural pelt has that sheen. A dye job left fur dull, like Kinache's pelt. Orenda noticed things like that. She had an artist's eye for detail.

They were in a rather animated conversation outside a tobacco shop. Kinache was obviously angry. His posture was rigid with outrage, his chin thrust forward. It made her curious. She slipped into the shadowed alcove of the doorway. From that vantage point, she had a clear view. They were talking only a few steps away. Orenda heard Kinache complaining about the injustice of the punishment he had received.

"Did you know about this?" he demanded. "Did you know they could do this to us?"

Tao took a step back. "Watch your tone."

Kinache winced, and his ears flattened. He seemed intimidated by Tao. Then he rolled up his sleeve and removed one of his silver cuffs to show the Zendali what the bracelet was hiding. A distinctive welt surrounded his wrist. It was strikingly bright against his dark fur. A web of white lines climbed up his arm, like a bolt of lightning against a stormy sky.

"They called this the sign of the splintered. It's a device that alters the implant. I tried a deep fur dye, but the mark won't take color."

"So, hide it. What's the problem?"

Kinache lifted his chin. He had a stubborn face. "If I inflict injury on others, I will feel *the victim's* pain in equal measure." When he saw Tao's doubt, he added, "A *brave* is willing to suffer."

A sly smile crossed Tao's face. "Cover it up," he said. "Let's meet at my place tonight. My father needs to see this, gather the others who have the mark."

Orenda waited for them to leave before she came out of the shadows. Her aunt must have been aware of this. Maybe Coso would tell her what it was. The council had marked them with this stigma. She felt the weight of this significant change in her chest.

44

THE ILLUSION OF SAFETY

T he Nisnap Reservation clinic was located in a longhouse built with logs of ancient trees. This building had existed long before and was part of an abandoned settlement. The reservation was built around it.

As they pulled through the entrance gates, Tokala gasped. "What's happened!" She drove the vehicle near the building and parked. "It's bursting full of patients, and more out on the porch! Are those bloody towels wrapped around their wounds?!" She jumped out of the car before Asha and Mora could respond.

"What's going on here?" Tokala asked her friend and assistant Idony, who had run out of the building to meet her.

"Farming accident. I've been bandaging the wounds, which don't need stitching. Her eyes were anxious and fully dilated. You should handle the surgery."

Tokala walked into the waiting area. The Pink female who had an appointment today was sitting. Next to her was a child.

"He knocked down a hornet's nest," Idony told Tokala.

He was covered in welts and gave Tokala a forlorn sigh, knowing his treatment might come last.

Tokala marched to the cabinet, took out a jar of ointment, and went back to the waiting room. "Tell your mom to put this on the stings. There is not much more I can do for you."

"I'm sorry, I could have done that. I was just distracted with the others." Idony apologized.

Tokala patted Idony on the shoulder as if to say it was all right. Then she talked to the pregnant Pink, "Unica, please go home and rest. We will do your exam later. I have to attend to the severe injuries first." As Unica and the child left, they passed Mora and Asha, who were in the doorway watching. Tokala saw their apprehension and made a go-away motion. "Don't worry, we'll get this sorted. Go do what you planned, Asha."

Tokala flipped through her intake papers and found nine severe injuries from the farm equipment accident. "Sort out the ones with the worst and deepest cuts and bring them to the back room one at a time. I'll clean and stitch. Then you can use the herbal salve and bandage. The broken bones will have to wait. We will set and splint them after. I will show you how. Let's get to it!"

Tokala soon realized the extent of the damage was worse than she thought. On closer inspection of the patients, and the towels soaked in their blood. These would all require immediate stitching. If they didn't have the implant to slow their blood loss, they might have bled out. *Idony should have taken care of the worst injuries first, but she was too frightened.* Tokala felt harried and panicked, wishing she had trained medics to assist her. Each and every one of these people was a priority.

"Why did you clean and bandage the minor cuts and scrapes first? You left the serious injuries without care!" Tokala felt a flush of annoyance and frustration. "You should not have waited for me. You know how to sew," Tokala admonished. "These injured farmers needed *immediate* care. Look how much blood they've lost! Get some supplies. We both need to stitch."

Idony flattened her ears at the rebuke. "They need sedation. I don't have access to that. You know I don't have the keys to those cupboards!" She wined. "I wouldn't want to cause them more distress by sewing them up without something to ease their pain. They're already in agony!"

"You would rather have them die?" Tokala knew she was being harsh with Idony, but her apprentice needed to be tougher, not meek, and indecisive if she was going to be an effective healer. "I understand your concern, but there will be times when your patient must bear the pain of treatment to save their lives."

Idony responded with every sign of shame: limp tail, ear-fans flattened, eyes cast down. Then Tokala was sorry. The Pinks are vulnerable. I can't speak in that tone. Tokala reminded herself. "We need to get to work," she said in a softer voice.

Idony met her eyes now, her ears stood out. An indication she was giving Tokala her full attention. Idony was a reservation Pink who'd been assisting Tokala for almost two years. She grew the herb garden. Her relationship with the healing arts began with her interest in how plants could be used to make herbal balms and tinctures for muscle aches or to treat rashes or cuts. By now she had done far more than making remedies and salves with her herbs. She was Tokala's unofficial apprentice.

After taking care of the worst cases, Tokala took notice of the quiet elderly fellow with cataracts who had been patiently waiting all morning. She'd brought a cure from the university that Algon had provided, which she hoped would remove them. She had not been trained in this type of medical procedure, but Algon explained the application, and it was actually very simple. Another gift from the Star People. "Loda, I am sorry I forgot you, and I don't have time for your procedure now, but I will come to find you when this is all over. Go home, please. No reason for you to sit here all day." He got up and ambled away, saying, "Thank you, doctor."

***

Asha used the main hall for her meetings with the community. It was a large structure, where families gathered to do collaborative projects, or where meetings about the farm were held. When Asha and Mora entered the building, they were faced with unexpected turmoil. A group of female refugees were having a fervent discussion. The others surrounded a small, middle-aged female. She was close to hysterical, keening like an injured animal. She was so distraught her words were incomprehensible. Several of the other residents were trying to calm her. "What has happened here?" Asha asked with concern as she approached the group with Mora.

A Pink with a long braid of red hair stood and pulled them aside to whisper, "Her daughter went missing a week ago."

Asha looked appalled. She opened her mouth to reply, but the Pink continued.

"Her daughter was found this morning on the far edge of the field. It was her body that got jammed in the harvester. Then the harvester overturned, causing other injuries to our farmers. It was not until they got the machine lifted that they found her mangled body." Asha and Mora were shocked and unsure how to comfort the grieving.

"Unica, this is my friend Mora. I wanted to include her in our sessions." Unica had white fur, bright red hair and striking blue eyes. She nodded solemnly to Mora. Only a little curious about the fact that Mora was Fog. She and the others were too distressed to pay much attention to their guests.

"Have the authorities been here?" Mora asked, not knowing how these crimes were dealt with on Wendat, or if the same department for the reservations handled investigations.

"Yes, they took her body just before you arrived."

"But the property is fenced, and those walls are tall. How did this happen?" asked Asha.

"We don't understand how she got there, but it wasn't an accident."

"How can you be sure? Maybe she ate something poisonous, passed out, and then the machine ran over her?"

The Pink was shaking her head. "No, they wanted to frighten us." Tears had soaked into the fine fur on her face. She broke down, sobbing, and Asha held her. Finally, she pulled away and tried to compose herself. When she glanced at them again, her eyes seemed haunted by the memory. "They scalped her. She had long blond hair. It was beautiful, and her whole scalp was removed. Then they dumped her body over the fence as if it were trash. It was at the edge of the property where the over-winter grain fields are, for livestock feed."

Mora gasped when she heard this, and Asha just looked furious.

"Our female population has been disappearing. It happens when they leave the reservations to do errands in town. It's been happening for a couple of years. At first, it was only once in a while. But in recent months, it is much too often to be anything but purposeful."

What did the council have to say about this? Asha asked her.

The Pink shrugged. I'm honestly not sure they know about it. We've made reports to the Sanctuary Officer. Then we never hear anything but excuses. The last time we tried to find out if there had been any investigation, the officer said they had probably just gotten lost or had run away.

Mora and Asha gave each other a knowing look. This was a case of negligence at best or outright collusion with bad intent.

"We are all refugees with a past that we're hiding from. They had no reason to leave the safety the council provided for us here. Besides, where would they run?"

"None of the cases was ever solved?"

"Not that we know." She looked like her edges were at loose ends, all her emotions frayed. "We have never had any reports about our missing females."

"They are always female?"

"Ours have been, yes, but we have heard that some males went missing on other reservations. None of us want to travel anymore, and it is difficult to get any business done for fear of running into trouble."

Asha turned to Mora. "Algon said you and Bi were in danger. This is what he meant."

"It will be hours before Tokala can leave," Mora said.

With a feeling of grim foreboding, the two of them took a seat and listened as the group talked about every Pink they knew who had gone missing, and how not even the sanctuary walls kept them safe.

"Unless those who committed these horrible crimes are punished, there is no justice!" The grieving mother said.

"I never thought of my safety," Mora said. "It wasn't in question before coming here. Now doubt is a breathless thing that slowly robs me of confidence. I can't even imagine the pressure the Pinks have had to live under here."

Asha took her hand and held it tight. Not knowing what to say. But hoping she could somehow protect her.

The redhead heard Mora's concerns. "We were given the promise of happiness when we came to Wendat. But we've always waited for it to be taken. We didn't know how it would happen, but we expected it. Now that it has started to erode, how will it end? Will we all be punished? Happiness was an illusion, and we were fools to think it was possible."

45

To Protect and Preserve

Mora allowed the Pink community to see that she was Fog to build trust in the community. It was a risk. She found no others of mixed race like herself at the sanctuary. The Pinks trusted Asha even though she was Zendali, but that didn't mean the Fog would trust her enough to come out in the open. If there were any of them in residence. They had more reason to hide.

It had been a long day. Mora felt emotionally drained. She sat in the back of the vehicle, lost in her thoughts, barely hearing what the others were saying.

On the way back from the reservation, Asha filled Tokala Luta in on everything they had learned from the females they'd spent the afternoon with. Tokala, in turn, told them she had spent most of her day stitching up the field workers.

"They did not say a word about what they had found or the brutal death of the young female!" Tokala complained. "They all were rather morose, and some seemed in shock. Now I understand why."

"I imagine they aren't sure who to trust," Asha said. "They suffered under hard conditions before they found their way to Wendat. The sanctuary provided a home for them, yet at this point, they are aware of their vulnerability, and they're frightened."

"Can we arm them so they're able to protect themselves? Teach them to fight?"

With astonished faces, both Tokala and Asha looked back at Mora. *Evidently, that's not an acceptable suggestion.* Mora deduced by their response.

"In our world," Tokala said in a tolerant but firm voice, "Pinks do not fight. They are never given weapons. If they were found with a weapon, it would break agreements made with the sanctuary office. I'm not sure what would happen to them, but no, this is not an option!"

"What you're saying is... they're not allowed to protect themselves, and obviously the government is not able to keep them safe. Can you imagine how disempowered they must feel now? To realize their numbers are being picked off one at a time whenever they dare to leave the compound, and they have to remain passive under the law?"

Neither Asha nor Tokala had a response. But they flattened their ears, showing they felt chastised.

"I have to assume that neither of you has considered how unfair the situation was?" Mora took their response as a signal she could argue her point. "Look, maybe it isn't supposed to be like this. They were told they would be safe here, but obviously, they're not, and being passive just makes them an easy target."

"I don't have any fighting skills to teach," said Asha, and Tokala nodded in agreement.

"Well, I do. I took self-defense training in college. I also took some classes in martial arts."

"What are you talking about? Tokala asked. Are you suggesting...?"

"Learning to fight would help. I'd like to teach them the basics. Then they can practice on their own. They also have tools, which they use on the farm, and knives for cooking. These are all weapons if you know how to use them. The Pinks need to be taught how to avert the dangers. They need confidence most of all. Those men you sewed up today, they were not silent because they were sad, Toka... they were angry! That's why they were unusually quiet. The Pinks have reached the conclusion that this violence against them won't stop. If you don't control the situation by showing them how to protect their families and the safety of their homes, some kind of chaos will erupt here. You cannot seriously imagine they will put up with this now. There will be a breaking point one way or the other."

"What do you imagine they can do?" Asha asked this with a doubtful tone because in her experience with the Pinks, they had no resolve to protest or revolt, which Mora was suggesting might happen here.

"Today we held vigil with a grieving community. They were not just mourning the loss of a daughter or a friend; they were bereaved because they've experienced the loss of a dream. They are losing hope. What happens when people decide they have nothing left to lose?"

Asha was starting to get Mora's point. Her eyes widened, and her ear-fans fluttered with her stress.

But Tokala shook her head sadly. "It is not our place to make that decision."

"How is teaching them fighting skills any different from giving them knowledge about their culture and languages? The two of you have been breaking the rules for some time, haven't you? If you really want to empower them, teach them how to be fearless. Give them hope."

46

CORRUPTION

Tokala dropped off Asha and Mora in their neighborhood. They were all unsettled after their trip to the reservation. During the remainder of the way back, they had been silent, each lost in their own thoughts and concerns.

"I'm going to go visit the Council elder to give her the news. I'm sure she will hear of it eventually, but I am disturbed by how many are missing, and the council does not seem to be acting to protect the reservation residents. It makes me wonder if maybe the disappearances are not being reported?" Tokala told them.

"Tell us what you find out," Asha said. "Mora and I will start on our mind-map project tomorrow. We'll be here if you want to drop by."

"By *here* you mean at Zamora's place, I assume?"

Asha smiled. "Right, unfortunately, I have no privacy at my house."

"I remember a time when you sought the attention of your father and brother."

Asha nodded. "I used to go unnoticed by them both. I'm now aware it was a good thing, but yes, I was bitter about their lack of affection growing up."

"You were free to discover who you are, Asha."

"True, I could do what I wanted, and they didn't bother me until I joined the Sisters' of Justice. Now they pester and insult me constantly."

Tokala nodded in understanding. "Be careful, see you soon." They waved as she drove off.

"I'm exhausted," Mora said.

Asha agreed. "Me too. I'll be here tomorrow. Have a good night."

They each walked a short distance to their homes. But when Asha entered her house, a heated discussion between her brother and father was taking place in the living room. She quietly moved down the hall and stepped into the pantry, which was between the kitchen and dining room. Now she had a distant view through the slats in the door and realized others were there as well.

Tao said, "I'm telling you, when I was hunting, I found Algon with a Fog female in the forest. She must be the same one Chayton and Askook tried to capture."

"You talked to Algon?" Ziyad asked his son.

"He said she was a traveler who hired him to drive her to the forest, and he didn't have her name, which is unlikely. Why would he take some random visitor to the Woodland Park? He's involved somehow with that Fog mongrel, I know it! But the more important question is... what was she looking for?"

"We will have a team search the area. I have a map of that park. Can you give me the exact location?"

"I suspect he knows her through Asha. Otherwise, why did she wear that cult outfit? I think they use the garb to hide right under our noses!"

"I thought there was some dispute about the female who attacked Askook. She didn't have Zendali features, and her coloring was unusual. Are we sure she's Fog?"

"The female I saw was definitely Fog; I can't verify if the other one was." Tao looked at Chayton, encouraging him to say something, but it was the medicine guardian's son, Kinache, who spoke.

"I think we are talking about two different females. The other one is maybe the result of some natives messing with the Pinks?"

"Isn't that the same?" Asked Tao.

"No, Son it is not the same. But it does bend our treaty with the council, which might give us some leverage. We'll make it a priority. The gang you've been managing... tell them to capture her."

Chayton spoke up. "She was working at the hotel during the awards dinner, which was sponsored by the university a few weeks back. She still works in the kitchen."

"I want to be on the team that captures her," Askook said. The overt hatred on his face was evident.

Asha was aware Chayton knew what Mora was, and he was redirecting the focus onto the other female, Bimisi. She couldn't imagine what Chayton hoped to gain by this, or why he would protect Mora. Actually, he thought she was Zamora, but he had been nothing but hostile to both of them. He had tried to rape Zamora once, and he had threatened Mora. Chayton was possessive and wanted control of her, but why?

Then Ziyad said, "Show me the markings of the modifier."

Asha watched through the alcove of the pantry, observing the three young men line up, Kinache, Chayton, and Askook. Who she assumed, was the one poisoned when they tried to capture Bimisi. That's what Mora had told her. According to Tokala, he had barely survived. He wants revenge. The thought of it gave her a chill.

They rolled up their long sleeves. Each had a kind of bracelet or leather armband on their wrist. When the jewelry was removed, a white ring could be seen. It was embedded in their flesh, and a web of lines that climbed up their arms had bleached their fur white. It looked like a lightning strike.

"Take off your tunics. I want to see how it connects to the implant." They did as they were told. Now they were in full view. White lines flowed through their fur, around their shoulders, and up the back of their necks. "I'll get a surgeon to remove them."

They reacted with apprehension. The room fell silent. Tao then informed his father that removal was too dangerous. "The council warned them, if they try to remove the modifiers, it will kill them."

Ziyad raised his brow ridge. "Humph," he snorted doubtfully. "Further investigation into this matter is necessary. With regard to the female at the hotel, we will stage her capture. Be ready."

Tao showed them to the door and then returned to the table where his father was sitting. "Do you think the council suspects we're involved?"

Ziyad gave his son a dismissive shake of his head as if his concerns about local government were unimportant. "We need to experiment and discover what effect the modifiers have."

Tao started to speak, but Ziyad cut him off. "And Tao, don't ever contradict me in public again."

"What do you want me to do?"

"Make sure they're with the team when the Fog female is captured. They need to witness the interrogation. Watch their reactions and record them. And the fisher's son, I'll contact the surgeon to remove his modifier. It's the only way to find out if removal causes death. Somehow, I doubt it."

Asha's brother was taken aback by this announcement. "Askook's been loyal. You know the Wen can go places we can't. If we cause even one of them harm, we may lose their devotion."

"In the condition they're in now, they will not be of further use to us."

"Chayton said he's willing to bear the pain." Tao chuckled. "He wants to be a warrior."

Ziyad laughed too and shook his head like the whole idea was a joke. "The Wen are not purebloods. Sure, they're dark, but still mongrels. They cannot be part of our order. I thought you understood that."

"I appreciate their commitment," Tao told his father with the earnest hope of swaying his decision. "Even the promise of membership gives them hope. It's been useful. They can bring in others to help our cause. Our scope is limited in this country. We need them."

Ziyad nodded, pondering for a moment. "Kinache and Chayton do have parents in powerful positions." The silence dragged on while he thought about the situation. Finally, he said, "You're right, they can still be useful. They can glean information for us. But letting them all suffer is a good test of their loyalty too. We need to find out how they react when they're near someone who's being harmed."

Tao agreed and was about to leave the room when Ziyad said, "The best use of the fisher's son is to observe what happens when we take it out. Just make sure the other two don't find out if he doesn't survive the experiment. We can tell them he went back to his family. They don't need any details."

Tao paused for a moment and then walked out of the room.

Asha and her brother had grown up here in Muwioni. Chayton and Kinache were his close friends. How long he had been acquainted with that other youth wasn't something she knew, but this had to trouble him. She didn't want to believe he was that brutal.

Asha was afraid to come out of the pantry. The house was too quiet; any movement she made would be heard. She crouched down and waited until finally her father went upstairs. Then she crept out the back way and headed to Mora's place.

Mora looked alarmed to see Asha at such a late hour. She was already dressed for bed. "I'm too tired to talk tonight, Asha," she said in a sleepy voice, then she noticed how frightened her friend was. "What happened? Come in, I'll make tea. Seems like you have something to tell me?"

"No, Mora, we have to get to the hotel and bring Bimisi here."

"She wants to be called Bi."

"Mora?" Asha looked at her with impatience. "Wake up, we have to go save her! I'll fill you in on the way."

47

SUSPICIONS

As Orenda searched for the art store, she considered what she knew of Kinache and Tao. They were mixed up in something. That she didn't doubt, but what?

Oddly, it wasn't Kinache's outrage or the marking which troubled Orenda the most. It was the cocky expression on the Zendali. She didn't sense empathy from Tao at all. He seemed too cavalier for the circumstances. Kinache, who she had pegged as smug and vain in the past, seemed desperate for this foreigner's respect. When she first met Tao, she had an inexplicable surge of panic. The way he scrutinized her that day at Holata Tyee's... had frightened her. She couldn't pinpoint why.

Not that she felt sorry for Kinache. She still didn't like him. He was a pretender like his mother, and Orenda was pretty sure he was involved in something untoward. But there was portent in the connection between these two young males. Something about them got under her skin.

It took her longer than expected to find the little shop that sold the paint, maybe because her mind was occupied by other things. It's possible she'd walked past the store and circled around more than once. When she finally got inside, she was delighted to see all the marvelous imported supplies they offered. It cheered her right up, and for a while, her thoughts of dirty deeds were suspended.

She bought more than she should have, more than was easy to carry. She now had several awkward bags of art supplies, and she was sure she couldn't fit them in the basket of a cycle, so she just trudged home on foot, cursing herself for not thinking about how much she was buying. Coso's place was all the way across town!

When Orenda arrived, she trudged straight to her room and deposited her supplies, then found her Great Aunt Coso having dinner in the garden.

"Orenda, there you are! Sorry, I started without you. I wasn't sure you were joining me for supper."

"I found the shop with the imported paints and bought a lot more supplies than I planned on getting. I didn't think about how far I would have to carry everything! It took me a while to walk home."

"You should have contacted me. I would have sent someone to pick you up."

Orenda looked thoughtful. "It would never have occurred to me to do that, Auntie. I didn't grow up with such options or privilege."

Coso nodded. "Of course, well, you're here now." She signaled to her aide, who had the kitchen staff bring her niece a plate.

"I saw something today that was disturbing."

Coso looked up with alarm. "Tell me what happened."

"Don't worry. Nothing happened to me. I just saw Kinache talking to a Zendali named Tao. I met him at Holata Tyee's that day."

Coso squinted her eyes and flattened her ear-fans.

"Kinache was angry," Orenda said, "and he showed Tao his arm. It had a white band around the wrist, which he had hidden with a bracelet. A webbing of white marks went up his arm. He called it a modifier."

"How did you come to witness this meeting and listen to what they were saying?"

"I hid in a doorway in the shadow. They didn't know."

"Please stay away from those two, Orenda. You are not studying with Holata Tyee. You have no reason to get involved with her son or concern yourself with what he is doing."

"The Zendali told him to go visit his father tonight and show him the markings. He said, to gather the others who have it."

Coso abruptly stood. "Let this go, Orenda. I don't want you getting involved in this! Excuse me, I have to make a call."

But just at that moment, Tokala Luta arrived looking frightened. "Pardon my intrusion, Councilor. I must speak to you now. Something terrible has happened."

"Follow me to my study then."

Orenda objected. "Auntie, please don't shut me out. I can't explain why, but I am already involved in this. Somehow it has to do with why I came. I need to know what is going on. I think I can help."

Coso considered the earnest faces of the two young apprentices and concluded that perhaps they could give her insight. They were able to see things differently. She did not want to discount the fact that the answers she needed might come from unexpected sources. "Yes, I accept that, but what we discuss stays between us, for now. It must be with my permission if you share anything I tell you. Do you understand?"

Both readily agreed.

In her office, she offered them seats while she attempted to contact Mato. When she didn't get a response, she searched for some files, then laid them on her desk and took a seat.

"Now, Tokala Luta, tell me your news."

48

THE TETHER

S ometimes Bi felt Far's presence strongly in the room. Now that she no longer communicated with her invigilator, she thought of a multitude of things she wished she had said. Bi realized that she'd let her own fear and doubt impede their friendship. She couldn't understand why she hadn't trusted her friend. There were always doubts holding her back.

In the dark, windowless room at the hotel, Bi sat in deep meditation. Entering a lucid state, she traveled to her Focal Space. Here she was able to call up anything she needed at will, a table, a map, or any other tool to assist her process or communication. It was a protected place where only those who had pure intent could enter.

On rare occasions, Bi might find other friendly spirit teachers who were no longer corporeal. Or dreamers visiting to give her important news or advice. Today she found one such spirit, an elder native of the Wendat tribes. He calmly gazed at her and spoke of only one mysterious thing: "You have a parasite. Tell my granddaughter to rid you of it."

When she was about to ask for clarification, he vanished.

She would have liked to know who his granddaughter was!

Bi could do nothing further to decipher what her mysterious guest meant. So, she put the enigma aside. She had a specific task in mind. Bi had saved memory objects that she wanted to share with Far. She was determined to find her. To somehow connect.

Transporting such objects out of one's own Focal Space was an arduous process for most students. Doing so took a steady mind. One must fix the objects and hold them in focus while they bring them into another dreamer's Focal Space. Bi had been holding them for some time, waiting for Far to connect, but maybe she had expected too much. She should have tried sooner to take them to Far.

She held the memory object of a gold medallion. It was the necklace worn by a Zendali business executive at the party. She also reconstructed the painting she'd seen once in a museum of the ancient emperor who wore it. Although now that she had to carry it out of her space, she shrank it to a more diminutive size. These objects looked real. She felt the weight of the gold in her hands.

Bi had been cut off from her invigilator since she got her implant. She had been so occupied with other things that she didn't spend time testing if there might be some way to repair the connection. "Far, what happened to you?" she whispered.

Bi sought her friend Far at her Focal Space. Hoping she could bridge whatever gap had been broken, frustrated by the barrier that the implant seemed to impose. But Bi couldn't enter. She was blocked. Finally, she grew tired of the effort to maintain a grasp on the objects she'd carried with her, and the connection dissipated. With her focus lost, she fell asleep, the words of her visitor in her thoughts. *A parasite? What did that mean? Am I ill?*

As she was falling asleep, she set an intention to find Far. Near daybreak, Bi entered a lucid dream. Far appeared, Bi reached out, attempting to speak to her. There was no response. Far didn't see or hear Bi.

Bi had two very different ways of using her gift. One was through lucid dreaming, which all spies were trained for. The other was astral projection. They had a completely different feel, and sensations. In lucid dreams, anything could be manifested. It was a magical realm and very fluid. Astral projection was the surveillance technique Bi could do from a meditative state. It was grounded in the physical world. Her spirit body would detach but lurk within the confines of the material world. She could direct it places, watch those who had no awareness of her presence, and listen to their conversations. This was how she was able to spy on the Zendali businessmen at the hotel. She needed to see them and have a visual reference, or maybe it wasn't so much *visual* as it was an imprint of their essence. Once she had that, she could find them. She had never done this through lucid dreaming.

Now, Bi had entered the Astral State through her lucid dream! This was unusual and had never happened before. She hovered in Far's environment, but instead of the two-way communication they were accustomed to, in the focal space, she was undetected and could not connect. The others in the room didn't realize she was there either.

Bi stilled herself to observe and try to understand what she was witnessing. Far was troubled, and uncharacteristically abrupt, as she spoke to a school administrator. They were asking for specific details, and Bi heard them speak her name. Bi had missed their questions. Far was receiving a warning.

"That is a serious accusation. What led to your conclusion?" The administrator had an admonishing tone.

It was unclear what concerned them because Bi missed most of the conversation.

Far was acting wary. "I just know it's true. I've seen..." Then she looked wildly around the room. "I mean, I... could tell she was lying."

"That will be all. You have deviated from the invigilator's duties, but I cannot ascertain exactly what you have been doing or not doing. We will investigate." The administrator waved her hand in dismissal.

Far turned to go.

"And Far, you have neglected your hygiene. Take care of it."

Far had not turned to face the administrator, which was rude. She tensed when accused of being unkempt. With no further word, she exited the administration office. A military commander confronted her in the hallway. "Are you certain your operative is a traitor?"

Bi was so shocked by the implication of this question that the lucid dream ended abruptly. Gasping as she sat up, looking urgently around the dark little room, unsure where she was. This was not foretelling a future event, as fever dreams would do. This was happening in real time! Her astral projection abilities had merged with her lucid dreaming!

Bi assumed the implant had blocked her ability to connect with Far. Because of this, her superiors had concluded she was a defector! She now had no way of getting a message to her invigilator. *Would Far be in danger by association?* Then, her mind flooded with indignant excuses and impossible-to-answer questions... *I'm doing my best! It's just so different from what anyone expected. I predicted it wouldn't be what they thought, and they didn't listen! Why would they decide I betrayed the Empire? On what evidence? Just because my invigilator can't reach me? If Far couldn't connect, wouldn't they assume that I'm dead?*

49

HARD TRUTHS

Mato was alarmed to find the two young men with his son at his home. There was menacing energy between them, a promise of confrontation. His first impression was that they intended to harm him in retribution for what the council had done. He quickly presented a calm front, acting as if he didn't find the situation dangerous. "You have something to say to me?" Mato asked his son Chayton.

"How could you let them do this to us? To me! Your own son!"

Mato considered how to respond. It was obvious that presenting facts about the crimes they'd committed wouldn't be useful in their current state of agitation. They felt justified in their actions. He was wondering *how* they had been corrupted, and yet he would not find out by merely questioning them. "Have a seat." He motioned to the sofa and chairs in the living room and took an armchair by the door himself.

They looked at each other, a little confused by Mato's easy demeanor. But they sat and now looked less ready to attack, a little more like the scared and confused teenagers that they were.

"I am not going to ask you what you're involved in, or why you are doing the bidding of criminals because I know you won't tell me. But neither am I willing to accept you're beyond redemption. Kinache, you grew up playing in this house with my son. I loved you like you were my own. And this youngster," he nodded toward Askook, "I'm sure would not be your friend if he weren't worthy of your trust. Whatever you're all involved in, I wish to appeal to your better selves. Please change your course. Give this modifier a chance to help you."

"To help us? You've condemned us to a lifetime of suffering, and for what? Because we followed the law? Obeyed the treaty you have with the Sovereign Nation? You and the entire council have been bending the rules for years, building those reservations, harboring traitors. Some of them are terrorists!"

The rage and the way his son spit out the words, punctuating each statement with complete conviction, shocked Mato. A feeling of deep remorse filled him. He'd lost his son. How had this happened? How had he not seen the signs?

"Aren't you going to say anything? You're more guilty than we are! You and your corrupt accomplices, and their rampant misuse of power, this sham of a government is infested with liberal practices undermining the foundation of our valuable foreign relationships!"

"Enough!" Mato stood.

Chayton also stood, chest puffed out, chin thrust forward, his slitted pupils reduced to pinpoints. All the signs of intense aggression. His fists clenched tight at his sides.

Mato took a step back, realizing his son's temper was out of control.

Chayton countered that by taking one menacing step toward his father, fist raised now to throw a punch.

Mato was suddenly filled with the kind of pain only a father can understand, a great loss, a recognition of failure. Suddenly Chayton began to groan, his eyes rolled back, his face contorted into an expression of agony. He first grabbed his arm, then put a hand to his chest and cried out, falling to the ground, rolling into a fetal position, tears wetting the fur on his face. He looked up at the other two standing over him. "Get out!"

Kinache and Askook ran for the door. When it slammed shut, Mato sat with his son and took him into his arms. Chayton resisted, but Mato held him tight. "Calm down now. The pain will dissipate when you let go of the anger, breathe, let it go."

Chayton started sobbing. After the pain eased, he pulled roughly away from his father. Resentful of the weakness he had shown in front of his friends, still angry about what his father had done to him.

Mato got up and started toward his study. "You should rest, son."

"There are things going on in Muwioni you should do something about!"

"Chayton, why are you so worked up about council business? You're not privy to all the details of what goes on in the city, and someone has distorted the facts and led you astray. Don't you trust me anymore?"

"How can I trust you when you punish the wrong people?"

"Are you denying you were involved in the attempted capture of a female in the forest?"

"She poisoned Askook!"

"I believe it is possible she was defending herself."

"She's Fog! An abomination!"

Hearing these words from his own son crushed Mato. "I don't want to hear that kind of talk in this house. Our people have always protected the refugees, regardless of their breeding. That is not going to stop."

"So, you admit the council is breaking our treaty with the Sovereign Nation? You *are* aware the Fog are being sheltered there."

Mato just stared at his son, unsure how to respond. The council had never admitted to harboring the Fog. There was nothing in their treaty directly forbidding the aid they gave the refugees. But Chayton was correct. The council had intentionally manipulated the situation.

"And I assume you will do nothing about Zamora, who is Fog?" Chayton said with bitterness.

"Are you talking about the young scientist you were in love with? You told me she was brilliant. You admired her! And now you want her detained, turned over to the Zendali, knowing they will harm her?"

Chayton's ear-fans flattened in frustration. "Zamora was a student at the university. She refused to put me on her team that designed the portal tech. I lost an opportunity because she didn't accept me! I'm better than the others, but she didn't want me! A *Fog* decided I wasn't good enough for her!"

"The way you spoke of Zamora, I thought you were dating her."

Chayton rolled his eyes. "We didn't date. I showed my interest, and she ignored me! Someone like her should have been grateful for my attention. But she wouldn't give me a chance. She's a mongrel who acts like a privileged bitch. Why should she be the exception?"

"Exception?"

"She lives somewhere in the city, not on a reservation. Did you know she's the one who actually invented portal technology? The university promised her diplomas! She shouldn't be allowed! It's your duty to put her in her place! She's deceiving everyone, walking around in public pretending to be a follower of Bicara!" Chayton looked away, his lip curling up in a smirk.

"She rejected you? Is that it? She wasn't interested, and you know her secret, so now you want to hurt her, show her who's in control?"

Chayton turned to his father with a look of utter contempt. Faced with the truth of the matter made him angrier. "The Sisters' of Justice are a sham to harbor fugitives!"

"The Sisters' who worship Bicara have sound principles. If you don't agree with their ways, you can ignore them. Let people believe what they wish. They are doing no harm to you."

"You are an ignorant old fool."

All the energy seemed to drain out of Mato when he heard disrespect so casually spoken. "You will not speak to anyone about Zamora. If you endanger her in any way, you will be cast out. The consequences will be more difficult to face than this modifier. You've been given one chance to adjust your behavior... take it."

Chayton was shocked his father would threaten to cast him out. It meant leaving the city, being sent far away. This was enough to sober him.

"Please leave the room. I have council business to attend to."

"Ever since Mother died, all you've done is work. At least now I have the support of people who see my worth." With such a painful truth hanging between them, Chayton left the room.

Mato saw messages on his receptor. Coso had been trying to reach him. He called her and learned about the death at the sanctuary. She also told him Tokala Luta suspected Holata Tyee and her son were involved with the Order of Amon Kuroo. He confirmed that this aligned with his recent intelligence but said nothing about Zamora.

After a sleepless night, where he worried about the fate of the young scientist his son had been infatuated with, he decided to contact her. He'd received some reports about the Portal contracts. He was aware that a Zendali delegation had won the manufacturing bid. Which was not what the council wanted. He also found that her university lab assistant, Algon, was in charge of production and was credited with her invention. The unfairness of the whole situation did not sit well with him. He had a strong sense there was more to it, and now this young female was at the heart of everything, a Fog, and an *inventor*. He was intrigued.

Zamora had her Receptor connection set to private, so Mato had to contact Tokala Luta to obtain her signal code. Even then, he had to leave a message and hope she would reply. He wasn't even sure what he was trying to do... maybe to warn her, or to pledge his support? To let her know she wasn't alone during a time of difficulty? Maybe knowing his son was trying to cause her harm made him act, to create balance. The only certainty he clung to was the need to protect her, and he didn't care what rules he had to break to do that.

50

Temporary Measures

A sha had contacted Algon to pick up a vehicle and meet them at the gates of the park. Mora still didn't feel like seeing him and wasn't at all pleased when she saw him waiting for them. She turned to Asha with a look of disapproval. "Was that necessary? If you have his help, why do you need me?"

"You need to get over your animosity toward Algon. He didn't intend to undermine you. But this is not about him or about you. Bimisi is in immediate danger, and there's nowhere else for her to stay except with you." Mora was sobered by Asha's deft rebuke.

They got to the hotel quickly. This late in the evening, most people were home from their jobs and having an evening meal. The streets were pretty empty. They parked in the front. Algon elected to wait outside in the vehicle. Asha and Mora went directly to the room where Bi was boarding. Asha signaled the door, and when Bi answered, looking surprised, Asha didn't waste any time explaining. She pushed past her and started gathering her things.

"What are you doing?"

"We'll explain on the way to Mora's place."

Mora added: "We need to relocate you to a reservation where they don't have access to you Bi. I told you before how dangerous this place is for you. I made a mistake in bringing you here. Please be reasonable. Asha overheard some men talking about capturing and torturing you!"

"Look, this is crazy. I am not going to a reservation. I am not Fog."

Asha looked at her with impatience. "You can stay at Mora's place until we make the arrangements. Don't argue with me. You are not staying here!"

Bi looked imploringly at Mora. "Please stop telling me what is best for me."

But it was Asha who answered: "Tell me now, if you're not Fog, what *are* you? This mess of fur dye you put all over yourself doesn't fool anyone. Did one of your parents mate with a Pink? You can tell me. I work on the reservations. I promise to do everything I can to protect you."

"It's nothing like that. I... all right, I will come with you now, and you can tell me what has gotten you so upset, but I won't promise to move anywhere."

Asha took it as a *go* and pushed Bi's backpack into her arms. "Gather up any other things that I missed ... hurry."

The three of them ran to the car, and Algon drove off.

"Did you see anyone lurking around, watching the hotel?" Asha asked Algon.

"Just normal tourists coming and going, nothing suspicious."

"Are you going to explain to me what has upset you?" Mora asked Asha.

"Yes," said Bi. "I think you should explain."

On the way back, Asha told them what she had overheard at her home. Then Mora told Bi about their trip to the reservation.

"If murder is happening on the reservations, why would you think I'm safer there?"

Asha and Mora exchanged a look. "She has a point," said Algon.

Just to be sure they weren't followed, Algon drove around the back streets for a while before heading to the foreigner's district. When they got inside, Mora noticed her Receptor Screen pulsing, an indication of an unknown number trying to reach her. She played the message and found that it was the Council member, Mato. The father of Chayton, who was requesting to speak with her.

Asha looked at her in alarm. "That can't be good, can it? What could he want?"

"Chayton knows I'm Fog. He threatened to expose me. I suspect he must have told his father."

"How did he find out? Algon, weren't you managing that selection process?" Asha asked.

"During the process of setting up the team for Zamora, Chayton passed my screening. I'm not sure how, because he has proven to be somehow involved with whatever Tao is doing. I should have found some indication of his affiliation with the Zendali."

"Maybe he hadn't fallen in with them yet?" Mora suggested.

Algon shrugged. "He did not seem to have any bigotry issues, or xenophobia, which I was screening for at the time."

"Why wasn't he chosen?" Asked Mora.

"I don't know. That was not my decision. The next stage of the selection process was an interview with Zamora. She remained veiled for that."

"So, he could not have found out at that point." Asha mused.

Algon nodded agreement. "As far as his technical abilities went, he passed or exceeded the other candidates. But there was something about his behavior that warned Zamora off. She decided not to accept him. Since he was already assigned to a different project, she didn't think he would be upset about not being chosen. But he persisted. Kept pushing for her to change her mind. Then something strange happened, and Zamora started meeting up with him and revealed what she was. It didn't make any sense to me. I told Asha about it, and we were both baffled."

"I don't think he has a clue where you live, and from what I heard my brother say, they can't tell who is a real member of the Sisters' of Justice, and who is using the veil to hide. So, there is that."

Mora came to her senses then, realizing that Bi was still standing in the entryway with all her things in her arms. She looked confused and tired. Mora felt suddenly guilty for getting sidetracked about her own welfare. It was clear they both needed to be careful.

"Welcome to the sisterhood of Bicara, Bi."

They all looked at Mora, then realized what she meant.

"Let me show you the guest room." She turned to Algon and Asha. "I think I can take it from here. We all need some rest."

51

SPARKS & LEADS

Yuma had been stopping by lately. He told Orenda he wanted to get acquainted, but he was pretty sure his mentor wouldn't approve. Still, he snuck away for quick visits quite often.

Orenda had set up her easel in the atrium off of her aunt's garden.

"The surreal worlds you paint are so captivating. How do you imagine such unusual things?"

Orenda didn't want to tell Yuma those places were from her dreams. She still felt protective of her visions. But she liked that they intrigued him. Rather than answer, she just smiled and shrugged.

Last week when he showed up, he brought her a tincture made with rosemary and lemon peel. This he made himself to remove the paint from her hands. Orenda was touched by his thoughtful caring. She also liked how sweetly proud he was when she accepted it. Ever since then, he'd come with a present for her.

Last week he had given her a balm for her lips, and some sweet bonbons made from cocoa beans and honey. She told him that he didn't need to bring her gifts. But the way he deflated at her words made her understand. These were more than kindness. They were love tokens.

Today he brought her a carved shell, a craft item from his homeland. It was an exquisite piece, and she loved it. The way her eyes brightened at the sight of it was all Yuma wanted. It pleased him to give her joy.

"But I can't accept this, Yuma. It's too precious and valuable!"

Yuma's disappointment was reflected in his body language. His ears flattened back, and he shifted from foot to foot.

Orenda realized she'd offended him. "I'm sorry. Are you sure you want to part with this?"

Then he smiled. "I would like you to have something from my tribe. Maybe one day you will visit my home with me?"

Orenda looked at him shyly and placed the carved shell on the ledge by her window. This was nearly a declaration that he wanted to partner with her, suggesting that she might want to meet his family. She wiggled her ears at the thought.

"It opens," he told her.

"Really?" She took the shell in hand again to examine it closer. Yes, there was a small seam... she put her claw in between and a lid popped up, revealing a small compartment. Inside was a translucent stone arrowhead.

"I found the arrowhead when I was a child."

"That must be an ancient artifact!"

"I have many. I spent a lot of time in old ruins. That one is small and perfect. You might use it for a necklace... maybe?"

She smiled because he already understood what she would like.

Orenda had never been courted before. The native youth in her village held her in such high regard as their future medicine guardian that they didn't see her as their equal. Normal friendships were awkward, and their deference made her feel like an outsider.

Orenda took up her paintbrush while Yuma talked to her. This was now their usual pattern. He would stay for an hour or so while she worked.

Yuma told her a little about his tenure with Holata Tyee, and it sounded like she was overbearing and secretive. She gave her son, Kinache, too much leeway, which he took advantage of by raiding their herbal and medical stores for his own experiments.

"He's not trained in medicine. You mentioned before he was training with a Zendali medicine practitioner? Is that what he needs the supplies for?"

"I wouldn't call her a *medicine practitioner*. Not like we use that title anyway, she's a sorceress."

"Is Holata Tyee aware of this?"

Yuma shook his head. "No, and I won't be the one to tell her. She adores her son. He can do no wrong in her eyes, and he's learned how to use her fondness to his advantage. Even after he came home with the stigma, she was fussing over him like he was a victim, rather than being upset about what he had done to deserve punishment."

"Stigma?"

"The Star People gave the council another invention, called a Modifier. A device that is paired with the implant to hinder violence. The marks created by the white band are distinctive wavy lines running up the arm."

Orenda turned from her painting to face Yuma. "I saw this! I was in the city looking for an art store and I saw Kinache with a young Zendali. He was showing him the marks!"

"Right, that would be Tao. He is the son of the Zendali ambassador, Ziyad, who is close friends with Holata Tyee."

Orenda put down her paintbrush. She wanted to say more, but she had promised her aunt not to disclose any information about the Order of Amon Kuroo and the locals who got mixed up with them. "Yuma, you should stay clear of Kinache. Don't complain about him taking supplies. Don't let him know you suspect him."

"Holata Tyee blames me for misuse, and also the mess he leaves. I am always cleaning up after him."

"It doesn't matter. Put up with whatever he does and act like you're ignorant of what he's doing. I'm serious. Dangerous people surround him. Don't reveal you're aware of these things."

Yuma looked askance at her. "Can you explain why you think this, Orenda?"

She didn't have a chance to answer. Asha and Tokala Luta, who came into the Atrium, interrupted them. Which was a good thing, because she wasn't sure what she was *allowed* to say in reply to his question.

"Yuma, I thought I'd find you here."

"How do you know I visit Orenda?"

"Doesn't matter." She smiled at him. She enjoyed being clever.

Asha gave her greetings to Yuma and Orenda. "Excuse me, I came to talk with your aunt," then she headed to the study.

Orenda commented on Tokala Luta's sleuth abilities. "She does always find you, Yuma. Maybe you're too predictable?"

Yuma gave Orenda a doubtful look. "More likely, she follows me."

"Yuma, I have better things to do!" She laughed and pushed his shoulder in a friendly way. "I actually tagged along with Asha, and I wanted to visit Orenda. I didn't realize you were here."

"But you said—"

"I was just messing with you."

Orenda enjoyed the way Tokala Luta teased Yuma. He was a little naïve, which made him gullible. Looking at the dynamics between the two of them, they almost seemed like siblings. Yuma had been in Muwioni for a few years, but he was still so unsophisticated, Orenda wondered how he had remained so innocent living in the city and working under Holata Tyee. She believed he was a talented healer, although his mentor didn't seem to value his skill. He generally kept his head down and did her bidding.

"What was it you came to see me about?" Orenda asked Tokala Luta.

"Have you ever encountered dark magic charms? And do you have any protection against them?"

This completely shifted the light mood of a moment. "What kind of magic, and what is the charm for?"

"To be honest, I am not sure." She took something out of her satchel that looked like a head, made of tar, shells and feathers. "Kinache made this. He pours blood onto this thing and puts offerings by it like an idol. He also made some amulets." She took something else out of her pocket and laid it on the table.

Yuma's intake of breath was audible. "Why would you take these? He will notice they're missing!"

"No, he won't. He's with his friend Tao. They'll be gone all afternoon."

"Yuma is right. You took a chance in bringing these here. These are not familiar, but they feel unclean. The energy is dreadful," she motioned to the effigy. "And that stinks of death."

Yuma seemed very upset by this breach of protocol. "Please take them back, Tokala. Make sure you place the items in the exact way he had them."

"I'm sorry I can't help you. If an insight comes to me, I'll tell you."

Tokala Luta thanked her. Then Yuma suggested they go right away and return Kinache's things.

Orenda took a break from painting to eat supper in the garden. Asha and her aunt came to join.

"Did the apprentices leave?" Coso asked.

"Yes, they had to attend to something urgently."

"I was updating Coso about Bimisi. We believe she is the one who Chayton and Askook tried to capture in the forest. We moved her to a safe location."

When Orenda looked confused, Asha told her. "Those two you were curious about meeting? One of them works at the Journeyer Hotel in the kitchen. I overheard a conversation which indicated she was in immediate danger. She's been boarding there for a few weeks."

Orenda looked excited. "Is she still working at the hotel?"

"I'm not sure. In my opinion, she shouldn't continue to go there, but she is pretty stubborn. I wanted to tell you I've met the other person from your drawings. And I will arrange a meeting for you as soon as I can."

"Oh! Such great news! Thank you so much, Asha!"

The three of them enjoyed their meal and chatted about other matters, but Orenda found herself somewhat distracted. She couldn't stop thinking about the two mysterious females who had been so much a part of her dream-world for years, and now she would meet them!

After Asha left, Orenda told her aunt what Tokala Luta had brought and what Kinache was doing. She had not been entirely honest with the apprentice. She had seen this effigy before in the eastern city when she was young. It was in the window of a backstreet shop that sold strange items for ceremonies. Her grandfather had told her to stay away from the place, and that this store was specifically for a Zendali religious sect. When she had asked why she should avoid it, he had said, "They're powerful gods, but not ours." She told her aunt everything she knew about the Zenda magic, which was not a lot.

"Asha mentioned two people from your drawings," Coso said. "What is that about?"

Orenda wasn't ready to tell her about them. "Oh, just some possible schoolmates," she told her. This was likely, as Orenda had visited galleries and artist functions in the city, making connections with the creative community before the school semester began.

As soon as she could disengage from her aunt, she retired to her room for the evening. Orenda couldn't stop thinking about Bimisi. The expectation of meeting someone from her dreams kept her awake. She finally decided to go to the hotel in the morning and try to meet her. She didn't have the patience to wait for Asha to make the introduction. Who knows how long that will take? Or if a formal introduction is even possible! At least now she had a lead, and she was going to follow it.

52

ZAMORA'S MOTHER

B efore Zamora was sent away from Zenda to live on Wendat, she discovered a journal
her mother had left for her. She took this with her and kept it in a secret place inside
her home library in Muwioni. She didn't shelve this cherished memento with all her other
journals. Only by happenstance did Mora find it.

She had set her Kav mug on the ledge of the bookshelf while searching for a specific
book. When she reached to move the cup, it bumped the edge of the molding and a narrow
tray popped out. Suddenly aware something had come loose, she looked carefully at the
open space to put the molding back in place, but then realized it wasn't broken. There
was a secret compartment, and inside was a book.

"I leave this journal for you, my daughter. Despite our traditions for the Golden to be
raised by their grandparents, you are my love-child, and I am your birth mother. They will
take you from me, but I wanted you to know I love you with all my heart, and I want to
keep you. You're all I have left of him."

These were the words of Zamora's Serwa! Mora closed the secret panel and took the
book to her bedroom, not wanting others to pick it up out of curiosity.

"I am sorry you will never meet your father, not that any Golden ever does. But yours,
despite being Pink, is brilliant and kind. I cannot write his name here; my father has made
me promise not to tell anyone, and especially not you. He will find your father a good
posting and won't speak of our crime."

"In all honesty, I can't imagine being with another mate. He is my best friend. Although my mother insists, I will wed soon to honor the bond arrangement. I will obey, if
for no other reason than to keep your father safe. I would not want him punished. I am
also to blame. But my price for these arrangements is my silence. You will never hear his

name and therefore have no way of tracing him. Don't be unhappy with me. This is for your own good as well as his."

Obviously, Zamora did have regrets. Asha mentioned she had wanted to search for him but did not have a name.

"I feel adrift in the pain of separation. Your father and I grew up together. I've never been without him. His absence is as shocking as it was meaningful."

"I hope I will grow to love my husband, as my mother assures me I will. I expect I will adore my children. Yet none of them will be as dear to me as you are. At this moment, I wonder if I will ever purr again. Will I ever know the tenderness your father gave me? My heart, quite literally, is broken."

Mora felt a chill, and her fur raised.

"I must put on an indifferent face. I can't manage a happy one."

It fascinated Mora to read the thoughts of this other mother, a different version of Serwa. She knew how fond her parents were of each other, how perfectly matched they were. How sad for this young Zendali to lose such a perfect love and be forced into an arranged marriage.

"At least I have an excuse for my melancholy when facing my husband's family. They were told my Golden child died. This will not prevent my status or the honor of a Golden wedding. The death of a Golden hatchling is not a misfortune befalling the birth mother. My parent's friends will be sorry for *their* loss, not mine. No one will know you live. No one can ever know you exist."

Mora raised her eye ridge. *What a horrible social system. Why give less value to a child because of their color?*

"I am sorry for the isolation you will experience shut away from everything in this house. You will have no friends and no culture. I hope you will not hate me for what I've done by bringing you into this world."

From what Asha had told her about Zamora's childhood; she had not suffered. She took the isolation in stride. I suppose that was partly because she didn't know what she was missing. Mora read Serwa's whole journal, staying up late into the night. Serwa told Zamora that her father had spent all his free time in the family library. Seems they had that in common. In other journals, Zamora had mentioned the library, her tutors, and a walled private garden. Her Zendali grandparents were not the most attentive or affectionate people, but they must have loved her to take such a risk. Apparently, she also forged a good relationship with her other grandparents, who were servants in the household.

Hearing the intimate thoughts of this version of Serwa made Mora wonder how much of her character and inner yearnings were like her own mother. She became aware of how little she knew about her mother's past. Mora had never thought of asking her about such things. Her mother guarded her personal issues and didn't share her feelings or fears openly. Well, Zamora's Serwa didn't dare be open about her true emotions either. The most important event in her life was also a crime that she had to hide.

Nonetheless, Mora could not help comparing the two mothers and wondered how much they were alike. Memories flashed through her mind; tears soaked into the fine fur on her face. Her mother had a good life. Her happiness was easy enough to read. Whatever her childhood had been like, the traumas she left behind, she was content in her marriage now. Mora made a promise to herself if she was ever able to return, to inquire more about Serwa's life before she immigrated to the United Colonies of Inoti.

Before falling asleep, Mora took the journal back to the library, so it would remain hidden in the secret compartment. Grateful for the gift that her counterpart's mother had left, it had reached further than Zamora's Serwa could ever have imagined.

53

THE BENEFACTOR

Mora had been working on the mind-map project Asha had proposed for about a week. When Asha arrived on the morning that they planned to visit the reservation, she took note of the pulsing messages, obviously unanswered, on Mora's wall screen. "What's that about?" she asked Mora.

"Mato, he calls every day."

"Persistent, isn't he? And you still haven't talked to him? Aren't you at all curious about what he wants?"

Mora shook her head. "I don't want anything to do with Chayton or his father."

Asha looked thoughtfully at Mora. "I've had occasion to meet Mato. He is a friend and colleague of Coso Winnemucca. I found him to be fair in his government dealings, and he seems to be a decent sort in general."

"I'll think about it," Mora said with a little stubbornness.

Asha pursed her lips knowingly. "Well then, let's review what we have ready. You mentioned there's enough... should we take what we have to the reservation today?" Asha had not really expected they would have an adequate mind-map completed for their reservation trip this time, but Mora seemed to think they did. "I was amazed that my history professor let me borrow the recording device for the whole summer," Asha said.

Mora smiled. "How *did* you manage to convince her?"

"I told her I needed it to prepare for my graduate project."

"Instead, you're spending time on things that won't advance your degree."

Asha's ear-fans sort of wiggled and then flattened back. "I can't think of this as a waste of my time. It's important."

"More than getting your degree?"

Asha gave Mora an eye roll. "I know…"

"Well, let me show you what I have then." Mora was filled with the sort of enthusiasm that was impossible not to notice, and it made Asha curious.

They had installed the recording device at Mora's place, in the second-floor library for privacy.

It only took a quick review of the material before Asha was astonished. "How did you complete such a vast amount of data in such a short time? And how do you have all this information in your head? It isn't even related to science."

"I also learned other languages from my world, and speak them fluently. My native tongue is Inreji, which is the dominant language in the United Colonies of Inoti. But this language the Pinks try to speak isn't exactly what I know. They have an antiquated, broken, and incomplete version of Inreji, which I can barely understand. I also heard a few phrases in other languages I recognized. I suspect the situation is the same for all the other reservations. They have fragments of their native languages which were preserved over time, but considering they weren't allowed to speak them, much was forgotten."

"And you're versed in all of them without an implant?" Asha looked at her in awe.

Mora laughed a little. "No, not all, but some. Essentially, with enough time, I would be able to rebuild a functional dictionary for each of the languages I learned, along with grammar, and rules of usage. However, we don't have the luxury of time. Instead, I chose some common phrases in those languages to get them started."

Asha was completely stunned. "I had no idea when I asked you to help me with the mind-mapping that you were capable of this! All I've been able to contribute are fragments of history, what their countries and cultures were like before the expansion wars."

"Asha, none of this would have happened if not for you! And what you contribute is very meaningful. It gives them context. They were once an advanced civilized people before the Zenda conquered them. This mind-map basically rewrites their history and nullifies what they've been told about being some kind of wild heathens who didn't have the ability for higher learning."

"This is already a staggering achievement, and you've only just gotten started" Asha's eyes teared up. "Thank you, Mora."

"I can help with the history and cultural part as well, or at least I can contribute by filling in what those cultures created in my world. I honestly don't have enough of your history to ascertain if any of those countries had the chance to develop as far here." She looked at Asha for any sign that she would be able to fill in those bits of Zenda history, but Asha shook her head.

"I'm sorry I can't tell you. So much of their history was suppressed."

"Well, maybe they did, and the Zenda claimed those advancements?"

"The Star People guided all of those civilizations in ancient times. For some reason, they removed themselves when the wars started and let the Pinks be overtaken. But I have no doubt they did help those cultures develop various higher learning skills. I have also visited some of the ruins in the territories. Those structures are still standing but quite damaged from the war. They are masterful designs, which could only have been built with a knowledge of advanced science and math."

"I'd love to travel in this world."

Asha looked sadly at her friend, knowing that would be impossible. "I can show you pictures."

"So, you think we have enough to get started?"

"Oh yes, I'm amazed at how much you've accomplished. I understand now what Algon meant when he told me, that you never sleep!"

"Once my mind latches onto a problem, I don't get much rest until I'm finished."

Asha's expression of mirth made Mora laugh.

"Yes, I realize this project may not ever be finished. But I will do what I have time for."

Asha thanked her again and then began to gather what they needed for the trip.

"If you don't mind, I will respond to Mato before Tokala gets here."

Asha tried to suppress her smile. "Sure, I'll be down when I finish here."

Mora went downstairs, found the receptor, and signaled Mato. She planned to leave a message, but he picked up on the first ring. "This is Zamora. You have been trying to reach me?"

Mato paused as if he wasn't quite sure how to begin. "I've been anticipating this call for some time. At first, I just wanted to warn you that forces beyond our ability to control mean you harm. But as the week went by and I had plenty of time to think about you and the fact that you were cheated out of ownership of your invention, I wanted to offer my patronage. If you have another project in mind, I am willing to sponsor you."

Mora couldn't believe what she was hearing. This sounded too good to be true. Part of her wanted to agree. An immediate impulse of gratitude filled her with hope and anticipation. She wanted to jump around Zamora's house with joy... but the practical or perhaps suspicious side of her was the one who spoke. "I'll think about it and get back to you."

"Of course, if you have questions, just let me know. I will make whatever you need a priority."

She thanked him for the offer and disengaged. Standing in her living room, staring at the wall, she considered all the possibilities, realizing that this could be her way back.

54

The Memorial Tree

T okala picked them up a half-hour later, and they headed for the reservation.

"You will not believe what Mora has done!" Asha was excited to tell Tokala about all they'd accomplished.

On the way, they discussed the mind-map, as well as how they might organize, in secret, some small groups for the self-defense lessons. Tokala was still hesitant about this idea; they were getting in deeper and deeper with regard to breaking the treaties. The mind-map alone contained much more than she'd expected. The work she did on the reservations was important, and the people needed her. She didn't want to risk being blocked from continuing if their illicit activities were reported. She feared the repercussions which might befall them if the wrong people were to find out what they were doing. So much uncertainty and danger surrounded this interference in the refugees' lives.

Mora and Asha argued with Tokala, who was still somewhat reticent about going further with the mind-map and teaching the Pinks to fight.

"A revolution cannot progress without the dissemination of knowledge," Asha told her.

"Don't you agree that such a great injustice must be reconciled?" Mora asked with a beseeching tone.

"They deserved to hear the truth! We owe it to them to give back what we can!" Asha implored.

"I can empower them, so they will protect themselves." Mora insisted.

In the end, their arguments swayed Tokala, even though she felt uncomfortable with the fact they had used the term revolution. "It is not our place to instigate a revolution or to encourage the Pinks to fight!"

But Asha convincingly countered this argument. "Young King Nak is the revolution-ary, and you can be sure that the traditionalists are going to push back on any of the changes he makes. All we are saying is, let's not let our Pinks get harmed in the process."

"He's not their king yet. But I get your point."

When they arrived at the reservation, however, they were faced with the consequences of the young female's gruesome death. A huge deciduous tree near the entrance of the compound was hung with the cut braids of all the resident's hair, both sexes. Attached to the branches with ribbons and colored string. A clear protest of the harm done to them, and the lack of justice for these acts of violence.

Tokala said, "Many of the tribes on Wendat have a custom of cutting their hair when they're in mourning, or during times of significant change."

"I think this is more than that," said Asha. "In the territories of The Sovereign Nation, when the expansion wars first began, most of the Pinks were hunted and killed. Scalps were taken as trophies, and for profit. Soldiers who took the lives of Pinks, were given a bonus for the number of scalps they collected. Long hair, especially lighter colors, was sold for decorative elements in the Zendali fashion industry."

"Their long hair decorates Zendali Garments?"

"More so in the past, but yes, and it is used to make elaborate wigs."

"But I was told the Pinks were all moved from their homelands?"

"Only the females who didn't fight back, and young children were taken for relocation. The prettiest and the most passive captives survived. Later, surviving Pinks kept their heads shaved or their hair cut short in protest. Or maybe for personal protection. Only those born and raised on the breeding farms let their hair grow long because they were required to."

"In the UCI settlers colonized this country, moving into native settlements, taking over their territories. The story was much the same as in this world with Zenda and the Pinks," Mora told them. "Living here in Muwioni only makes the truth of that tragedy more obvious. Too much was lost in our world. The native cultures and languages are nearly non-existent. It was somehow easier to accept before I had personal knowledge of what was missing. Now that I've met the native people here, the loss is a raw place in my heart."

Tokala saw that Mora had tears in her eyes. What she had admitted was devastating.

Asha brought Mora back to the present when she said, "Do you know why they call them Pinks?"

Mora shook her head.

"They don't have a double layer of fur. If you look at any Zenda native, we have a thicker pelt consisting of two layers," Asha said. One is a soft, fluffy underlayer, intermixed with a second layer, which is a little longer, and glossy. If you look closely, or part our fur, even then, you won't easily view the epidermis on a Zendali. But the Pinks have only one layer of short silky fur. Their pink skin can be easily seen underneath. Their fur is most often white but can be other pale colors... No matter what color the fur is, their epidermis is pink underneath. And one more thing: if you cut into the flesh, it is also pink. If you cut into Zendali flesh, it is dark."

"We have only one layer of fur as well," Tokala interjected. "The Wen are closer to the fair races. Our epidermis is darker, but if cut, the flesh is pink. Our skin color usually matches our fur. It is only the Zendali who have such a thick pelt, and dark meat."

Mora had never really paid attention, but she had a double layer of fur like Asha. It was just lavender instead of Indigo. Another sign of her Zendali bloodline, like the Mane.

Asha continued with the history of the fair races. "Some Pinks in their homelands had a tradition of shaving the body fur to decorate their skin with abrasion and ink to make permanent designs. Then their fur grew over them, but the pattern showed through. They were called tokens, amulets, and charms. I think maybe they were some sort of hereditary mark, a clan identifier, or perhaps symbols from their pagan spiritual beliefs. They were beautiful, intricate designs, like woven knots, patterns, or fanciful creatures. The soldiers who sold scalps took advantage of the interest in these graphics and developed a market for the skin that had charms etched on it. They began to cut these markings from the dead, as well as taking their scalps. The long pale hair, and these unique symbols on the skin were highly coveted. City people paid a high price for them."

"Oh!" Mora's eyes grew wide with shock.

"These skins were used to make handbags, jackets, and other collectible items. At some point, when the expansion wars were over, they made captives replicate these designs on themselves. In this way, they maintained a retail advantage for their merchandise. A gruesome thing, considering the captive Pinks must have understood why they were asked to mark each other. Also around that time, they started the breeding farms, culling the females and a few bucks to raise the products they later marketed. Some residents on the reservations escaped from these Pedigree Farms, as they came to be called," Asha said.

Tokala asked, "Is it the reason why many of them had short hair when they arrived?"

Asha nodded. "Yes, they likely sold their long hair for passage with a fishing vessel, or tradespeople who were shipping Zenda products to this country. It is highly valued and expensive. But also, they may have cut it for protection. The farm did give them safety of a sort. They didn't allow their Pinks to be harmed by outsiders. They must have been aware they might be killed by someone who would take their scalp after they escaped."

"Do you think they knew their hair was used as a fringe on garments in Zenda?"

"It's possible. Someone might have told them. Most of the breeding farms also ran a side business, providing sexual services for the sailors who frequented their ports. So, they did have access to people who might talk about things the breeders didn't tell them."

"They forced them into prostitution?!"

"Surprisingly, from the reports I read, they wanted to interact with the travelers, regardless of what was expected."

"Why would they?!" It was Tokala who was most offended by this.

"Maybe because the sailors brought news of the outside world? That is also where most of our Fog came from too. Some escaped by to stowing away on the boats, or occasionally the sailors would willingly assist them. Especially if they were the ones who impregnated them. It was a high crime to create the Fog. It motivated them to get the prostitute to safety."

"Why would the breeders endanger their business and take such a risk?" Mora asked.

"For the same reason most people break the law, money. It was *very* profitable. The females that the farm prostituted were not their prime breeding stock. They were less than perfect specimens. Later, when laws prohibited prostitution, they gave the imperfect stock to the Market Economy Services for placement elsewhere."

"Even after they found their way to Wendat, they kept their hair short. Only in recent years have they felt safe enough to let it grow." Tokala pointed out.

"How long did this go on?" Ask Mora.

"Oh, the breeding farms are still in operation, but Nakhadot's father, King Nebtawi, set very strict operational laws forbidding prostitution. Most of Nebtawi's laws are not popular among the ruling class, but by law they should be imposed."

"I can't imagine! That is so sad," Mora said.

"However, before Nebtawi came into power, the farms had expanded in scope. They also became a market for transplant organs, exotic luxury meats, as well as hair and skin for fashion and household items. They even used the bones for jewelry."

Tokala looked horrified. "This is unknown to our people!"

"The government agents are supposed to enforce all regulations that King Nebtawi was able to put into law. But I have heard the Amun, who are essentially in control, are notorious for letting infractions slide when it benefits them."

"If the council knew how they used the Pinks in Zenda, they would be furious! It was our understanding they were merely living in service to the Zenda. This is much worse!"

"Why do you think the tourists from Wendat aren't allowed visas to the mainland of Zenda? You can only travel to the territories which are set up for tourism. You cannot go to the mainland where the breeding farms are, or the continents where mining or other industries use Pinks as their workforce. These are all off-limits, not only to the Wen but most Zenda citizens never see how Pinks are treated in such places either. A lot of these things would offend any sensible person."

"Then you're saying the average citizen is ignorant? Surely, they can't all be!" Tokala had become rather distraught by Asha's report. "Why have you never told me these things before?"

"My father has some private ledgers and histories, which tell a different, or rather a more complete history of our country than we were told growing up. I don't know why he has them. Being a historian, I could not resist reading them, even though he would be furious if he knew I was riffling through his office, or taking things he had hidden."

Tokala looked shocked and said in a quiet voice, "Asha, please tell me you put them back."

Asha nodded. "Of course, I did, but now I'm determined to do something about it, and I'm furious! My people have become desensitized to the horror of it all. They don't see it for what it is. Even I didn't know the whole truth."

"But do the people in Zenda support this?" asked Mora.

"No, not all of them. It's complicated. Most people are vaguely aware that some atrocities happened long ago, and they think this was just what happens in war. They are all conditioned and schooled to think Pinks are not advanced. They accept the lie that Pinks are a sub-species who can only learn simple tasks. Citizens of Zenda actually believe they're helping the Pinks who live and work among them by providing them a living and safe labor conditions. They're basically ignorant of the facts because the government successfully suppressed that information. They created a narrative that the Zendali citizens could be comfortable with."

"But they eat the meat of Pinks? Use their organs for transplants?" asked Tokala.

"Well, yes, the transplants are culled from Pinks, but the law supports the fact that they are freely given, and documented evidence shows that the Pinks agree. However, the sale of Pink flesh as exotic meat was outlawed by Nebtawi."

"I sense that isn't the whole story," said Mora.

Asha nodded. "It still happens. Pink meat is a black-market item. It's served as exotic foodstuffs to patrons who are fully aware of what that means. I suspect mostly to those who are members of the Traditionalist Party, which is led by the Amun. They controlled the royals for generations."

"That is disgusting," Tokala said.

Asha agreed. "Most importantly, our young King Nakhadot... I mean, the prince,"—she smiled at Tokala, who always corrected her— "is against any practice that brings harm to the Pinks. He is adamant about reforming our society. His father, Nebtawi, gave the Pinks a choice. It is not true autonomy by any means, but he required the breeding farms, the research facilities, and any other business that uses Pinks for labor, to prove they were told exactly what was expected of them, and a recorded acceptance is taken during the contract process. At the age of maturity, every Pink can choose if they will remain in place or be reassigned."

"You mean they are told this will happen, and they still remain?" Tokala exclaimed.

"Yes, surprisingly, the perks of the lifestyle outweigh the cost. Some prefer to stay. The record must show the Pink agrees to all the terms of their employment. And those terms also must be fully documented to prove the Pink making the commitment was told explicitly what will be expected of them."

"How could any of them agree to stay?" asked Mora

"This new law made every institution clean up its act and treat its resident Pinks with more care and respect. It also created a competitive environment, where the employer had to offer benefits, improved living conditions, and better food. In addition, entertainments are a big decisive factor."

"They put themselves at risk for a few treats and distractions?"

"Yes, exactly. To get them interested in staying, these companies offer a joyous, contented lifestyle."

"Until when? At what age are they culled?"

"Well, only the breeding farms cull them and usually at around thirty, but sometimes sooner if a vital organ is needed. The corporations have testing processes for all ages, so the only harm which may happen is a side effect of a drug, or if a disease is purposely induced, which they don't have an adequate cure for."

"I thought you said the laws protected them from harm?" Tokala was indignant.

"The laws require the companies to inform the Pinks what might harm them. They give their Pinks a choice. If they want to take the risk or not. But taking higher risks will bring higher rewards, so they usually agree. It is a gamble that often pays off. Even if they die, their family gets the reward."

Mora's hair stood up in a chill along her arms. Asha continued...

"Restrictions were put into place to ensure the farms and corporations don't abuse the Pinks. For example, they completely shut down the use of Pinks for sexual entertainment. High fines and even imprisonment would be the punishment for the sex trade."

Mora shook her head. "The last king started these regulations—Nakhadot's father? Why didn't he continue with his revolutionary plans?"

"His plans were suppressed. I wish I knew the answer to that question. Now his son is taking up the banner for the revolution Nebtawi only dreamed of."

Tokala, still fixated on the conditions of the Pinks in Zenda, asked. "Why would anyone agree to be kept like that, and used for their parts?"

Asha rarely saw Tokala lose her cool, but it was understandable why she was upset. Tokala had worked closely with the Pinks for years.

"Several generations have passed, those Pinks grew accustomed to being enslaved. They have also accepted what they were told about their kind. Then suddenly they were offered things they never expected to have. It is not as if there are good choices. Private household service would be the next priority option, a chance to be valued and protected by a wealthy family. Pretty much every household has them, but families are selective when taking someone into their home. Pinks who would seek a different life are left mostly with the dirty end of service labor as members of the Market-Economy job force. Those jobs are more labor-intensive. Surprisingly, the two most prestigious placements are the breeding farms and the companies who use Pinks to test their products."

Mora and Tokala looked at Asha with knitted brows, as if such a situation was incomprehensible.

"I still have to ask why?" Mora just couldn't accept anyone would choose it.

"The lifestyle. In those places, the Pinks are given comfort and leisure, the best food and entertainment. They're treated like pets or prized livestock. They would rather live happy lives with all the wealth of luxury offered for thirty years than a lifetime doing something harder."

The anger on Tokala's face was unmistakable. "I feel sick," she told them.

Mora felt it too. The Zenda really did treat Pinks like livestock. They did not consider them equals. The creeping sensation of danger was finally settling into her soul. She was terrified. "These residents on the reservations cut their long hair in protest, but also to signal they had had enough. I think our solution will be well received."

Tokala had a new resolve. "I fully support your plan now. I'm sorry I didn't understand what was at stake."

As before, Tokala spent the afternoon at the clinic. She checked on the men she had patched up on her last trip and found they were all healing without infection. She tended to her pregnant patient, checked if Loda's eyes were better, and a few other female issues. No new problems had to be dealt with.

The other two loaded the mind map into every resident's implants. They came and went from the central log house as inconspicuously as possible. Mora and Asha also presented their idea for teaching self-defense. The Pinks were more than grateful.

On the ride home, Asha and Mora shared how well the languages and history were received, how it lifted people's spirits and gave them something else to focus on.

They warned the Pinks to be discreet. But they knew it was only a matter of time before what they had done would be discovered and investigated. It was only a matter of time before this insubordinate act would get the attention of the council, or even worse, the Zendali.

"Who can predict what sort of punishment will come our way because of this?" Tokala said with a degree of trepidation.

"It's not something we can prepare for," Asha said.

"We can only try to be resolute in the face of what frightens us, I suppose, but if we are even a small measure as brave as these Pink have been, we will be all right."

55

MISDIRECTION

Bi wasn't at all annoying as a roommate. Mora begrudgingly decided she should stay. She refused to be sensible about moving to the reservation. Mora couldn't fault her for it, though. She also didn't want to live in isolation and do farm work. Bi insisted, against all caution, that she would continue her work at the hotel, saying she was safe to come and go in the daylight, and she worked the morning shift. In the evenings, she preferred the privacy of her room. They really only saw each other in passing or shared an occasional evening meal.

Mora had helped Bi scrub off the plant-based color from her fur, and they both marveled at her lustrous golden pelt. Then Mora taught her how to dress in the garb of the Sisters', hoping it would give her more protection in the city.

After Bi first walked under the veil, she told Mora how she enjoyed having a more casual passage to and from work. "Before wearing the Sisters' garb, I spent all my time in that closet-like room at the hotel or in the kitchens. Now I'm able to interact with people, and they don't have a clue who I really am."

Mora suspected that wasn't true, but she knew Bi would insist on going, anyway.

***

Orenda had been following the young stranger, whom she suspected was Bimisi for several days. She began by watching the hotel to see when she arrived for work. Then followed her when she got off her shift. Orenda wasn't sure how to approach her and was considering different options. What she did notice was that there were others watching and following her as well. She saw Tao with a group of Zendali youth. They watched the kitchen exit, in the alley. But Bimisi always came and left through the front entrance with a public view. There were occasionally native youths who also tried to follow her home. Orenda knew they were part of Tao's gang because she had observed them conferring at different times. Bimisi was obviously aware of them too and always managed to lose them on the way by taking various circuitous routes through public markets and other busy shopping centers. Bimisi would confound Orenda's efforts to follow as well, and when she lost Bimisi, she would watch the gang to see who they met up with, and what they did.

A few days into this routine, she finally decided to go into the hotel and just ask for Bimisi. The one she was seeking stood in the hallway, wearing the black garb and veil of the Sisters' of Justice. "Why have you been following me?"

She's perceptive, Orenda thought, *didn't realize I was so obvious*. "I meant you no harm, but there *are* some dangerous people watching you."

"You came to tell me that?"

Orenda pulled her sketchbook out of a satchel. "No, I came to show you this." She held it out. "Please... just take a moment to look."

Bi reached out and grabbed the book while keeping her eyes on Orenda. "What is this?" She opened it and started flipping through the pages. It showed illustrations of Bi and Mora, and also there were scenes of the Eastern Empire, her homeland, her house, her room, and the Brainery Institute. This book contained too many secrets. She closed it with a snap. Looked up at Orenda trying to see what the intent of this might be, because it didn't make sense. "Who *are* you?"

"My name is Orenda. I came from the eastern part of Wendat. I'm a seer and trained under my grandfather, who is a medicine guardian. The problem is, the only things I ever see in my visions are you and this other one. I don't understand why, because I don't know who either of you are, or why I seem to be connected to you."

Bi understood then, Orenda was a dreamer like herself, or at least she had the gift manifested differently, or someone trained her in a different way. "I am a seer too."

Orenda's eyes widened. "Oh! Are you acquainted with this other one? Is she like us?"

"I know her, but no, she's a scientist."

Orenda looked puzzled. "What is the connection then? What do we all have in common? There must be a reason for this. Do you think we're allied for some important cause?"

Bi showed her conflicted feelings as her ear-fans wobbled out and back. "Let me get my things. If you can keep up, I'll take you to meet her. Just be prepared. She won't be happy about it."

Orenda smiled and nodded.

***

They left out the front, just like tourists, and walked alone to the market as if they didn't have a couple of gangs watching their every move. "Be ready and follow me." They came to a juncture in the path where a transport was parked. It was stacked high with crates of vegetables. Bi pushed Orenda behind it and followed, signaling her to be quiet. At that moment, one group passed them. Then she crept around the vendor and behind a curtain. This led to stairs; they went down quietly. Orenda whispered, "What is this place?"

"A passage to the other side of the market. Only the vendors know about it." When they emerged on the other side, she directed them to a bank and through a hole in a hedge. On the other side was a dry canal. "I didn't know this was here."

"It's for runoff during the rainy season. Most of the year the canal is dry, but you don't want to be caught here when there's a rainstorm. It floods fast."

They took this channel all the way across town, then climbed up some stairs and out onto a street across from a park. "Where is this?" Orenda asked. She was disoriented and had never been to this side of town before.

"Around the corner is the gate to the Foreigners Park, and beyond that is a housing development. This small village is typical of Zendali architecture. We're not far from the university." She pointed in the opposite direction from where they were walking.

"So that's how you were able to evade being followed?"

"That is one way. I take different routes through the city. When you're being followed, never take the same path. The more predictable you are, the greater the chance of getting caught."

Bi had her own fob disk for Mora's door. Before they entered, she said, "Mora won't be happy I'm bringing you here. I'm not sure what she will do."

Orenda nodded, understanding why she needed her privacy. As expected, Mora wasn't pleased about the intrusion. The one rule she had imposed when Bi moved in was no outsiders in the house, no guests ever. Bi had readily agreed. She had no friends in

Muwioni anyway, and she didn't expect it to be an issue. Now here she was with a native in tow.

Bi casually introduced her. "Mora, this is Orenda. Please sit down so we can talk."

***

Mora was furious but trying to keep a lid on it. *How dare she so bluntly tell me to sit, like it's her right to dictate what to do in my own home!*

Orenda followed them to the table and accepted the cup of tea Bi put before her. Mora was staring at her, and the indignation she radiated was intimidating. Bi explained Orenda had moved from the east coast to attend college, and she was living with her great aunt, who was the council elder Coso Winnemucca. This was not news that made Mora any more inclined to like Orenda. She didn't enjoy exposing her face to strangers, especially not anyone who had connections to the government. But Bi could be very determined. As she was telling Orenda's story, Mora was only half-listening to the conversation.

"Orenda's family expected her to follow tradition and study with the local medicine guardian Holata Tyee," Bi said.

That got Mora's attention as she realized this was the female Tokala had told her about.

Bi went on to say Orenda had not come to study medicine. Instead, she was going to study art. Mora had started to relax when she realized Bi had ties to her other friend, but she still didn't understand why Bi and Tokala wanted her to meet Orenda. It was not as if they had anything in common. Mora was also distracted with thoughts about setting up a new project and didn't have time to just sit and chat with art students.

With encouragement, Bi pushed Orenda to show Mora her sketchbook. She watched the indecision on their faces, and it made Mora curious. This was obviously something she didn't often share. All right; her interest was piqued. The drawings must be exceptional. Orenda got a big book out of her satchel and opened it on the table. She turned it around so it faced Mora and turned the page.

There was a drawing of Mora surrounded by buildings from her world! "What!" She looked up to see the two of them staring at her with a look of expectation.

Orenda continued to turn the pages. Every surface was covered with drawings of Mora. With detailed sketches of her home world. And of Bi, but she wasn't focused on those at the moment. Mora tore her eyes from the page, looking up at Orenda and Bi, who were still watching her. She put her hand out, her fingers trembling. To stop the shaking, she placed her hand on top of the open book and closed her eyes for a moment, taking a deep breath. She could feel her throat constricting, a rise of panic overwhelming her.

Finally, she said, "How?" It came out as a sort of croak, and she found she could not articulate anything more definitive. She could not process what this all meant.

Orenda responded in a calm, patient voice, as if she were trying to reassure a frightened animal. "I'm a dreamer. That's why my grandfather chose me to follow him as a healer and seer. But my dreams seemed more like fantasy, unreal, and sometimes like nightmares. Strange, impossible places and two unknown females haunted my visions my whole life. I never seemed to dream anything else."

"You gave up on medicine and came here to study art?"

Orenda nodded. "Yes, and then I saw you both in the city, dressed in black and covered in veils." She turned the pages in the book to show Mora a sketch of two figures dressed in the garb of the Sisters' in a market.

Bi pointed at the date on the page. "Mora, this was drawn weeks ago, before Orenda arrived in Muwioni and before I started wearing the robes."

Orenda was nodding. "When I saw you in the market the other day, it was just like this dream had come true!"

***

"She's been following me to and from my job for days," Bi told Mora. "Today she came into the hotel and asked to see me, then showed me this book."

Mora was still alarmed, a perplexed expression on her face as she flipped through the pages, too stunned to say more. "I don't live in a magical world. I don't believe in mystical things, palm readers, psychic mediums, and any form of divination... well, I have always considered them to be ways to cheat people out of their hard-earned money." Mora looked at them with some degree of bewilderment. "Yet lately, these convictions are being challenged, and this..." she indicated the book she still held. "I cannot explain."

There were hopeful expressions on both faces. They didn't interrupt. They understood she was still working through it.

"These drawings are also very... personal. They make me feel exposed and uncomfortable. I'm sorry, but it just doesn't seem possible! This could all be fake..." As her anger surfaced through the confusion, her fur stood on end. Mora stared at the two of them, her ears flattened back.

They sat before her, uncertain and dismayed.

"This is a liability." Mora's sharp tone made her words sound ominous.

Which was not what either of them wanted to hear. They looked at each other, not knowing how to respond.

Bi stood. "Orenda, would you excuse us, please? Mora, can we talk privately?" Bi walked to the staircase, and Mora reluctantly followed.

When they reached the top floor, far enough away not to be heard, Mora said, "Is she some kind of spy?" Her anger now obvious, she was fuming.

"For some reason, you are even more upset now than when we first arrived," Bi said. "You are letting your suspicions cloud your reason."

"What does Orenda actually know about us? Asha told me about a Zendali faction in Wendat. What if *she* is their informant?"

"What?" Bi was surprised, then it dawned on her why Mora might think that. "No, she is a dreamer, like me. I'm sure she has no such agenda. She just feels we are all connected in some inexplicable way, and I agree with her."

"You don't even know her, Bi. I'm bewildered at your naïveté."

"The book," said Bi.

"That book could have been created to fool you, which it obviously did."

"Mora, you need to look at the whole book, read the notations, talk to her. This was not a ruse. It's real. I understand this because I'm a dreamer too."

Mora turned away, paced back and forth, sighing in exasperation. "You think I'm angry, Bi, but what she showed us, it's like the ground opened under me."

"It *is* terrifying, I agree. Please take another look, Mora."

Mora shook her head. Not wanting to believe it... but finally she stood straighter and seemed to have resolved her initial discomfort. "I will take a closer look at the book. Just tell me first what you hope to accomplish with this connection?"

"To be honest, I don't know. I just strongly felt that you had to meet her and see that book."

They returned to Orenda, who was calmly sketching and sipping tea.

Bi apologized and invited her to sit in the living room and asked if Mora could examine her sketchbook.

They moved to more comfortable seating, and while Bi chatted with Orenda, Mora became absorbed in the artwork.

Finally, Mora said, "How many of these books do you have?"

Orenda wasn't surprised by the question. "A chest full. I've been drawing in journals for as long as I can remember."

"You have these with you?"

Orenda nodded affirmatively, then had a flash of comprehension across her face. "You're worried who might see them?"

"I most definitely am. Is your chest locked?"

Orenda nodded again.

"Can you have the chest brought here?"

"Do you want to see them all?" asked Bi.

"I'd like to, yes, but I want to be sure no one outside of this room gets their hands on them."

"I can bring it here if you don't mind storing it? The trunk is big and really heavy. My father thought I was silly to bring it here, but I couldn't leave it behind."

Mora agreed and said it would be fine. "Let me get you a ride home. It's getting late."

Orenda left feeling she had accomplished something important. She finally had contact with the people of her dreams.

***

When Orenda arrived at her aunt's place, it was dark, which was odd. Usually, there were lights on at this hour. Maybe she was out? But then she noticed the gate stood open and unlocked, and the door was wide open too. Not thinking about danger, she ran into the house. It had been completely ransacked. Some of her aunts' precious artifacts were broken, the shards littering the floor. Papers everywhere, blowing in the breeze from the open door, furniture broken or tumbled over, as if the intruders were looking for something. It was dead silent now, and Orenda was pretty sure no one was here. She called out to her aunt and then looked more carefully at the papers littering the floor. They were from her auntie's office. She followed the trail of documents and pushed open the door.

Coso lay on the floor, blood pooled around her head. She had been beaten badly. Orenda felt for a pulse and found she was still alive, but her breath was shallow. Orenda's tears obscured her vision. She managed to contact the emergency service number. While she waited for them to arrive, she gently cleaned the wound on her aunt's head, her scalp had been cut all around one side as if to remove it. Orenda's fingers trembled. The sight of it gave her a deep, shuddering chill. She wet a clean cloth in alcohol and wrapped it tightly around her aunt's head to hold the loose flap in place, then covered her body in a blanket. Finally, coming to her senses, Orenda contacted her aunt's associate, Mato.

Mato and the emergency van arrived at the same time. When he saw his friend being taken away, and the state of the house, he looked at Orenda in shock. "Where are the household staff?"

"I didn't see anyone else. I didn't want to leave Auntie Coso to look for them."

"All right, you go with Coso to the hospital. I will deal with all of this."

Orenda's tears were still flowing. "This was all my fault."

Mato looked at her with a bewildered expression. "Why would you think that?"

"Because there was a young female I wanted to meet. She works at the Journeyer. I was looking for an opportunity to approach her when I noticed she was being followed by a gang. Then I started watching them. They're all trouble-makers. We were seen leaving the hotel and were followed. But we cleverly slipped away and lost them. The gang members must have recognized me and thought I brought her here."

"It is not your fault what they did." Orenda was sobbing now. "Look at me." Mato gently turned her face. "There is no way anyone could have foreseen this kind of violence. Don't blame yourself." He looked out at the emergency van. They had finished loading the stretcher into the back. "You better go now. I'll come to the hospital when I finish here."

56

Failure & Regret

Orenda sat by Coso's hospital bed all night. When Mato arrived in the morning, he apologized for taking so long. He looked terrible and obviously hadn't slept. Orenda was still so distraught she had no concern for anything else. She didn't think to ask about the others who were in service to Coso. They were mysteriously absent when she found her aunt.

"How is she?" Mato took the other chair near the bed. Coso was still unconscious.

"They stitched her head. Half her scalp was cut around her head like they planned to..." Orenda's eyes welled up with tears, and Mato nodded with understanding. "They said she had some other head trauma, a beating. They aren't certain if there will be permanent damage. I should have seen this. I'm a worthless visionary! What will my grandfather think if he learns I had no warning of this?"

Mato looked at her sadly. "Not everything in our path is meant to be seen in advance. Some things need to happen, even terrible things, which lead ultimately to knowledge."

"I don't understand why such awful things should be allowed to happen," Orenda said bitterly. "My grandfather tried to warn me that *how I see* will naturally be different from any other medicine practitioner... and that I shouldn't consider such a difference as a failure. But how can I not be frustrated with myself when I wasn't able to protect my family?"

"I understand how you feel. Also, hard as this is to accept, please consider what would happen if we didn't have this warning." At his words, Orenda cringed, and her ears flattened back. Mato continued. "If you had advanced knowledge, you might have prevented the attack, but we wouldn't have been warned of how bold and confident these criminals have become. Something worse might have happened."

Orenda snorted in exasperation. "My grandfather, Ezno, always knew when harmful things would befall the tribe. He was able to be of service to them. I don't have his abilities." Tears glistened in the soft fur on her face. "It just isn't fair!"

"Whatever gave you the impression the world is fair? We all must bear our burdens. Your aunt chose this path to help her people. She willingly put herself in harm's way so justice could be done. If she had not been attacked, we would not understand there are elements out of our control. Now is the time to seek a solution, and believe me, Orenda, we will find who did this, and they will be punished."

"What happened at her house? What did you find after I left?"

Mato sighed deeply and looked down. "I'm not sure how much of this I should share with you. Why burden you further? The only thing we need to do is sequester you in a safe place until this is over."

Now Orenda sat up straight with her eyes ablaze. Her expression of indignation was just like her aunts when she was determined. "I am not a child! If you think you can keep any details from me, you are dead wrong. If you will not tell me what happened, I will investigate on my own!"

Mato looked a little alarmed, then shook his head, looked sideways at her in resignation, giving her a half-smile. "So, it runs in the family. I never could get my way with Coso either. All right, I will tell you what I can. But some confidential details I will remain undisclosed for now, as the investigation is in progress. Is this acceptable?"

Orenda nodded and sat silently, waiting for him to tell her.

"The intruders were looking for something. Part of the damage was due to their search for what they assumed was hidden. At first, this looked like the work of vandals. Maybe that was what they wanted us to think, and why they made such a mess. But they were searching for something specific. They beat Coso for information. She is a stubborn old bird, and I doubt she would cooperate under any sort of duress."

"Do you think they tried to scalp her because she refused to give them what they wanted?"

"No, I think that was the action of a zealot. We found a bloody yard tool on the floor of the office. We surmise that a member of Coso's staff tried to save her by attacking the perpetrator. This is a bold act, considering they're Pinks, and as such are strictly forbidden by our treaty with Zenda to wield weapons of any kind."

"But they protected her!"

"By law, this could still mean serious punishment." He paused and looked thoughtfully at Orenda, who was sobered by this information. "Of course, the council will take these unusual circumstances into consideration, and they will not be charged with a crime."

"But they acted to save her, at their own risk."

"Yes, they were willing to safeguard her at their own peril."

"I'm worried about them. Do you think they might have been killed?"

"We did not find anyone in the house. Whoever broke in may have taken the servants hostage, or maybe the household staff fled after the attack."

"They would never have left her. They were like family."

"Even if they thought she was dead? Orenda, they were all Pink, maybe they were afraid of the consequences?"

"Where would they go? And where is the person they hit with the yard tool?"

"These are the questions that need to be investigated."

"That isn't good enough, Mato! If they have her staff, they will harm them, especially if they fought to save her."

"We're doing everything we can and following every lead."

Orenda suddenly thought of her trunk and journals. "I have to go back!"

"What? No." He was shaking his head with firm determination. "That is a crime scene. We can bring you some clothing, but you can't enter the house. Surely you understand? Please let me keep you safe."

"Mato, I need the trunk. I need to find out if anything is missing."

"Did you have valuables in this trunk? I don't think they cared about robbing her. A lot of valuable items were left untouched."

"What's in the trunk is only valuable to me. But the contents might be harmful to people I care about."

Mato looked confused with her answer, but he understood that she would insist. He signaled his assistant. "Take her to the house, have her trunk removed and let her take some clothing, then take her to the safe location we discussed."

"Thank you, I'll return as soon as I can. Will you stay with her?" Orenda asked.

He nodded. "Today I can, but—"

"I know you have an investigation to manage, but I don't want her to wake without one of us here."

When they arrived at the house and were able to view the damage in the light of day, she froze on the doorstep. It was worse than she remembered. Surprisingly, her trunk had not been opened, maybe because she'd thrown some clothing on top. Various unfolded items draped all down the sides. Her room was not very tidy, which in this case, meant the trunk was easily overlooked. She packed some clothes and toiletries, leaving most of her things in the closet. When her trunk and case were in the vehicle, she gave the driver Mora's address. "I have to drop the trunk at this house. Take me there first."

57

HIDING IN PLAIN SIGHT

Mora looked groggy when she came down to the kitchen in the morning. "I couldn't sleep," she announced without really looking at her housemate.

Bi looked at her a little sheepishly. "I guess that's my fault. I'm sorry."

Mora shrugged, which was a good sign.

"I made some breakfast. Have a seat."

Mora sat and accepted a cup of Kav, prepared just the way she liked it, with the Mella plant cream. She looked up at Bi in surprise.

"Is it weird that I remember what you like?" Bi asked.

Mora smiled and shook her head. "No, it's nice, thanks." After a moment she added, "I came to some obvious conclusions that I was too upset to see before."

Bi sipped her tea with a hopeful smile. "Tell me."

"Well, of course, the clear fact that Orenda would not have been able to observe our faces in public, and doubtful that even if she was told about us, she would not have been able to render so many drawings of our likeness."

Bi smiled, looking just a little bit cheeky. She even wiggled her ears, but smartly didn't say anything. Mora felt the judgment in her attitude though, like Bi was thinking... *the smart scientist finally sees the obvious.*

"Yes, I admit I could have come to this conclusion sooner, but I was quite literally shocked!"

"I was too Mora, truly, I almost fainted when she opened her journal to get my attention."

"Those drawings were too detailed to doubt. And she made notes on those pages, which indicated that she didn't fully comprehend what she was seeing. She wrote about how disturbing the visions were. No one could have described all of that to her."

Bi nodded in agreement. "I had come to the same conclusion by the time I decided to introduce you to her."

"Do you think she has shown them to anyone else?"

"She said they were a secret, that she never even shared them with her grandfather, who was also a visionary."

"Why would she keep her visions from him?"

"Orenda told me she had a sort of premonition, a strong warning, telling her the visions were only for her, not for the tribe. If she considered speaking of them, she would feel unwell, and that would stop her."

Mora shook her head. "Is that... what I saw in her journal... Is that what your visions are like, Bi?"

Bi considered how to respond. "Not exactly. Orenda is a visionary and a dreamer. We share these skills. What she sees is vivid and seems to have been directing her to find us, for whatever reason. There was only one focus. She told me she had never had a vision like her grandfather about what she calls useful things, or about othlike,er members of the community. Which, of course, was expected of her as a future medicine guardian, so she decided the occupation wasn't the right path for her."

"How do your visions differ?"

"I'm a lucid dreamer; I can direct my spirit body to travel. I communicate with other spirits, who are my guides. I have prophetic dreams, which show me things that could happen. Maybe what I do is more like Orenda's grandfather, I'm not sure." Bi left out how she used to be able to contact other living dreamers in her homeland. Her connection had been cut around the time she got her implant, so including this fact didn't seem to be necessary.

Mora thought about everything Bi explained, then she said, "I believe you."

Bi looked at Mora agape. "You didn't before?"

"To be honest, no, not actually. I accepted that you believed these things, but all the unusual talents you describe are completely removed from my personal experience." She looked a little uncomfortable and paused. "Magical things are imaginary. Something out of a children's storybook. And I never cared for those silly tales."

"Stories are rooted in truth. Just because you didn't experience these things yourself doesn't mean they aren't true or never happened."

Mora smiled indulgently. "I wouldn't go so far... I am a *see it, to believe it,* sort of scientist."

Bi shook her head. "Not true. What do you think your inventions are? They were once nothing more than an idea, another kind of vision. You gave form to that notion, bringing it into the physical world. A lot of people would consider that magic. And who is to say you don't have spirits guiding your work?"

Mora chuckled a little but had no reply. She sipped her Kav.

At that moment, someone signaled at the door. Mora turned on the wall screen and saw Orenda on the doorstep, so she pressed the disk to open for her. Bi ran to greet her.

Orenda stepped into the house. It was evident from her expression that she was upset.

"What's wrong? What happened?"

"While I was with you yesterday, someone broke into my aunt's place and..." She couldn't finish and started to sob.

Bi stepped forward to embrace her. Orenda let herself be held for a moment and then stepped away and composed herself. "I think that gang recognized me when we left the hotel. When we lost them, they thought we might have gone to my aunt's place."

Bi and Mora looked at each other. Mora stepped closer and said softly, "What did they do?"

"They beat Coso. Then they tried to scalp her! They ransacked her beautiful home like they were looking for..." Orenda's pause was gripped with sorrow. Her throat choked on the words. "Maybe looking for us," she said finally. "Maybe they thought we were hiding there."

A chill ran through Mora. She was thinking about what happened at the reservation. "They were gone when you got home?"

Orenda nodded. "I called the emergency services, and they took her to the hospital. She is still unconscious."

"You can't stay at her house now. It's not safe," Bi said, looking at Mora.

"That's what Mato said. He forbid me to stay there. Because the house is a mess and... a crime scene." Orenda squeaked out the last part.

"All right, I think Orenda should move in here with us," Mora said to Bi. "If you don't mind sharing your room?"

Bi was surprised. "Really? I mean, I never imagined you would be open to another house guest!" She paused. "Yes, of course, I am happy to make space in the room for her."

Mora nodded. "I figured you would be agreeable. I think she needs our help, and I won't deny that something inexplicable brought us together." She paused, realizing this was not a very important point in light of what was going on. "It's confusing, but also intriguing. I don't understand how this happened, but I accept that a link between us exists. The safest thing for everyone is to have her here, and all those journals, under this roof."

Bi smiled, encouraged by this new development.

Mora asked, "Orenda, is your trunk safe? Or did they take it?"

"I have the trunk with me. Mato arranged for me to stay at a safe house. When I went to pack my clothes, I insisted that they put the trunk in their vehicle. I was just going to drop it off here for safekeeping."

"Let's unload your things then, better have you stay with us."

"What should I tell the driver?"

"Say as little as possible. Tell him you'll talk with Mato later."

The driver was conflicted when the three young females insisted that he leave Orenda. They also made him promise not to disclose the address. Saying that Orenda would be moved to another location by the Sisters' of Justice. He told them Mato wouldn't approve. The perpetrators were most likely involved with the Order of Amon Kuroo, and this house was in the heart of the Zendali community. She would be right under their noses until the Sisters' moved her. But Orenda refused to go with him. Finally, he gave in and drove away.

Of course, they didn't plan to move Orenda. They had all decided they were meant to be together, for some inexplicable reason. Mora started to think about what it would mean to have a third person, whom she didn't know, here at her home... suddenly the gravity of the decision she'd made hit her... she took a deep breath in an attempt to calm the panic. *I'm going to start a new project, and I'll be at the lab most of the time anyway. This shouldn't be a problem...* but her anxiety was taking over her reason. *I hope she doesn't have any annoying habits.*

Bi noticed her expression. "Don't worry, Mora, I'll see that she understands your preferences."

Mora looked at Bi with respect. *How does she know what I'm thinking?*

58

DISCLOSURE

M ora realized it was too awkward to keep her secret from her housemates, especially as her home was one of the few places, she was able to speak openly with Asha and Algon. Telling them the truth would alleviate the worry of some compromising information slipping out. She'd also been exposed by Orenda's drawings, and she imagined both of them had unspoken questions about those strange places Orenda saw in her dreams. She spent the night in doubt, especially after the reaction she'd gotten from Tokala. But she'd come around... *I think she believes me now.*

The morning came with resolve. Mora decided to reveal her true origins. She went to the guest room, which her guests were sharing, and woke them up. "We need to talk."

She headed down and made breakfast. By the time Orenda and Bi came to the kitchen looking confused and a little worried, she had the table set and asked them to join her.

"Is something wrong?" Bi asked.

Mora shook her head. "No, and this is not about you, *either of you.* This is something I need to tell you about myself." She gazed at the confused faces of her two exhausted friends and felt guilty for putting this on them, considering everything else that was going on. "I need you both to promise me that what I tell you will remain our secret. Even if you don't believe me. You cannot talk to anyone about it. Ever."

They both nodded in agreement. Bi seemed puzzled, but Orenda had an excited look, ear-fans perked up, and stuck straight out.

Mora noticed Orenda's look of anticipation and found it a little odd. Ignoring whatever that meant, she decided a straightforward disclosure was best. "The places you drew in your sketchbook? The strange cityscapes—that is my world. That is where I'm from."

They both looked at her, uncomprehending. Then Bi said, "How ... what do you mean? Is there an undiscovered continent on Hadot, or an island maybe?"

Orenda was shaking her head. "No undiscovered lands or mysterious unknown countries exist in our world. What does it really mean, and how is it possible?"

Mora suddenly realized how hard it was to explain and hesitated to continue. If someone in her world had made such claims, she would've just laughed or silently thought they were crazy. She'd never have taken them seriously. *I may as well give it a try.* "I'm from an alternate world. My Hadot is the same. But different. I ended up exchanging places with Zamora after an accident with our portal experiments."

Orenda's face lit up with a huge smile, but not the sort of *she's demented* smile. This was a real, happy smile. Then she threw her head back and laughed. Both Bi and Mora looked surprised. After what happened to Coso, Orenda had been despondent, and they had both been doing everything they could to help ease her worry. Hearing her laugh was a wonderful relief.

Orenda caught her breath, looked at Mora with happy tears, and said, "Thank you! I can't tell you how good it feels to discover I'm not crazy!"

Now, Mora smiled too. "Well, that was easier than I anticipated."

But Bi was silent and offered no confession. Instead, she kept the focus on Mora. "If you traded places, do you have a way to go back to your world?"

"No, not yet anyway, and I don't have time to tell you any more specifics right now. We all have things we need to do today. I have to dress and go now. I wanted to tell you both because Asha and I might talk about things relating to my situation, or I might be ignorant of how some things work here in Muwioni. It's easier if you understand why I'm... well, sometimes clueless."

Bi suddenly got up to clear the table and do the dishes. Her mood had become distant, like she was avoiding further discussion.

"Bi, are you still planning to go to work at the hotel? You don't have to. We have enough credit to live comfortably here. It might be best if you don't go until all of these problems settle down."

Bi ignored the question, like she was stalling, thinking... she washed the dishes with a little too much vigor.

"Bi?" Mora said, trying to get a response.

Bi turned to Mora finally. She had a faraway look.

"I've been talking to you. Didn't you hear me?"

"I'll be fine, Mora. I will be extra careful. Don't worry. Ask Orenda. She can tell you I know how to get through the city without anyone following me."

Mora was dissatisfied with her answer, but she couldn't force Bi to stay in the house where she was safe. "Orenda, any news about Coso?"

"No, I'm going to hang out here this afternoon. I have some research I need to do, but I plan to stay at the hospital tonight. The hospital staff put a cot in her room, so I don't have to sleep in a chair."

"Let me know if I can help."

Orenda looked at her, puzzled. "To be honest, I'd like to tell you not to distract Mato. I am aware he's helping you with something. I just want him to focus on finding out who hurt Coso, and where her household staff has been taken."

Mora nodded. "You're right. He should not be absorbed with other things at this time. But what he is doing for me won't take long, so don't worry. He's organized a team of people to do interrogations. He's told me they are exploring every lead. I don't think he will be inattentive with this investigation. Not that he would be with any crime of this nature, but Coso is his dear friend and college."

59

WITHOUT A TRACE

Orenda spent much of the night at the hospital again. Coso still hadn't woken from her coma. Mato checked in on her again in the early morning. He'd changed his uniform but still didn't look rested. "Seems like neither of us is getting any sleep. Did you find anything yet?"

Mato shook his head with a somber expression. "There's no trace of what happened to Coso's staff. The blood we found at the scene is at the lab, and we should have a match today. If we can find one of the attackers, they might give us more insight into the situation. Other than that, unless she wakes up and gives us more information, we have very little to go on."

"How did they do this in the middle of the day without anyone seeing?"

"That isn't actually the case. They just made sure every witness was removed."

"So, there'll be no justice. If my aunt never wakes up. What then?"

"I am posting two guards at her room here, night and day. No one enters who isn't authorized. You will be contacted if she wakes, Orenda. You should go and get some rest. And where are you staying, by the way?"

"You think they will come to the hospital and try to finish what they started, so she can't identify them!"

"It's doubtful, but we're taking every precaution."

"I trust you, Mato. But I would rather not say where I'm staying, for the same reason."

***

As soon as Orenda left, Mato contacted Mora. He was pleased that she had agreed to his offer. "Let's set a time to discuss your new project." He was also curious how Orenda knew her, but he didn't feel it was appropriate to ask.

"This is a priority for me, and I know you are busy, so just tell me when and where."

"If you can send me what you need in the way of a workspace, with specifics, I will start the process. Does it need to be a *clean lab*? Knowing your requirements will help me find a suitable location. Also, I'll need a list of materials and supplies."

"I think it would be wise to acquire the location, and all the materials, in a way that can't be traced back to you. Is it possible?"

Mato was silent for a moment, thinking about this request. "You expect sabotage?"

"That is one possibility. I can think of several others. Better to be cautious. I am also going to need an assistant. I have the process worked out reasonably well now. I don't need a whole team, just an extra set of hands."

"Do you have someone in mind who is qualified?"

"I think so. I need to contact him and see if he's interested."

"Zamora, do you mind my asking what you plan to create?"

"First, my friends call me Mora. Second, I thought it was obvious? I'm going to build portals to transport people."

"You honestly think that is possible?"

"I know it is."

"But the university said the portal technology was limited to inanimate objects."

"What I built for them is. They will also not be able to transport larger objects. They don't have the skills or ability to upscale."

The revelation of what Mora was planning to do left Mato speechless. He realized why she wanted to keep everything secret. Finally, he said, "Transporting people will change everything."

"That's right. And this technology has to remain in the right hands. You lost the manufacturing of the other portals due to the university's greed and its ties to the Sovereign Nation. This will stay under the control of the United Tribes of Wendat. Algon doesn't understand my designs. He can't build anything new for the Zendali. He can only follow the design that I gave to the university. No one else can do what I can. I will send you my requirements encrypted. I will have Orenda hand-deliver the encryption key."

"Orenda? Do you know her?"

"Yes, and I am aware she will see you at the hospital."

60

A New Design

When Mora closed the connection with Mato, she contacted Ohpa. She had planned to leave him a message, but when he saw it was Zamora's signal, he answered right away.

"Zamora, I'm so happy you called!"

"I urgently need to talk to you. Do you want to meet in person at my place? I need help with a new project."

"Yes, I can come over this evening. Do you need me to assist you?"

"No, Ohpa, I need you to be my partner. I am limited by my inability to be in public view. I will make you my partner and give you the credit. My investor will create the paperwork if you agree?"

Ohpa was silent on the other line for so long she thought she'd lost the connection. "Ohpa?"

"Yes, Zamora, of course, I am honored you chose me. I feel unworthy."

Mora then realized he was overcome with emotion, and it sounded like he was crying. "Ohpa, can I trust you to say nothing of this to anyone?"

"I will do anything you need, yes, certainly, you can trust me."

While she waited for Ohpa to arrive, she worked on her design. Lost in her calculations, she was surprised when the door chimed.

She welcomed him in and made tea. It took very little time for her to explain everything to Ohpa. "The portal machinery we built at the university is in production now. It can only transport inanimate objects. It will not scale up. The company producing it doesn't understand the technology, and they won't be able to use it to transport anything alive. We will build such a portal for the living to use."

"We are building a portal to transport people?!"

Mora smiled at his surprise. "This week we will meet the investor and sign the papers. When the lab is ready, you will be contacted again with the location. Then we will get to work."

Without further discussion, she pushed Ohpa to leave, saying she had too much to do.

What she didn't explain to him or to Mato was that she would make an adjustment so only she or Zamora could use it for cross-world transportation, allowing her to return to her timeline and Zamora to this one. She realized a multitude of alternative worlds must exist. She still needed to figure out how to select the correct one. How to choose the one she came from was still a mystery. Her back-door feature would be necessary in case she ended up in the wrong place. She was also concerned that her portals wouldn't allow other people to do cross-world travel. Once Mora's portals were in distribution, any portal location might be accessed to receive her (or Zamora's) genetic signature without anyone knowing their place of origin. At least, that was her plan.

Another thing Mora didn't tell anyone is that she made a back-door to the University Portal design as well. She had the power to make changes to them remotely or even shut them down. No one else understood the design well enough to detect it or *fix it*. She planned to build a portal interface to access or divert things shipped with those devices because she had a feeling it would be useful for the Wendat council.

Algon was unaware of the back-door. Mora had planned to tell him about it until he ended up working for the Zenda Corporation. Asha had told her he'd been forced into long hours on production for wide distribution, especially in Zendali and the Territories. Which she found suspicious. What was so urgent? Mora agreed with Asha's concerns, but for now, Algon was a pawn in someone else's game.

61

Shadows & Dreams

M ato contacted Mora in the early morning. She informed him who her partner would be, and he agreed to meet with Ohpa to sign the documents.

Mora liked his professional attitude and how quickly he acted on his promise. It assured her that she'd made the right decision. Asha arrived as she was ending the call.

The first thing Mora said to Asha when she walked in affirmed her confidence. "You were right about Mato."

"You finally found out what he wanted?"

"I did. He's going to fund my new project. I'm asking you not to mention this to Algon because of the conflict of interest. Can I trust you to keep this between us?"

"Why did you tell me at all?" Asha said, obviously annoyed. "I hate keeping secrets from him, and I'm a terrible liar."

"Well, not so terrible, considering all that you've kept secret from your father and brother." Asha tipped her head from side to side.

This was a typical body expression Mora had seen used in Muwioni, meaning something like: *It could be so. I'll think about it. You got me there,* or *I'm unsure.* It seemed to have a lot of uses.

"I had to tell you," Mora said, "because once a site is chosen for my lab, I'll be busy with the new project and that means we need to do as much as we can for the people on the reservations in the next few weeks."

Asha looked a little disappointed. "I thought we could do a lot of good for the Pink community if we continued to work together. And I have experience with how it goes when you or Algon are working on your science projects. It's total immersion. You hardly sleep or eat! I won't see you at all once you start, will I?"

Mora wiggled her ear-fans and smiled. Amused that Asha was calling her work a "science project," she pursed her lips.

"Zamora has that same expression when she's trying to decide how to say something difficult, or when she doesn't want to commit," Asha said with a degree of annoyance.

"I will still make the occasional visit to the reservations with you and Tokala. But you're right. Most of my focus will be redirected to my other work. Don't worry, we will be able to deliver a great deal of information to the Pinks. Also, once I give them the basics of self-defense, they can pass it on to each other."

"I hope so because that was your idea, and you're the only one who can teach self-defense. They have put their faith in you. And you were right about giving them something to look forward to. I've seen a difference in their attitudes. The expectation that they'll have the ability to safeguard their community made a huge difference."

At that moment, Orenda came in after spending the night at the hospital. She set her bag on the floor and headed for the kitchen without noticing who was sitting with Mora at the table.

"Orenda?" Asha was completely amazed to see her. "I didn't realize you two had met." She turned to Mora. "This is the one I was telling you about!"

Mora smiled. "I figured that out." Then she got serious. "I guess you haven't heard what happened to her aunt yet?"

"No, I didn't hear anything." She looked at Orenda. "What happened?"

Orenda sighed. "If she had just left it alone and waited for you to introduce me, this might not have happened."

Asha had an apprehensive posture. "What happened to Coso?"

"I went searching for Bi. I know you said you'd tell her about me, but I was too curious. I left the hotel with her and came here. But there was a gang of young Zendali watching. They were with your brother, and he must have recognized me. They followed us, but we lost them. I guess they decided we went to my aunt's place."

Asha looked at her calmly, resigned to the fact that her brother must be involved in activities she deplored. "Did they cause a disturbance then?"

Orenda gave Asha a look that morphed between resentment and exasperation. "They must have thought I took Bi there."

Mora said, "We don't know that's why, Orenda. You are just assuming and making connections that might not be factual. It could just be a coincidence. You have to stop blaming yourself."

Asha looked suddenly frightened. "Tell me the whole story. It sounds like something awful took place!"

Orenda broke down, sobbing with her hands covering her face. Mora had noticed that tears were always close to the surface and easily triggered, so she looked at Asha with concern.

Asha crossed the kitchen and took Orenda into an embrace; over her shoulder she asked Mora, "What did they do? Is Coso hurt?"

Orenda gently pulled away and wiped her tears. "They beat her and tried to scalp her."

Mora noticed how shaky Orenda was. That wasn't all emotion. "When did you last eat?"

"I don't know, and I don't have an appetite. I haven't gotten a good night's sleep in a while either. I'm just so exhausted."

Mora made her sit down and brought her some leftovers and tea. "Eat that. I don't want any arguments."

Orenda looked up at her as if to say again that she wasn't hungry, but thought it was better not to disagree. She pushed the food around on the plate and took small bites.

Mora could see Asha was eager to find out more details. But they waited until Orenda finished playing with the food and told them she would go rest. They both hugged her and tried to comfort her.

Orenda wasn't informed about what happened on the reservation. Mora surmised that those incidents had to be related. But she didn't want to say anything else that might worry her friend.

Once Orenda was in the guest room, Asha said, "Please tell me Coso didn't die."

"She's in a coma. They had to shave her head to stitch the cut that went halfway around her head. She had other head traumas as well from the attack. Her face is a mess of bruises, some big contusions. There are a couple of broken ribs from being kicked when she was down. They're not sure if she'll have permanent brain damage."

Tears soaked into Asha's face, gleaming on her indigo fur.

"Don't start falling apart on me, Asha. We have work to do. This whole situation is getting out of control."

Asha nodded and rubbed at the wetness, trying to dry her face. Then she reached for her tea and quietly drank. "What is the council doing about it?"

"Apparently, Muwioni doesn't have a police force, detectives, or a national guard. And the country has no army."

Asha acknowledged the point Mora was making. "This society was not prepared for such violence. They didn't have these problems in the past. So, Mato has been trying to fill all of those roles by himself?"

"I assume he's coordinating a team and building an investigation. I am not able to glean a lot of information from my brief talks with Orenda. Of course, they want to keep this quiet. There will be nothing about it on any public channels," Mora said.

"In the past, before the Star People gave us the implants, the people in this country were not unified. Tribes were separated without a universal language. They also raided other groups and killed warriors from different tribes that invaded their hunting grounds. It wasn't all peaceful. Each tribe was governed differently. However, one thing that seemed to have been common among all people of Wendat, was that crime within each community was almost non-existent."

"That's why they didn't need peacekeepers?" Mora asked.

Asha shrugged. "Peace Keepers? Interesting concept. In Zendali they are called the Guards. They're enforcers."

"It still seems unreasonable that they never formed an official security department here," Mora said

"The justice system in each region varied, but any wrongdoing was not a matter between individuals but between families, clans, towns, and nations. If someone committed an offense, it was not just the immediate victim that would be seeking justice, but the victim's community... and not just the one who committed the crime who was guilty, the restitution fell on that person's entire family or community. Basically, they kept their people in line by giving them support. It is still their basic philosophy, but now they have a council of elders in each region who govern."

Mora shook her head. "If you don't mind my saying so, Asha, this doesn't sound like it could work in a denser population."

"You may be right. Maybe that is the problem the cities are facing now?"

Mora was intrigued. "And that is why there's no official agency to deal with crime in Muwioni?"

"Not just here, but the whole country! I suspect there will be after this incident though." Asha looked away for a moment, then tapped her claws on the table in a nervous way. She obviously had something else she wanted to say. "Mora, you know those books I scavenged from my father's desk?"

Mora's fur stood on end. "Don't tell me he knows."

Asha shook her head. "I don't think so, but there was this symbol on all of them, the head of a Kuroo wearing a crown. Around the bird's head in a circle it says *Wandrona Protects the Pure*. I've also seen that same trademark embossed on other documents in his office. I think that is the seal of the Amon Kuroo."

Mora had been suspecting Ziyad's involvement in that ancient order since she'd seen him at the awards ceremony. Algon had recently been going on about it to Asha, but she didn't want to believe it. "Do you have any idea who among your compatriots are members of the Order of Amon Kuroo?"

Asha looked aghast. "No! And if I did, I would tell Mato!"

"Then it's time you told him about your father and brother."

Asha cringed, but nodded. "I have no loyalty to anyone with those beliefs."

"As far as the immediate situation on Wendat in the major cities, there needs to be some investigative body created. If they don't get these crimes under control, the perpetrators might return to Zenda without a trace and without any restitution possible," Mora said.

Asha looked troubled. They sat quietly sipping their tea until Asha said, "I honestly hope I'm wrong about my father and brother, but I'm worried you and Algon might be right."

When the silence lingered with those worries, Mora stood up... "Let's put our energy into something positive."

Mora nodded her agreement. "Asha, this is something unrelated, but I have been meaning to ask you." She hesitated, still unsure if it was wise. "My parents in this world, can I find some information about them?"

"I was wondering why you didn't ask me sooner. Especially after you looked for your Pink companion," Asha said this with a sardonic tone as she raised her browridge.

Which gave Mora a wave of guilt. Of course, she should have asked sooner. Her ear-fans flattened back, and a rush of excuses ran through her mind.

"Zamora was not in the least sentimental," Asha said. "She never talked much about her family. But I did some digging into her past... out of curiosity."

"Without her knowledge?"

Asha did that head tilt, side to side. "It was when we first knew each other, and I had to know if befriending a Fog was wise. Of course, at the time I thought she was just a ward of Ekon Darigo, and that can mean various things."

"How did you figure out he was her grandfather?"

"My research showed that his daughter Serwa had given birth to a Golden, and the baby didn't survive. It was the right date to coincide with Zamora's birth."

"No one would think to do a search like that because everyone thought Serwa's hatching died," Mora said.

"Why do you want to find Zamora's parents? If you don't mind my asking?"

"Well, I *am* close with my family, and I love my father. He's a brilliant teacher, kind and generous. I miss him every day. I miss my mother too, and her cooking." She smiled. "I miss the playful interactions my parents would have when I went there for dinner."

Asha gave Mora a sad look. "I can give you reports about her grandparents, who still live in Zenda. But I found that Zamora's mother died in a mysterious accident, along with her second unborn child." She paused when seeing Mora's disappointment. "I did end up sharing this information with Zamora. She asked me to try to find her father, but I had no success. She was never told his name. All I discovered was that around the time Zamora was born, a young Pink male transferred from their household to a mining colony on Ujarak, in the territories. The dates corresponded to the time her father was removed from the household. The name was missing from the file. We thought it might have been him. I'll send you what I have about them."

"There are uncountable loose ends. Sometimes they seem like shadows or dreams."

Asha gave her a rueful smirk. "Now you're starting to sound like Bi and Orenda."

62

Evasive Maneuvers

Asha had stayed late with Mora, working to complete their mind-map for the reservation. When she arrived home, it was dark and quiet, which wasn't usual. She signaled the lights in the entryway to brighten, then saw her brother Tao sitting at the table in the dining room with a malicious expression on his face. She jumped. "You scared me! Why are you sitting in the shadows?"

Her brother stood and quickly crossed the distance between them. He grabbed her head covering and veil, ripping them off. "When are you going to end this ridiculous charade?"

He had grabbed her plaited crest with the fabric, causing her to cry out in pain. She was afraid to say anything in response. She knew that Tao could be violent. She didn't want to antagonize him further.

"We suspect there are two females in Muwioni wearing garb like this who are Fog. Your native..." he held back the derogatory slang... "was seen with one in the forest."

Not knowing how much he had discovered, she wasn't sure how to answer. She chose to deny any knowledge of them. "I don't know every member of the sect."

"I don't believe you! Do you think we're fools? You and your rebels are hiding under all of this, he grabbed the fabric on her sleeve, twisting her arm."

"I'm not hiding anything, and you're hurting me, Tao, stop being rough!" She jerked her arm out of his grasp. They were shouting now. Her father, Ziyad, entered the room. When they were children, he always protected her from Tao's temper. She looked at her father now, waiting for him to tell her brother to go to his room or not to harm her. But instead of defending her, he laid his own heavy hand on her, his fingers gripping the back of her neck. He leaned in close and said in a low voice close to her ear, "You'd better hope that I don't discover my own daughter is allied with mongrels like that."

A chill ran down her back, lifting her fur. Asha had no time to respond before he pushed her down into a chair. She looked up at him and asked, "What did I do to make you suspect me? Why are you treating me like this?" She acted with indignation, using innocent hurt feelings as a way to avoid whatever was coming.

In a stern, menacing voice, her father said, "We are going to have a talk now, Asha, and you're going to tell me everything you know."

"Why are you speaking to me as if I'm a misbehaving child? What makes you so sure I know anything?"

"Everything leads back to your cult."

"That's ludicrous! What leads do you have that make my Sisters' guilty? What exactly are you basing this on?"

Ziyad looked at his son and nodded, a signal for him to speak.

"I saw Algon in the forest with a Fog female. He told me she had paid him to drive her there, and he had no idea why or what she was looking for."

"If that is what he said, then that is the truth. He had no reason to deceive you, especially over some random traveler who wanted to go to the forest."

"Who told you she was a traveler?"

Asha was flustered now. "I just assumed, if she lived here in the city, she would just find her own way to get there."

"Since when is your native giving rides to strangers?"

"I have no idea; we haven't talked about it. Look, I know Algon wouldn't do anything purposely to break the treaty. He's a rule follower."

"There is another sighting of a female of mixed origin who was working at the hotel. You were seen talking to her during the awards dinner. Later, she began to wear the garb of your Sisters'. Why would she do that, if not to hide who she is?"

"That young female at the dinner was Wen, not Fog. She was not supposed to be serving at the party. She had work to do in the kitchen. All I did was tell her not to annoy the guests."

It was actually Mora who had interceded on Bimisi's behalf, but if they think it was her, that is just as well.

"If that is true, why did she suddenly become a follower of Bicara?"

"I am not aware that she has. Are you sure that the female you saw wearing the garb of the Sisters' isn't the traveler you were talking about, just staying at the hotel?"

Ziyad looked up at his son. Asha had chosen the right answers—they didn't know anything for certain. They only assumed.

Tao was getting more agitated. "She's lying! She knows something!"

"You were seen leaving the university late at night from the science wing. What were you doing there?" Tao demanded. "Did you take something?"

Asha honestly knew nothing about this, and her eyes widened. "I often leave the university late, but not from the science wing. What does that have to do with me?"

"Where have you been tonight?" Ziyad asked her.

"Studying with friends."

"Your tests are over. Why do you need to study?"

"In my senior year, I should present a project for graduation. I've been doing research for that."

"Who are these friends?"

"No one you know."

"I want their names. I want to know where you are at all times!"

Asha looked up at him defiantly. "I will not involve my friends in your petty, narrow-minded desire to control me!" Asha had a temper too–it just took a lot to provoke her.

Ziyad backhanded her. "You will do what I say, and you will never speak to me like that again!"

In the next moment, Asha saw the ghost of regret on her father's face. He knew he had gone too far. But Tao was still furious.

Asha could feel her eye swelling shut. She stood and gave them both a defiant glare, then ran crying from the room. Asha was thinking, *my mother divorced father for exactly this sort of abuse.*

63

Avoiding Discovery

In the early morning before it was light, Asha arrived unannounced at Mora's place. It took time for the door to open. Mora was standing in the living room looking only half awake. Her mane was a kinky, snarled mess, having come out of the braids. She was about to complain about being woken up, but then she saw Asha's swollen face.

"What happened to you?"

"My brother and father had a serious talk with me last night."

"Oh, my goodness!"

"There's nothing good about it."

"It's only an expression."

"We will have to be careful now, where we meet and work, and I think we should find a room at the university to finish what we started. I don't want to lead anyone to your door."

"Come sit down. We better put some ice on that."

"It won't help now. I'm all right, really. It will heal. Let's get going before the city is awake. I have an idea."

Mora got herself dressed, they both put on their veils, and headed out. For the first time, Mora became aware that unlike most of the houses in this community, her door was located on the side facing a partition wall, which hid her entrance quite effectively from the street. Also, a walkway led to a path behind the house. This was shielded by a stand of trees and thick brush. The residence was built to give Zamora privacy and options, so she could move to and from her place unseen. Instead of turning in the direction of the university, Asha headed toward the city. "Where are we going?"

"We're meeting the Sisters' of Justice. You need to become more familiar with them. They know Zamora, but well, you might need them now. They've agreed to walk with us." Asha had a rigidly straight back as she walked. There was determination in her defiance. "Safety in numbers."

Asha led her toward the courtyard of an old school. "They live here."

When they entered the gardens surrounding the Sisters' headquarters, a group of ten Sisters' stood waiting quietly, hands folded behind them, like soldiers at ease. Mora had never seen so many of them together. It looked a little spooky. Asha went to the group and spoke quietly to one of them, then lifted her veil to show her face. With her dark fur, the bruise was not as obvious as it would have been on someone with Mora's coloring. Yet, all the Sisters' reacted with a sharp intake of breath or a small cry of concern.

"They will accompany us to the university, and then return when we want to leave. Until this trouble settles down, they will give us their protection and support," Asha said. "Which basically means they're going to follow us everywhere we need to go."

Mora was impressed. The entourage of Sisters' definitely made her feel safer. After walking a few blocks in silence, she began to relax. She had been shouldering a lot of stress, and overwhelming doubt. Her mind was constantly comparing her own world to this one, and realizing time and again how much better this one was. Regret curled tightly in her heart because her kind had no place here. There was so much beauty bound up with dread. Not that she could stay, but sometimes she was tempted, despite the dangers.

"Sometimes I'm really sad I can't stay here."

"Even with all of this going on?" Asha asked.

"There is a possibility I won't figure out how to get home, even if I complete the portals. I still don't know how to target my world for the return."

I didn't realize you were facing such ambiguity; you always seem so confident."

Mora laughed a little. "I try not to think about it."

"I imagine that is what keeps you sane through all of this."

"It's the little things I notice."

"Like what?" Asha asked.

"Well, of course the styles and fashions are more noticeable in your world because they're so completely different from what I'm used to."

"Are you interested in fashion, Mora?"

"Not... really. I never used to be. I guess I didn't have time for it. I had several changes of clothes, which were all the same. I didn't have to think about what to wear. And now with these robes, it is also not something I need to consider. However, I do appreciate the beauty I see here, and find the differences interesting. Don't you ever miss it? Dressing up, I mean?"

"No." It was a sharp reply, and after a moment she added... "Such things remind me of my mother, who was fashionable to the extreme. She cared only about her wardrobe, shoes, and jewelry. Always seeking the newest and best to impress her friends. She had to have something new for every party. All her time was spent shopping or at spas preparing for her events."

"Is your mother deceased?"

Asha was quiet for a moment, and Mora felt like she'd asked too much, and the inquiry about private matters was overstepping.

"No, she is very much alive and free to party and do whatever she likes. She left us because my father is violent. He beat her one too many times."

Mora mulled that over, not sure what would be an appropriate answer, all things considered. "She must be beautiful."

"Yes, she's beautiful to look at, but very self-centered. I think I associate fashion with her, and the lack of caring she had for her own hatchlings."

"I'm surprised she left her children with an abusive husband!"

"Well, in that she had no choice. He insisted on having full custody and then moved us here. I was only six years old. My brother, eight. We haven't seen her since. But I see photos of her published at events. She's quite popular, always elegantly dressed, and still attractive."

They walked in silence for a while longer, then Asha told her: "A few of the Sister's have said that they've been approached by a young male, thinking they were Zamora."

"I was wondering how Kai and Chayton knew it was me, but they were just guessing, and sometimes got it right."

"They also asked about Bi. I guess word got around that she might be a native-Pink mix. They want to know what tribe she claims to come from."

"I actually never asked her. I don't think Orenda knows either."

"It would be dangerous if they found the tribe who broke their treaty. They will use it as an excuse to make trouble. Something awful is about to happen. I can feel it."

"So, all these years the Wen have actually honored the agreement not to mix? No secret love affairs or rapes resulting in children?"

"None I've heard of. The reservations are closed communities, with safeguards."

"But they can come and go freely, right?"

"They are not forced or restricted to that place, but they willingly choose to remain isolated for their own security. You have to remember these are refugees who escaped. They stick to their own."

Mora nodded. "You told me life for the Pinks is better now after the changes imposed by Nakhadot's father, King Nebtawi. Are fewer Pinks trying to escape than before?"

"I am not privy to that information. Maybe my father is. The conditions have improved, but they're not free. The Pinks are useful to the Zenda society. They don't want them to integrate or be independent, and the conservative faction especially doesn't like that they're given a safe harbor here. Nevertheless, boundaries exist that neither country will cross. The Zenda who mix with Pinks would create a Fog child. There is no name for a child who is a Native-Pink mix, as it had not been done. Doing so would be putting themselves and their offspring in jeopardy. I believe your friend Bi might be the first."

"But you think she would be safe on a reservation?"

"They offer sanctuary to immigrants who are in danger. This is a different case; I am not sure if they could. If it becomes public knowledge, then it will be a problem. The council would have to negotiate with Zenda about the broken treaty. It would put them at a disadvantage. Let's just say at this point, it is already a tenuous situation."

"You still think she should go to a reservation in the meantime, though? You don't think she's safe at my place?"

"I believe they're hunting for her. What do you think?"

Asha's question was said like a challenge. Mora realized her friend was still upset that she had gotten Bi a job at the hotel. No one could be sorrier about it than Mora was herself. It was incomprehensible why Bi insisted on continuing to work there.

They walked in silence until Mora said, "After what happened to you last night, I would say we are all in danger."

64

DREAD AND DESPAIR

The following morning, Mora was again rudely awakened at an early hour. It was Algon who kept signally the door until she answered. When she let him in, he was frantic, gesturing and speaking loudly, and most of what he said didn't register because she wasn't quite awake.

"You seem beside yourself, Algon. You need to calm down. Do you want some tea?"

He shook his head and refused to come to the kitchen. He remained in the entryway looking anxious and worried.

"They know who you are, or more precisely, they know *what* you are. You and that other one you're harboring here. You're in real danger. Did you see what that monster Ziyad did to Asha? Imagine if he can abuse his own daughter like that, what he would do to you!"

"Asha told me they have suspicions, but no proof. We will be fine, and anyway, it's not your problem."

Algon was shaking his head vigorously and pacing. "No, Mora, no, you don't get it...Tao sounded certain. He knows I'm involved! Don't you understand what they will do if they catch you?"

Mora was too tired to deal with this. "Don't worry about it. I won't be here long."

Algon looked up sharply. "You're building another machine? Let me help you."

"I don't need your help."

"I thought you had forgiven me."

"I have forgiven you, Algon, but I have not forgotten you took credit for my invention, and you're profiting from it. That's not as easy to let go. I resent it. I'm sorry."

"I did all I could for you and Zamora. I'm not safe either after being seen with you. Tao followed us that day in the forest!"

"Well, now I understand what this is all about, you're worried about yourself?"

Algon looked extremely frustrated. "You are so quick to take offense." His ears fluttered nervously. "You've twisted what I'm trying to say." He looked imploringly at her. "Don't be unkind, Mora. I kept your secrets, I helped you when you got here, I didn't tell Tao anything when he came and tried to press me for information. But I can see where this is all going. I can't pretend things are *normal*. How can you? If they find you, they will find out Asha and I were involved."

Mora had all but forgiven Algon for what she saw as a deliberate betrayal. Her bitterness had shifted to acceptance over the last few weeks while she and Asha had been working together. But despite Algon's insistence that Zamora knew she wouldn't be credited, she could not get over how unfair the outcome was. Now, this felt like he wanted her out of the way so he and Asha would not be guilty by association, and it really pissed her off. "You're just worried if you're seen as my accomplice that your security will be compromised. You might lose your new job overseeing the replication of my technology for the Zenda Corporation."

Algon swallowed hard and looked uncomfortable. "It's not like that."

"No? All you've said since you got here is how compromised you are because of me!"

He shook his head. "I don't want Asha hurt."

"You assume that I would purposely put her in danger? She is the one who asked me to work with her, not the other way around."

"Work with her? What are you two doing? She won't tell me."

Mora ignored that question. "If you cared at all about Zamora and me, who made that job of yours *possible*, you would be ready to defend our rights of ownership! Instead, you're trying to get rid of me!"

"Mora, it is a simple fact that you have no rights for me to defend."

She looked at him with complete contempt. "I think you should get out of my house."

"To be clear, Zamora would have been compliant. Her prospects would have been different, but opportunities would have come. She's more realistic about how this world works. But you can't be managed like that, can you? You have bigger expectations; you... You glorify your worth."

"And that is unacceptable here?"

"You know it is! Look, we will protect you, but the world is not ready for your freedom. If what you've done became common knowledge, it would disrupt the balance, and our treaties with Zenda would be in dispute. It might even start a war! That's how dangerous you are."

Their fighting had woken up Orenda and Bi, who came down to see what was going on.

Now, the three of them stared him down with fury in their eyes. He turned and left without another word.

As soon as Algon stormed out, Orenda busied herself in the kitchen, while Mora paced in the living room and fumed internally at the accusations Algon had thrown at her.

"Mora, please sit with us. He's scared and angry. Don't let him rattle you so much."

The three of them sat at the table with tea and breakfast plates.

Mora was too upset to be hungry, but she ate anyway. She might otherwise go all day without a meal. She waited nervously for Asha to arrive. They'd planned a trip to the reservation, but Mora was now more worried about Asha than she had been. She didn't want to admit it, but maybe Algon had a point. She had pushed her friends to do more for the Pinks than they had planned to do. It put them at risk.

"Are they speaking their native languages on the reservations?" Bi asked Mora.

Orenda looked at her oddly, but answered. "Pinks don't have memories of their ancestor's cultures or languages."

When Bi noted Orenda's odd expression, she reworded her question with more detail. "Do the Pinks tend to gather according to race or culture? Do they speak their native languages at all? Do they have memories of their homelands?"

Mora didn't find Bi's inquiries strange or realize how peculiar this line of questioning was. "During my visits to the reservation, and my interactions with the people, I found some had phrases, stories, and myths, which were memorized from their countries of origin. These were secretly passed down in an oral tradition. But there are only fragments."

Mora, Asha, and Tokala had told no one about the mind-maps they were creating, so Bi and Orenda weren't aware. Nor was Algon. The fewer people who knew what they were up to, the better.

"If the Pinks had no formal education, what are they taught once they join a reservation?"

"Their mind-maps include knowledge of any work produced by that collective, and also other useful things about farming and what they need to be self-sufficient."

Orenda looked thoughtful. "From what I've heard, their lives are much the same as we live in our native communities."

Her friends had managed to get Mora out of her bad mood. Despite their own worries, they made an effort to cheer her up.

Just when Bi was clearing the table from the morning meal, Asha signaled Mora's Receptor. "I am with the Sisters' down the street near the park. Can you join us now? I suggest you walk the path behind your house so you're not seen. We can meet Tokala in town. I don't want her picking us up here."

"What about Bi?"

"What about her? She should stay at your place. Tell her not to go out."

"Bi? Are you staying home?" Mora asked her.

Bi rolled her eyes up, like she was thinking. "I will be fine on my own. Don't worry."

65

ABDUCTION

B i finished her shift in the kitchens and was told to take out the trash. For several weeks, she had avoided using the staff entrance by the alley that went directly to the kitchen. She sensed that the alley wasn't safe for her. No one had complained yet about her not using the staff entrance, but it was only a matter of time before someone decided to report her. Working in the restaurant meant doing whatever the kitchen manager told her to do. She was a large, imposing native with dark green fur; they called her Madam Mukwa. She had thin lips that were usually pressed tight together with judgmental indignation, because no one did anything right. She kept her long hair in a tight bun and wore an apron so crisp it could probably stand on its own. Mukwa wanted Bi to take out the trash, which was in the alley.

Bi exited the kitchen door and stood on the raised stoop, where she had a pretty good view in each direction. A premonition made her pause. Something was familiar in that niggling way of a dream recollection. Danger lurked in her awareness. Nervously, she looked around. The alley *seemed* empty, just a line of compost receptacle bins for the gardeners to pick up and the big trash bin on the other side. Maybe my mind's playing out the worst-case scenario. This was the middle of the day, and the whole kitchen staff knew where she was going. She went down the stairs toward the bins. Letting go of the breath she had been holding with a sigh. She shook her head. I'm getting paranoid. She lifted the trash bucket to dump it into the bin.

That's when five shapes appeared, seemingly out of nowhere, and surrounded her. Suddenly the dream flashed into her mind, the one that had been waking her up at night. These men in Kuroo avatars were a living nightmare, with red beady electronic eyes. The totems of the extremist Zendali Order. She spun around to discover they were on all sides.

Out of instinct, she threw the bucket at the one in front of her, hoping to create an opening to push through, but he barely moved. The bin bounced off his shoulder and dropped to the ground. One of the men stepped toward her and yanked the headpiece and veil off her head. Then he looked at the others and nodded.

As they were dragging her away, she looked at the kitchen window. Madam Mukwa was standing there watching with a smug expression. Bi didn't bother to scream, and she didn't resist any further. This would not be reported. She would just disappear with no one to tell her friends what had happened. They put a black bag over her head, tied her hands behind her, and lifted her up. After carrying her a short distance, she was roughly thrown in the back of a vehicle.

Bi paid attention to the movement of the hauler as it bumped along the cobblestone road and made a few turns. She recognized the water falling from the garden towers and the warble of the train tendrils as it left the station. They drove in silence then, on the smooth road out of the city. At one point, they pulled off onto a dirt road and waited.

Someone talking outside said, "How long?" After a pause, he said, "That wasn't the plan!" Next was a lot of cursing. The guy wasn't happy. Then he kicked the vehicle and directed his swearing at her.

They waited as darkness came. She really needed to pee. Finally, they got a signal to proceed. The road wound down a narrow path with a lot of potholes. They slowed down to navigate around them, but it was agony on her full bladder. A scraping sound as the transport moved through bushes and trees told her the road was overgrown.

When they stopped, they didn't take her out, but closed all the doors and walked away. She couldn't hold her full bladder any longer. The warm liquid soaked her garments and then turned cold. She listened to the night birds and frogs. This was somewhere in the mountains. After a time, the men returned, hauled her out, and carried her up some stairs and through a place with wooden floors that creaked as they walked. "She stinks," said the one carrying the upper half of her body.

The house was otherwise quiet. They carried her down some stairs to a basement. She had never seen a place built with a basement in Muwioni. A damp, rank stench, like something had spoiled, made her gag. She heard a rattle of keys, and then she was in an enclosed space. They cut her bindings, took off the hood, and left the room. The door was closed and locked.

They had dressed in black, their faces covered with masks, but not like those who captured her, who wore the Kuroo Avatars. When the last one was closing the door, she stared at his wrist, which had a strange welt-like band embedded in his flesh, not a bracelet, but something fused into his skin beneath the fur. What caused that? She wondered.

She examined the room. An old cellar, maybe? The stone along one wall had poor mortar. Dampness trickled through the cracks, leaving a stain. A different kind of stone was near the ceiling where a window had been walled up. *So that must be level with the ground outside.* The building was on a slope. The other walls were built of weathered wood. Which was also not a very common building material in these parts. The Wen believe that trees have souls. They were therefore very selective about what they culled from a forest.

The floor tiles were chipped and broken in places. Grime filled the crevices and cracks. They provided a cot with an old blanket. A wooden chair and a small table were against the opposite wall. The only thing on the table was a large clay container of water. A covered bucket sat in the corner, which she assumed would be her latrine. *Looks like they plan to keep me here for a while.* Which she took as a good sign. No hasty plans to dispose of her.

Her jailer returned and told her to undress. She didn't move. "Take off those filthy wet clothes!" he yelled. He held some folded garments. She stripped down and stood shivering. Not because of the cold, but she was afraid. He put the other clothing on the chair. "Kick those over." She did as she was told. He gathered them and left the room. When the footsteps receded, she took the clothes and got dressed. They gave her no undergarments. The loose pants were too big, but they had a draw-string waist, which she tied tight to keep them up. The shirt had long sleeves and buttoned down the front. Made of rough natural fabric, plain, and utilitarian. She was still shivering, the shock of her capture catching up to her awareness... she went to the cot, covered herself with the blanket, and curled into a fetal position with her back to the wall. The bed smelled unclean, like sweat and dust.

No sounds came from the house above, but a scraping noise came from somewhere nearby. It was intermittent. There was nothing familiar about this. She was certain it wasn't an animal rustling outside or within the walls. It felt like it was some sort of resolute undertaking, purposeful, and mysterious. A small thing, but it made her uneasy.

She should have expected this. Mora and the others warned her. Now she had to face the reality of those dreams she had been ignoring lately. Whoever was behind this, she would find out soon enough. She lay still, listening to the scraping until she fell asleep.

Bi dreamt of a wall panel that she pried open to reveal a crawl space in the wall. A cavity just big enough to squeeze into. Inside the wall, she moved with sideways steps along the dark passage. This led toward the scrapping sound. She didn't have a chance of escaping in the dream. A loud bang jerked her awake. Before she could move, someone had grabbed her arm and roughly pulled her off the cot. Her feet were bare; the floor was cold. She began to tremble. He took her hair in one hand and twisted, pulling her head back to expose her throat, just as another entered with something in his hand. When he got closer, it alarmed her to see he had a collar, like hounds wear. He placed this around her neck and locked it.

The two men were talking in a Zenda dialect she didn't know. When she got the implant, it came with mind-maps of the most common languages. This was something else. While the two of them attached the collar, a third slipped in and put a plate on the table. From their tone and gestures, she gathered they were saying nasty things about her.

They left and locked her in. Her fingers reached up to the collar, feeling the rough edges made of thick leather. The big metal ring hanging from the front was cold. She couldn't see how the thing was attached. She tugged it around and found a lock, which was solidly latched with no give. With a sigh, she stopped gripping and pulling and let her hands drop. Her eyes fell on the plate. Bread, and a small bowl of hot cereal. Must be morning, she thought. Her stomach growled at the smell of the food.

Before eating anything, she wanted to inspect the room and find that loose panel. She dropped to her knees and began to push on all the slats of wood, testing if any boards were loose. They didn't look exactly the same as the panels in her dream. The room was small, and before long, she'd checked every wall. Nothing.

She sat down and ate. *Pretty good fare for a prisoner*, she thought.

A sedative was in the food. Soon after finishing the porridge, she was dizzy. She stood and stumbled to the cot, falling onto the mattress and blacking out.

When she woke from the drug, she was seated in a chair in a bigger room. A heavy metal chain was attached to her collar, then extended behind her to a wall.

"Good, you're awake." This was said in Neofinagh, the universal tongue of the Sovereign Nation.

Bi tried to look past the glare into the shadow of the room. A light was shining at her; a tall figure was somewhere behind the brightness. A hulking shape moved there, but she couldn't make out any features. The voice was deep, resonant. A gruff, throaty sound, giving her the impression of someone imposing and harsh. He was not one of the men who had been in her cell to attach the collar. They had been younger and had exhilaration in their voices, as if eager to fulfill some long-expected desire.

"Let's start with where you're from."

Bi squinted at him. When she didn't answer, an electric shock stung her mid-section. She looked down and saw wires extending from the ground. They attached to braces around her legs, as well as a band around her stomach and another at her diaphragm, close to her heart. The shock made her heart skip a beat.

Someone in the room grunted, and others moved around in the back.

The interrogator ignored what was going on behind him. "That was just a little pinch. Expect more pain if you don't cooperate." His voice sounded like a professor giving a lesson, so normal, without emotion or malice. Not at all like she would imagine someone would speak when they were going to torture her. He gave her another shock. This one had more of a bite. Her body jerked rigid, rising up slightly against the restraints, then flopped back in the chair when it ended.

Someone in the room grunted as if in pain. *What is going on?* She wondered.

"I'm from a village northwest of here along the coast." She had time to embellish her cover story after doing more research on the tribes that actually lived in that region.

He shocked her again. "Let's give up on that charade, shall we? Tell me where you come from?"

Now more than one voice of pain came from the back of the room whenever she was shocked. It seemed to hurt them more than her. Are they shocking someone else too?

"I'm from the Hagawa tribe in the Northwe-st-ahga ..." Another shock cut off any further speech. That one was sharp.

Someone behind her interrogator cried out and fell.

"We've done our research and know for a fact that is not true. As I said, you can give up that story. What we have *not* discovered is how you got into Wendat. Have you escaped from one of the territories or were you born on a reservation?"

They think I'm Fog, and they will kill me when they finish the interrogation. "Why would I be on a reservation?"

"Why were you wearing the garb of the Sisters' of Justice? Do they harbor your kind?"

"I'm not a member. I just took the garments for cover, so I could work."

"Who gave them to you?"

She couldn't think of an answer quickly enough.

Another shock, more painful with each successive application, as if her nerves were getting more sensitive to the abuse. At least they don't suspect I'm from the Eastern Empire. I can't imagine how much worse this might be if they discover who I really am.

This time, she heard more than one person moaning in agony. They seemed to react each time they zapped her. Maybe they're hooked up too. But why?

When she refused to give an appropriate answer, her inquisitor increased the intensity. The shock became unbearable. She screamed, the others screamed, the room was filled with pain. Then she blacked out.

66

THE POWER OF CONFIDENCE

Tokala waited for her friends in the courtyard of the Sisters' of Justice residence.

For the past week, the Sisters' had been escorting Mora and Asha everywhere. Tokala watched the procession from a distance as it moved through the street... some heads turned. People stood aside in awe. It's one thing for one or two of them to walk through the market, just a passing curiosity, but a full procession of these Sisters' in black with veils made an impressive sight!

Tokala had the vehicle ready. As soon as Mora and Asha joined her, they drove to the reservation.

There wasn't much to do in the clinic, so Tokala closed up after she'd seen her last patient and went to find her friends.

In the longhouse, Mora and Asha were without their veils and robes, down to their black bodysuits, which were the undergarments worn below the Sisters' robes. Mora used Asha to demonstrate the moves, and her students followed along. Mora had chosen a handful of residents who looked the fittest, a mix of each sex. This was the sixth group she'd instructed that day. Two more were waiting for instruction. The sweat was pouring off of the two of them, and their garments were wet with perspiration.

Mora instructed them in the basics of self-defense. She taught evasive moves for the females, and unexpected points of vulnerability to immobilize their attackers. The males were taught more aggressive maneuvers to take advantage of their height and strength. She gave different applications to each group, so they could share what they learned with each other. All the residents were attentive and responsive. And some of them had surprised her by using their tails to trip their partners or grab a limb. This was a whole new element she had never considered, and it was an encouraging sign. They were thinking for themselves.

After the last group finished, the Pinks gathered around Mora and Asha, hugging and thanking them. It was as if they had cast a lifeline during a storm. Tokala patched up a few scrapes and bruises from practice. The residents all had a satisfied and hopeful outlook after such a morale boost.

While Mora and Asha were getting dressed, Tokala was waiting on the sidelines for them to finish. A few of the mothers approached her shyly to ask for a favor.

Then Tokala came to her friends and said, "They have a request."

***

Mora and Asha followed Tokala to meet the group, who were waiting with bashful expressions. Their reticence seemed out of place after their dynamic workout. With concern, Mora wondered what had happened. "Is there a problem, was someone hurt?"

They all vigorously shook their heads. Yet the group looked oddly discomfited and sheepish, like there was something they were afraid to share. "You've given us so much... we're hesitant to ask."

"I'm happy to help. What can I do for you?" Asha tried to sound reassuring.

"Names... we want to give meaningful names to our children. Names from our heritage. Would you know of any you can share with us?"

Asha showed signs of remorse. Of all the things that they had lost, this had to be one of the saddest. "I'm sorry, I don't know any."

But Mora spoke up. "I can make a list for you."

"The native children have powerful names that fit who the child will grow to be." The resident looked like she was trying to find the right words to describe what she meant.

"Names with significance?"

She nodded enthusiastically. "Yes, do our ancestors' names have such meanings?"

"Yes, of course, they do. Maybe not in the same way that the people on Wendat name their children. I am not sure how their naming ceremonies work. But, for example, your husband is named Osgyth?" She nodded eagerly. "His name means War God." The Pink looked astonished.

"No wonder our masters didn't let us use the names! Do you know more?"

"Your name, Zoete, means sweet." She was a small female with white fur, pale blue head hair, and blue-grey eyes. She smiled shyly. Mora had taken note during their interactions that she was gracious and kind to everyone.

"What about me?" another female said.

They all crowded in, saying, "Me! Me next!"

Mora laughed. "You have taken names from your ancestors?"

Zoete answered. "Only some of us remember, and there aren't enough names for all of us or our children."

Mora was tired, but she faced the one who asked to be next. Idony, had a buttercream fur color, bright yellow head-hair, and her eyes were blue. "Your name means Goddess of youth, and your husband is Sonam. His means the sun." The crowd that had gathered gasped and whispered, squeezing closer, hoping to be chosen next. Mora spoke to Enwalla, a sturdy, big-boned female with white fur, and black head-hair. "Your name means royal." This caused some of the others to tease her in a kind way, and they all laughed. "Your husband's name, Gunus, means mighty." Mora chose a tall female next—Snorri, who had white fur, and white head hair. Her blue eyes were keen and focused. "Your name means smart or sharp-witted." Snorri looked proud and stood taller. Unica, who had white fur, red head-hair, and green eyes, moved forward. Mora told her, "Your name means unique, and your husband Axwel's name means Great Stream." The last one was a slight female with ghostly blue eyes so pale they were nearly white. Her name was Frost, and she had pale pink fur and matching head-hair. "Your name describes the beautiful pattern that moisture makes when frozen on a windowpane or covering the forest on a w inter day."

By this time, the entire group was in tears. Enwalla said, "Those are all fitting names! But so much has been forgotten. Some of us still use the names the Zendali gave us." The others were nodding and looking hopefully at Mora, and saying that others would want to know about their names or have something more meaningful.

"Let me take some time to make a list. I promise to give this my attention. You'll have them soon." Mora had a hard time leaving. They were all crowding around as she tried to cross the property. Some had run to tell others about their names, and then a few new people were running after her, saying, "Do you know mine?"

"Next time," she told them as she got into the vehicle. When she closed the door, she said, "I feel like a celebrity!"

Asha pushed her veil back and looked at her. "How can you remember all of those strange names and their meanings? Or did you just make that up?"

"I told you I have an eidetic memory. Learning about old names was a hobby of mine as a child. It's called onomatology. Languages are constantly changing. For example, even though some of these Pinks speak a version of Inreji, I can barely understand them. My version of that language is different, more modern."

"And you recall everything that you learned?" asked Tokala.

Mora smiled. "Seems like I do."

Mora nodded. "Back to my original point, I was specifically interested in personal names and their origins. But the meaning seems to have stuck in my memory as well. Most of these people took names from their ancestors, they are no longer in common use in my world. They're old-fashioned."

"But I thought you said some unused knowledge will fade over time."

"I said that about the mind-mapping. I am not sure exactly how eidetic memories differ from the mind-mapped. However, memories of things I learned as a child are still very clear. I can view those pages like looking at a book in front of me now. I remember what I learned, even though I haven't thought about onomatology in years."

Tokala looked impressed. "Could those names then be used to trace where their ancestors originated?"

Asha said, "Of course! Mora, if you know the origins of the names, then that would give us a clue about their lost cultures."

"Maybe that could be our next project," Tokala said.

Mora looked at her friends. "About that, I haven't wanted to drop this on you both, but I will start my new project soon, and I won't be able to devote as much time to the reservation work."

67

Escape

Through a haze of near senseless gloom, Bi's eyes fluttered slightly open. She was being carried toward a room. As consciousness tried to return, she observed what was nearby. A stern native female was speaking. "I *told* you she couldn't take that much! If you want her to live long enough to tell us anything useful, then try something else. This is not effective. And get those idiots out of here." She pointed. "Put them in a room... Not *that* one. Are all your acolytes dimwitted?" Bodies were dragged past her, three unconscious males. One she had seen in her room with the white band on his arm.

The gruff voice spoke. "That one is her son. Put him in her transport."

They dumped Bi onto a cot and left the room. When the door slammed shut, she sat up and realized she wasn't in the same room. This one smelled. No chair or table, no water to drink, no bucket either. Maybe that meant they didn't plan to keep her alive much longer. Perhaps she proved to be more resilient than expected.

The old native female had said, "Try something else."

What might they do next? Bi's fur raised as a chill swept through her. She got up with some difficulty. Everything hurt. *These panels look right.* She began to examine the walls. Halfway through the first section, one board moved at her touch. This had to be it! She pushed and felt the panel slip aside, yes! The crawl space was narrow, but Bi was small. She moved inside and grabbed the panel, adjusting it back into place. For additional protection, she took a loose board from the floor and braced it against the panel so it couldn't move.

She had to wiggle sideways to stand, but she managed to leverage herself up in the cramped area between the walls. Awkwardly, she began to sidestep along inside the gap. She moved within the confined space as quietly as she could, the dark gloom was punctuated with occasional light spilling through the cracks of the panels. At one point, she heard whispered voices and moved close to the wall to peer through a wider crack. The room on the other side had a dim light, enough to view a room packed full of Pinks. They were beaten up and dirty. No cots or chairs or other furniture anywhere that she could see. Everyone huddled on the floor. One of them was using a sharp stone to cut through the thick leather manacles attached to another's foot. Now she knew what the scrapping sound was. This room must be next to the room she was originally placed in. There was nothing she could do for them unless she got free, so she kept moving to the end of the building.

Here, it was complete darkness. She put out her hand as a guide, pushing her way through spiderwebs and other indistinguishable fuzzy things. As she moved through the dark, the fear of being trapped grew into an overwhelming certainty. When she came to a wall at the end, she nearly broke down sobbing, without hope of escape. Her heart was pounding, the panic rising. *It's a dead-end!*

It was a slight breeze on her side that alerted her to another passage on the left. Carefully, she took the turn and saw an outline of a door in the distance. Her heartbeat quickened with excitement. However, she came to the end of that passage sooner than expected. It was too small to be a door and had no latch or handle. Her fingers explored the edges where the light came through. She felt points of something sharp. This was a board nailed in place from the outside. She would have to force it, and that would make noise. It was also daylight. Any movement might be seen.

A decision had to be made. If she waited, they would come to the room and find her gone. They would be on alert and actively looking for her. If she left now, during the daylight, guards might be outside, and they would see her escape from this hole.

She decided to loosen the board enough to peek out. She braced herself against the wall joints, holding herself up at the height of the board. Putting her feet on the wood, she pressed until she felt it move a little. Bi repeated this as the nails slowly let go, and one end popped open.

She lowered herself down, and took a step forward. With the edge of the board in hand, Bi peeked out. It was frustrating. She could see very little. There were flagstones on the ground, a patio? Beyond that was long dry grass, and then a forest of trees at the edge of the property. Nothing between the house and the forest to hide her escape. *All right; I have to run for those trees.* She also noticed that it was late afternoon. By the color of the light, the sun would be setting soon. She pulled the board back into place and decided to wait until dark.

She slipped down the wall to rest in a seated position. The space was wider here, and she was able to sit with her knees up. The next thing she was aware of was an alarm and shouting. Somehow, she had dozed off, and it was fully dark. Well, they discovered the room was empty.

She quickly pushed out the board and shimmied through the opening. She looked all around and up, but no one was in sight. Bi took a moment to replace the board as firmly as she could and then ran for the forest.

No guards were outside yet. They must assume someone released her. Eventually, they'd expand their search. She ran barefoot, stumbling often, hoping not to break a bone. She really couldn't see anything clearly. Maybe it was a blessing that there was no moonlight to guide her in this overgrown woodland.

More than anything, she wished she had her shoes. They'd removed them, and nothing was available to wrap her feet with. The ground was rough with roots and sharp things. Wincing as she ran, the ground dug into her tender soles. She had to tolerate it and keep running. It was only her panic and the fact that she couldn't see that kept her moving forward. If it were daylight, she might have taken one look at the dense thicket and decided it wasn't possible to penetrate.

Bi stumbled into some sort of wet muck, her toes sinking into the sludge, up to her ankles. The sound of water running over stones informed her that a river or creek was nearby. The deep runoff turned the creek into a seasonally deep watercourse, cold with snowmelt from the mountains. Nevertheless, the water might be her only escape in case they used hounds to track her. She took a few steps, but fell on the slippery stones, bruising her knee. Reluctantly, Bi lay herself down in the cold water, shivering uncontrollably as it soaked through her garments. The cuts on her bare feet stung. She let the water carry her body along with the current. Occasionally, she bounced or knocked against boulders, adding more bruises to those they had given her. But by this time, Bi was so numb she didn't care.

She didn't know if the current was taking her towards the city or away. But it hardly mattered. She just had to get as far from that house as she could. Bi tried to picture maps of the area, but the only water feature she recalled was the ocean. Where this creek was, and in which direction it moved, was a mystery.

It wasn't long before her mind wasn't able to hold a rational thought. The water was deeper and moved slower here. She felt as one with the heavy depths that pulled and pushed her along. Drifting like wreckage cast off in a storm, Bi imagined herself back in the sea, her little boat overturned in the storm. *They didn't find me.* She'd been holding her head up, away from the water, but it became too much of an effort. Finally, she relaxed, letting herself fall back. The river became a snake, viciously biting her head. In her delirium, she winced as the fangs penetrated her skull, filling her brain with venom. Then she lost herself completely in the swirling torrent.

She woke at dawn on the sandy bank. She must have lost consciousness again. How she managed not to drown was her first thought, or die of hypothermia. Her implant must have saved her. Pale sunlight filtered through the trees. The forest was not as dense here. She sat up and coughed out water. Her lungs were burning. She was shivering so hard that her teeth hurt as they chattered. Her yellow fur stood on end. She had to move and warm-up. Bi stumbled to her feet and found that every muscle ached. She could barely walk. Her feet were swollen and covered with small cuts and scrapes. Bruises throbbed across her torso. Lifting her shirt, she saw a blue-black color under her fur extending from her chest to her hips. The damage went all around. Her back was tender, too. An examination of her ankles exposed the same injuries all the way up her calves. Lacerations from her run in the brush crisscrossed her exposed arms, neck, and face. At least the creek had washed them clean. The fabric of her garments was also torn in places. She removed the pants and shirt and wrung them out, then reluctantly put them on again.

She was exhausted, but if she was going to survive, she had to move. Bi was trained to push through pain. It still took considerable effort to climb up the bank. At the top, she found a path. Uncertain of what direction to take, she chose to follow the flow of the creek.

As the morning sun rose higher, the warmth on her shoulders seemed like a small blessing. The moisture in her clothing began to steam and evaporate. Walking helped as well. Her muscles relaxed, and her teeth stopped chattering. In the sunlight, she examined her pelt. The coloring was much lighter than any Wen she had seen. Also, her fur was not green but yellow. She'd lost her Sister-cult robes that hid her difference, and she was exposed, in plain view.

As she neared the edge of the city, Bi saw a clearing ahead. She walked out of the forest and onto a road. A few older buildings here were surrounded by plots of land and gardens. Cautiously, Bi stayed off the main road, working her way through the neighborhood. She walked the back streets and alleys or took pathways through their gardens. As people woke up and came outside, she got quite a lot of curious stares. She didn't stop to ask for help. Her goal was to make her way to Mora's place, which she hoped was not being watched by their enemy at this hour.

Finally, into the city proper, Bi went to the canal that had often been her shortcut through the city. But it wasn't dry, it too was flowing with a seasonal excess of water.

Exhausted and defeated, she sat on the steps wondering how she would navigate the city looking as she did. Then she spied a small ledge along the side of the canal, a feature of its construction. The narrow ridge was just above the water level, and barely wide enough to walk on, but it was possible. This made her progress slower, but eventually, she emerged across from the foreigner's park. It was still early enough that few people were out and about. She took the path around the backside of the house.

Bi stumbled onto Mora's porch, hoping someone was home. She didn't have her fob disk to open the aperture. The bag she carried to work was still in a safe cupboard at the Journeyer Hotel. She signaled the door, and it opened immediately. Mora's face looked shocked at the sight of her. "Where were you? We've been so worried!"

Bi moved past Mora, into the safety of her home.

Orenda surveyed Bi's condition. Fear and worry were expressed in her body's response to her friend's obvious medical needs. Her ear-fans flattened back, her slitted pupils expanded. Then Orenda pulled Bi into an embrace.

Bi moaned a little in pain.

Orenda, let her loose. "You're damp and cold!"

Mora was less emotional, more practical. "Let's get you into a hot bath and some dry clothes. Where did these rags come from?" Mora asked.

Bi had not yet said a word. She looked to be in shock.

Mora continued talking as she led her friend toward the bathroom. "And then we want to hear what happened. And what is this?" Mora touched the collar.

In the room they shared, Orenda helped undress her friend. When she removed Bi's tunic, she gasped at the sight of the massive bruising.

Mora was still running the bath. "Mora! Come here, you have to see this." Mora ran from the bathing room at Orenda's urgent call. A stern look replaced the worried one when Mora saw Bi's injuries. "Let me find something to remove that thing from your neck."

Orenda was nearly in tears. "You need a healer. I don't have the necessary supplies with me, and these wounds need attention."

"No" was all Bi said.

Mora ignored that and said, "I'm calling Tokala. We can trust her."

Orenda nodded, then said to Bi, "I don't have any of my medical salves or tinctures here."

Mora returned with a tool in her hand and turned the collar around to look at the lock. Bi was standing naked and shivering.

"Almost there." Mora was looking very determined. The lock popped open, and Mora pulled the thing off. "I want to know all about this."

Bi just walked to the tub and got in, closing her eyes as she slipped down into the warm water. "Let me soak for a while."

The other two moved out and started to close the door to keep the warm air in the room. "Just call if you need anything."

"I'm starving. Do we have eggs?"

Orenda smiled. "Sure, I'll make you some."

Mora and Orenda looked at each other with wide eyes. The dog collar hung limply in Mora's hand.

68

UNCOMFORTABLE TRUTH

All through the day, Mora and Orenda tried to get more of the story out of Bi, who was still evasive and stubbornly quiet.

"Why would you put herself in danger like that?" Mora asked with exasperation.

"Why go to the hotel at all?" Orenda asked.

When Bi admitted to having dreams about her capture that had informed her of the escape route, they were astonished.

"You allowed yourself to face such danger when you had a perfectly safe place to stay out of harm's way!" Mora exclaimed.

But Bi refused to explain.

"Mora," Orenda said, "I have this niggling hunch that keeps trying to surface."

"Like a premonition?"

Orenda shrugged. "A sort of sinking feeling that there's more under the surface, more than what Bi is willing to share. It's disturbing, because Bi isn't being entirely honest and I don't know why."

When Tokaka came over with healing salves and herbs for pain, Bi refused to tell her anything. She allowed the healer to tend to her wounds, but then she turned her back and curled up on the bed. Making it clear she wasn't open to more discussion. They let her rest.

Before Tokala left, she said, "Holata Tyee brought Kinache home with some sort of illness. She refuses to let Yuma or me examine or treat him. She just spends hours fussing over him herself. But she is in an awful foul mood, and I better not stay too long." Tokala left, saying she would check in on Bi soon.

Later in the day, Asha came over, discovered what had happened to Bi, and began to put some of the various events together. She went with Mora into the bedroom to ask Bi questions...

Can you tell me anything about the people who captured you? Any distinguishing marks? Anything which might identify them?

Bi told her about the strange white band on the wrist. And how the fur above it was marked in a white pattern.

"Those marks on the arm of the youth. I've seen them recently at my house," Ahsa said, "on three native males who were talking to my father. The bands are called the modifier stigma. The council put them on those three because they keep getting into trouble, and partly due to what they tried to do to Bi."

Bi turned to Asha and looked attentively for more information.

Asha continued. "One was Askook. He's the fisher's son whom you poisoned with your ring when he tried to capture you. I think Mato's son Chayton was with him. Also, Holata Tyee's son, Kinache, was involved in some way. Those three now have this new modifier that makes them experience the pain of anyone they harm."

Bi's slitted pupils expanded with the realization of who else was in that room experiencing her pain. She had enough contact with Asha to trust that she wasn't involved in what her father and brother were doing. She sat up in bed to respond to Asha's inquiries.

"When I was being questioned, they shocked me. The contractions became more painful as they turned up the voltage. Every time they hurt me, there were others in the back of the room experiencing my pain. When they carried me out, an elderly native female directed some of them to carry the unconscious males to a different cell and put one in her vehicle."

"So, they were there too. But who was this native female? Did you recognize her?"

"I looked at her, but my eyes were tearing and blurred."

"Hold on just a minute." Orenda, who had been listening, got her sketchbook and opened it to a page. This was a drawing of an older native with a smug face. She had her chin tilted up in a defiant expression. "Do you recognize her?" Orenda turned the page to show a few other drawings of the same native, from different angles.

"Yes, it's her. She has a mole on her nose. I was focused on the long hairs coming out of it. And those bushy brows. I'm sure she's the one I saw."

Orenda turned to Asha and Mora. "This is Holata Tyee. She must be involved in whatever Ziyad is doing. I assume the male with the deep throaty voice is your father, Asha?"

Asha looked angry. She nodded. "What should we do? Who can we tell? Can we trust Mato?"

Orenda was about to agree that it was the right thing to do. When a signal came in on her personal Receptor device. It was Yuma. He started to tell her something when Orenda told him to hold on. She motioned to the others and said, "Let's move downstairs for this." To Yuma she said, "I'm going to put this up on the Receptor Screen so everyone can hear you. All right, Yuma, can you continue?"

"Sure... Oh, is that... Mora?"

Immediately, Orenda realized her mistake. Yuma had never seen Mora or Zamora's faces.

Asha started cursing while searching for the control to turn off the visuals at their end. The others followed Asha's frantic reaction and showed surprise, as they had never heard her swear. Mora was particularly amused because the curses were kind of cute. In the Neofinga language, she had basically said *thunderbutt* and *stinky toadstool*.

Then Yuma apologized for the interruption. He was obviously not sure how to handle the frenzy he had caused. "I'm sorry, Mora. I would never tell anyone."

"It's all right," Mora said. "Stop, Asha. Everyone, please calm down. Yuma, are you alone?"

"Yes, I am now. I mean, I am alone in the clinic."

Orenda was in tears now. Mora reached out to comfort her, petting her head. "Relax, I trust Yuma. He may as well be part of our growing secret circle." She laughed a little at the absurdity of it all. "Yuma, I take it you had something urgent to tell us?"

He didn't see Bi because she hung back out of sight. Yuma was shy, but also very worried. He looked at Orenda. "Are you sure I should say this to everyone?" He looked quickly at Asha.

"Asha knows about her father and brother, yes, you should tell us all. Go ahead."

"I was just telling Orenda I overheard a conversation. Holata Tyee and two men were talking. Well, actually shouting, and she was telling them to shut up and act normal. I was watching when the men left. It was Ziyad and Mato. I think something bad happened."

Orenda sat down on the couch like she had lost her last hope.

Mora and Asha looked at each other.

Orenda thanked Yuma for contacting her and told him she would try to see him soon.

Mora was thinking about how she had agreed to build a new machine, thinking she would be helping the council, but if Mato was mixed up with Ziyad, she might be putting an even greater tool into their hands, and she couldn't let that happen. Yet if she abandoned the project, she had no hope of returning to her world. "Now I don't know what to do."

"I do," said Bi.

The other three turned to look at her.

69

Secrets & Confessions

When Bi announced she knew what they should do, everyone was surprised. She had not been speaking much since her escape and torture. Until the conversation with Asha and Orenda, which confirmed Holata Tyee was in some way involved in what Ziyad was doing.

"I've given this a lot of thought. I have decided that I must now tell you who I am." She had such a sober expression. She tried to keep a brave face, but her ears nervously twitched. "By telling you, however, I will commit treason. I'm not sure what kind of punishment that will mean for me."

Mora, Orenda, and Asha looked at her in confusion. "Bi, what do you mean?" asked Mora.

"I am from the Eastern Empire. My Empress sent me here on a mission to gather information about the shadow people." She looked at Asha. "That's what we call your kind."

Almost in unison, the other three said, "Eastern Empire!"

Once Asha recovered from the shock of it, she said, "Your country has been in isolation for generations! Stories about the East are like fables. The thought that any of us in Wendat might ever meet someone from the Eastern Empire... well, that seemed so remote that it wouldn't even enter our minds as a possibility!"

Having come from another world, the idea of Bi coming from the mysterious Empire wasn't such a shock. "But how did you manage to come here, Bi?" Mora asked.

"How I got here is not the story I need to tell you right now."

"You are a spy?" asked Asha. "But you're so young!"

Bi nodded affirmatively. "I am also a lucid dreamer. My kind, who have the gift, are trained from childhood to be spies."

Silence followed while the others mulled that over.

Then Orenda said, "So the places in my drawings are images of your homeland?"

Bi just stared at her. Everyone understood that was obviously true. After a moment where she gathered her courage, Bi told them: "I regret having to deceive you for so long. But urgent matters require me to share what I've learned now. It all somehow factors into what is happening here, and I need you to help me figure it out. Then together we can use all of our gifts to stop something terrible from happening."

The other three nodded distractedly, each with their own internal processes going on. They seemed at a loss for the right response to Bi's confession.

"I do not believe Mato is involved, or in an alliance with the Order of Amon Kuroo. What Yuma overheard must have been Mato confronting the other two. I believe we must trust him, and in any case, with Coso in a coma, we have to entrust someone in authority with what we have learned. I doubt very much he would be so close to Coso if he were corrupt."

Orenda looked hopeful. "I sense you're right about that. She has a good intuition about people, and Mato was her closest confidant."

"We need to inform him of Coso's people who are at that house where I was taken. If they can be recovered, they can tell us a lot more about what took place at Coso's home during the attack."

"But how?" asked Asha, weren't you blindfolded in their vehicle? And when you got away, you floated in the river for... how long? Maybe hours."

"I recall the way. I've memorized the sounds I heard, and the feel of the road. It might be enough to guide Mato's team to their door, but it will at least bring them close."

Asha was nodding her approval. "We also need to inform Mato that those three males, including his son, were present when you were tortured, and about my father and brother and Holata Tyee."

Mora looked at Orenda. "Do you think Mato will be going to the hospital today?"

"He's there this morning, but will leave soon. We've been taking turns, so one of us is always with her. He goes when he can take the time away from the investigation. Sometimes he checks on her during the day, sometimes at night."

"Contact him and ask if he can meet us at the hospital tomorrow morning. That seems like the safest place for us to talk."

70

BREAKING THE BOND

Orenda and Mora were already at the breakfast table. They'd gotten up early and needed to leave soon to meet Mato at the hospital.

When Bi came walking into the kitchen, a floating spirit followed her. At the sight of the apparition, Orenda jumped up and threw the whole dish of salt into the air above Bi's head. The spirit looked astonished that Orenda could see her and promptly winked out of existence.

Bi ducked to avoid the salt. "Why are you throwing salt at me, Orenda?"

"Not at you! At the spirit who has attached herself to you!"

"What do you mean?"

Orenda, squinting her eyes, walked in a circle around Bi. "Oh! You're tethered to someone. I assume if you don't know that, it's not something you chose or agreed to?"

"Tethered?"

"Someone has connected themselves to you energetically. Have you noticed that your dreaming abilities were inhibited, or have you felt exceptionally exhausted lately?"

"Yes, but I thought it was because of all the stressful things that happened."

Orenda flattened her ear-fans. "I see your point. Sorry, of course, you're exhausted after what you went through. I meant before all of that... recently?"

"My abilities have changed. There were ways I used my gift previously that I can't now. I thought it was the implant."

Orenda was shaking her head. "The implant should not interfere with your gift in any way."

"Could this be Holata Tyee's doing? Did she attach something when I was a captive?"

"I will ask Yuma and Tokala what they think. But I doubt it. This was a young female with pale fur."

Bi stood there in shock. "It can't be."

"It definitely was. I think she's been spying on you. Unfortunately, I was never around to catch her doing it until today."

Bi was still speechless. Standing in the same place and looking bewildered.

"Not to worry, I'll ask Yuma and Tokala to bring over the necessary items and herbs. We'll do a ceremony to cut those cords."

That word suddenly brought back a memory for Bi. "Cords? As in cording? My friend and lover from the institute, Far, she told me once we were corded. She is also my invigilator now, the one I was reporting to."

"Well, now you know who it is. Why didn't you ask her what that meant if you didn't understand it?"

"I thought it was some silly romantic thing. I never imagined that it would give her the ability to find me here and watch me like that! If it's who I think it is, she's never shown the ability to astral project."

"Do you have the ability? Because if she's corded to you, she can feed on your energy and do what you do. She's obviously been using the tether to find you."

Mora stood from her seat at the table with her dishes. "We'd better go now, Orenda, or we'll be late. Bi, can you please sweep up that salt before it gets spread around?"

As they left, Orenda turned to Bi. "We will do the ceremony tonight. She won't be able to follow you around after that."

Bi got chills. "What if she heard what I confessed to you?"

Orenda shook her head. "If she had been around then, I would have seen her."

"Wait!" Bi shouted as the two were about to exit. Both were stunned by her sudden appeal. "Orenda, your grandfather... what does he look like?"

Baffled, Orenda gave Bi a bewildered look. "He's very thin. His fur is speckled with white because he's old, and he has kind eyes. Why do you ask?"

"He came to me once and said I had a parasite, and to ask for his granddaughter's help. But I didn't know you yet."

Orenda smiled knowingly. "It seems that Enzo is watching over us."

71

Fortune Favors the Just

Mora and Orenda walked out onto the path behind the house. At the end of the block, they stopped when they found some of Tao's gang members were in the Foreigners Park.

"They've been following me to the hospital lately," Orenda said.

"They are watching Bi and me too, not that we've left the house often." Mora said this with trepidation. "I hope they haven't figured out where we live yet. I've tried to elude their pursuit. With so much attention on every robed figure, we can't be too careful."

Quickly, they crossed the main road and ducked down to the canal, which was flooded, but Bi had told them about the ledge. They went only as far as the next stairway, and Mora suggested they part ways.

"Change of plan, Orenda. If members of that gang are roaming around, I better go to the Sisters' estate. It's close to here. I'll wait for them to accompany me across town."

Orenda looked uncertain. "Are you sure you can get there safely?"

"I hope so. It's just down the street. I'll only make you more of a target by going with you now. If you feel safe crossing the city by yourself, you can go ahead to the hospital and ask if Mato will wait for me."

Orenda nodded agreement. "I'll explain why you're late, but he might not be able to stay for long."

"If he can't, tell him I will reschedule, but that it is urgent."

***

As this was an unexpected visit, Mora had to wait while the Sisters' finished their morning chores or prayers or whatever it was the Sisters' did, she wandered into a room filled with iconography, paintings of the Goddess Bicara covered the walls, some with altars and candles before them. Carved onyx statues stood in the alcoves, the eyes inset with white marble and amber.

Representations of the Goddess looked much the same as the Zendali royals. She assumed this cult grew out of that country. Bicara had ancient roots. The religion spread to Wendat and the territories. Now, followers from every nation were indistinguishable when shrouded in the veil and robes.

These paintings made Mora wonder why people anthropomorphize the sacred. Gods and goddesses were often painted to look like the mortals who worshiped them.

Depicted here, Bicara had large eyes with slitted pupils, fan-shaped ears, and dark indigo fur. It was interesting to note Bicara also had a full mane, not a crest. A crest was more common. As Asha had informed her, it was only royals who had that much head hair. Mora understood now that the mane tied the Goddess to the Royal lineage. She wondered if that was symbolic or if she was once a mortal from the pureblood line.

A round table sat in the middle of the room, covered in a milky white cloth. Mora ran her finger over the intricate embroidery, tracing the cosmic symbols as they spread across the sheen of spidersilk. An ornate box was in the center of the table. It didn't occur to her that it might be forbidden or rude to open it. Without hesitation, she flipped the lid. Her ears wiggled with delight at what she found inside. "Oh! How beautiful!"

It was some sort of card deck. Rendered with delicate hand-painted images and embellished with gold leaf. These were no ordinary cards, though. Each one seemed to tell a story that included Hadot's heavenly bodies, symbolically represented as people. The two moons: Ifa the bright first moon, shown as male in princely form. Ife, the second... or *lover's moon*... was a young female, dressed in a soft flowing gown. Followed by Tiku, the symbol of death, this one showed a skeletal figure in a dry and ravaged landscape. Orphic, a rare gas giant, was a symbol of something precious, adored, and loved. This card had a richly dressed figure in robes and jewels. The planet Fulgent had a reflective quality. The card represented vanity and self-importance. It showed a female looking into a pond at her own reflection. Cherche was a small ice planet. Which was furthest from the sun. A symbol of the seeker. The card showed a person following a long road. Savior is the planet seen on the horizon in the north at sunset. Ships navigate by it. Which is why this planet was commonly considered a symbol of what is found, or discovered. An odyssey completed, a war won, a conquest, and the hero. This card showed a sailor in uniform on a ship, following the star. Last was Amity, a planet with rings and several moons. She was a symbol of peaceful relationships and resolution. It showed an image of two hands clasped. One had white fur, the other, indigo. Mora raised an eye ridge at the implications... *Now that is interesting.* She thought.

After those major cards were others with words etched across the top and bottom: ignorance/knowledge, attachment/generosity, aversion/acceptance, pride/shame, envy/support, gluttony/moderation, lechery/decency.

Mora was so engrossed in her examination of the cards she did not hear as the sister approached so quietly behind her. Startled, several cards dropped onto the table. "Oh, I'm sorry I..." she bent to recover the cards and return them to the box.

The sister was one of the Wen whom they called an oracle. She had removed her veil. Showing a placid face without emotion, which for some reason made Mora feel she had been sacrilegious by touching their cherished things.

"I'm sorry for the intrusion," Mora told her.

The oracle walked forward, pulled out a chair and motioned for Mora to take the place across from her. "I am Kinywa. The cards are for divination. You're obviously curious. Would you like a reading?"

"I don't have time now. I have an important meeting at the hospital." Mora was also of the opinion that all such things were superstitious. She considered anyone who fell for such nonsense to be gullible.

"No, it is I who must apologize, because you'll need to wait longer than usual this morning. We didn't expect you today. The Sisters are not ready to leave. I promise this won't delay you."

"Sure, why not?" Mora didn't want to offend the Sisters' who had been very accommodating. *No harm in letting this one go through the charade if it pleases her.*

"Have you had the divine guidance of Bicara before?" Kinywa was aware of the reading given to Zamora a few years ago, yet this female, who called herself Zamora, shook her head in the negative.

Mora took a deep breath, not letting her ears wiggle or her mouth betray her amusement. Nevertheless, the Oracle understood she was a skeptic.

"Members of our sect who have a powerful connection to the Goddess and are able to foresee the future are called the Oracles of Bicara. My name is Kinywa. I am a native of Wendat. You already know Kehanet, who is Zendali."

Mora nodded. She didn't know Kehanet, but Zamora must have, so she played along.

Kinywa watched Mora carefully and found it curious that although she nodded to affirm that she knew the other Oracle, Zamora honestly did not recall Kehanet had done a reading for her.

Kinywa motioned for Mora to take a seat. She handed the whole deck of cards to Mora and told her to mix them well and touch every card. When she was done, she tried to hand them back to Kinywa, but the oracle told her to stack them before her, cut the deck, then make one stack again. Mora obliged, thinking it was a silly ritual.

"The cards are laid in this manner: the top card represents the issue in question." She turned over the card labeled Cherche, the seeker. "Below we place three cards. The first represents the past." She turned over the card, and it said Attachment. "This card also speaks of passion, yearning, a desire to fulfill a goal in your case. The next card represents the present." She placed the card that said Orphic. "You are in possession of a rare talent or thing, something highly valued. The next card represents the future. By this, we mean what is likely to happen unless something significant alters your path." This was the card Envy. "I cannot say yet if it is you who will covet something, or if others will want what you have. Let's see what comes next."

By this point, Mora's attitude had changed, and she was intrigued.

"I will lay two cards below each of those three," Kinywa continued. "They will give us particulars relating to the card above. The first card below relates to the past, which concerns the issue of attachment." The card read Ignorance on one end, but it was turned upside down, and the top said Knowledge. "The opposite of ignorance is knowledge. It means you have something meaningful to contribute. The next card below these previous two cards represents the present—something rare and valued." The card said Pride. "Perhaps you have reason to be proud, but you should be careful it doesn't blind your decisions."

Mora looked at her with respect and thought. *I suppose that is deserved.*

The next card went under Envy. In the position of the future, it was Avarice. "There will be those who wish to take from you... something you create. They aim to cheat you."

Mora was astonished and waited nervously for the other cards to be placed.

"The last three cards will give us understanding and resolution, what has been, led you to the present and will follow you into your future. You must choose if you wish to follow the path you are on, or if you need to make changes to alter the outcome.

The next card in the line of the past was the Savior. "You have the ability to lead others. Your actions are a guiding light, and your destiny is tied to that goal." She looked up into Mora's eyes and could see this resonated with her. The next card in line with the present was Amity. "This shows you have developed peaceful relationships and trust." The last card under the future line was Flugent in a reverse position. "Fulgent is reversed. In some cases, this card is more than vanity. It is symbolic of deceit. When reversed, it represents true vision and correctness. Sadly, difficulties will follow you, but in the end, a resolution will come, and it will be to your benefit. Fortune favors the just."

Mora sat for a moment, overwhelmed with a sense of awe, staring at the cards. This was another instance where magical things conflicted with her scientific predisposition. *How does this work? How is this possible?* Then, the oracle broke her concentration by gathering the cards and returning them to the box. She stood, gave a slight bow to Mora, and left the room. Mora became aware she had not even thanked the oracle for the reading. Not long after Kinywa left the room, a group of Sisters' came and told her they were ready. It almost seemed like they *wanted* her to wander into this room. Mora suspected nothing about this was coincidental.

Mora suddenly suspected that this organization, which followed Bicara's teachings, was much more than anyone suspected. *Perhaps Lady Justice was not a theological figurehead after all. Maybe they were more than a religious organization? Could the symbolic knife they wore as a charm have more meaning than cutting through deception and duplicity?*

***

Unknown to Mora, the Sisters' had indeed developed a network of secret agents and operatives throughout Zenda and the Territories who worked as the unveiled in city government offices, corporations, schools, and entertainment industries. They worked with and among the Pinks to protect them, and they sought to remove those who were in the greatest danger, relocating them to safety.

In Wendat, they were just beginning to build their organization. Zamora had joined because of her kinship with Asha, and she accepted the ideological precepts of Bicara. She did not, however, involve herself in more than a weekly meeting at the temple. For her, it was only a safety net. She was never made aware of their true calling. Zamora was too focused on her own work. The idea that others needed saving was not on her mind.

This was the understanding of the Oracle Kehanet, who had done a reading for Zamora. The judgment was simple: Zamora would not be committed to their cause. She was allowed to join the Sisters' of Justice, but she was not privy to their secrets. Her interactions were always on the periphery. She was a believer, not a doer.

Kinywa, was of a different opinion now, although admittedly somewhat confused. She was aware Kehanet's previous reading for Zamora, was the basis for the Sisters' judgment and decision. But Kinywa had a suspicion, no, more of a conviction... that this female, who called herself Zamora, couldn't be the same they had met before. First, because she had no foreknowledge of the divination process, the cards appeared to be completely novel to her. And secondly, because the reading was so divergent from the first. Readings did not diverge so radically. A path forward might change an outcome, but the lifeline, the goals, did not change. No individual could alter their path so completely. Kinywa didn't know how this was possible, but the cards didn't lie. This one had completely different intentions, and therefore her path diverged greatly from the other one. She decided to bring her discovery to the congregation.

72

Love & Lust

Mora spotted Kai when she was walking with the Sisters' to the hospital. He was watching the whole group, obviously trying to determine if she was among them. Just as they were about to enter the hospital, he caught up with them and reached out to take Mora's hand. She reacted instinctively with a turn, jab, and throw, putting him down. Kai, on the ground, was wincing from the punch to a tender area. "What do you want, Kai? Why are you following us?"

"Zamora, I mean you no harm. Please, I need to speak with you."

This all happened so quickly that even the Sisters' didn't expect this reaction from Mora. She thanked them and said she would find her own way home.

Mora took out her receptor and signaled Orenda. "I'll be up there in a minute."

Kai was standing now, looking disheveled, his pride hurt more than anything else.

Turning back to Kai, she said, "Let's go inside. We can talk in the waiting room."

Kai followed her in, and they sat in the back of the room, away from the other people. He looked a little bewildered. Mora had already settled on a judgment. He was pompous and entitled. He was a player. Overconfident, because he expected to have anyone he pleased. Evidently, he had toyed with Zamora for a while and was used to having his way with her. Of course, Mora's lack of interest would be upsetting.

"I'm busy with more important things Kai. I don't have time for whatever this is."

His expression changed to a resigned sadness. "All right, I'll get to the point. My friend Chayton, did something to you a few months back. I was surprised when your attitude toward him changed."

"You're jealous of something you think happened between me and Chayton? Kai, I don't want anything to do with Chayton, or with you for that matter."

He hung his head. "I deserve that. But no, I'm not jealous. I found out he was getting some sort of charms from Kinache. He's been using dark magic on you."

Mora shook her head. This nonsense again. She closed her eyes. "Don't worry about it. I already found out."

He looked at her, expecting to hear more about how she discovered it. But realized she wasn't going to say. "I'm sorry I didn't respect you, Zamora. It was wrong of me to take you for granted. I didn't know how I felt about you until you became... distant."

Mora looked at him without any concern. She just wanted to end this and go upstairs to talk with Mato. She was trying to think of what to say, so she could disengage from this silly drama.

"My parents, they would not allow us to be together, not if they found out what you are, you understand? So, I didn't take what we had seriously." Kai told her.

She still couldn't think of what to say. Mora just didn't care, and she felt nothing in return. She recognized he was suffering over Zamora, but that was his loss. *He should have treated her better.* She thought.

He reached for her hand. "Zamora, don't you understand what I am trying to say? I'm in love with you."

She pulled her hand away and abruptly stood up. "Get over it, Kai, because there is no future for us."

Then, with a clear conscience and absolutely no regret, she left him sitting there in complete shock.

When Mora entered Coso's room, Orenda looked up. "Mato was called out. He said he would come back."

Mora took a seat to wait with her.

"When you arrived with the Sisters' I was looking out the window. What did that guy want from you?"

"Kai? He and Zamora were lovers. He's distressed because I'm not giving him any attention. It's probably because no one has ever rejected him before. And now he's discovered that he loves her."

Orenda was smiling. "So, what did you tell him?"

"I told him to get lost. But he did confirm Chayton was dabbling in dark magic charms Kinache made for him."

***

Then Mato walked into Coso's hospital room, looking stressed and unkempt. He saw Mora with Orenda and closed the hospital door. The air was full of mystery, all the unspoken bits and pieces of what they each knew. Their unsaid certainties hung in the air, as if those truths existed in the form of energy, but were not yet made real by expressing them in words. You could feel the totality of those secrets ready to burst out.

Orenda sensed something more, something personal. The council elder was suffering with. "Mato, what happened?"

"My son, he's in another room, here at the hospital." His head listed to the side, and his chin started to tremble.

Orenda and Mora looked at each other, suspecting the fullness of this drama would be hard for the council elder to accept.

Mato covered his face for a moment, then stood straighter. "It was a reaction to the Modifier."

They were all silent. Mora and Orenda understood what had happened. But before they could tell him, he revealed something else.

"We found another youth, Askook. His modifier was removed, and as we warned, it killed him."

"Where was he found?" Asked Mora.

"He washed up on shore near Rayfin Harbor. We assume he'd been on a boat. I tried to contact his parents, but they were not to be found. Maybe he had some altercation when he returned to his family? Maybe he tried to remove it on his own? We won't know until we can talk to them. I confronted Ziyad about that particular youth, because he'd been seen in Tao's gang. But he insisted Askook left to join his family, and he knew nothing of his demise."

"There is more to it than that. We have learned things you need to know."

"Bimisi was kidnapped. They hooked her up to an electric device that caused a lot of bruising and physical damage. We think your son and the other two were in the room when she was questioned."

Mato's ear-fans flattened and his fur stood on end.

"Bimisi escaped, but she is still pretty fragile."

Mato closed his eyes and took a deep breath. "I'm glad to hear she is safe now."

"Yuma and Tokala Luta have seen Holata Tyee and Ziyad together, whispering of secret things. Bi also believes he and Holata Tyee were involved in her kidnapping and torture."

Mato's eyes widened. "But she hasn't met them. How does she know this?"

"Orenda showed her drawings of the medicine guardian. Bi confirmed it was her."

"She saw Ziyad too?"

"No. But her interrogator had a deep, throaty voice like his."

Mato shook his head. "It's not enough."

"Asha overheard her brother and father order an experiment on Askook to discover what would happen if they removed the modifier."

"Unfortunately, this is still just hearsay. We have no proof they were involved in his death."

"Bi saw a room full of Pinks in the house where she was taken. She thinks they could be from Coso's house. Maybe they can tell you what happened and give testimony about the crimes?"

Mato's ear-fans pricked up and straight out. "That is hopeful news! Yes, we need to send a search party immediately to find them." Then he paused and sat down with a sigh, as if defeated, which was not the response Mora and Orenda expected.

"What you have told me confirms my suspicions, and fills in some gaps. The only problem is that we have no hard evidence of Ziyad or Holata Tyee's involvement. No credible witnesses of their crimes. We have rumors, and that is not enough to charge such powerful people with these crimes."

"Bi says she can tell you how to find the house."

He looked up at that. "Yes, of course. We should rescue them. I will notify a team. When can we speak to your friend?"

There was a pause, then Mora said, "She is still on the mend, so maybe a remote conversation would be best? I can arrange it." She paused. "Ah, she might not be willing to have a visual connection, only voice. Will that be all right?"

Mato agreed. "If we can find the house and free the Pinks, we will have their testimony. But they are not citizens, and their word against Holata Tyee and Ziyad, who is the Zenda Ambassador..."

The implications hung in the air. It still was not enough to even call them in for questioning.

Then Coso said, "There is proof."

In unison, everyone looked at the bed to find Coso was awake!

73

Lost & Nameless

Coso explained to Mato where the hidden security devices were throughout her home and garden. He had retrieved visual evidence of the mayhem Tao and his gang had caused there, and also of the attack on her. He now had evidence of the brutal treatment of the council elder and the kidnapping of her staff. Coso's health was improving, but she remained under observation at the hospital with guards for her safety.

Mora arranged for Bi to speak with Mato's team. She described what she had discerned during the drive to the house where she was held captive. Bi told them the sounds she heard in passing, the train and other landmarks, where the road was smooth or bumpy, and when the vehicle turned. She told them what she remembered of the house itself and the rooms she had seen. Now it was their turn to reconstruct that path and to search for the house.

"Are you heading out then?" Bi asked Mora as she gathered their things to meet Asha.

"We finished the mind-map we made for the Pinks, or at least as much work as I have time for."

Bi had been curious about what the mind-map consisted of, but since both Mora and Asha seemed more than a little secretive about it, she didn't ask. Bi understood secrets.

"Asha is staying at the hotel now?"

"Yes, she took a room there after her confrontation with her father and brother, but we decided a trip out of town was a good idea, at least while Mato and his team conduct the investigation."

"Where are you headed? Is it far? Do you know anything about the place?"

Mora smiled. Bi had been a little restless stuck at home. It was obvious she would like to join them on their adventure. "We're taking a trip to the Meex reservation, which is a day's journey and will require an overnight stay at least. I know their primary crop was ferrebast, which has many uses, but they don't process it there. Other native companies make rope and clothing from it, as well as oil, and medicine. Acorns are their second crop. The government built the reservation near an ancient grove. Traditionally, acorn was a staple food for the Wen. The Pinks still harvest and process them."

"Well, I guess I'm staying put. I have plans with Orenda and Yuma for a ceremony that should release the parasite, as Orenda's grandfather called my spy companion. Evidently, my invigilator has the ability to astral project and spy on what I've been doing here in Wendat."

"I've been considering the ramifications of everything I learned about Far," Bi said. "I've ended up with more questions than answers about what she's been doing back home... and *why*. I don't understand why she cut communication and has neglected her responsibilities as my invigilator."

"You're in good hands with Orenda and Yuma. I'm sure the ritual will go well." Mora hugged Bi. "I'm sorry you can't join us. Please stay inside and be careful. We are still in danger here."

***

An entourage of Sisters' met Mora near the park and took her to meet Asha and Tokala at the train station. Just getting on the train already lifted some of the stress Mora had been carrying. "This was such a good idea, Tokala, thank you for suggesting it."

"I think getting out of town and meeting some new people will take our minds off things here. We all need to distance ourselves from the trouble in Muwioni."

The trip required a train ride north and then a drive west toward the coast. Upon arrival, Mora's first impression was pure fascination. This was an older, more established community.

As they followed a path through a large vegetable garden, which was for the reservation's personal use, Mora found everything charming and asked their guide a multitude of questions.

"Where does the water come from to make that pond? The other reservation didn't have one."

"We diverted a small creek." The Pink was confident and proud in a way that made Mora feel grateful that this new home gave these refugees such determination and a sense of purpose. In contrast with the other reservation where enough of their residents had gone missing that they were losing hope.

Their guide had continued to explain the whole process... "To make the pond, we dug a deep hole, covered it with clay and stone. Once it was baked in the sun for a season, we ran the water from the creek through it."

"How clever, and then the creek water flows out the other side keeping it fresh! Are those fish in there!"

Their guide was pleased with Mora's enthusiasm, and happy to talk about their lively community. Mora was impressed with the way everything was organized. It was also a little like going back in time, as there were few modern conveniences here. The other two had been to this reservation often and were familiar with everything and everyone.

"It's nice to see you in good cheer, Mora," Tokala said.

Asha turned back and smiled at Mora. "I have never seen this side of you, Mora. You're like a curious child here." And she laughed. Then with a more sober thought she added... "or maybe it is more accurate to say I have never seen this behavior in Zamora. You are different."

Mora shrugged. She had no idea how she differed from her counterpart, but nothing was going to dampen her joy on this day. The three of them continued to wind through the pathways, and their guide showed them where they raised large furry rodents and several types of fowl, which Mora assumed were their protein source. She also saw herd animals in a field, which might provide milk.

"This community is constructed just like the other one! All the buildings are laid out the same, except it's used very differently." Mora commented as she hurried along trying to keep up.

Asha agreed. "The other reservation has a big open space when we enter. Meex wisely uses that area for gardens because their community is more densely populated."

"I read that there is a population limit for the reservation?"

"Yes, when a reservation reaches maximum capacity, new births only follow deaths, unless someone transfers to a different reservation. But most are not at a zero-growth rate like this one. Some are below capacity, and Pinks are encouraged to transfer to them. If a reservation has a sparse population, they struggle to keep up with production because they don't have enough laborers required to stay independent."

The thought and care that went into creating the reservations impressed Mora. They were true sanctuaries and so unlike the native communities she had seen in her world, where the broken and destitute indigenous people lived in poverty and often struggled with addiction. This underlined the injustice all too clearly.

As usual, Tokala had a full day of patients to tend to, so she went to the clinic. It was identical to the other one. Mora and Asha set up in the main hall to share their mind-map of languages, history, culture, and a list of names with meanings, which is what they had already given to the other reservation community. They had planned to offer self-defense in the evening, but no incidents of assault or missing residents had happened here. Meex was more remote, and harder to reach. Consequently, only a few people showed an interest in Mora's fighting techniques. Those who did, seemed shy and uncertain if such training was permissible.

The main hall was private and protected from outside view. They both felt welcome and safe enough to take off their head coverings. Which made it more comfortable when interacting with the residents. It was maybe halfway through the day when a male entered with the next group to receive the download for his implant. Mora suddenly stopped what she was saying and stood up.

"What's wrong, Mora?" Asha asked, but Mora stood frozen and stared across the room. Then she raised her hand to her mouth, just touching her lips, like she was either in awe or afraid of something. Asha stood as well, and then all the others turned to see what Mora was worried about.

"He's my father." She said this not in the common native language, but in a lesser-known dialect from Zenda, that she and Asha could have a private conversation in.

"What?" Asha said in surprise.

"Well, I mean, Zamora's father. I know that's him because he looks exactly like my dad."

"What are you going to do?"

"I'm not sure. I don't want to upset him, but I really want to ask how he got here and where he was before. I want to know everything!"

"Mora, you better calm down. Let's finish our work here. We plan to stay overnight. You have time. Think carefully about how you want to approach him and what you want to say. You're not going to tell him who you really are?"

Mora looked at her. "No, I'll tell him I'm Zamora, but did he know what they named his daughter? How do I tell him he is my father?"

"Exactly, so ease into this. Give it some thought."

When he got close, and it was his turn, she learned through an introduction that he was a teacher in the community. He had taught the residents things which were not traditionally mind-mapped for Pinks at the reservations. He had already begun the work that Asha and Mora intended to do.

"Asha, he has an eidetic memory, too. I got that ability from my father."

Mora then greeted Zamora's father. "What is your name?"

"They call me Teacher here."

"Did you have other names?"

He looked at the two of them. His tone was friendly, but his suspicion was clear. After all, he was taking to a Zendali, and a Fog. "Why do you ask?"

Mora decided that honesty might be best. "I think you're my father."

He gave her a dispassionate stare, not at all the reaction her own father might have had to such a statement. But this teacher had a different life. "Why would you think so?"

"I have an eidetic memory. This means that if I read something or see a document, for example, I remember everything as if it were a picture before me. I think you have this ability as well, and at some point in your early life, perhaps you had access to a library?"

He swallowed hard. Sitting stiffly in the chair. He looked sideways at the reservation resident who organized the mind-mapping and said in a quiet voice, "How did you say you knew these two?"

"They are close friends of Tokala Luta, whom you know well. I think you can trust them."

He nodded and turned back to Mora. "Give me another reason to believe you."

Mora recalled the story of Zamora's childhood and how she came here, everything that Asha had told her about how the social system in the Sovereign Nation worked. The youth are encouraged to explore their sexuality before formal unions, which are often political matches. A child born out of wedlock is called a Golden Egg. This event is praised, and proof of fertility. As is customary, the grandparents become parents to these children. The birth mother goes on to marry and start a life with her husband and his family. Zamora was careful not to put anything incriminating in her journals. They told Mora only a little about Zamora's childhood in Zenda, but nothing about her family relationships. Fortunately, Asha had been told a lot about Zamora's personal history, which facilitated Mora's conversation with her counterpart's father now.

"I was born to Serwa Darego. It was discovered that my father was the son of the servants. They had grown up together and were friends. But he was sent away, and I was never told his name. My grandparents made the difficult choice not to kill me, as the law required, but raised me in secrecy until they were able to send me here to Wendat."

By this time, he had tears soaking the fur on his face.

"Which reservation do you live on?" he asked.

Mora had no easy answer to this question. She chose an abbreviated version of the truth. "I live in the city in hiding. I wear these garments as a follower of Bicara, so no one can see that I am Fog. This is a secret which only a few friends know. You mustn't tell anyone, please."

He seemed to ponder all the ramifications of this news, then he offered some of his own history. "When I was friends with your mother, I was called Omo Adun. This was her affectionate name for me. It means sweet one. I did in fact have access to the family library, and I read every book. Which prepared me for when I was sent away to a mining facility on Ujarak, where I used the name Omo until they began to call me Teacher. I helped the miners gain literacy. Ultimately, I had the support of the manager. We helped each other. He was a good Zendali. Having knowledge others didn't possess gave me an advantage, and eventually, with the help of this manager, I escaped. But that is a long story, not for today."

"May I call you Omo then?"

He looked sad and shook his head. "I left that life behind me. Here I am called Teacher."

"Have you been teaching here for long?"

He paused again, obviously uncomfortable with her inquiries. "No, I arrived recently, only a few months ago. When they asked me what I could do, I suggested teaching would be the most valuable skill I could offer.

"Should I call you teacher?"

It took him a while to answer. Mora realized that if she was his daughter, having her call him teacher was odd.

"No," he said. "I have heard that you gave us a list of names of our ancestors. Perhaps I will choose a new name for myself. The names from the past tag us to contracts in Zenda. All of us are careful to let them go. Just in case something changes, it will be more difficult for us to be returned to those who own our contracts."

Mora's ears flattened back. "That is sensible." Then she smiled. "Would you allow me to suggest a name?"

He chuckled. "I'm curious what you would choose."

"I would choose Thal Liams. The first name means valley. The second one means resolute protector. That is what you are. A protector of this new home."

"Two names! And a good choice. I like them."

She couldn't mention that her own father had those names.

"How do you know this Zamora? And how did you recognize who I was?"

"I wish I could tell you. There are so many things I hope we will have time to share."

"I have the feeling you don't expect to return to our community anytime soon."

"We live quite a distance from this reservation, and I have important work in the city. I'm a scientist." At this, he reacted with pointed interest. "We are staying overnight, though. You and I will have tomorrow to share and learn about each other. And of course, I will try to return when I can."

"How were you able to study and become a scientist, being Fog?"

"It's complicated, and a long story." She smiled at him warmly and reached out to touch his hand. "I'll tell you tomorrow."

Mora's day with Zamora's father was bittersweet. He was a fascinating fellow and a wonderful teacher, as was her own father. It was difficult to leave, knowing that she might never see him again. But at least she had found him, and if Zamora returns, she can now have a relationship with her father.

When they got on the train, returning to Muwioni, Mora confessed. "I feel terribly homesick for my own family. Having time with Zamora's father reminded me of what I've been missing."

Her friends, sitting on either side, put their arms around her in sympathy.

Mora found herself talking about her worries, which was something she had never done before. Such a luxury required knowing someone intimately enough to know they could be trusted. "I have to admit that even though I need to return, I am incredibly sad to lose contact with all the friends I've made here."

"We will miss you as well." Asha told her with sincerity.

"In my world, the conditions never presented themselves, I suppose. I've given it a lot of thought. I've changed so much. *You* have all changed me." This was a nervous attempt at a confession that made her uncomfortable.

"What do you mean?" Tokala asked Mora, who had a sort of befuddled expression.

"Well, unusual circumstances brought us together, and we *needed* each other... that never happened to me at home. I don't have friends really, not back there."

Asha did that side-to-side head tilt. Mora supposed it meant she sympathized.

"There are other concerns weighing on me too. The pressure of what I still need to accomplish to get back, and the uncertainty of accomplishing that."

"But you have funding now, and you're designing your portal. Don't you feel confident that you have all you need?" asked Asha.

"The time to build it is limited. You realize there are forces at play in the city which could easily put a stop to everything I'm doing. No, I don't feel confident! Not because I can't do the design, but because there are those who would prohibit me from working."

Tokala nodded in understanding. "Your success would prove a point."

"Exactly. If the Order of Amon Kuroo found out what I'm up to, they would try to stop me. I might die fighting them, or be forced onto a reservation for my own safety."

"Mora, I think your worries are exaggerated a little, Tokala said.

"Maybe. But the worry tears at my heart. What if I had no opportunity to complete the design? I would never return to my world."

74

DESIGN IMPROVEMENTS

N ow she needed to build something bigger, to accommodate a living form. But she wanted it to be trim and modest compared to that first monstrosity she had built in her lab at Inoti University back home. She often wondered if her machine was also ruined, and if it was, did Zamora work on a redesign in her laboratory, with her Algon? She was taking a risk by assuming she'd have a portal to accept her back home, but she tried not to think about that end-game. Her mind had to be clear to get this new machine assembled.

When Mato announced the new lab was ready, they planned to start the following morning. Ohpa showed up before Mora was ready, of course.

"When you said you'd meet me here, I guess I should have expected you'd be early." What she meant was eager.

"I wanted to be sure you'd get to work safely."

She had just finished breakfast and had a Kav cup in hand. "Want some Kav?"

Ohpa wrinkled his nose. "Tea, maybe?"

While Mora prepared a cup of mint tea, Ohpa walked around her living room with a look of awe. All the transparent wall-panels in Zamora's house were covered with diagrams and calculations. Examining her mathematical equations and summations of infinite sequences, and marveling at this view into her mind, Ohpa's ear-fans stood out and kept fluttering with his appraisal.

She joined him, handing Ohpa the cup. "My primary focus is on the internal workings at this point. I've been in full immersion mode lately." She laughed, knowing it was a lot to take in.

"Have you been working night and day on this? Do you ever sleep or eat? How did you get so much done so fast?"

"Fortunately, my roommates brought me food and encouraged me to eat. But mostly I've been napping in that chair and never make it upstairs to bed."

"You must be exhausted!"

"No, that will come later. Right now I am driven, *possessed,* with a need to complete this. It keeps me going."

Mato had already met with Ohpa to sign contracts in advance. The agreement gave Zamora a percentage of the profits. It was split three ways, which Mato insisted on, even though he was putting up the money for the build and for the warehouse. He told Mora he was sure that the proceeds from the distribution of the portals would be more than enough to make back his losses and enough for them all to be wealthy.

It was agreed that Ohpa would be listed as the inventor. Mora began to understand why Zamora made the choices she had at the university. She was also driven to do the work, to make the dream a reality, no matter who would get the credit. Still, Mora knew it would sting if she stayed here, not to be recognized for her achievements, but it was becoming less important to her as the project progressed. *Maybe Zamora is more altruistic than I am?*

The warehouse was an older building on the edge of the industrial district of the city. It had been emptied and abandoned for some time. It was scheduled for demolition in the near future to make room for new developments. But Mato was able to secure it for a few months. After the design phase, they would look for another building for manufacturing.

This building was cleaned in preparation for Mora and Ohpa. She could still smell the disinfectant. Clerestory windows let in a surprising amount of sunlight, and the skylights were made of energy crystal, which absorbed sunlight and generated enough power for the building. The windows were old, manufactured before the production of domes, which were more commonplace now. All that mattered was that they still worked.

The other walls and hallway were without windows, giving them privacy. One entire wall was covered with transparent panels, like in Zamora's home. Mora marveled at those magical surfaces, which were written on with a type of light beam stylus. It was efficient and clean. She would miss them when she went home. These thoughts were more often on her mind now that going home felt possible. She began to take note of all the wonders that were unique to Zamora's Hadot.

The warehouse had a security system in place. The front entrance let into an entryway, where a guard's booth would remain unattended. They wouldn't be using a guard. The fewer people who knew they were there, the better. A double-door system with a security pad installed. An entry code was required to enter. In the hallway, another secure door opened with a fob.

There was a small room next to the factory floor with a cot, a small kitchen, and a bathroom. Mora suspected the little room had been used as an office in the past. She was impressed with the care Mato had put into the set-up. He seemed to think of everything. After a full tour, Mora expressed her gratitude, and Ohpa was too overwhelmed to speak. Not just with the huge wonderful laboratory setup, but to be favored by Mora and given this opportunity.

"I think that is everything you asked for. Everything from your list of supplies and parts is on the main floor or in those closets and cabinets. The receptor screen will send messages to me directly if you just ask it for Mato. Let me know if you need anything else. Otherwise, I have other work to attend to."

Mora walked with him to the exit and thanked him in a distracted sort of way, her mind was already focused on her work. On the outside, the building looked abandoned. The grounds were in disrepair, with untrimmed trees and bushes and overgrown weeds. A surrounding walkway was cracked. The ferrebast building had been whitewashed when it was in use but was now peeling. Overall, it looked sad and derelict, which made it perfect.

As Mato was leaving, she thought of Coso. "How is the investigation going? I hear that the council elder will be released from the hospital soon."

He turned and paused, looking past her to be sure Ohpa was still in the laboratory and could not hear what he was going to say. "We retrieved recordings of the events at her home from her security system. We're holding off on direct confrontations until we can find out what Ziyad and the other Zendali nationals are planning. What your friend Bi told us was very helpful, as far as knowing others involved and who they are. We now have them under surveillance. It seems to be a big operation that they want to protect at all costs. But we still don't know what they're up to."

Mora looked thoughtfully at him, her brow furrowed. "Do you think Coso will be safe at home?"

He shook his head. "I advised against it, but she won't listen. I have set a team to watch the property."

"Were you able to find the house where her staff was held?"

"Yes, they were found. Again, thanks to your friend Bi. Otherwise, they would have perished. The house was empty except for the locked room where they were kept. They had not eaten for several days. They were suffering from dehydration as well as injuries from beatings and rough treatment. But they are being taken care of now. They all wish to return to Coso."

"Thank you for everything, Mato, and for keeping me informed."

"We would not have gotten this far without your help and the informants you brought to us. It is I who should be thanking you."

Mora watched Mato leave through the back access point. They all agreed it was wise to use it from then on. When she returned to the lab, Ohpa was studying the piles of components on the main floor with a discerning eye. It took a moment before he noticed Mora was back. He looked up and beamed a huge smile at her. She was wondering what his relationship had been like with Zamora, and hoped that they would work well together because there was no turning back now.

"All right, my friend, shall we get started?"

75

ANTICIPATION

B i missed Mora. She almost never left the new laboratory now. When she did come back to Zamora's place for a shower and change of clothing, she would catch up on news about Coso and the others. Mora had invited Asha to sleep in her bed since she wasn't using the bedroom, and even though the house was close to Ziyad, it was no less safe than the hotel. Either way, they both had to be extremely careful when they came and went. Bi was giving Asha a few lessons in that regard.

Mato had advised Asha to stay in hiding until his investigation was over, but she was still sneaking out with Tokala for their work at the reservations. Asha, staying at Zamora's place made it easier for Mora to get updates about what was happening with the Pinks.

Orenda had told her she was thinking about moving back with her aunt, but Mato had asked her to wait. He was worried about her safety. He had told her that the fewer people his team had to keep an eye on, the better. In any case, Coso's staff were returned, and they insisted they were perfectly fine and able of taking care of Coso's needs.

***

On this day, Orenda and Bi were eagerly waiting for Mora when she came home. They were both smiling. This was a different kind of excited energy, not the sort of dreadful... *we are in danger* anxiety, which they had been experiencing lately, but rather something her two friends were bursting to tell her.

"What's going on?" Mora asked with wariness.

"Something amazing," said Orenda. "As far as I know, this has never happened."

"Can you be specific, please?" Mora understood this was happy excitement, but she was tired, hungry, and overworked and did not have much patience. She wanted them to get to the point.

Bi answered her. She was not as excitable as Orenda. She had not grown up with the openness the local people shared regarding the Star People. For her, they were more of a legend. Most people in the Eastern Empire thought they were mythical beings, something from stories you made up to entertain children. When she confirmed they were real, and she knew for a fact that they once had a relationship with her ancestors, that opened a lot of questions she didn't have a way of answering. Seeing them here, in person, amazed her as much as it did Mora. But never would she ever have thought this would happen. "The Star People, they requested a personal audience with us."

Mora stood there with a puzzled expression.

Asha had come down when she heard Mora arrive and caught the last statement. Before Mora could respond, Asha said, "They what?" The others turned to look at her.

"They asked to meet the three of us—Orenda, Mora, and me," Bi said.

"When?" asked Mora.

"This evening, just after sunset, so we can travel safely through the city. They contacted Orenda yesterday and gave her the coordinates."

"Then I better shower, change into something clean, and eat. And I need a nap. I was up all night."

"I'll make you some food," Orenda offered.

"Before we go, I wanted to share something with you all." Bi brought out a small book. "I am not an artist like Orenda, but when I first arrived here, and after I was attacked by Askook and Chayton in the forest, I evaded capture by entering a cave. I had dreams about the entire event for months. That's how I was able to find the hidden entrance. The cave was used by the Wen long ago but must have been forgotten. Inside, the walls were covered in amazing petroglyphs, which tell a story about the Star People. I tried to copy them into this notebook." She laid her little book on the table so the others could take a look, then Asha squeezed in behind them to look at the drawings.

Asha was the first to comment. "This means they were watching the Wen long before their official contact. And they were seen too! The natives might have thought of them as gods."

Orenda was fascinated by the art. "This is amazing, Bi. I hope one day you can show me where this place is."

"The story interests me most," Asha said. "This is our history! I'd like to make a copy."

As Mora wandered away, Asha asked more questions about the figures Bi had drawn.

Mora excused herself to shower while her friends continued to chat about the aliens, and Orenda cooked breakfast.

***

Mora was so wrapped up in her own work that Bi's drawings were a distraction she chose to ignore. She was close to completing her portal design but had still not come up with the solution which would identify the alternate timelines. She knew she had a working model. The machine accurately transported people from one portal to the next in this world. She had tested the new portal herself. But her back-door access to other timelines was still in question. They were already making plans for reproduction and distribution. Mora hesitated to announce the product until she was satisfied with the model and had done more tests.

Her mind was completely focused on her portal design and function. As she showered, fixed her hair, and dressed, she was going over every detail of her design in her mind... As she ate, surrounded by her friends, she hardly noticed what the others were talking about or doing.

On the exterior, her portal looked like a capsule, similar in appearance to the lift in Zamora's house. It was a clear, round tube. But the top was domed and made of energy crystal. On the base was a round plate containing all the mechanical components. A portion of the tube extended up from the base, waist-high, made of ferrebast. Along the edge were the controls and buttons that programmed the destinations. She expected destination hubs would be set up in major cities first.

Mora's mind reached out to various memory imprints from books and scientific journals she'd read. Everything from string theory and quantum field theory to super-symmetry, and every aspect of fundamental physics, in an attempt to solve the puzzle of the multiverse. She even reviewed an ancient Old-World document about atomism, which proposed infinite parallel worlds that arose from the collision of atoms. She was not going to dismiss even the slightest chance that inspiration might come from an unexpected source. The physics community had been debating the various multiverse theories for ages.

Here in Wendat, she did not find a single reference to theories related to a multiverse, which she found rather strange. Now she had proof that they exist, or rather, *she* was proof they exist. Yet she still didn't know how it happened. She only knew, beyond any doubt that there are parallel worlds, and she wanted to get back to her own without getting lost.

76

TOUCHED BY THE STARS

Orenda's coordinates led them to an elegant penthouse apartment in a building set aside for council members who visited on business trips from other regions. The building and the apartment were unlocked. Someone prepared it for their visit but didn't stay. They were instructed to wait outside, which was puzzling, and they were questioning what it meant when they were traveling up the lift. Entering the place alone, like they were trespassing, gave them an odd sensation of not belonging.

A striking view of Muwioni was the first thing to capture their attention. Floor-to-ceiling windows looked out onto a large garden terrace. Now they understood. They moved through the apartment without a care, eager to meet the Star People on the terrace, but they were alone.

The sunset's last glimmerings were reflected on the surface of the tallest crystal domes. The setting sun painted the sky in an orange blush; the fluffy clouds were tinted green against dark purple storm clouds further away in the west. They could see beyond the city limits as the sun dropped behind the mountains.

Bi was standing at the railing of the terrace, looking east, and suddenly it was all familiar. She was here long ago, in a fever dream. She turned to the others. "I've been here before, in a lucid dream!"

The other two came near and stood with her. They also turned their attention eastward as the first moon rose over the horizon. It was huge with a reddish tint. "What do you call the first moon to rise again?" Mora asked.

"We call the bright moon Ifa, the chief's son," Orenda answered. "The Zenda call him the prince, a herald of change."

In the distance, close to Ifa, a bright spot of light appeared, and it was moving. No one spoke. They were all captivated by this unusual sight. As it came closer, it looked like a shining golden orb. Transfixed now, they could hardly breathe. Then it split into three and shot forward. Caught off guard, they had no time to react. They were each encased separately in an effervescent semblance, which lifted their bodies slightly to float above the terrace.

They hovered with their arms at their sides, their palms spread open and their fingers wide apart. Their heads were tilted back, and their eyes rolled up. Seemingly supported by the light-force surrounding them. The force which held them was like a pulsing heartbeat. Information flowed into their implants. Images flitted through their minds, filling them with new understanding and knowledge.

Then the energy within the orb was pulled up and back, the luminosity was swallowed into the implants at the base of their skulls. A sensation like liquid light pouring into them, a floodlight igniting in their heads, tingling shivers running across their bodies. Then suddenly, they were once again on their feet. A little shaky and disoriented.

The night was dark. Ifa now was higher in the sky. Maybe an hour had passed in what felt like only a moment. No lights were illuminating the apartment. Everything around them felt peculiar, in a way they couldn't vocalize... remote, might be the right word, as if the place were now stranger than before. Their paradigm had shifted, making the world a little unfamiliar. The city glowed below them, and the sky was full of stars. They only had to look at each other to understand they all were experiencing the same sense of awe.

They stood for a while in silence. When it was apparent, there would be no personal contact with the Star People, and they'd gotten what they came for, they moved inside. The empty darkness of the place was bleak and gave them pause. Mora stopped in the living room. "Wait, let's sit here for a while and talk. I think it would be better to share what we received with each other and no one else, at least for now."

Orenda and Bi agreed. They signaled the orb bulbs for the soft glow they provided. In the penthouse, they were removed from the street noise. They sat for a time still pondering the experience. It was like coming off a boat and not having your land legs yet. A sense of disorientation stayed with them.

Bi was the first to speak. "Before I came here and when I was still in training, I had this vision, and I didn't know what it meant. It differed from any other lucid dream I'd had. Usually, I was shown a way to avoid trouble, or I was warned of difficulties to come, people I could trust, people I should be wary of. This vision was different. I had no way of knowing it was related to the Star People."

The others said nothing, and after a moment Bi continued.

"One of the first things I saw when I arrived at Wendat was that cave with ancient pictographic stories. I recognize now it's a story of transference. Something came out of the sky to touch the tribal members. The drawings showed a circle surrounding the figures, with lines radiating out from each of them. This, what we just experienced, has happened before. If this is how they transfer knowledge to us, why do they need to show themselves at all? Why do they come and meet with your council?"

Mora answered because she understood the power of recognition. "Letting themselves be seen has a psychological impact on the population. It leaves no doubt there are those unlike themselves, the alienness is sobering. It leaves no doubt that they are in control and far more advanced. It renders respect from the masses."

"The Wen don't fear them," Bi said. "Do you think the implants remove such worries?"

Orenda, who didn't have such sentiments about the Aliens, raised her brow ridge. "The Wen have benefitted from our relationship with the Star People. If the implant suppresses instinctual fear of others, who are unlike ourselves, that is helpful. Fear would breed mistrust, and panic."

"I suppose that is true." Mora agreed. "I admit to having questions about their intentions. Misgivings, you might say. But this experience..." She struggled to describe her feelings. "I'm just overwhelmed with gratitude."

The three of them shared generalizations about their experiences. All spoke of a sense of completion. Even though the tasks they were given were nowhere near finished, they described a feeling of being supported and empowered. The confusion and worries they'd had before were removed. Leaving contentment in its place. They described it as euphoric. All heavy concerns lifted.

"I assume we each learned something different here today. Do you want to share the specifics of your experience?" asked Orenda.

"I can't share the details," Mora said, "but I have the answers now. I understand how to get home."

Bi looked at her. "What about Zamora? She's in your world. What will happen to her?"

"I have the fundamental principles of multiverse travel now. She can return home too, but that will be her decision. Honestly, I don't know Zamora. Just because she's my counterpart doesn't mean we have the same values. I have more questions about what happened to her there, and what she's done in my absence. But I can't let all of that worry me at this point."

Bi nodded. "I learned I must also return home. I have a new mission. But not without some difficulties along the way. Orenda, I need to meet your aunt and tell her who I am."

"I know. I'll arrange it as soon as Coso is well enough to return to work." She was quiet for a moment, then shared more. "I was also told I will be a medicine guardian. It was not the path I wanted, but I finally understand why I'm different and how it serves a greater purpose. Now I also see clearly how the three of us are connected, and why we had to meet."

77

PREPARATIONS

When Mora and her roommates arrived back at Zamora's place, Tokala and Yuma were waiting for them. As soon as they all got indoors under the lights, the three of them were sobered by what they saw. Their friends had been in some kind of skirmish. "What happened?"

"Asha and I had just returned from the reservation," Tokala said. "I was picking up Yuma to buy medical herbs and other supplies. We do the buying every month, but because Kinache keeps messing with our stores, we were running low on some items, and Holata Tyee blamed us."

"What happened next?"

"When we stepped out of the vehicle, Asha and I... we were surrounded by a gang wearing Kuroo avatars. They grabbed and bound Asha and held me back as they put her in another transport. They were speaking a Zendali dialect which I wasn't able to understand. I can't tell you where they took her."

"And how did *this* happen?" Mora was referring to the scuffs and bruises both of them had.

"Yuma was coming out of Holata Tyee's compound to meet us. He jumped the one who was holding me. I also struggled, trying to get free, but there were a lot of them and it was impossible to stop what they were doing to Asha. They even laughed at us, threw me to the ground, and drove off with her. I should have taken those self-defense lessons. I felt so powerless."

"Let me clean those cuts. I have the supplies you left here for Bi in the bathroom." Orenda went to fetch the ointments and bandages.

"Have you notified anyone else, Mato maybe?" asked Mora.

Yuma shook his head. "No, we came directly here. We weren't sure who to trust."

Mora activated her communication device and put in Mato's personal code. He answered immediately. "Mora? It's late. What's wrong?"

"Asha was taken; it was that gang that runs with Tao. They wore the avatars of Amon Kuroo. So, we can't identify them. They also assaulted Tokala Luta and Yuma."

Mato started to ask specifics about what happened, but Mora stopped him. "Hold on, let me put you up on the receptor screen and you can ask them yourself." Mato's face appeared larger than life, looking worried.

"Yuma, when you came out of Holata Tyee's compound, was that when you were first aware those youths were at the house? They were not previously inside with the medicine guardian?"

"Honestly, I'm not sure. I was in the stockroom almost all-day doing inventory, preparing to go with Tokala when they got back."

"So, it is possible they were in the house and came out before you did when they realized someone had driven up?"

"I did hear some people talking with her, but I didn't look to see who it was. You might be right. I'm sorry, I can't be sure."

Mato pursed his lips and looked upward, like he was thinking. "Were any Wen involved in the abduction?"

"I don't think so. The Order of Amon Kuroo doesn't let the Wen wear their Avatars. All Order members are Zenda purebloods. They promise membership to the local youth, but it hasn't happened as far as I'm aware. The native avatars are usually family totems."

Mato nodded, wondering how this young fellow had so much information about a secret organization that he and the council were only recently made aware of. "Any other details you're able to provide that might help us identify those who took Asha?"

Tokala Luta came forward. "Maybe... Asha behaved differently with one of them as if she knew him. They argued in a more personal way. I think he might have been her brother Tao."

After a moment of silence, Mora asked Mato, "What did you learn from the security recordings at Coso Winnemucca's place?"

"We have identified all those who were involved, and have those recordings as well as the testimonies of her staff."

"Then what are you waiting for?"

"Algon finished production of the first batch of portals, and they were shipped for distribution in Zenda a week ago. We just learned this today. The portals should be in place by now. We believe the Order of Amon Kuroo is planning to move something through these portals."

At that moment, Bi stepped up to be seen by Mato. He had talked to her previously, but he had never seen her face. "I know what they will do."

Mato realized who she was. "Hello Bi, what information can you give me?"

"They are going to bring weapons to Wendat. The kind which isn't allowed by treaty, and would never pass inspection at the importation docks. They plan to kill the Pinks at the reservations. All of them, all reservations, will be attacked at once. This will put the treaty between your countries at default, and while Prince Nakhadot is occupied with this, they will take over his throne and kill him if they can. You should warn them all!"

Mato was alarmed. He had found the information Bi gave him previously was, in every way, accurate. He had no reason to doubt her now, but he was stunned by the details she had just outlined. "Everywhere, at once?"

"Yes, and the one who is directing the operation is staying at the hotel." She gave him a description of the delegate she had seen who wore the medallion from her country. "Wait, I also have a drawing of him." She picked up her notebook and held an open page up to the screen. "This is the one. Sorry, I am not a talented artist like Orenda."

Mora thought about the weapons. "Mato, this might be a good time to tell you I can stop them from sending the weapons through the portals. But I need to go to the lab where I built the interface."

Mato had a doubtful expression. "How can you stop them, Mora?"

"I installed a back door into the design of the portals that the university sold to the Sovereign Nation."

"Which means what, exactly?"

"It means I can turn off the portals if necessary, and it seems like this is one of those circumstances where that would be advisable."

"Are you telling me you saw this coming?"

Both Orenda and Bi were looking at her in surprise too.

"I'm not a visionary." Mora shook her head. "I kept thinking things didn't quite add up. I was also mad about how the university treated me. And Algon getting all the credit for my invention." The others were staring at her, so she said defensively, "You have to admit, despite my hurt feelings, there was obvious favoritism going on in regard to the production contract. It looked like they were working too closely with Zendali investors, supporting their bid. What I did was insurance. I guess I never expected I would actually need to use it."

"Well, I'm happy you did. I will have someone pick you up and take you to the lab. Considering we don't know when they're planning to transport the weapons, we should disable the portals as soon as possible."

Bi was shaking her head. "I disagree. You need to have evidence of their illegal actions. You need to catch them with those weapons in hand."

Mato considered her suggestion. "I would agree if we knew where they were going to bring them in. But once they're armed, they can kill my team as well as the Pinks."

Mora asked, "Don't you have an arsenal for defense?"

"We don't produce the kind of weapons that the Sovereign Nation does. We didn't need them."

"Well, what do you have to protect yourselves? Honestly, you never imagined you might go to war with them?"

"No, and I suppose it was naïve to trust their treaty."

Mora huffed in exasperation. Thinking about her own world and all the treaties the natives agreed to, which were broken. "What weapons do you have, Mato?"

"We make tranquilizer rifles, which are used when culling animals from a herd or to tag them when monitoring migrations. Also, there are batons with an electric charge, enough to disable someone momentarily. We have crossbows, used for hunting, and various hand weapons like knives, the axe, and other kinds of blades designed for other uses."

"The Order of Amon Kuroo will have gathered all of those as well."

"Their visas do not allow them to obtain or possess weapons."

"And you think those laws will prevent them? It's why they endorsed your wayward youth. The Wen could buy the things which foreigners could not."

Orenda added: "We also have blow-guns. They're more popular on the southern continent of Wendat, but we have some of them here, they can be used from a distance to shoot poison darts and take down an attacker."

"Do we have anyone here skilled in their use, though? If not, someone could easily disable a member of our team if the dart didn't hit the right target." Yuma countered.

"I have an idea," said Bi. "Mato, could you come here so we can discuss this in person? Then, if you need to take Mora to the lab, you can go together after we talk."

Tokala Luta stepped closer and said, "Meanwhile, make contact with all the reservation Sanctuary Officers. Inform them of the imminent attack, and tell them to notify the Pinks of what is coming, so they can prepare."

78

Discovery

M ora contacted Algon, asking for the list of locations where the portals were distributed on Wendat. She watched him on her receptor screen. He had the bewildered look of someone exhausted, and he was also distressed and annoyed.

Algon was reluctant at first, hedging. "That's confidential. I am not allowed to say."

She had to explain what they suspected the Zendali investors were using the portals for. Realizing this was a criminal exception, he finally agreed to send the list to her and Mato.

"I used to see all the ways you are like Zamora, but now I cannot help but be painfully aware of how much you are not. You're selfishly focused on your own losses, and your actions are careless. You have no idea how what you do impacts everyone around you."

"Well, thank you for your concise appraisal of my worth."

"Your worth? You cannot fathom how narrow-minded that sounds. They took Asha today! Do you have any idea what they will do to her?"

Mora's indignation was abruptly extinguished at the mention of her friend's abduction. "Yes, I am aware, Algon, they will press her for information, and I have seen the evidence of her father's temper."

"The two of you created a mind-map giving the Pinks cultural data. Did you really think it wouldn't be discovered? I'm sure she has taken all the blame onto herself. That is true friendship, Mora. But they will do more than press her for more information, because your Mind-Map contains details she shouldn't know."

"How do you have this information, Algon? Did Asha tell you?"

"I overhear conversations. The investors are always hanging around, waiting anxiously and pushing my production team to work longer hours. I heard them talking about what you two did."

She was sobered by the fact that Asha was at risk for something she had chosen to include, some history and accomplishments of those countries in her world. "We understood discovery was likely at some point. But we both agreed it was something we wanted to give them. How is what I did selfish, Algon? I put myself at risk for the Pinks."

"You just wanted something to do because you lost control of your portal technology, right? You were angry and bored, and you don't like to be idle. But you didn't consider how breaking our treaties would cause repercussions? Don't think the Pinks won't be punished as well!"

"You mean I don't think about how my actions affect you? Because you find it inconvenient to be associated with the Fog while working for a Zenda company! And in regard to what I did with the Pinks, Asha and I had our priorities straight!"

Mora stopped abruptly. She had been shouting and realized this exchange revealed a lot of resentment on both sides. She thought they'd resolved things between them, but obviously, there was still some anger under the surface.

"Look, Algon," she said with a sigh, "arguing about this won't help. I need to get to work on this for Mato."

He pressed his lips together, clearly still angry.

"It's not likely her own family will do much harm to her," Mora said. "We will find her."

"Her father is the leader of the Order. Or at least he is taking lead, here in Muwioni. What matters is simple. Ziyad is more concerned with finding you and Bi than he cares about his daughter's welfare, and he is convinced now that she knows who you are. He believes she has betrayed their country. They're saying she's in league with radicals, and by radicals he means the Fog."

"Radicals? That's rich, him calling us radicals!"

"Now do you understand how dangerous your actions have been?"

"Are you going to turn me over to Ziyad to save her, then? Is that your plan?"

"Exposing you would only bring suspicion onto me. It would not help Asha."

"Then tell me why you are wasting my time with these accusations?"

He shook his head dejectedly. "I don't know how to help Asha. I'm furious with you both and scared."

Mora realized now that his eyes were watering. He was trying to hold back his tears.

"I'm worried," he said with exasperation. "And I'm powerless to help her."

Mora felt sorry for him. "All right, I understand, Algon. We will rescue Asha. And then we will find a way to keep them from taking her back. Would she be able to ask for asylum?"

Algon looked surprised. The thought had not occurred to him. "That has never been done. Only the Pinks and the Fog seek asylum. There has never been a need for a pureblood to seek refuge here."

"Well, there is a first time for everything."

79

DISGRACE

Bi was right. Catching the Order of Amon Kuroo with the weapons was necessary, but they only needed to find one transfer point, and Algon had provided the crucial list of where the portals were installed in Muwioni.

Mora discovered one of the portals was set up in the house where Bi had been captive. She notified Mato, who was already organizing the teams for the local defensive response. He also contacted the other councils. They had appointed deputies and were coordinating various groups to take action on every reservation in Wendat. In the city of Muwioni, Mato established teams who were currently on their way to each remote village near the west coast reservations.

When his local team had rescued the Pinks who work for Coso, he ordered his team to leave no sign of entry. They released the Pinks, documented what they found, and then covered their tracks as they left. Obviously, it worked because the rebels seemed confident that their hideout had not been exposed. Mato's team made it look like the Pinks had escaped on their own. Considering there had been no consequences from the escape of their prisoners; they carried on using the safe house.

The utter stupidity of the foreign agents surprised Mato. Hearing they had returned and set up a portal at that location showed him how confident they were. "Either they're very bold or completely foolish. Be careful."

With a degree of wariness, the squad advanced, looking for traps or any surveillance equipment like Coso had installed at her home. But they found nothing of the sort. Mato's team surrounded the building at a distance, hidden by the foliage. They remained out of sight, waiting for his orders.

Mato didn't trust Algon with their plan, but to get his cooperation, Mora had explained to Algon they expected to find Asha at one of these locations. Algon had been more than willing to help once he understood what was at stake. Mora also chose not to tell Algon about the back-door access to the portals. Now that she was at her lab with her interface device, she could see when any portal was activated. She took a guess that Tao and Ziyad would be at the local safe-house, where Bi had previously been taken. She hoped the portal there would be one of the first to be used.

As soon as that portal was activated, Mora shut down all others. She let the transfer take place at only the location where she expected to find Ziyad. Several other portals were stopped mid-transfer. She was not sure what the result would be. Maybe some of the equipment would come through. It could deform the items during the transfer process because it was incomplete. Or would her actions prohibit the shipment altogether? She had never done experiments with partial transfers. Mato's team waited for the assailants in the house to come out. When they emerged, they were wearing the Avatars representing the Order of Amon Kuroo. Black-winged birds with red glowing eyes, and they carried rapid-fire projectile weapons. They had organized for an assault. Several vehicles were standing by, ready to transport them.

***

Surprise was Mato's only advantage. His team immediately took down three of them with tranquilizer darts. When they fell, the others began to shoot into the trees. Two on Mato's team were shot, but not killed. They were bleeding badly. A blow dart hit another member of the rebels, who was holding a weapon and looking confused. His avatar winked out as he fell, the weapon clattering to the ground. The remaining target with a weapon tried to run back into the house. "Shot him!" Mato yelled. An arrow sailed swiftly and pierced the escaping rebel in the back.

Having heard the weapons fired, others ran out of the house. Mato's team deployed another round of tranquilizer darts, which took out only two of the moving targets. The rebels were also firing their weapons as they ran, but in their haste, the projectiles mostly hit the ground or their own transport vehicles. Someone on Mato's team threw an axe, cleaving the forward shooter's head. The remaining assailant stopped, seeing they were caught, put down his weapon, and raised his hands in surrender.

Once all the assailants were bound, Mato's team entered the house and found several native youths inside. They were not wearing the Avatars like the others. Gunfire burst through the walls, hitting the furniture but missing the extraction team. When their ammunition ran out, tranquilizer darts took the last of the native youth down.

"Find Ziyad!" Mato ordered, and the team moved through the house to clear each room in search of the Zendali in charge.

When they returned to the main room, they shook their heads. "Ziyad isn't here. But we found his daughter."

Asha was locked in one of the rooms. She was wearing a collar like they had put on Bi. Her arm was broken, and they had tortured her in the electric chair. They carried her out unconscious.

When the Avatars were all deactivated, they found it was Tao who surrendered. He was leading this group of rebels and preparing for a raid on the local reservation.

"Where is your father?" Mato demanded. Tao stared back in defiance and refused to speak. Mato didn't honestly expect him to reply, but he spent a little of his frustration by shouting at him.

As his team was loading the prisoners for transport, Mato got a call from Mora.

"The other portal station is closer to Nisnap reservation. There must be other rebels there. Do you have a team on the way?"

"There's a team in route to cut them off. The rebels are unarmed, right?"

Mora sighed with frustration. She'd blocked the transfer of artillery, but that didn't mean they won't have other weapons, which she'd already warned him about. "Don't count on it." She warned.

Mato made a groaning sort of sigh, indicating he understood.

Mora was about to disengage when something occurred to her.

"Did you discover why the reports of missing Pinks were not reaching the council?"

"We brought in the nephew of the sanctuary officer. That was his job. After hours of questioning, he finally admitted that he had tossed out those reports. He was bribed."

"Disposed of them? Bribed! Did he tell you why? Is he in cahoots with the Amun Kuroo? What about the officer himself? Is he reliable? Do you trust him to warn the residents?"

"I don't know Mora. We notified him. We haven't gotten a response."

80

Unexpected Fallout

I nside another forest cabin near the Nisnap Reservation Farms, a contingent of young Zendali and a few Wen youth waited for Tao.

"Get Tao on your receptor. He's late! Tell him that mongrel gadget malfunctioned!"

The native youth cringed, not wanting to be the one to bring Tao that news. "We don't need the Zenda armaments. The Pinks don't fight."

Another Zendali approached. "I just tried to reach the other team. No answer. They must be on their way."

The young Zendali in charge kicked the portal and cursed. The much-anticipated firearms clogged the machine in a mangled mess, broken and worthless. He and the others had been excited to use them. They had joked about the bloodbath such an instrument would cause. "We have explosives?"

The native answered. "Yes, from the mining company, we took a whole box."

With a sardonic smile, he gave the order to proceed. "If their gate is closed, we'll blow it open!" They were all splintered, ramped-up on adrenaline, and eager for the fight. They wanted to prove themselves, and they were not about to back down.

Time was also an issue. The attacks were supposed to happen all at once. The entire gang was overly confident in their prowess, having been encouraged toward violence for months.

The Zendali in the lead clapped the native recruit on his back. "You're right. The Pinks will be easy targets. Brute force should be enough. You want to be a warrior, right? Grab a knife, let's take some scalps!"

Armed with hunting knives and a crossbow that none of them were trained to use, they headed out.

By the time Mato's team arrived at the cabin, the place was empty. They found some broken and mangled parts in the portal box. At which point they realized the radicals had chosen to go forward without the artillery. Recognizing the gravity of the situation, they left in haste, expecting to find a massacre on the reservation.

***

"Have you intercepted the rebels?" Mato shouted into his receptor device.

"We're too late. The place is empty."

"Are they armed?"

"The portal is full of mangled weapons, I assume none of them came through whole."

"Use any means possible to stop them."

"You're giving permission to kill?" This wasn't the Wendat way, but nothing about this situation was normal.

Mato paused before answering. "If they resist, do what you must. We have had casualties here. Expect them to have acquired other weapons. They're dangerous, and they intend to kill."

"We have reports that native youths are among this group."

"They are in league with the Zendali rebels. They have made their choice."

Recognizing the gravity of the situation, they left in haste, expecting to find a massacre at the Nisnap reservation.

81

ΛTTΛCK ΛT NISNΛP

Z ote ran from the lodge house and grabbed the bell that was sometimes used to call general meetings and began to hank the cord. The clang rang loud and harsh, sounding an alarm through the Nisnap community. Pinks began to run tward the building and gather. Zote shouted to the crowd, "They're coming for us! The Zendali are attacking! The Sanctuary officer just called to warn us."

Osgyth stepped up next to address the crowd. "Get your tools! Warn anyone you meet. Prepare for engagement!"

Everyone dispersed. As they ran, they told others who were headed toward the lodge to get their weapons.

The community began to gather in the clearing near the gates. Moson, Ganus, Xwell and Burn were some of the biggest men in the community, well-muscled from their heavy labor. They moved with confidence, passing out tools and knives to anyone empty-handed.

The sanctuary officer arrived, skidding through the open gates. He jumped from his vehicle with haste, unsure what to make of the gathered Pinks. Instead of following his advice and hiding in the root cellars, they were armed with tools! The sanctuary officer was beside himself with stress, and his eyes grew wider when he understood they planned to engage their attackers.

"What is happening here? What do they think they're going to do with those farming implements?" The officer asked. He was shaking with fright.

"It might be best if you leave, wait this out in the safety of your home," Zoete told him.

"Go home?" He asked in confusion. "Even if I wanted to, it is too late!" He was a small native, accustomed to the security of his desk job. He had never had to deal with any trouble of this kind.

"I believe you're out of your element." Frost told him as she gently touched his shoulder to calm him. "You had better come with us."

The officer looked around him with wild eyes. "This is wrong. You will all be killed. You need to hide!"

Frost, who was pregnant, took him aside. "That is a good idea. Would you be willing to go with me and the children into hiding? To protect us, of course."

He readily agreed, and Frost led him to the root cellars.

The big-boned, no-nonsense female Rosewallon had picked up the fighting arts Mora taught them like it was second nature. She gathered all the able-bodied women and organized their plan of defense. They all had cropped their hair after the brutal death of one of their own.

"You might die today, but if you do, it will be protecting our home and a future for our children."

No cheer followed, only solemn nods and some tears. They realized she was right. This might be the day they lost loved ones, or they might die themselves, and it was worth the risk.

Snorri was the second biggest female in the camp. Tall, robust, and especially strong. She'd been practicing with some tools. The scythe was her weapon of choice. Now she took a stand in front to address the others, holding her weapon high. She was filled with the kind of fury and indignation that tends to motivate others.

"We have suffered for generations!" she said. "This is our chance at freedom. It is an honor to defend our home with our lives. If we don't, there is nothing worth living for! So, put aside your remorse and fear. Now it is time for payback! Let's make Mora proud!"

As if to punctuate her declaration, a loud boom shook the ground, and the gate burst inward, the wooden fragments scattering like tiny sharp arrows, some finding flesh to pierce. Although bloodied from this, the Pinks stood ready and did not run. Rebels dressed in the Avatars of Amon Kuroo ran through the entrance, blades in hand. A fearsome sight.

The Pinks did not run. Wielding their sharp tools, they stood ready to engage. There was some confusion. The rebels expected a slaughter, not a fight. An arrow was shot by a Zendali with a bow, but it flew wide and hit the building. Mason threw his axe at the archer while he was fumbling with the bow, trying to notch a second arrow. It cut deep into the man's shoulder, nearly severing it from his body. Blood spurted out and covered the other attackers near him. He took a few steps as he attempted to pull the axe away, yelling in agony.

Then, someone in the community blew a horn. A haunting sound, blown loud and clear, followed by a war cry from some old fable in the histories Mora had given them. With an impassioned display of rage, the Pinks rushed forward, penetrating the ranks of their attackers. It was all so unexpected. Pinks were known to be docile creatures. They were supposed to cower and run.

These young Zendali who were devoted to the Order, were from wealthy nationalist families. They had never actually fought anyone with knives or engaged in any sort of hand-to-hand combat. The only drills they had practiced back home were in the use of the rapid-fire projectile weapons. They knew how to pull a trigger from a distance and hit a target. But there were no such weapons in their hands and no safe distance from this mob.

In a state of shock, the Amon Kuroo acolytes stood frozen in place as the Pinks ran, screaming in fury toward them. Their scary black avatars with burning red eyes were designed to put awe and fright into the minds of anyone who encountered them. They had no effect on these Pinks. The rebels were bumped and thrashed from every direction. Their avatars blinked and scuttled.

The natives among them were bewildered to see their heroes looking foolish. The Order had made them into the vilest sort of bullies and taught them the power of intimidation. But on this day, everything was falling apart. They didn't feel proud anymore. They too, were clobbered under a barrage of garden tools. Nothing could have been more demoralizing.

The action got messy. One of the Amon Kuroo came too close to Snorri, threatening her with his knife and using ugly profanity. She chopped off his head with one quick slice of her blade, and the red eyes of his avatar winked off. Seeing this, the other females surrounded their attackers and moved in. Avoided most of the jabs from the raider's knives and in some cases were able to disarm them. After that, they kicked and beat them down until Xwell intervened. "It's enough. Tie them."

Zoete was on her back while one of the Amon Kuroo cut a gash into her pale blue hairline. "You stupid bitch, you robbed us of our trophies!" The raiders had expected considerable profits from taking scalps after their kills, but the Pinks in this community had cropped hair. Blood soaked into Zoete's facial fur and quickly soaked her hair. She squirmed and tried to dislodge him, but he was kneeling on her shoulders. Suddenly, he slumped forward when Moson hit him on the head with a shovel. He kicked the unconscious Zendali off of Zoete and then turned to catch another with a low gut punch with the end of the shovel handle.

Ganus was in a headlock. He'd forgotten everything Mora taught him the moment the fight began. There were ways to get out of such a hold, but it was too late. Instead, he managed to stab the leg of the Zendali who was choking him, and the hold released just enough for him to turn and punch his attacker in the face. The Kuroo Avatar deactivated, revealing the terrified face of the Zendali youth. Ganus hit him again to knock him out.

Several fights were happening at once. It was a melee of furious action. Burn used his tail to trip his assailant, who was about to hit him, then gave him a punch in the throat which left him gagging on the ground. Unica knocked her attacker off balance then pinned him down with a pitchfork through his wrist and clothing. This Zendali was screaming as his blood soaked the ground. One by one, the assailants were subdued and then bound.

"You'll have trouble over that," Burn said, he pointed to the head on the ground.

Snorri still held the scythe covered in the Zendali's blood that had sprayed all over her.

"Are you hurt, or is all of that his blood?"

"Just minor injuries, don't worry. I will take the punishment. I am not sorry."

At that moment, Mato's men arrived, screeching through the crushed gates in a mad rush. The Amon Kuroo had a good head start, and they expected to find the Pinks dead or overcome. Instead, they found all the raiders on the ground, bound, and tied.

Evidence of violence and damage was apparent, crimson dripping from cuts into the Pink's wan fur. Swollen eyes and broken noses. A few were limping around, or on the ground nursing an injured arm or rib. But all the Pinks were alive! Even more shocking, the Amon Kuroo and their native accomplices were utterly defeated.

One Zendali had an axe in his shoulder. He might lose the arm, but he was alive. Only one fatality, too obvious to miss... Snorri stood over the decapitated head. "Did you do this?" The leader of Mato's Squad asked her.

She nodded. "It was either him or me. I defended my home."

The team was speechless. Then the leader turned to the others in his squad. "Gather the assailants." He faced Snorri. "I know it was self-defense, but what happens now will depend on a decision by the council. I'll have to take you with us."

Snorri nodded. "I expected as much."

She wasn't taken as a prisoner, nor was she handled roughly. The men were all a little in awe of her. The blood changed her pale fur to crimson. It was a sobering sight. As they walked toward the vehicle, the team leader asked her, "Are you hurt? Do you need a doctor?"

"I think I just need a shower." She smiled a little at him, and his eyes got wide with respect.

82

JUDGMENT

C ouncil member Coso Winnemucca stood at the front of the council chambers, where all who entered could see she was on her feet and somewhat recovered. Most of the hair on her head had been shaved for the surgery to reattach her scalp. That side of her head now sprouted a light grey fuzz. Through it, the red scar circling her crown could be seen. At the sides and back of her head, some long hair remained, this was braided with beads and shells, the work of her niece Orenda, who insisted she not cut it.

The other members of the council were seated, facing the crowd. "This will be rather historic, I imagine," Coso spoke softly so only Mato, who was beside her, could hear.

In response, he chuckled. "That's putting it mildly."

Not all reservations had fared well during the attacks, even with some warning and the help of the deputies the councils appointed to protect the Pinks. No one was prepared for such an incursion. There had been no violence between the tribes in generations. The only saving grace was the fact that the aggressors weren't able to arm themselves with high-power weapons. All portals failed when Mora shut them down. The Amon Kuroo were reduced to fighting the deputies and Pinks in hand-to-hand combat with nothing more than knives. They tallied injuries and deaths on both sides. The Pinks at the other reservations were unprepared and lacked the confidence or know-how to fight. Most of the Pinks who tried to defend themselves were killed.

Snorri, who had acted in self-defense, was given a room with a shower and clean garments. She rested there until it was time to face the council.

Ziyad was found on a private yacht prepared to flee the country with some investors from the portal company, along with the Golden twins and a few other wealthy Zendali. Mato's team also took Tao and the local members of the Order into confinement pending this trial. The other members of Amon Kuroo who were detained at the reservations were all brought to the council today for judgment.

Also in attendance at these hearings was Chief Achak Tawa Kuroo. His family totem was a Kuroo. Having been especially offended by the appropriation of his family totem, he made the off-season trip to Muwioni to observe what measures would be taken to correct the damage to his honorable tribe.

Chief Achak Tawa Kuroo wore traditional clothing; he was not swayed by the fashions of foreigners. He frowned upon anyone who put foreign culture above native tradition. He despised coming to the cities where the old ways were being replaced by eccentric imports like avatars and other foreign styles and products. The darkening of native pelts to look more Zendali offended him the most. The Chief was an acquaintance and staunch supporter of Dean Comcomly Hardihood and agreed wholeheartedly that something had to be done to diminish the foreign influence on Wendat.

His dark greenish fur and rusty brown hair were salted with white, showing his age. Everything about him looked weathered by the elements. He was stoic and grim. Tall, and lean, with big ear fans that stuck out from the side of his dominant cheekbones and a high forehead. His lips were thin, and his nose protruded from his face more than was common. His hair was very long. The front portion pulled up into a pompadour and painted with white clay. The remaining hair hung in two long braids wrapped in white leather laces, ending with black Kuroo feathers. His entrance into the judgment hall caused people to turn and stare.

The chief scowled at the Zendali in custody, who were bound to their chairs on one side of the room, thirty-five in total. A few others were hospitalized. They would share in the judgment of the council set forth after today's deliberations. No doubt these foreigners were ignorant of what would happen to them today.

Waiting for the session to begin, the council members were quietly talking among themselves.

Coso, looking at the faces she was about to pass judgment on, said, "They expect special privileges. Look how smug they are."

Knowingly, Mato smiled at her. "Their guards overheard them complaining. Ziyad assured them that this fiasco would soon be over."

"Then our judgment will be a rude awakening."

"They believe themselves untouchable, and above the law of this country. They expect to be deported. I imagine they miss the comforts and entertainment of home." Matao said.

Ziyad and Tao were both bound and gagged. They had both been very vocal, Ziyad making demands and denying involvement, and Tao had been cursing and yelling threats. Now they burned with fury as they stared at the council. Coso wondered how they could cause so much damage without ever suspecting what they chanced to lose.

Snorri sat alone on the other side of the room, also facing the council members. As it was unlawful for Pinks to wield a weapon, she expected a harsh punishment. But she bore that guilt without remorse. Chief Kuroo took a seat next to her. She looked at him with some apprehension, her ear-fans flattening back, not understanding his intent at first. He did not turn his head, but he felt her fear. When he saw through the corner of his eye that her hand on the arm of her chair was trembling, he reached over and covered her hand reassuringly with his. He still didn't look at her, but she realized he was present to give his support. She straightened her back, lifted her chin, and tried to look brave.

The council government in each district had conferred. Deciding on a unilateral punishment. All members of the Amon Kuroo and any natives associated with their order would receive the same judgment today. The Order of Amon Kuroo was banned from reentry to Wendat. It was Coso who delivered the judgment for their northwest council.

"The Order of Amon Kuroo is now listed as a terrorist organization, and those who are affiliated with this organization here in Wendat, and in The Sovereign Zenda Nation have broken the treaty with Wendat. We have spoken with Prince Nakhadot, the true royal heir of Kemel, a descendant of King Nebtawi." She paused as a loud murmur rose from the Zendali, interrupting her speech. They looked at each other. A few glowered with vicious hostility.

A wealthy, pompous Zendali sitting behind Ziyad spoke up. "You have no authority to pass judgment on a citizen of the Sovereign Nation!" This was the one Bi had gathered information about at the hotel. His company bought the Portal contract. Then, produced and distributed the portals to import weapons. Coso also discovered that his ancestors had fought in a war with the Eastern Empire.

"Oh, but we do. When you applied for your visa to our country, you were required to receive our implants, and you were given documents that outlined the conditions for your stay in Wendat. Did any of you read that agreement?" She watched them look at each other with trepidation. "I find it curious that not one of you took the time to read what you signed. Especially since some of you are businessmen." She looked at the Zendali who had complained and then at Ziyad. "And some of you were the cunning masterminds behind these hostilities, for which you will be judged today." She shook her head, then continued. "That document clearly states that you will be held accountable under *our* laws while you are on our soil. You all agreed to this."

The room erupted in a clamor of complaints and bellowed curses.

"That is enough! You will be silent, or you too, will be gagged." The crowd quieted. Now they looked less assured of their fate. "Yes, that is correct. We have had communication with your prince. You evidently have no idea what is taking place in your own country."

Coso paused for a moment and turned to Chief Achak Tawa Kuroo. "I believe you have something to say before I continue."

The chief stood. His voice was deep and commanding. "You have appropriated our tribal identity for your criminal enterprise, bringing shame on my people by association. Reparations will be made to our people and to the Pinks for the injuries and lives you have taken. All your properties and credits have been seized to begin the process of mending your wrong deeds." Again, a stirring of moans and whispers went through the crowd. Exclamations and objections were made. The chief ignored them. "In addition, your Kuroo Totems will be destroyed and forbidden. No one will hide behind this disguise again, perpetrating unforgivable acts of war! And yes, we consider this a call to war." Having said his piece, he sat down again, waiting for Coso to continue.

She stood again, looking at the Zendali for a moment as she thought.

"But that is what you planned, isn't it?" she said. "You wanted a war. You wanted to gain control so you could continue the expansion wars of your ancestors. The Order of Amon Kuroo believes in the doctrine of the pure-bloods. You are radical nationalists of an old tradition." She looked at the chief. "It is unfortunate that the identifier of this ancient organization is the Kuroo, but they did not appropriate it from your tribe."

The chief looked as if he was about to stand in objection, but Coso Winnemucca held up her hand to stop him, a gesture meaning wait.

"The Kuroo is an ancient Zendali symbol of devoted love," she said. "It was the sacred companion of Wandrona. Therefore, long ago, it was adopted as the mark of the faithful for this secret order. They were bound by their belief that only the purest blood should rule the earth. They were the architects of the expansion wars."

Another murmur ran through the room, and Chief Kuroo looked displeased but did not object.

"However," Coso went on, "what these men do not realize is that the Kuroo also represents change, transformation, and intelligent insight. We need to adapt as times change and new information becomes available. Without the ability to change our course as we gather new evidence, we become dogmatic and stagnant, tied to the rules of order that no longer have meaning in our modern world. I pity you all because you have been misled and corrupted. The very people you relied upon to guide you, twisted your hearts and minds into something ugly." She was speaking to Tao and the members of his gang when she said these words. "Nevertheless, you are all old enough to make decisive choices, and you chose to bring harm to others. For this, you will be punished."

Now the complaints came all at once, an incoherent howl of agitation. Coso let them express their disapproval. And at the same time, she motioned to her colleagues, who brought forward a table that was piled with white rings. When the men saw what was before them, they became silent. They all had seen what had happened to the native youth who were fitted with the modifier. Some of them had been present when the Fog girl was tortured, and they understood the gravity of this device. Ziyad and Tao even more so, as they tried to remove it from Askook, resulting in his death. This was a permanent liability, which put him and the members of his order at risk.

"All members who took part in the violence, who were involved in the planning of this insurrection, or in any way broke treaties with Wendat, will be fitted with the Modifier, marking each of you with the stigma of a criminal. The devices which you see on the table before you were constructed to work in tandem with your implants. They're called modifiers because they're designed to encourage and amplify empathy, which you all seem to lack. If you ever cause harm to anyone again, you will feel their pain. If you are even in the room where someone is being harmed, you will feel their pain. It will be unavoidable, and you will suffer whatever they experience. This includes the suffering of animals, so it is unlikely any of you will hunt again or harm your pets. They are implanted on your dominant arm so that your every action will be a reminder of your crimes."

She paused for a moment while the other council members began to fit the white bands on the accused, who were bound to their chairs. Ziyad and Tao struggled, but the others accepted them with resignation.

"The Modifier is irreversible. If you attempt to remove them, it will be fatal." As some of you are aware, considering you experimented on one of your own."

This accusation caused a round of whispered questions.

"We have found the body of Askook. His modifier was surgically removed, and as promised, it killed him."

The room was suddenly silent as that sank in. The betrayal was clear. All the young members of this group had befriended Askook.

"His body was dumped in the sea. When his parents were questioned, we learned they were on the other side of the continent during the time Askook was killed. He could not have returned to his family, as all of you were led to believe."

As the manipulation and lies were coming to light. Some of the Zendali boys looked ashamed.

The council members moved through the rows fitting the modifiers on every wrist.

Coso continued: "To reiterate our Judgement... All your properties and business assets have been seized to help pay for damages. The Kuroo Avatars will be destroyed and outlawed. The Order of Amon Kuroo is registered as a terrorist organization. That means no further entry to any port, at any time, on the continent of Wendat. And you will be blocked from ever using the portals."

"This modifier is a gift. An opportunity to gain a new perspective. You were told that you were special because you could *Splinter*, but in truth, you were defective. Incapable of working in harmony with your implant and with others who are different from you. The modifier will give you incentive not to splinter. As long as you do not choose violence, you can live without pain. We hope you will choose to live in peace."

When the modifiers were activated, pain clawed up their arms, bleaching their indigo fur to white in the wake of its flow, resulting in the characteristic lightning bolt trace. Once their cries died down, Coso spoke: "This will become known as the Sign of the Splinter. In your country, it will mark you as a criminal. Perhaps not all of you are aware yet, but the tides are turning. Nakhadot has his own army, it is doubtful you will overthrow him." She wanted to say more, but she did not have day-to-day reports on the revolution in Zenda. At this point, it was chaos there. But she chose to believe the outcome would be favorable.

"Finally, there will be deportation for those from the Sovereign Zenda Nation. You will not be returning to the life you led in the past, your assets at home will be seized by your government. Your family members will be investigated to determine if they had any part in your treasonous plans to overthrow the rightful King. Further punishment will be a decision for your government." Again, she was extrapolating on the recent conversation she had with one of Nakhadot's close associates. But these Zendali didn't know any more than she did. Her goal was to remove the hope of escaping punishment.

Coso paused. The room was dead silent now. "One of you will have an opportunity to receive a less severe sentence. The first of you who will testify to the crimes your organization has committed over the last few years will receive this accommodation. We assume the missing Pinks from our reservations have been murdered. Their families want to bury their dead and give them the honor they deserve. We ask that one of you tell us where they are. If you can do this, we have the word of Nakhadot that you will receive a lighter sentence. You will have the night to consider. If you wish to confess, you will have an opportunity to contact us. As we do not have a jail, you will be held on a vessel in the harbor."

Ziyad looked up in anticipation. But Coso understood that hopeful expression and put an end to his expectations. "Your luxury yachts have been confiscated. You will be returning to Zenda in one of our retrofitted steamers. The rooms are small and very basic but should be comfortable enough. This vessel will be set on an automatic trajectory to Zenda. You will be locked inside until someone known to your prince arrives with the passcode to release you. We recommend that you be judicious with your provisions. The civil war in your country may be so distracting that you will be forgotten."

83

JUSTICE

When the captives from the Order were escorted out of the council chambers, they brought in a new group. These were Wen who had been inducted into the organization. Chayton and Kinache were among them, as was his mother, Holata Tyee. While they were getting seated and cuffed to the arms of their chairs, Coso turned to the Pink female Snorri.

"I asked you to join us here today to be a witness to their judgment, Snorri. There will be no decree against you, because you acted in self-defense, and as a warrior defending your family. What you and the other members of your reservation were able to do was commendable. You took one life, but you saved many others. When this is over, the council will be revising our treaty with Nakhadot Hotep Kemel after his coronation ceremony. We expect to have the opportunity to offer your people more freedom and better opportunities. We would like to start by offering you a job."

With tears wetting Snorri's face, she shyly expressed her gratitude. "I expected to be punished. Thank you for your understanding and kind words." She rubbed the tears from her face and wiggled her ear-fans in anticipation of the job Coso had offered.

"We would like you to lead the training of our new patrol. Mora explained to us what she taught you, but she will not be available to do the training. She has offered to work with you and Rosewallon for a short time. You were her best student. I believe you are the one who might be available to travel and teach because you're unmarried?"

Snorri's eyes brightened, and she smiled just a little. "Yes, I would be honored. Thank you for the opportunity."

"What has taken place in our cities has led us to understand that we need a peacekeeping contingent. We would like it to consist of both Wen and the fair races."

"Would I be a peacekeeper after the training?"

"Yes, with a high rank, we want you to travel to other cities and teach self-defense. The attack on our sanctuary reservations has shown us that we are wholly unprepared for violence. We need to learn how to defend our democracy. Before you agree to take the job, you must understand that it will not be easy traveling away from your home, and not everyone will be as accepting of you in that role because of the color of your fur, some Wen might resent learning from a Pink, because the negative influence from the Amon Kuroo has spread through our communities, it is all too pervasive now. That will change in time, but the way we see it, if they can't accept you as their teacher, we don't want them on our team. We're interested in peacekeepers, not people with prejudices that might influence their decisions."

"Yes, I am willing, and I understand that it may be difficult. I will accept that challenge."

Now the chief turned and smiled at Snorri. He took her hand as he rose to his feet. She was a tall, big-boned female, which meant he didn't tower over her. She only had to lift her chin a bit to look into his eyes. In his other hand was a pendant made of silver. Etched onto the surface were lines in the shape of an arrow with feathered quills at one end.

"This symbol represents the life force of all living things," he said. "It points to the heart of a warrior. Today, we thank you for your courage. Let this serve as a reminder that you will go through life without fear." He placed the talisman over her head. It was the perfect length to rest against her heart.

Snorri was usually not the type of person to get emotional, but there were tears on her face and this time, she didn't wipe them away. She just smiled and said, "Thank you."

84

REHABILITATION

The council had asked both Mora and Asha not to wear their robes and veils as an exception. They had complied. Asha was apprehensive as she knew her father and brother had been taken into custody, and when she asked Mato for details of the situation, he was vague.

Mora, Tokala Luta, and Yuma picked Asha up at the hospital. When they arrived at the Council building, Algon was waiting for them. He gently hugged Asha.

"I'm sorry. I haven't been to see you. I was detained; they just released me."

"Do you know what to expect?" Asha asked him.

"They didn't tell me."

The group sat together in the waiting area outside the chambers. They knew the proceedings had begun in the early morning, but they were told to arrive later in the day.

Asha's physical wounds were significant. It would take time to mend. It was the emotional aspects of recent events that troubled her more deeply. Learning about her family's involvement in the attempted slaughter of her friends at the reservation was devastating. Asha's bruises were not obvious under her thick indigo pelt, but her wrist had been fractured when Tao wrenched her arm when she was captured. It was splinted and wrapped now. The throbbing ache was a constant reminder of what they had done.

Asha and Mora had already confessed to Mato what they'd been doing on the reservations. They expected there would be some repercussions for breaking the treaty agreements.

"I don't know if I will even have a job now." Algon told Asha.

She darted a look of annoyance at him. "Don't let Mora hear you."

Yuma and Tokala sat on the other side of Asha, looking like two small boats adrift on the sea. Asha nudged Tokala. "Hey, what's the matter with you two?"

"They took Holata Tyee and Kinache. Not that we didn't expect her involvement and all, but what will happen with us now?"

"Tokala, she wasn't a very good teacher. She treated you both badly."

Yuma, who was listening, nodded agreement. "But still, we had hope of a future. Now I might have to leave the city."

Tokala squeezed Yuma's hand. "You just don't want to leave Orenda."

He tilted his head side-to-side, fluttered his ears, and smiled a little.

"We were up half the night." Tokala told Asha. "It took us hours to put things back in order after Mato's team searched the property."

The doors to the inner chamber opened, and Coso herself came out to invite them inside. The other council members sat behind a long table on a raised dais at the front of the room. To the left were the Wen, who had gotten mixed up with the Order of Amon Kuroo, including Chayton and Kinache. In addition, Holata Tyee and a few native business owners who marketed Zenda products like the Binkies and Avatars were looking hostile and uncomfortable in their seats.

As their small group followed Coso in, they were led to the chairs on the right side, which were mostly empty except for Snorri and an impressive-looking chief in full regalia. After taking their seats, Coso Winnemucca ended the recess and called the meeting to order.

They set a second table up in front of the seats on the left side of the room. It contained a pile of what looked simply like white circles, but everyone, by this time, knew what they were. Coso stood to address the room.

"This is a judgment day, which we hope will be the beginning of rehabilitation for our community. The council has reviewed all the evidence. Because this was a country-wide event, we deliberated with the other three councils to reach a unanimous agreement on how to punish those involved. No one will escape justice. We have already dealt with the foreigners. Now we are faced with the damage done by our own people."

She paused while she spoke quietly to the seated council, then she turned and faced the room again, looking directly at the old guardian in the back of the room. She was not wearing her elegant clothing or fine jewelry now. Her hair was a tangled mess, and she looked angry.

"We will first address the misdeeds of the medicine guardian Holata. You will no longer be addressed with the honorific Tyee, as you have disgraced your profession. We have seized your property and all your assets to make reparations. We cannot excuse the corruption and treason you involved yourself in. You and all the others will be given the modifier. The council mandated that you and your son must leave this city. However, finding a place for you to go posed a dilemma. No other territory on Wendat wanted you near their youth."

Holata glowered at Coso.

"But finally, we found a remote settlement in the far north. They needed a medicine guardian badly enough that they agreed to accept you into their community. This will be your second chance. We hope you will learn to serve them with humility."

Coso addressed Kinache next. "You were on the security footage in my home. Your actions against this council and your involvement in the attack on the reservations have earned you banishment from this city. You will accompany your mother to the north. You may not leave the village for any reason. We hope you will respect this opportunity and find the support and care you need to heal. If you don't, you will be cast out on your own."

Asha was both impressed and confounded by the leniency of the council. In her opinion, they deserved far worse. She tried to whisper something to Tokala, but she just shook her head.

Coso was speaking now to the other young Wen. "Our modern cities lack the tribal support to help guide our youth. This was a deficiency in our society. We overlooked your needs. As a result, you lost the values of our culture. You have turned away from the Sacred Prime and allowed yourselves to be indoctrinated into a hostile foreign organization. We failed you. Your families failed you. We give you the Modifier to atone for your actions. This is your chance to let go of the resentment and loathing which has corrupted your soul. Give it a chance. It will help you to learn tolerance. Your families have all agreed to focus their attention on your recovery. They will support you on a new path. None of you committed murder, but you did cause injury, and for that, you and your family will pay reparations to the Reservation."

Some of them looked horrified that the council would force them to make amends to the Pinks.

Coso continued, "In other regions of our country, the sanctuaries were not able to defend themselves as well, which resulted in a number of deaths. The Wen involved will be stripped of their possessions and banished, and their families will pay reparations. Each of them who is banished will be sent alone to a remote location, and all villagers in the surrounding area will be warned not to interact with them. Because they are city youth without survival skills, it is unlikely they will survive the winter alone. Keep this in mind as you all move forward in your lives. If we discover you have continued in your vengeful activities, we will banish you as well."

Chayton and Kinache, who sat in front, already had the modifier. While Kinache looked at the council with barely contained malice, Chayton looked resigned, even remorseful.

Coso then addressed the Muwioni citizens who had colluded with the Zendali. Some were business owners. Others had well-placed jobs that made them useful, like the kitchen manager Madam Mukwa who assisted in Bi's capture. "You are old enough to have known better than to get involved with a criminal enterprise. Unfortunately, your family will also pay for your crimes. Your businesses have been shut down; your financial credits transferred to a reserve account to pay restitution. You and your families will also work in service positions assisting in the recovery of those you've harmed. We have seized your homes and all your possessions. We have arranged for a group home outside of the city proper to house you. It is more than adequate for all of you. But there will be no luxuries or comforts. Moving forward, a host has been assigned to direct your work schedule. If you deviate from your assigned duties in any way, you will be banished. If, however, you pay your debt and adjust your behavior, you will be able to reestablish a home in the city. It will take a lot of time and hard work to regain your independence."

Some of the business owners looked ashamed, while others appeared to be willfully defiant.

"We want you to understand what has happened here," said Coso. "And I am going to ask Asha, who is the daughter of Ziyad and a historian, to tell you the truth about the Order of Amon Kuroo which you aligned yourselves with." She motioned to Asha, who had not expected this.

Asha stood, realizing what Coso wanted her to say. But there was another reason the council elder wanted her to be seen. She wanted the accused to face one of their victims and see all of her injuries. Her bandaged wrist, her split lip, and swollen eye, the way she winced when she moved because her body was so badly bruised.

"The Order of Amon Kuroo is, or was, created by radical nationalists who were convinced they were the original people, the Purebloods. Our nation learned about genetic molecules and polynucleotide chains long ago. They discovered deviations in those who lived on other continents. It showed two main subspecies. This imperfect science was the basis of the Expansion Wars. The Zendali royals backed the nationalists in those days. The Amun became advisors to the royal family and were closely related through marriage bonding. They wanted war because it was advantageous to have more land and slave labor."

At the mention of slaves, a rustle of disquiet went through the room. Asha paused to compose her thoughts and then continued.

"The Amun first organized the secret cult of Amon Kuroo, using their influence to manipulate the government and royal policies. Zenda colonized the lands of the fair races because of the directive given to them by a jealous war god called Wandrona. He told our people that they had dominion over all other creatures. And the fair races were nothing more than livestock to them. When they lost the war with the Eastern Empire, they chose to take a different tactic when they approached Wendat. Which might have had something to do with the fact that the Star People had given your country valuable technology and advancements. What the Zendali did not tell you, well... it is not even in our official history, is that the people of Wendat also have those deviant gene markers. The Wen are no more pure, by Zendali standards, than the Pinks. The Amon Kuroo would have no qualms about eradicating your people. They could hide the fact you aren't pure because they've brainwashed their citizens into thinking pale fur meant less intelligent, animalistic even. But you... well, you *looked* acceptable. Especially after you began to dye your fur darker to be more like them."

The Wen awaiting punishment stirred and whispered.

"They accepted this treaty arrangement because it is politically advantageous for them to do business here. The fact is, you are not purebloods, and the Order of Amon Kuroo would never have let you join. You simply had access to things they needed, so they made you do what they couldn't. They despised you all, deceived and perverted you. They had absolutely no concern for your well-being." Asha sat down. She had a bitter expression. There was no getting away from the fact that her own family had corrupted these youths. She was angry and ashamed.

Asha observed the youth while she was talking. Their expressions changed from an attitude of indignation to a sort of despondent acceptance. They had been fooled.

"Thank you, Asha. You're safe from any further harm. Your father and brother are being deported. We have appropriated most of their assets to pay restitution to those they have wronged. You, however, will keep your family home, and you will be given a permanent visa if you wish to stay in Wendat. It will be up to you to make a living and support yourself, but you are free to remain in Muwioni."

Coso signaled the other council members, who stood before the tables with modifiers. They moved forward and began to fit them on the Wen prisoners.

Asha tried to smile to show her gratitude. She couldn't think of anything to say. Her head was pounding, and she was exhausted. The room filled with the painful moans of those being fitted with modifiers. Their discomfort gave her a mixture of satisfaction and regret. She agreed with the punishment, but felt in some way guilty for the damages.

The Council elder addressed Tokala Luta and Yuma next.

"With Holata no longer in residence, the city would like to offer her home to the two of you. We realize you have not completed your apprenticeship, but we have a solution for that. We will discuss this privately. For now, rest assured your future here is secure."

Asha squeezed Tokala's hand. The relief on her friends' faces lifted her spirits.

There were only two more judgments. But before the council continued, Coso had the Native youth, the business executives, and Holata removed from the room. It was instructive for the medicine guardian and her son to learn what would happen to their home, to understand what they had lost. But it was not necessary for them to remain in the court at this point. When they were rounded up and ushered out, Algon was next.

"Algon, we spent a great deal of time investigating your involvement with the Zendali company, who employed you after they bought the production contract from the university. We needed to understand how much collusion was involved, what you knew, and what you did for them. If it had not been for the help you gave to Mora and Mato, we would have come to a very different conclusion. After our deliberations and study of the evidence, we have decided your entanglement seemed to be a legitimate interest in the business. We believe you were unaware of their plans and were misled. This does, however, leave the question open about who will run the company now that it is government property. Would you be interested in continuing your role as the operating manager?"

Algon's apprehension caused a cold sweat to seep through his fur and dampen his shirt. There was a visible release of tension when the council absolved him of wrong-doing. "Yes," he managed to say. "I would be grateful to continue working on the portal production."

"Good, one more thing, however, we understand you were not the actual inventor of this technology, although you were given credit?"

Algon stammered, "that... that was the university's decision."

"Right, we have spoken with them. They will answer for their greed and misappropriation in regard to this technology. We are still investigating the board members and the decisions they made. Zamora is to be awarded the honor of her invention, as it was her creation. She will receive a percentage of the profits, as will you, but your percentage will be less than what you negotiated in your previous contract, as you don't actually have any rights to this technology. The records are being amended. We are aware she is Fog, and we intend to open our universities to all the fair races."

His voice was soft when he answered. He was embarrassed. "That's fair."

Mora was addressed next: "Zamora, we owe you a great deal, for your invention, for your cooperation with Mato during the insurrection, and for the training you gave the reservation inhabitants. You gave them the means and the confidence to defend themselves against their attackers. Because you have shown us beyond any doubt that the fair races are capable, we will no longer allow them to be oppressed. We will negotiate a new treaty with the young King Nakhadot, who, I have been told, is amendable to reformation. Soon the world will be made aware of your good deeds and your genius. It will change everything. Are you ready to face that future?"

Mora's eyes were tearful. "I... I'm grateful, and honored. Yes, I hope to live up to your expectations."

Coso smiled. "You already have. But understand one thing clearly: just because you and other Fog have new freedoms here, you will still be a target for those who follow the old ways of your country. You must always be cautious. You can now move freely without the garb of Bicara's sisterhood unless you choose it."

"I have a request, if I may?"

Coso paused with a look of curiosity. "Go on, what is it?"

"My father, he's a Pink, living at the Meex Reservation. I need to find out if he survived the attack. And could he come here to Muwioni for a visit? I'm working with my partner, Ohpa, on new portal technology. I'd like my father to see what we're doing."

"Your father? Are you sure of this?"

"I'm sure."

"We will look into it. Give us his name, and we will bring him here if he's able to travel."

"This concludes our judgment regarding the insurrection. Tokala Luta and Yuma, if you will remain here for a private discussion, the rest of you are free to go."

***

When Mora, Asha, and Algon left the inner chambers, Orenda was waiting. They thought at first that she had come to meet them and find out what the judgments were, but she stood and headed for the chambers. "I'll see you afterward, and we can talk then," she said in passing.

When Orenda entered, Coso Winnemucca told Yuma and Tokala Luta she hoped that her niece would become their new mentor. "I realize she is close to your own age, but she has had more years of practical experience in all aspects of medicine, and Orenda is skilled in ceremonial practices, too, which you have not learned from Holata. Orenda can guide you in those studies, and I am sure that together you will rise to be a formidable cooperative, as I can see you are already friends. Is this acceptable?"

Orenda was hesitant, but the Star People had told her that medicine was her path. "I agree with one condition: I still want to study art. I would choose to diversify my endeavors until I complete those studies. Art will always be a part of my visionary practice, and I want to gain the skills the university has to offer. If that is admissible, then I agree."

Both Tokala Luta and Yuma were nodding in agreement.

Yuma said, "I believe we have much to learn from Orenda. We will make her schedule work for us."

"It is settled then," Coso said. "We will designate the compound previously owned by Holata as the local medical clinic and home to those who practice there. If you choose to take on new apprentices at any time, that will be your decision, Orenda. If any of you choose to move and practice elsewhere, it is also your right to do so. I trust you will be sure someone capable remains in service to this community."

Orenda nodded her agreement.

Lastly, Coso said, "Holata and Kinache's personal effects have already been removed."

Tokala and Yuma looked relieved.

"That concludes our business for today. Orenda, you are always welcome at my home. I hope you will visit often. I wanted you to know about this arraignment, as it is now safe for you to move out of Zamora's place. You can move to the clinic property and make it your home."

Orenda reminded her aunt that Bimisi had also been kidnapped and that restitution should be made. "They used the same electric shock torture on her. She also suffered, and her injuries were extensive."

"Thank you for reminding me," Coso said. "She is the one responsible for rescuing my staff. These crimes will be added to the charges against the Order of Amon Kuroo, and funds will be set aside for Bimisi. I'd like to meet this elusive stranger and discuss restitution."

85

FOREBODING

While Mora was helping Orenda pack her belongings, Bi entered the room with a look of disappointment. "Are you sure you want to move out?" she asked Orenda. "I'm going to miss you."

"Oh, Bi, I have some good news! My aunt wants to meet you, and the Muwioni Council is offering restitution for the harm caused by the Order."

Bi peered at Orenda with apprehension. "She what? Really, to me? But she thinks I'm a native. When does she want to meet? I mean..." She looked nervous. Her ear-fans fluttered and then folded back.

Earlier, Mora had started telling Bi about the judgment day but had stopped to help Orenda pack because Yuma was bringing a transport to move the trunk and her other things. "Bi, you told me before that you needed to speak with her, anyway."

"Yes, but she may not be predisposed to do me any favors once she learns who I really am."

Mora was folding clothing items and placing them carefully in a satchel. "Bi, do you plan to tell her then?"

She looked thoughtful. "I don't think I have a choice. Since getting the implant, I've been cut off from communications with my country. I have no way to return, and I have no further mission here. Yet the Star People showed me I *would* return and told me I have a greater purpose, to unify our nation with Wendat. I'm unclear how to return or how someone like me can accomplish what they want me to do. I need the council's help."

Orenda reassured her. "The information you gave to Mato helped them understand how the Order planned the attack on the reservations. Without you, there might have been more people killed. And in any case, you have caused no harm here. How badly could they judge you?"

"I entered your country illegally. I spied on people who had legitimate visas to be here."

"Who just happened to be a radical conservative sect who wanted to eliminate the Pinks!"

Bi smiled. "But I didn't know any of that when I came here."

"You, me, and Mora were destined to come together here for a reason. We were guided by the Sacred Prime."

"I hope your council perceives my actions in such an equitable way, but I've had enough experience with government officials to realize that is not normally the outcome. They judge according to their rules and laws. Our wishes and hopes and good intentions have little to do with it."

"I've never asked you about your country, Bi. We are all so curious to know more. What was it like growing up in the Eastern Empire?" Mora asked.

Bi's expression was conflicted. "I have chosen to talk about the Eastern Empire, but to be honest, by doing so, my people will think I betrayed them, and consider me a conspirator."

"That sounds rather dire. Why wouldn't you be able to talk about your country?" Mora asked.

"Well, I was not supposed to expose my origins." She gave them a half-smile, like that point should be obvious. Then she looked more serious. "I've learned things I shouldn't know because of my abilities. I spied on my own people. The knowledge I have about our history and the inner workings of the Eastern Empire is a secret. The preferences of the royal family, and the opinions of the Empress, are not commonly known by our citizens. I developed opinions and attitudes based on knowledge I should not have had access to."

"So, because of your Gift, you are more aware of the inner workings of your government? The other spies are also visionaries, wouldn't they come to the same conclusions?" Asked Orenda.

"You recall I was surprised that Far could astral project?"

Both Mora and Orenda nodded.

"I possess an ability that no other student of the Brainery Institute has ever reported being able to do. I have had this talent all my life. Which is also rare. The Gift usually makes itself known during fever dreams at puberty. I assume Far was able to project herself to me because of the cording."

Orenda was empathetic. "I sense you're deeply concerned about this, Bi, but I don't have enough context to understand why."

"I have never told anyone that I could astral project. If my government knew... it might cause a dreadful result, not just for me, but the entire school. Can you imagine if the royals knew I could spy on them? They would suspect everyone with a gift; they would shut everything down!"

"Don't you think you're being a little paranoid, Bi?" Mora asked.

Bi shook her head. "No, not at all, I have had a lot of years to think about the ramifications."

"But your insight into the veracity of the Empire would be valuable. You could give an honest perspective in any negotiations. This would be exceptionally important for our council," Orenda said.

Bi smiled. "You are describing treasonous behavior. That would be considered a sort of disobedience, which my country would never forgive. My attitude toward the Eastern Empire is radical. I have never admitted that to anyone. It would mean my death. Since being here, I have gone even deeper into perversity."

"You're saying that knowledge is dangerous?"

"Of course, because I should not have any *way* of acquiring it." She smirked. "Don't you see, I am the perfect spy, but I can never tell my own country how good I am."

"Yet the Star People believe you will unify our countries. You should trust in that." Orenda told her.

"I believe it would be beneficial for our countries to forge a union, or at the very least, open trade. But how can I facilitate such changes when I am so low in our class system? My Empress would not even grant me an audience! Why would my superiors listen to what I think? I can't divulge the information I gathered in secret, and those secrets inform my opinions. To be honest, I'm not sure how much to say. In my heart, I feel complete transparency would serve the greater good, but such honesty is rarely appreciated, especially if it paints anyone who has power in a bad light."

Mora nodded her understanding. "In my country, we had people come forward to inform on the government and make some secret things public. Usually, they became political prisoners or had to flee the country to avoid arrest."

Orenda looked worried. "Bi, if you need more time to think about it, we will understand."

Bi gave them a sort of dubious half-smile. "Well, you realize... if I tell you all of this history without Asha present, she will be unhappy."

That was true, and it lightened the mood. They all laughed.

"I have an idea," Mora said. "I still have the Mind-Mapping equipment here. We can record it while you tell us. Then both Asha and the council could have access to whatever you want to share. You can take time to consider the contents of the recording and maybe edit what you present to the council members."

"Can it work like that?" asked Orenda.

"I think so. Asha knows more about mind-mapping than I do. Normally I subvocalize what I'm recording. Asha just thinks what she wants to record, but I can't record her way... my eidetic memory pulls up visual reference pages relating to what I'm thinking. But if I say the words softly to myself, the recording stays on track." She smiled at Bi. "It should work just as well when you're speaking out loud."

"Let's try it," Bi said with some enthusiasm.

The three of them moved into the library, and Mora put the headpiece on Bi, and turned on the machine. "Just talk normally."

"All right, here goes... a little overview of my country: The Eastern Empire is ruled by a matriarchy. This wasn't always the case..."

Bi talked about the social, and political history of her country until Yuma arrived. Orenda went to let him in and they started to carry out her trunk.

Mora asked Bi: "What will you do if you return to your country?"

"I'm not sure they will value me as a spy any longer if I'm not able to contact my invigilator when I'm on a mission. Or at least I have not been able to do that since I got my implant here. If I can't do what I was trained to do, then I have few prospects."

Mora interrupted her. "Your invigilator is someone at the institute you report to in your lucid dreams?"

Bi nodded. "The invigilator is also Gifted. My invigilator was a close friend from my school days, Far. She is the one who corded me."

"Have you had any other contact with her, or have you had the feeling you're being watched?"

"No, the ceremony broke my connection to Far, I'm sure of it. But before that, I observed her reporting to my government."

"Reporting about what?"

"I must have misunderstood. She is not only my invigilator; she was my close friend. She loves me . . . at least she said she did."

"Bi, there's more to this. I can see that it upsets you. What are you not saying?"

"I think she was telling them I am a traitor."

Orenda had just come back up to the library and caught that last sentence. She and Mora both reacted at once.

"What?!"

86

Eastern Empire Ambassador

O renda took Bi to meet her aunt Coso Winnemucca. The council elder's home was a large compound surrounded by dense shrubbery, which gave the courtyard a private feeling.

"I'm glad to see the house restored." Orenda told Bi, "There were broken windows." As they entered the house, Orenda seemed to be taking inventory, she led Bi through the rooms toward her aunt's home office. "Most everything is back in place. Except a few sculptural pieces are missing from the shelves. But at least it looks like a home again, not a crime scene."

The Pinks, who lived with the council elder, greeted Bi with profuse gratitude. Their ears wiggled, and their tails were held high and twitching with happiness. All the attention made her embarrassed. The eldest of the servants hugged Orenda, a rumble of her purr was loud enough that Bi could hear it, a sign of contentment.

Orenda patted the servant on her back. "I'm so happy you are all home and safe."

"Thanks to your friend, we are well." She smiled at Bi shyly. "Coso is waiting in the garden for you."

Tea and cakes were set out for their meeting. Coso stood and bowed slightly to greet Bi and welcomed her to sit.

"So good to see you, Orenda. Are you settling in at your new home?"

"Yes, and thank you for sending my things over."

Coso spoke then to Bi. "I hope this informal setting will put you at ease, Bimisi. I understand you have something important to tell me, and Orenda seemed concerned. She wouldn't tell me what was troubling you."

Bi sat a little stiffly in her chair. The garden setting had the opposite effect on her, making Bi realize how much trust she had been given, and how shocking her news might be. The Council elder might think she had taken advantage of her niece, or maybe her deceptive entry into their country was worthy of punishment.

Her anxiety was building as she imagined all the negative repercussions. Suddenly, she couldn't take a breath. Her throat constricted as a raspy sound came out unbidden. She had never had a panic attack before, yet she had also never cared so much about something as important as this.

When Bi started to hyperventilate, Orenda realized what was happening. "Bi, it'll be all right, try to calm your breath." She rummaged in her bag and brought out a jar, opened it, and stuck it under Bi's nose. "Here, inhale deeply."

Bi did as Orenda asked, and the herbal fumes had a calming effect almost immediately.

The council elder was now confused. "What is this all about, Orenda?"

"Bi needs to tell you in her own way. She's just nervous."

Bi looked up at Coso, admonishing herself silently. This is not the behavior of a trained operative for the Eastern Empire. She gathered her courage and managed to speak with a steady voice. "I apologize for my nervousness. Thank you for seeing me today. My name is actually Bi. Just Bi."

Coso nodded for her to continue.

"I came to your country illegally. I am from the Eastern Empire."

Coso's ear-fans perked up. It was not the reaction Bi expected. The council elder stared at Bi for a moment before she smiled knowingly. "Now, some things are making a little more sense. Please continue and tell me why you came."

"You must have heard about our war with the shadow people?" She paused. "I mean the Sovereign Zenda Nation? When it ended, a shift in power occurred. Our country became a matriarchy ruled by the Niyama family. The Empress still lives in fear of our country being invaded."

"You came here to spy on the Zendali?" Coso asked?

Bi nodded. "I am a gifted Lucid Dreamer; the Zendali business executives were in my visions. This foretold that I would travel here. My mission was to gather information about the Zendali, and find out if Wendat was colluding with our enemy."

"You are very young for a spy."

Bi smiled shyly. "Instead, my attempt at gathering information led me to discover they were planning to attack the reservations here. I informed your niece, Asha, and Mora, and they told Mato."

"I understood you took part in the rescue of my household staff as well, and that you were captured and tortured. I expect the Order of Amon Kuroo thought you were Fog? They wanted to find out where you were from?"

"Yes, at first, they thought I was Fog like Mora, but I don't have Zendali features. Finally, they assumed I was native, and my parents broke their treaty and mated with the Pinks, because I'm mixed... and have green eyes."

"But you didn't confess your origins?"

"No, that would be unwise. If they were to discover the truth, it would put my country in danger."

"They might have killed you."

"Yes, I believe they would have... if I had not escaped."

"Didn't the people who sent you here realize your appearance would pose some difficulty for you... that you were too pale to blend in with our population?"

"We were cut off from the rest of the world for so long. The last time anyone from the Eastern Empire traveled to Wendat the people here had lighter pelts. They were not as dark as they are now. Also, I am considered dark in my country. An unflattering trait."

Coso looked doubtful. "I think they made a lot of assumptions and sent you into a dangerous situation. May I ask how you were able to relay your information to your superiors? Is there some technological advancement that allowed you to contact them?"

"I'm trained in a School of Lucid Dreamers. We are trained to be spies from a young age. When one of us goes on a mission, we're assigned another dreamer as an invigilator. We can meet in our dream-space to communicate. However, once I got an implant, I was no longer able to contact her."

"The implant should not have interfered with your Gift, Bi. Are you sure there isn't another reason your invigilator blocked the usual discourse you shared?" Asked Orenda.

Bi recalled the conversation she'd watched Far have with the military officer. *Are you sure your agent is a traitor?* The reality of her homecoming suddenly became clear to her.

"There might have been a misunderstanding," Bi said. "I told you, Far reported that I defected. I thought... oh, of course you're right! She has purposely blocked me from contact."

Bi's mind was racing with the ramifications. She had not given it credence. *How could I have ignored the significance of that vision?* Then she knew why, and it squeezed her heart like a fist. She didn't want to admit to herself that Far would betray her.

"You have been a courageous, Bi," Coso said. "I'm sure your Empress will reward your heroic work here."

Bi's pupils dilated in alarm. "You are wrong about that, Council elder. I will most certainly be arrested." Her ear-fans flattened against her head. "You think I'm brave? The more I learn, the more frightened I become. I have failed my country. If I cannot be a spy, I will have no value to them."

Coso's brow furrowed. She seemed to be contemplating how to respond. Orenda stared at Bi with apprehension.

"On the contrary," Coso said, "you have not failed. You have accomplished a great deal. You will have value for us as an ambassador, and I would like to appoint you as such."

Bi released a breath she didn't realize she was holding.

"You don't need to give me your decision today," Coso said.

Bi shook her head, a motion which at first seemed to be a refusal. "To tell you the truth, I am afraid to go home. I wanted to stay in Wendat. But the Star People told me it's my destiny to unite our countries."

"Star People told you?" Coso looked from Bi to Orenda for clarification.

"I'll tell you about it later, Auntie. But Bi, Mora, and I had an experience recently. They..." Orenda searched for the right word, "instructed us."

Coso widened her eyes with interest.

"I don't know how to do what they want," Bi said. "But I suspect that accepting your offer would be the first step."

Coso nodded. "If you believe you're returning to some sort of indictment, then you are proving your bravery once again by your willingness to accept this offer. I find that impressive."

"Well, you shouldn't. I simply have no other option. To answer your other question, I was never told how I would be retrieved. Maybe they didn't expect me to succeed, or perhaps my survival was unlikely. If you understood how little regard someone of my class is given, you would realize the possibility of failure outweighs any hope I have of success. The only thread of confidence comes from the fact that the Star People have seen an outcome I cannot fathom. And now you have entrusted me with this title."

Coso raised her eyeridge at that statement. "Surely, they value you more than that. In regard to the issue of fur color, more people in the Sovereign Territories and especially here on Wendat have lighter fur than it appears. Natural shades are rarely seen now, but I remember when I was young, seeing much more diversity."

"My government wasn't completely mistaken in assuming I would fit in."

"You are still fairer than most, Bi. However, not everyone here is as naturally dark as they seem. It has become fashionable to use the fur dying salons to fit into the Zendali standard of beauty."

"In my country, people sometimes do the opposite and bleach their fur white."

"The conventions of beauty can be demanding if you care about that sort of thing," Orenda chimed in.

"Because of the Sovereign Nations taboo on the Fog, citizens who had lighter fur started to use the dye shops to avoid suspicion. I suppose. Also, the Zendali have had a great impact on fashion and style in our country in recent years. Our youth lean toward the Zenda's ideal of beauty. Perhaps for financial reasons, they also hope to get business connections with Zendali companies."

Orenda was nodding. "A light-furred citizen will not rise to positions of power in the Sovereign Nation. Even people in our cities depend on business relationships with the Zendali, like Algon. Many Wen have changed their appearance to gain approval from the foreigners."

Bi considered the similarity to her country's norms. "Sometimes parents kill dark children like me when they're born, just like the Zenda kill the Fog. The government doesn't approve of slaying babies, but they don't punish anyone for it either. Parents don't want to raise a daughter who can't be a householder or a son who won't find a mate. They don't want to be remembered as having faulty genetics, either. Those of us who develop the gift redeem themselves in their parents' eyes, and the shame is removed. But you're right. Our society is prejudiced too. Only one prefers dark hatchlings and the other fair. The only place in this world where someone like me might live without dishonor is here."

"If you become our ambassador, there are secrets I would impart. However, you must officially accept the assignment. Only then will I be completely transparent." Coso told Bi, which also peeked Orenda's interest.

Bi nodded and waited for Coso to continue, taking note of the council elder's serious expression. When she didn't speak, Bi realized she was waiting for a decision. "Oh, you want me to...Yes, I agree to be an ambassador between the Eastern Empire and the United Tribes of Wendat."

The council elder signaled to someone on her staff, who was waiting by the entryway. They brought a document and placed it on the table. It was an official-looking parchment. A pen and an ink pad sat next to it. "Put your thumbprint on the paper and then sign it."

"You were prepared for this? How did you know?"

Coso smiled. "Mora let something slip when we were in the middle of the insurrection. I doubted her, but now you have confirmed the truth of the matter. And hard to fathom as it is... I believe you. I also must add that you are very gutsy. Anyone who would go through what you have, and come through it with such self-assurance, has my approval."

Bi did as the council elder asked and signed the document, adding her thumbprint.

"You didn't read it?"

"Should I not trust you?"

The council elder just tilted her head. "I am trustworthy, Bi, but it is a reasonable practice to always read what you sign. You can only ask questions or debate the finer points before you make an agreement."

"Wise advice. I did not grow up with choice. I will be aware of this with any future documents I am asked to sign."

"Some broadcasts coming out of Zenda, recorded by Prince Nakhadot, reveal the origins of the Zendali. You should watch them."

"I assume they're relevant to the secrets you spoke of?"

"Yes, he reveals many secrets hidden for centuries. We are all related. Everyone on Hadot is connected genetically, except for the Zenda bloodline, which is different. They are obviously compatible with us. We can mate with them, but they are a separate species from everyone else."

Bi had a previous conversation with Asha, which raised questions about this topic. "It is a curiosity."

"You don't look surprised. Did you already listen to the recordings from Zenda?"

Bi looked at Orenda, who nodded. "No, not yet, but I'm interested. Asha told us in a private conversation something along these lines. She also mentioned there were Zendali in the past who came here to attend school, or for business, then matted with the Wen. That must have darkened your population to some degree?"

"Yes, many in the past integrated into native families and adopted our culture. I suspect the Amon Kuroo put a stop to that in recent years. Perhaps your friend Asha will mate formally with Algon before long?"

Bi smiled. "Yes, I'm sure you're right about Asha and Algon." After a reflective pause, she said, "I'm still curious why the Sovereign Nation chose to make trade agreements and treaties with your country and not ours."

"It was partly the timing. They approached us after the war with the Eastern Empire. I believe they thought the Star People had something to do with the atomic bomb your ancestors used against them."

"Actually, the Star People warned my ancestors not to produce atomic energy and forbade them to use the bomb. But they did it anyway. That's why they abandoned us. Most of our people have no idea aliens walked among us. They've become a fable."

"It is with the consent of all Wendat councils that we look forward to forging a new relationship with the Eastern Empire Bi. You will be famous for your efforts to unite our countries."

Bi smiled at that, and then shook the council elder's arm when it was offered, grasping elbows in the Muwioni tradition. "I am officially a treasonous a double agent." Bi joked.

Coso tilted her head, understanding the irony. "All we can do is try. Don't you agree it is time to end the suspicion between our countries and avoid hostilities? We hope the news you will take back about Prince Nakhadot and his reformation efforts will also help."

"People are already calling the prince *the young king*. Why is that? Just how old is he?"

"He's fifteen, Orenda replied. So, you can imagine why he wasn't taken seriously by the dowager Queen and the older population who've controlled the country since his father's death. But he will be king soon. His coronation is greatly anticipated by his followers. They already call him king, because putting a crown on his head is only a formality. The older generation argued that traditional values are worth maintaining. Nak's grandfather, Amahte' Amun, is staunchly opposed to giving Pinks any concessions. He even tried to steal the throne for himself. But I think Nakhadot's father Nebtawi was already leaning toward reformation."

"What inspired Nakhadot to view his country so differently?"

"Well, this is just speculation, but he was mostly raised by his nurse, who was a Pink. I haven't caught the full story, but she was killed recently. You really should try to catch the broadcasts; they're causing complete pandemonium in Zenda."

Bi watched the council elder, and suddenly a wisp of intuition came to her. "Council elder, were you referring to another secret you wanted to share, unrelated to what Prince Nakhadot has revealed?"

Coso smiled as if she were waiting for the question. "Yes, Bi, as the formal ambassador, you should know my family is related to the Niyama bloodline."

Both Bi and Orenda stared at her in shock, unable to reply.

87

FINAL INSTRUCTIONS

When Orenda and Bi returned to Zamora's place, Mora, Asha, Algon, Tokala Luta and Yuma were all waiting. "What happened?" Asha was first to ask.

"You're looking at the Eastern Empire Ambassador!" Bi smiled. "But of course, everything depends on my own countries' willingness to open its borders and negotiate a treaty with Wendat. I am sure it won't be that easy. I may be arrested as soon as we pull into the harbor."

Orenda gave Bi one of those head tilts, side to side. Mora was still curious how many meanings this gesture had.

"Haven't you had any visions about it?" Orenda asked.

"Not yet. I have no indication of what is really going on at home. It's frustrating. But at least I can move around this city freely without fear of being found out. I didn't even realize how much it worried me." She got teary-eyed. "I've grown to love this city and my friends here. Having to deceive everyone was painful. Lying got more difficult as time went on. Maybe I'm not cut out to be a spy."

Mora could sympathize since she'd had the same experience.

Everyone laughed and hugged Bi.

"Maybe you shouldn't go, Bi," Tokala said. "Why not stay here with us?"

Bi hesitated, not wanting to go into all the reasons, but before she could answer, Yuma changed the mood by holding up a container of golden liquid. "I think we should celebrate!"

Mora looked uncertain. "I thought you didn't drink spirits, or that the implants canceled the effects of the alcohol?"

"This is not alcohol. It's Pluma," Yuma said. "A blend of herbs that helps visionaries see better. In small amounts, it has a mild uplifting sensation, and it's delicious. We use it during special occasions, and this is certainly a time to celebrate for several reasons!"

"Did you make it yourself?" asked Orenda.

"Tokala did. She's a better herbalist than I am."

They sat in the living room. Mora had attempted to make one of her mother's recipes. Asha and Algon had picked up some food from a local restaurant.

The door chimed, and Mora let Ohpa in. He took a plate of food and something to drink, then joined the others. Mora sat next to him and addressed their group of friends. "Ohpa and I have an announcement. We would like you to be the first to know we have built a portal that will transport the living to various destinations here in this world."

Ohpa took note of the way she said *this world...* and gave her a questioning look. Which Mora ignored.

"Congratulations on completing your project, Mora, Ohpa," Algon said. A look of regret crossed his features, then he forced a smile.

"Thank you," Mora said. "We already have a factory site and will be setting up for production later next week. Ohpa has partnered with me on this one, and he will be overseeing the process and then the distribution."

Ohpa was almost bursting with delight. His eyes sparkled with happiness.

"I have one more bit of news. My father is arriving tomorrow, so I'll need you to bunk with me for a few days, Bi. I want to share with him where I live and show him the portals. We will install one near his reservation, so he can come to the city when he wishes."

Everyone but Ohpa had heard how she'd found Zamora's father, so this news was not exactly astonishing to them, but Ohpa gasped. "How did you find him? How do you know it's him?"

Mora just laughed. "That's a long story, maybe another time?" She reached across and pinched his ear, which had a startling effect on him. *Damn,* Mora thought to herself, *why did I do that? This drink must elevate emotional responses.* Ohpa was now staring at her in that love-sick manner he used to have. She turned away and started gathering her guests' plates. Then Ohpa jumped up and started to help her.

Asha could read the dynamics and knew the history of Ohpa and Zamora, so she interceded. "Give me those," she said to Mora. "We'll clean up. Come with me, Ohpa."

Mora sat back down with relief. "So, Bi, Orenda is no longer rooming with us, and now you will be taking a journey home too?"

"The Council Elders say within a month or two. There are preparations to be made."

"What about you, Mora?" asked Algon. "Did you find a way to return to your world?"

"Yes, I have. I know how to adjust the portals now. Soon, I will also leave. I wanted to tell you that I do appreciate all you did for me here, Algon. I'm sorry for treating you so badly." Mora flattened her ear-fans. "I was just so angry."

He was shaking his head. "No, Mora, I am ashamed of taking over your work like that. It seemed like the only option at the time."

Mora looked at him sadly.

"I mean, I could have refused, I guess." He looked up at her. "I hope you can forgive me."

"Best to ask for Zamora's forgiveness, Algon," she said. "None of this belongs to me. But I have a feeling she would understand better than I did."

They all talked and laughed until late at night, for this was the first time they had been together without heavy concerns weighing on them. Bi excused herself, saying she needed to sleep, and that was the signal for the others to leave. Ohpa was the last to go. He seemed to linger, maybe hopeful that Mora would ask him to stay. She instead treated him in a business-like manner. "Ohpa, this is a list of where we should distribute the portals. Can you be sure they get installed in these exact locations?"

He took the list to examine her request. "Those that are here on Wendat, there is no problem. Those in Zenda and the Sovereign Nations Territories, I will do it if they allow."

"If you offer free installations with low-cost transfers, I think they will be willing. Oh! And there are limitations imposed on who can travel to the mainland in Zenda. You will need to engage those parameters to meet their travel restrictions. I left all the instructions for those modifications at the lab. Also, criminals who have modifiers will not have access. I programmed it into the portal matrix already. They will automatically be rejected, and the portal will notify the authorities. You might want to write that into the contract, so they're aware."

He was nodding as she outlined these things. "You left very detailed instructions and notes on all the exceptions. May I ask... why are you leaving all of this up to me?" He stuttered then. "I... I don't object to it, I... I'm only wondering."

Mora thought about what to reveal and decided not to tell him she wasn't Zamora. The fewer people who knew about the other timelines, the better. "I will be traveling for a while, now that we're finished. There are some things I have to do. I'm leaving you in charge, and Mato will oversee any necessary legal matters. You're welcome to hire assistants and other staff, and you should... you will need them once the portals are in production. It is all in your hands. For the time being, you will be in charge. I trust you completely."

He looked crestfallen at the news that she would be going away. "By the way, I signed the new documents today that give you credit for the invention."

"Thank you for agreeing to do that, Ohpa. Your share of the profits will remain the same. You will be wealthy, and you can fund any personal project now that you have an interest in."

He smiled at her. "May I embrace you, Zamora? If you're going away, I'll miss you."

She wrapped her arms around him and said into his ear, "You're a good friend. Thank you for everything."

Then, she practically had to push him out the door. Ohpa seemed persistently hopeful that she would engage him in a more intimate encounter.

"I'll see you at the lab again," she said. "I'll be there to show my father around tomorrow."

88

Sentimental Allure of Happiness

"I feel like a walking freak show," Mora said in almost a whisper.

Thal smiled at her with understanding. "Just ignore them."

Mora had picked up Zamora's father at the train station that morning. They spent the day wandering around the city and got quite a lot of stares as Mora chose not to wear the garb of Bicara's Sisterhood and was unveiled for the first time in Wendat. People were not accustomed to seeing a Fog person at all, and seeing a Pink with one, wandering around like a tourist was a strange sight. Zendali who lived and worked in the city, were especially struck by this unusual sight.

A group of Zendali females were shopping in the city center. They wore the latest Sovereign Nation fashions and stood out in the crowd. After all that had happened recently, she was taken aback by how boldly they behaved. But then she understood the average tourist who wasn't associated with the Amon Kuroo may not yet be aware of what happened at the reservations. The council had not publicized the details, giving the Pink community time to recover. Official announcements of government policy changes would only occur after a formal treaty had been signed with Nakhadot. The broadcasts from Zenda had caused some of the Zenda tourists to extend their visas to avoid returning to their country during a brutal civil war.

Mora and Thal watched the visitors from the shadow of a fruit stand at the market. As the Zendali passed by, Mora thought they were like walking art installations. Something which belonged on a fashion runway or in a modern art museum. But she didn't mention this, assuming no such thing took place in Muwioni.

The Zenda visitors entered a shop across the market, into which they had to duck down a bit to fit through the door. Between the towering platform shoes and their hair-do's, they were quite tall. "I think they must be wigs, don't you? I can't imagine they would sleep in those," Mora said to Thal.

"Even when I lived in the capital, I witnessed nothing quite like that!"

"Do you remember much from the years you grew up in Ekene?"

"I remember everything."

Mora nodded, knowing her father had an excellent memory. Clearly, his counterpart did too. "The people who visit Muwioni from Zenda and the Territories are always elegantly dressed in fancy outfits. The males as well." *Flaunting their wealth,* she thought.

Thal laughed at what she had said, a loud, scoffing sort of guffaw, full of scorn.

Mora looked sideways at him. "Have you not seen them? You don't agree?"

"I don't know. It seems all of their attention is on the surface of things. It rattles me. Do they really have so much time to waste on decoration? This ostentatious show of wealth... does it matter? It's garish and pretentious. Does it really impress you?" He stared at the bewildered look on Mora's face, the heat of his annoyance burning out. "I assume you don't mind my candor?"

Mora hadn't seen them like that. Her view was influenced by the prevalent temperaments and customs of people on the west coast of Inoti, where artistic expression was common, and the art scene was quite eccentric. Wild outfits and costumes were more the norm, and especially prolific during festivals. She was used to the crazy fashions at home and didn't pay them much attention. Yet here, she observed everything with a degree of wonderment because the styles were entirely unique to her experience. None of it had any deeper meaning for her. But this version of Thal admired simplicity and usefulness. On the reservations, people dressed in a modest or practical way. Most of their clothing was hand-woven and handmade. Seeing these outfits must be outlandish or grotesque to him.

"No, not at all. I prefer honesty."

Thal looked a little sheepish. He obviously held some animosity toward the Zenda. More bitterness than hatred, but of course he had recently seen some of his friends harmed during the Zendali insurgence. Shortly after which he came to the city and saw these tourists.

Mora suddenly felt a flood of emotion. Chagrin and shame were her dominant reactions. She had misread the situation. How could she not? Mora was someone out of context. She replied with a meaningless comment. "Zenda has influenced the clothing styles in this city quite a bit."

Not wanting to spoil the mood of their day together, they both chuckled at the understatement. It felt forced and awkward.

Thal noticed Mora's embarrassment. I hope I didn't offend you.

Mora gave his arm a squeeze. A reassuring gesture.

They bought some vendor food at the market for lunch and ate in silence as they wandered the bazaar. Mora kept an eye on what interested him. He stopped to examine some old books, lovingly leafing through the pages. The stall keepers gave them wary looks but didn't openly object to their handling of the merchandise. Thal didn't seem to notice the bookseller's discomfort, or he didn't care. But Mora did, and she found their attitude offensive.

When the two of them walked away, he told her: "You mustn't let them know they upset you."

"What?"

Thal was looking intently at her.

He read the situation clearly. He just didn't show any sign of indignation. Mora acknowledged that she understood. "I have not gone unveiled in the city before, I still have a lot to learn."

"It will take a few generations, you know? For people to adjust to having us actively among them."

Mora thought he might be right. But she didn't want to talk more about those social struggles. She would not be here to watch that transformation. With a lighter tone, she changed the subject. "Do you want to see my lab?"

***

The tension of their outing at the market dropped away as they walked into her creative space. Mora sighed with relief as she felt the rigid strain in her shoulders release. Now, she was in her comfort zone.

Thal walked across the room to the transparent writing panels that were scrawled with Mora's calculations. She didn't expect Zamora's father to discern what the symbols meant. Her own father did not. Physics, or science in general, was not her father's field of interest. He'd visited her at the Inoti university and never showed support for her project. On reflection, she suspected he didn't believe the project was feasible. He avoided talking about it, so he wouldn't reveal his lack of confidence.

But when this version of Thal started to ask her specific questions, she realized he had a deeper grasp of her creative process than anyone who had assisted her at either university. "Where did you study physics and math?" She asked him without thinking.

Thal looked at her oddly. "I'm self-taught, of course. Your grandfather had an impressive library in the family home. I was fortunate to have access. I often discussed subjects of interest with your mother, Serwa. We would study together. If I had questions, she would pester her professors to find my answers, even if the subject wasn't something she cared about. At times, I must admit, I was frustrated by not having direct access to the teachers. But Serwa was always considerate in regard to my preoccupations." He chuckled. "She ended up with a reputation for her studious behavior and constant questions at her school. The other kids teased her for acting like a Golden instead of being more social."

Mora was familiar with the library from stories Asha had told her about her counterpart, Zamora, who spent most of her time as a child with those books. She was home-schooled too. Mora smiled at Thal and answered as she assumed Zamora would have. "I loved that library too."

She quickly changed the subject, not wanting him to ask any specifics about the library, or inquire about favorite books, which she would have no knowledge of.

She showed him the prototype of the portals and told him where they would be installed once production was underway.

"We will place one near the reservation. I will program all portals so you can travel without charge, and move freely to the city when you wish."

He looked at her with surprise. "You want me to come again?"

"Yes, of course, you are always welcome. You're my only family! I will give you an entry disc for my house, you can stay at my place whenever you like." Realizing she wouldn't be around much longer, she added: "I am sad to tell you; however, I'll be traveling for a time, it might be awhile before I see you again. But I have a library. You might enjoy borrowing a few for your classes."

Thal never expected in his lifetime to have this kind of freedom. "I'm not entirely sure what you're suggesting is permissible, Zamora, but it's kind of you to give me your trust and to be so generous."

"The council is renegotiating the treaty with the Sovereign Zenda Nation. After the insurrection and the attacks on the reservations, they have reason to restructure how they live with the Pinks. The council elder, Coso Winnemucca, told me herself... Pinks and Fog will now be allowed to use the universities."

"Are you sure?" Zamora's father, being a teacher on the reservation, looked at Mora with astonishment. "This would mean I could prepare the reservation youth for college."

"Yes, I'm not saying there won't be some period of adjustment, as you said it can take years for people to accept the fair races as equals. The native students will no doubt be more open to these changes than the foreign students from Zenda. I expect some aversion, even hostility, but it's a way forward for our kind."

"I am extremely doubtful that xenophobia will be that easily removed from society."

"I didn't say this would be easy. But a shift in policy is a welcome change, don't you think? Sure, we will have to endure criticism and prejudice, but it's worthwhile... isn't it?" She was looking at his doubtful expression.

"This happened because of you, Zamora. You have proven to the government we're more than they were led to believe. I'm so very proud and humbled that you're my daughter."

Mora's own father praised her scholarly achievements as she grew up. Her parents were supportive, especially as she advanced beyond most other children in her age group. But when Zamora's father told her this, her emotional reaction was intense, and his recognition of her accomplishments was somehow more meaningful. She had actually done something here, which made a bigger impact and helped the refugees.

In her life, she had never reached outside of her personal goals to consider that her actions might make a difference for others. Well, of course, aside from the fact that portal technology will revolutionize travel. But that is a genuinely abstract thing compared to this. Thal's praise also made her aware she had wanted her father to believe in her. To have confidence in her talent. His counterpart's compliment made her tear up. She blinked the tears away and smiled.

"Let's go home. I want to introduce you to my friend. She's from the Eastern Empire." Thal stood in place, dumbfounded. "Will you never cease to amaze me, Zamora?" She laughed as she pulled him toward the door.

On their way out, she found Ohpa was entering the lab. While passing in the entryway, she introduced them. "Ohpa, while I'm away, if you need any assistance, you might want to employ my father. He actually understands my work. I think he would be of some help to you." Both Thal and Opha looked at her in surprise.

"He... he understands all of that?" Ohpa waved in the direction of the calculations on the screens.

Thal smiled shyly, and then tilted his head, side to side.

Mora had a huge smile on her face. She patted Ohpa on the shoulder. "He *is* my father," she said, as if that should explain everything. She hugged Ohpa again, and they left.

***

Over dinner, Bi told them about the plans for her return to the Eastern Empire as an ambassador. Thal was obviously fascinated with someone from this mysterious country, and through his eyes, Mora came to understand how remarkable it was that Bi had come here. She had known the young spy for quite a while before learning where she was from. And then, of course, not having grown up in this world, the impact of the revelation was not as meaningful to her as it was to the others who had lived with this world's history.

Casually sitting together, visiting and sharing stories, Mora was starting to feel some doubts about returning to her own world. In so many ways, Wendat was better. This world was cleaner, more natural, and more advanced due to the Wen's relationship with the aliens. And now, her kind had a place here. Socially, things were changing for the better. She could be part of making such a wonderful transition happen.

But sadly... no, she shook her head because that fantasy was unrealistic. Besides, she missed her own family, and she longed for the company of her lover, Fen. *If I could bring them here...* she thought. No, this is not our world. It's time to go.

Seeing Mora shake her head, Bi thought her friend was responding to something she'd said. "What is it, Mora?"

"Nothing." Mora smiled. "I'll just miss you."

89

FINAL FAREWELL

"I hope I haven't overwhelmed you with all my questions," Mora said.

Thal's eyes twinkled with delight. "Not at all. I like that you're curious."

Zamora's father had been with Mora for a couple of days. She asked him every question she could think of. All the details about his life. Where he went when he left Ekene, all about the mining colony, how he traveled to Wendat, and the process of getting asylum. She discovered he had not been here for very long, but already he was a valued member of his community because of his knowledge and teaching experience.

It was a melancholy parting for Mora, as she didn't expect to see him again. He was so different from her father. They took divergent paths, had separate interests, and, of course, vastly different life experiences. Though they were also alike in character and temperament. In the evenings before bed, Mora wrote everything in a journal, which she would leave for Zamora, along with the name he had taken, and how she could contact him at the Meex reservation.

When Mora took Thal to the train, she tried her best to smile and not show him she was a little heartbroken to part ways. Maybe it was because she missed her own father. But she felt regret for having so little time with this version of Thal.

* * *

On her last night in Wendat, Mora hosted another get-together for her closest allies and friends. Which made her realize that she actually had established more meaningful relationships with people in this world than she had at home.

Zamora's place was filled with everyone Mora was close to. They were laughing, telling stories, and debating their various points of view. There were curious, interesting conversations going on, and the contrast to what she normally heard at dinner parties back home was significant.

The Inoti crowd she and Fen hung out with was focused on very trivial things much of the time. She felt a sort of funk settle in her chest. Doubt mixed with loss. She was going to miss this.

At the party, Orenda again asked Bi if she had any premonition dreams about what to expect when she returned to the Eastern Empire.

"Yes, I started to have some strange, inexplicable dreams. I'm not sure how to draw any conclusions. I've seen people I know, but they're behaving in an unexpected manner. It gives me an unsettled feeling. The only way to understand it is to return and face whatever is waiting for me."

"That is pretty much how my visions have always been," Orenda told her, and they all laughed about it, knowing better now why they were destined to meet.

Bi told them that Coso had some strategy sessions planned before her departure to the Eastern Empire. And that Istas Moki, the vice president of the university, was enlisted to accompany her on the return trip as a representative of the government of Wendat.

"Why Istas Moki?" Mora asked.

"Istas Moki has the greatest knowledge of the Eastern Empire, or rather of the old Empire, before the matriarchy," Asha told them. "Before Istas Moki took an administrative role, she taught history."

"Coso told me she would be the best asset they can provide," Bi said.

"Istas Moki also speaks Shin. The language of the Old Empire," Asha told them.

"The modern language of the Eastern Empire incorporates the most common dialect from our northern clans called Utta. Our modern tongue is called Shinutta. Only scholars would be able to understand the old language," Bi said.

"I imagine this would be a dream come true for Moki. She has always been fascinated with your country. Well, what she knew of it," Asha told Bi.

"Istas Moki approached the Council when she learned I was in Wendat, and requested the opportunity to accompany me. I haven't met her yet. She might regret her decision when we get there. I'm not sure the Empress is ready for open borders."

"She was one of the few people who supported me when I was at odds with the university board," Mora said. "I think she will serve as a good representative, and hopefully, she will be useful."

Bi nodded. "I will be mind-mapping the basics of Shinutta, before our departure. I don't have your gift of perfect memory, Mora, but I can at least give those who travel with me enough of our modern language to make introductions and everyday conversation."

Mora said, "I don't have the visionary gifts that you and Orenda share. But I can honestly say that doubt... and a feeling of trepidation are constant, now that I have a way home."

They sat in a sober mood until Mora felt she had to busy herself to stop her worried thoughts. "I'll just check on something in the kitchen."

90

The Key

The candles had burned low. A few guests lingered in the living room, their voices soft and blurred. In the kitchen, Mora was putting leftover food away when Asha came close behind her. Mora turned to see concern in Asha's dark eyes. Her shawl was drawn tightly around her shoulders, and her ears twitched nervously.

"You're really leaving," Asha said. It wasn't a question.

Mora gave a small smile. "You sound disappointed."

"I'm... concerned." She tapped her claws on the counter, then looked up, as if she had decided something and couldn't afford to hesitate. "You should know something before you go."

Mora stilled. The sharpness in her friend's tone got her attention. "What is it?"

"My father and brother," Asha said, lowering her voice. "They were planning something. I found this in the house."

Mora's throat went dry. She took the folder and opened it. The page was filled with symbols and words in an ancient language. "All of these kept on paper?"

Asha shrugged. "Evidently the Amon Kuroo doesn't trust new technology. Paper can be burned. But my father had no time to do that. I believe this describes some sort of weapon," Asha continued, her voice taut. "They call it the *Key*. And they mean to use it before the solstice festival. If the country were not in unrest, Nakhadot would be having his coronation ceremony around that time. That's when he comes of age. The Amon Kuroo oppose the reforms that the prince intends to implement. This Key is their weapon, and they intend to use it to stop his revolution."

"What exactly is this Key? A physical weapon, or a poison of some sort?"

"More likely, it is some sort of magic," Asha told her. "I heard them once talking about it, but I didn't know the significance."

Mora's heart pounded as she read the file. She noticed a pattern that related to points of access and delivery. She didn't know what was to be accessed or delivered, but she worried that if Nakhatot's people were not able to be at those locations, to see what was taking place, he might lose his advantage. Her mind leapt to the portals. To her new machine. "Asha, can you warn the prince of this threat?"

Asha shook her head fiercely.

"I don't have proof. This is all I have, and it's not conclusive. They're speaking in code."

The folder lay open on the kitchen counter. Mora scanned it, looking for clues. Some seemingly random elements stood out. "But look, there is a pattern. These points intersect, and that word, tasarut, I've seen it somewhere..."

"It was on the cover of those books I showed you. From my father's secret drawer. It's a word from the Zight dialect," Zamora said. "It has several meanings, depending on the situation. It can mean to master something. It can speak of something critical or pivotal. It can be a ticket, gateway... or... a key!"

"Somehow, all of these symbols relate to the Key," Mora told her. "And these lines," she followed them with her finger across the page, "lead to specific locations."

Asha shook her head. "I don't see it, Mora. This is not a map. Nothing here matches specific locations in Ekene. In any case, I can't take mere conjecture to the prince. Why would he even grant me an audience? I am the daughter of Ziyad. Who is now known to be a member of the Amon Kuroo." She picked up the folder. "I've studied enough history to recognize that when old powers are cornered, they strike before change can take root. That's what my father intended. I don't believe he has any leverage after what took place here, but who knows what the Order back in Zenda has already put in place." She stepped back toward the door, her shawl slipping loose, her expression bleak.

"Maybe you can show this to the council..." Mora suggested.

"No. What's the point? They wouldn't know what to do with this."

The candles had burned low. A few guests lingered in the living room, their voices soft and blurred. In the kitchen, Mora was putting leftover food away when Asha came close behind her. Mora turned to see concern in Asha's dark eyes. Her shawl was drawn tightly around her shoulders, and her ears twitched nervously.

"You're really leaving," Asha said. It wasn't a question.

Mora gave a small smile. "You sound disappointed."

"I'm... concerned." She tapped her claws on the counter, then looked up, as if she had decided something and couldn't afford to hesitate. "You should know something before you go."

Mora stilled. The sharpness of her friend's tone got her attention. "What is it?"

"My father and brother," Asha said, lowering her voice. "They were planning something. I found this in the house."

Mora's throat went dry. She took the folder and opened it.

"This describes some sort of weapon," Asha continued, her voice taut. "They call it the *Key*. And they mean to use it before the solstice festival. If the country were not in unrest, Nakhadot would be having his coronation ceremony around that time. That's when he comes of age. The Amon Kuroo oppose the reforms that the prince intends to implement. This Key is their weapon, and they intend to use it to stop his revolution."

"What exactly is this key? A physical weapon, or a poison of some sort?"

"More likely, it is some sort of magic," Asha told her. "I heard them once talking about it, but I didn't know the significance."

Mora's heart pounded as she read the file. She noticed a pattern that related to points of access and delivery. She didn't know what was to be accessed or delivered, but she worried that if Nakhatot's people were not able to be at those locations, he might lose his advantage. Her mind leapt to the portals. To her new machine. "Asha, can you warn the prince of this threat?"

Asha shook her head fiercely.

"I don't have proof. This is all I have, and it's not conclusive. They're speaking in code."

The folder lay open on the kitchen counter. Mora scanned it, looking for clues. Some seemingly random elements stood out. "But look, there is a pattern. These points intersect, and that word, tasarut, I've seen it somewhere... Oh, it was on the cover of those books you showed me. From your father's secret drawer."

"It's a word from the Zight dialect," Zamora said. "It has several meanings, depending on the situation. It can mean to master something. It can speak of something critical or pivotal. It can be a ticket, gateway... or... a key!"

"Somehow, all of these symbols relate to the Key," Mora told her. "And these lines," she followed them with her finger across the page, "lead to specific locations."

Asha shook her head. "I don't see it, Mora. This is not a map. Nothing here matches specific locations in Ekene. In any case, I can't take mere conjecture to the prince. Why would he even grant me an audience? I am the daughter of Ziyad. Who is now known to be a member of the Amon Kuroo." She picked up the folder. "I've studied enough history to recognize that when old powers are cornered, they strike before change can take root. That's what my father intended. I don't believe he has any leverage after what took place here, but who knows what the Order back in Zenda has already put in place." She stepped back toward the door, her shawl slipping loose, her expression bleak.

"Maybe you can show this to the council..." Mora suggested.

"No. What's the point? They wouldn't know what to do with this."

"But they have influence; they could help you get an audience with someone in Ekene. The prince needs to be warned!"

"And what would I tell them? I know this is meaningful somehow. I just don't know where it leads."

"But, Asha..."

"I'm telling you because I can't carry it alone. The Amon Kuroo moves in shadows. By the time the world sees what they've done, it will already be written in the histories as inevitable. But you and I know it isn't. Someone chooses. Someone always chooses." Her facial fur was wet. Mora, I'm going to sneak out now. She nodded toward the living room, where their friends were still in party mode. If they see me, they will start asking questions. She pulled Mora into a tight hug, "Be safe," she said.

Before Mora could say more, Asha had disengaged, backed out of the door, and was gone... swallowed by the night. Like only the Zendali could with their dark indigo fur. Mora stood alone. Someone laughed in the other room, and it gave her a chill. "What is this Key?" she said quietly to herself. She had thought that her leaving this world would be of no consequence. Everything seemed on the right track; restitutions had been made. She imagined that sending the portals to Zenda would be enough. But now she knew they might fall into the wrong hands. Her eidetic memory had imprinted what she had seen. With time, she might be able to make sense of it. *Someone needs to alert the prince about this Key*—before the solstice festival.

Maybe Zamora will know what to do.

***

Yuma found Mora alone in the kitchen and drew her back into the group. The rest of the evening was focused on more pleasant topics. But Asha's parting words remained with her. A shadow casting doubt on her decision to leave.

People stayed late again. Bi had gone to sleep on the couch. As before, Ohpa was the last to depart, offering to stay and help clean up, which Mora knew was code for stay the night and cuddle. She just had the feeling he was the cuddling type. "Thank you, Ohpa, but tomorrow is an early rising. I will clean up in the morning. I just want to sleep now."

He nodded and headed toward the door. His disappointment was unmistakable. She tried to ease him out with care and a few sympathetic parting words. She was beginning to understand how his relentless optimism had won Zamora's attention.

* * *

In the morning, Bi packed her few possessions. She would be staying in one of the council lodgings during the preparations for her journey. She and Mora found it hard to say goodbye; both were uncharacteristically tearful. Their futures were so uncertain.

Council elder Coso Winnemucca sent her aides to collect Bi. Mora held her tight one last time. Then, as the vehicle drove off, Bi looked out the back of the bubble dome. Mora felt the future tipping away into the unknown, and it was unsettling.

91

The Long Way Home

Mora was alone in the converted factory where they had built her new portal prototype. She lingered there, admiring her invention; she couldn't be prouder to see her brainchild in material form. They were calling it a Transit Portal. It reminded Mora of an old-fashioned Mobi-booth before the invention of the HelioLoop. And the clear capsule at the top looked like a Blazerocket. She remembered one of her first conversations with Algon when she came to this world. He was curious about Blazerockets. She smiled now, remembering how astonished he was to hear they had ventured into space with them. In her version of Hadot, they connected their communication system with StrataKites. Evidently, the stratosphere in this world was only occupied by alien ships. While her world didn't have all the wonders that the aliens had gifted the Wen, her version of Hadot did have a few impressive inventions, like their communication system, which was superior to what they had here.

Mora wished she had a Holo-Lens with her to take some pictures of her portal. They did have holography here, but they called it optography, and the device was called an Optic-Lens. Zamora didn't own one. The surge of disappointment was almost a good enough excuse to put off her departure. Almost... but there would always be another excuse. The mystery and threat of the Key, the distribution of the portals... There would never be a perfect time to leave. *Hopefully, Zamora will finish what I can't.* She sighed. *It's time to go.*

She went to her settings panel and entered the codes to access her world-line. This back-door option was only available to Mora was alone in the converted factory where they had built her new portal prototype. She lingered there, admiring her invention; she couldn't be prouder to see her brainchild in material form. They were calling it a Transit

Portal. It reminded Mora of an old-fashioned Mobi-booth before the invention of the HelioLoop. And the clear capsule at the top looked like a Blazerocket. She remembered one of her first conversations with Algon when she came to this world. He was curious about Blazerockets. She smiled now, remembering how astonished he was to hear they had ventured into space with them. In her version of Hadot, they connected their communication system with StrataKites. Evidently, the stratosphere in this world was only occupied by alien ships. While her world didn't have all the wonders that the aliens had gifted the Wen, her version of Hadot did have a few impressive inventions, like their communication system, which was superior to what they had here.

Mora wished she had a Holo-Lens with her to take some pictures of her portal. They did have holography here, but they called it optography, and the device was called an Optic-Lens. Zamora didn't own one. The surge of disappointment was almost a good enough excuse to put off her departure. Almost... but there would always be another excuse. The mystery of the Key, the distribution of the portals... There would never be a perfect time to leave. *Hopefully, Zamora will finish what I can't.* She sighed. *It's time to go.*

She went to her settings panel and entered the codes to access her world-line. This back-door option was only available to Mora. It would revert to a normal designation when she was gone. That was it, nothing else to do. She looked around the room; her calculations still filled the memory boards. Her papers were strewn around. *I really am messy*, she thought. Yet somehow it made the place look *right*, like it was well-used and as homey as a laboratory could be.

She had said all her goodbyes. She had even contacted Mato and Coso to let them know she'd be away for a time. They didn't ask where she was going, and she kept the conversation casual. As far as the business was concerned... maybe Zamora would return to take over, but Ohpa was in charge now. The three of them had no idea that Mora would leave this world.

"Hopefully, Zamora will appreciate the deals I've made here," she said out loud, because no one was around. "It will set her up for life." Mora smiled at all she had accomplished in such a short time.

This was a maiden voyage for her new machine across world-lines. This should be smoother than the last trip. There was a big *unknown* that worried her. If there weren't a portal on the other side to receive her, she might just evaporate into nothing. She grimaced at that thought.

"No reason to keep stalling," she said to herself as she put her finger on the button. "Be brave, Mora."

Her destination was logged; she pressed the activation lever. A hum emanated from the platform. The chamber began to glow. Gravity vanished. There was a soft sensation of levity. She watched herself coming apart as her physical form disappeared into particles of light. The transfer happened so quickly. It was only a blink of time, and suddenly she was in another place. She felt herself lean back against the bulkhead. Closing her eyes, she took a deep breath. Finally, the vertigo passed.

It was dead quiet and mostly dark. She had chosen to come at night, expecting her portal to be at her university laboratory. She didn't want to materialize in front of people and have to explain where she came from.

But this was not her university. It was a huge hangar. There were a few workstations set up across the way, but the place was so big it looked empty. Around her were the pieces of her original portal design. There were scorch marks, and some materials were warped. It was put back together in an ad-hoc sort of way. A chill ruffled the fur on her arms as she realized how lucky she was that this receiving platform was still functional.

She stepped off the platform and searched in her backpack for a hand lamp. It had a powerful beam for such a small device. The radiant glow illuminated the nearest wall. She saw a series of cabinets, a ladder, shelves with a lot of odds and ends, parts... and a door! Suddenly, she heard a noise, maybe an outer door closing, then footsteps. She turned off the palm light and ran to the nearest workstation, ducking down behind the desk. From where she hid, they wouldn't see her if the door opened. A wedge of the far wall was in view; it began to glow. *Oh, that's a window.* An Inoti guard was shining a light into the room from a hallway. Next, she heard a Mobi signal. The guard answered, "No activity," he said. There was a pause while he listened. "Who knows what caused the power surge? There isn't anything here." He walked away through the outer door.

She quickly explored the room and noticed the crates stacked against one wall had the Ministry of Signal and Order logo: MSO. The wallboard calculations showed a concerted effort to understand her code. Paperwork was piled on the desks. All seemed to be government directives. She also saw a schedule for the Signal Enforcement Guard. *The SEG? Why are they involved?*

So, it's a guarded facility. I wonder if the doors are locked. She waited and listened and then ventured forward. On the wall near the door was a roster. Two names astonished Mora—Chayton was under a list of programmers, and his father, Mato, was the military officer in charge. *Why should I be surprised? Of course, their counterparts are involved in portal tech here. But why does the MSO have my portal?*

The inner door was unlocked, but she noticed there was a keypad on the outside, which meant an access code was needed to get back in. The same was true of the outside door. She opened it just enough to peek out and saw that the hangar was, in fact, at an airport.

She snuck through and stayed in the shadow of the building. The moonlight was bright enough in the open areas that she might be seen. As she rounded the edge of the compound, a guard stood with his back to her. She quickly backed around the corner, out of sight. *Maybe the opposite direction then?* She went the other way. She turned that corner. There was a dark expanse shaded by some taller buildings, which seemed to be unoccupied at this hour.

There were no lights on. But when she ran that way, a motion-censored light flashed on, illuminating the whole area.

"Frack!" She kept running, and the light cycled off. *Maybe there's only the one guard? No, he was talking to someone. There must be at least two.* She reached a wire fence, but at the top of it was a roll of barbed wire. *It's like a prison facility!*

She searched the ground and finally found something useful. It was dirty and caked with mud, but it was a good-sized canvas scrap, maybe an old tent or awning. She climbed partway up and threw the doubled tarp over the barbed wire. She had to go back down for her bag. Feeling the pressure of every step that prevented her escape, Mora climbed up, threw the bag over first, then climbed onto the canvas. Some barbs still poked through and stabbed her. She managed to jump down but landed awkwardly. She reached up and tried to pull the canvas loose. It wouldn't budge. The barbs had grabbed the fabric, and now it was stuck and flapping loudly in the wind. *They will know someone climbed over if they find this.* Tugging harder, adding all her weight to the end that hung over the fence, part of it tore and fell. She gathered it, shaking out the dirt.

She didn't want to waste any more time loitering there. Perimeter guards might be close. Mora grabbed her bag and ran. There was no sign to give her a clue about where she was. She hoped to find a road. The thought occurred to her that maybe she was just running into the wilderness where she would get turned around in the dark and lost, but she kept running to put some distance between the facility and herself.

Mora took cover behind a row of tall bushes. From there, she dashed further into the trees. She stuffed the torn canvas beneath a bramble bush, hoping it wouldn't be found. She could only see where the moonlight shone in the clearings. She stumbled and fell a few times, aggravating her bruised ankle. This forced her to slow her pace, favoring her injured foot. She was determined to limp as far as necessary to find safety. When she finally stopped for a breather, in the silence of the night, she could hear someone in the distance yelling. *Maybe they saw the tarp and suspected an intruder?* She put the hand lamp back in her pack.

She was suddenly startled by the thumping whop-whop of a WingSkater approaching her position. It paused, hovering above her. Even though the trees and shadows covered her instinctively, she hunched down and froze. At this time of night, they could only see her if she went out in the open. Mora started to doubt her plan. *Would a road be safe?* She wondered. *What is this place? Since when does the MSO have secret, secured operations?*

In her panic, it felt like the WingSkater had hung above her for an eternity. While she cowered, her mind worried over what would happen when they apprehended her. But it had only hovered briefly above her location and then flew off. The noise faded... going further away, and back toward the facility. She stood and ran in small bursts, keeping to the shadows, moving away from the compound.

Eventually, the tree line ended at a road. She saw a sign with two arms. One pointed back from where she had come. It said: Dramhail Dur Station. The other pointed forward and said Crater Rock Bay. She was familiar with that seaside town. Mora calculated the distance to her home. It wasn't far if she could drive. If she had a vehicle, this road would take her to the speedway, which would get her into town in no time. But sadly, she didn't have transportation. And her HelioLoop was not on her. She had no way to contact a friend to pick her up. Mora crossed the road and tried to walk along a path that wound through scrubby little bushes and trees. She hoped they would hide her if the WingSkater came back, or if any MSO haulers came down the road.

It must be near second-moon, she guessed. The road was dark and empty. She'd bruised her ankle when jumping off the fence, and it was starting to swell. Progress was also hindered by the rough terrain. Finally, she was forced to leave the forest and walk on the road. She could move faster on the paved surface. But she was still worried the Signal Enforcement Guard might be hunting for her. This state of fearful anxiety followed her into town. Every unexpected sound startled her. She had never realized how the night was full of hooting and howling creatures.

She kept walking. Her foot became more inflamed with the effort. Finally, she made it to the little seaside town of Crater Rock Bay. At this hour, nothing was open. She walked down Main Street, passing the Kav shops, restaurants, and a boutique. Even in the dim light, the painted buildings looked garishly bright. *Of course, the implant... colors will be more intense here.* She continued along the treelined road. Flowers were blooming in pots and hanging baskets. She walked past the apothecary, a tourist shop, and a boutique. It was all like a painted postcard of a distant memory.

She tried the door at the little seaside hotel, hoping to find a late-night clerk at the desk. But it was locked. The lobby was dark and still. An old standing-clock on the street told her it was past the hours when any sensible person would be awake.

No hope of finding a hauler stop here, either. It was not a major interstate route, just a small coastal road with no traffic at this time of night. She walked down to Higs Road, which she knew led into Brighton State Park. *Looks like I'll be walking all night.* She had hiked these trails some years ago. They would lead to Diamond Hills and West Wellin farms. Then she could cross the Inoti University campus. From there, it wasn't much further to her house. Mora lived in Southpark, near Newbridge Lake.

About an hour into the trek, she realized that these must be the same woods Bi would have traveled when she arrived in that other world on her way to Muwioni. How quickly her mind wanted to grasp onto what felt real. Walking through that little west coast town, it was like touching ground after being at sea. The other world where she had lived for several months was beginning to feel like a long-complicated dream.

Mora tried to keep a good pace, but her ankle still throbbed. Her little palm light wasn't enough. The trail was rife with obstacles. She tripped on roots and trudged through puddles. She rested only a little now and then when she stopped to fill her water bottle at a creek. By the time she crossed the university campus, students were meandering around.

Everything was *normal*, yet at the same time surreal in contrast to Muwioni. And much more colorful than she remembered. Mora had become a stranger to her own world. When she got to her house, she was exhausted. She had no key, but she knew where the spare was in the backyard.

The gate was locked on the other side. She had no energy to climb over the fence. She decided to knock on the front door, but got no answer. She knocked harder. Nothing... it was silent. *Maybe no one is home. Maybe Zamora isn't living here.* Just when she started to step off the porch, the door opened, and she saw herself. Zamora stood frozen in the doorway, her hair unbound, her eyes wide, her mouth actually hanging open in astonishment.

"Mora?"

Thank You

Visit my website to receive a free copy of my novella Jojote, which is set in the same world as Inverse.

https://margotconor.com/

You will also find updates on other books in this series, which are in production.

If you enjoyed this book, please consider leaving a review on Amazon and Goodreads.

Accolades

My developmental editor, Lera Komissarova, of Websman is the only person to read the first draft of Inverse. With her persistent guidance, I learned to see the story differently. She believes that words should flow like music, and she pushed me to go deeper into the emotional depth of my characters. Thank you, Lera, for believing in me and for all your support and kindness over the years.

I'd also like to express gratitude to my mother, who always supported my creative journey. I did not learn until after she passed that she also was writing stories. I feel such deep sadness that she never shared with them with me.

Credit goes to my critique partners: Maxie Jane Frazier, Donnetrice Allison, Sabrina Robinson, and Asher Sund. Thank you for all your advice, corrections, and suggestions. There is no doubt that with your help this book was improved. I feel very fortunate to be a part of our group. You are all amazing writers, and I can't wait to see your books in print.

Last but *never* least, much gratitude to my wonderful husband, who gives me the time and encouragement to follow my writing journey. I feel so fortunate to have his support.

This book would not have happened without each person mentioned here. You all contribute to my success. If there is one thing I have learned during this process, it is that we need to support each other. That is how our dreams come to fruition.

www.ingramcontent.com/pod-product-compliance
Lightning Source LLC
Chambersburg PA
CBHW020508020726
47493CB00001B/233